In Due Season

Early Canadian Literature Series

The Early Canadian Literature Series returns to print rare texts deserving restoration to the canon of Canadian texts in English. Including novels, periodical pieces, memoirs, and creative non-fiction, the series showcases texts by Indigenous peoples and immigrants from a range of ancestral, language, and religious origins. Each volume includes an afterword by a prominent scholar providing new avenues of interpretation for all readers.

Series Editor: Benjamin Lefebvre

Series Advisory Board:
Andrea Cabajsky, Département d'anglais, Université de Moncton
Carole Gerson, Department of English, Simon Fraser University
Cynthia Sugars, Department of English, University of Ottawa

For more information please contact:

Siobhan McMenemy
Senior Editor
Wilfrid Laurier University Press
75 University Avenue West
Waterloo, ON   N2L 3C5
Canada

Phone: 519.884.0710 ext. 3782
Fax: 519.725.1399
Email: smcmenemy@wlu.ca

In Due Season

Christine van der Mark

Afterword by Carole Gerson and Janice Dowson

Early Canadian Literature · WLU PRESS

Wilfrid Laurier University Press acknowledges the support of the Canada Council for the Arts for our publishing program. We acknowledge the financial support of the Government of Canada through its Book Publishing Industry Development Program for our publishing activities. This work was supported by the Research Support Fund.

 Canada Council Conseil des arts
for the Arts du Canada

Library and Archives Canada Cataloguing in Publication

van der Mark, Christine, 1917–1970, author
    In due season / Christine van der Mark.

(Early Canadian literature)
Includes bibliographical references.
Issued in print and electronic formats.
ISBN 978-1-77112-071-5 (paperback).—ISBN 978-1-77112-072-2 (pdf).— ISBN 978-1-77112-073-9 (epub).

    I. Title. II. Series: Early Canadian literature series

PS8543.A3816 2016   C813'.54   C2016-902315-X
                                                                              C2016-902316-8

Cover design and text design by Blakeley Words+Pictures. Cover photo courtesy of University of Calgary Special Collections 695/01.1.9.4. This edition of *In Due Season* is published by arrangement with the author's estate. Text copyright © 1947 Oxford University Press (Canada).

© 2016 Wilfrid Laurier University Press
Waterloo, Ontario, Canada
www.wlupress.wlu.ca

Contents

Series Editor's Preface by Benjamin Lefebvre   vii

In Due Season   1

Afterword by Carole Gerson and Janice Dowson   319

Series Editor's Preface

Christine van der Mark was born in Calgary, Alberta, on 17 September 1917, of Dutch and English ancestry. While teaching intermittently in rural Alberta schools, she completed an undergraduate degree in English literature and an M.A. in creative writing, both at the University of Alberta, where she also taught composition. She submitted as her M.A. thesis a draft of her first novel, *In Due Season*, which would be co-winner of a prestigious award sponsored by the Toronto branch of Oxford University Press and New York publisher Thomas Y. Crowell. After she married economist Thomas F. Wise in 1949, his career and graduate studies took the family to a number of locations, including Montreal, Pakistan, Connecticut, the Sudan, and Ottawa. Her work following *In Due Season* includes the novel *Honey in the Rock* (1966), three unpublished novels, and a number of articles for periodicals such as the *Christian Science Monitor*. Although some sources give her date of death as 1969, she died in Ottawa on 13 January 1970.

In *Unnamed Country: The Struggle for a Canadian Prairie Fiction* (1977), Dick Harrison refers to *In Due Season* as "[t]he most accomplished" of a group of "less romantic novels" in which "the land is portrayed as harsh and potentially sinister" (124). In his entry on van der Mark in *The Oxford Companion to Canadian Literature* (1983),

Harrison adds that the book "explores, from a distinctive female point of view, the human costs of pioneering" (812). Indeed, the *Globe and Mail*, in its report on the book as one of two winners of the Oxford–Crowell competition, had seen this sort of reckoning as one of the novel's innovations: "Life in the new settlement, complicated by the continued absence of a shiftless husband, shows the ironic balance between increased material prosperity and increasing spiritual hardness and isolation" ("First" 10). The novel is also groundbreaking in its depiction of a complex community in which Aboriginal and Metis residents interact with European settlers from a range of ethnic backgrounds.

In Due Season was first published by the Toronto branch of Oxford University Press in 1947; it was reprinted, from the same plates, in a new edition by Vancouver publisher New Star Books in 1979, with an introduction by poet Dorothy Livesay (1909–1996) and an afterword by van der Mark's eldest daughter, Dorothy Wise (1950–2015). This Early Canadian Literature edition uses the Oxford edition as its copy-text and contains the full text of that edition. It lets stand inconsistencies of spelling, capitalization, hyphenation, and punctuation, with the exception of some minor corrections for clarity. It also makes one substantive correction: on page 274 of this edition, the phrase "what's happened to Mike since the trial" has been changed from "what's happened Mike since the trial."

The University of Calgary holds an extensive Christine van der Mark fonds that includes manuscripts, typescripts, correspondence, photographs, and miscellaneous papers.

BENJAMIN LEFEBVRE

Works Cited

"First Novels Win Fellowships in Oxford–Crowell Competition." *Globe and Mail* 1 Feb.
    1947: 10. *ProQuest Historical Newspapers*. Web. 26 Feb. 2016.

Harrison, Dick. *Unnamed Country: The Struggle for a Canadian Prairie Fiction*. Edmonton:
    U of Alberta P, 1977. Print.

———. "van der Mark, Christine." *The Oxford Companion to Canadian Literature*.
    Ed. William Toye. Toronto: Oxford UP, 1983. 812. Print.

Livesay, Dorothy. Introduction. *In Due Season*. By Christine van der Mark. Vancouver:
    New Star, 1979. i–iv. Print.

van der Mark, Christine. *In Due Season*. Toronto: Oxford UP, 1947. Print.

———. *In Due Season*. 1947. Vancouver: New Star, 1979. Print.

"van der Mark, Christine." *Encyclopedia of Literature in Canada*. Ed. William H. New.
    Toronto: U of Toronto P, 2002. 1163. Print.

Wise, Dorothy. Afterword. *In Due Season*. By Christine van der Mark. Vancouver: New
    Star, 1979. 365–72. Print.

In Due Season

Be not deceived; God is not mocked; for whatsoever a man soweth, that shall he also reap.

This is the story of a woman, alone, forced to work like a man to wrest a living from the land. This is the story also of a pioneer community. There is the constant passing of seedtime and harvest, and the pushing back of the wilderness. The community grows and develops; the woman degenerates in spirit. For it is the very soul, as well as human blood and bone, which goes into the building of a new land.

All names and characters appearing in this book are fictitious.

Chapter I

1

The day was sullen. Dark clouds were banked up on the western horizon. Dust sifted along the rutted prairie roads in a dry, choking wind, which blew teasingly in the hollows and over the rough hills, promising rain, and bringing only gloom. Deserted buildings stared blankly, their loose shutters and shingles flapping, their fences disappearing under the soil. Now and then a hawk rose with the wind, or beat his great black wings under the clouds. Not a green blade of grass could be seen on the harsh rolling prairie that lay brown, and gaunt, and scarred beneath the April sky. For it was spring.

Dry brown Russian thistles rolled across the yard of a grey bleak home that leaned a little to the east. Rusty cars stood there, and teams with drooping heads. Little whirlwinds of dust blew through the barnyard into the faces of the men gathered there who sat or leaned in weary attitudes, or walked about, examining a pathetic array of machinery. They wore denim overalls turned up at the ankles, showing broken boots. Their jackets, patched and ragged, open down the fronts, showed a variety of work-shirts, all with the collars turned up and the points sticking outwards. Caps with broken peaks, and hats bashed and shapeless were being constantly pulled forwards and shoved backwards, as decisions were made. Under the brims, the faces looked hard, lean, wind-bitten, frost-bitten, with fine lines about the eyes, deepened now with dust.

Tied to a rail, a horse stood patient and sad, her coat matted with dust, her ribs prominent. The auctioneer approached her in a business-like way. His ready chant was tossed on the wind.

"What-am-I-bid—what-am-I-bid—what-am-I-bid— Gentlemen!" His round smooth face flushed a deep red as he performed a sort of rhythmic dance to his words. "What-am-I-bid-for-this-horse?"

Like a show, old Benjie Farrel thought. A show at the Stampede where someone sang and danced, and the crowd watched and paid. Even the tattered black and tan dog, Gypsy, sat upright, alertness in his gold eyes. The old man got down off the hay-rack from where he had been watching. He tottered a little, going up to the group.

"That mare looks mighty poor," Rod Graham drawled.

"Sure was a tough winter on stock," Benjie sighed.

"What-am-I-bid—what-am-I-bid— Gentlemen!" the auctioneer chanted again. Benjie put his hands in his pockets, his face a mask. Beside him, Rod continued to regard the mare without interest.

"Five dollars!" a moustached farmer boomed from the crowd, pushing his way forward. With eyes like little hard pieces of brown glass, he looked over the beast, rubbing the dispirited head with a gnarled hand.

"Who'll-make-it-six? Who'll-make-it-six? Gentlemen!"

"Here comes Lina and the wife," Rod muttered as two women crossed the yard. "Hope to God Della ain't figgering to buy nothing."

"Is the little red saddle sold, Daddy? Mrs. Graham was thinking to buy it."

Benjie and Rod turned to the big fair woman who towered above Mrs. Graham, her head with its large knot of light hair firmly poised.

Benjie nodded. "Yep, Lina, Jed Carter got it."

6

"We don't need the thing," Rod growled.

"Who'll-make-it-six? Who'll-make-it-six."

"Six!" shouted Jed, a lean, shifty-eyed man watching Lina from the hay-rack.

"If Rodney is to ride clear to Randon for high school, he must have a saddle!" Mrs. Graham stormed. "You good as promised!"

"Six! Six! Do I hear seven? Who'll-make-it-seven?"

"Rodney going to high school?" Lina asked with interest, her clear blue eyes on Rod's face. "He done well, that kid."

Rod looked pleased.

"Who'll-make-it-seven? Who'll-make-it-seven?"

Lina looked over Benjie's head at the mute figure of the horse beside which the auctioneer danced about.

"Poor Lady wintered bad."

Rod glanced sharply at the woman's averted face.

"Seven!" he yelled.

Mrs. Graham went white with fury.

"Rod Graham, what in heaven's name!"

"Eight!" Kent's hard brown eyes glittered.

"When you wouldn't get the kid a saddle . . ."

"I was just stepping up the bids!" Graham wagged his head with a pleased grin.

Lina smiled. "That was just swell of you. Thanks awfully."

"Nine! Do I hear nine? Going . . . Going . . ."

Benjie winced as though under a blow as the auctioneer's hand dropped.

"Gone to Jim Kent for eight dollars!"

"Well, I must get back to the house. Are you coming up for a cup of coffee, Mrs. Graham?" Lina asked tranquilly.

"I don't know but what I should stay here and watch this man of mine!" Mrs. Graham felt in the pocket of her fraying tweed coat and brought out a greyish handkerchief to wipe some dust from her eye.

"Oh come now, some coffee'll do you good." Lina took her arm persuasively.

Indoors, Lina in her decent black dress tidily covered by a gay print apron, handed out sandwiches and coffee to a small group of women. The house had a desolate look, for it had been stripped of its curtains, furniture, and floor-coverings. She had saved scarcely anything; the visitors were accommodated on old apple boxes. The kitchen linoleum, in an untidy roll with the word SOLD chalked across it, leaned in a corner. New owners from time to time hauled away various pieces of furniture piled up in the back porch. The sombre light of the late afternoon showed the women weather-beaten, their shoulders drooping as though with heavy burdens. From under matronly hats, their hair straggled in blown wisps. Their eyes were patient. Among them Lina's child, golden and fragile, moved shyly with a plate of bread and butter. And Lina, among these resigned figures, seemed strong, the eyes in her tanned face a blue blaze of life.

"More coffee, Mrs. Brown?" she asked in a deep throaty voice as she advanced upon the small visitor with the coffee pot in her hand.

"Oh no thank you, really. It was very good." Mrs. Brown got up, drawing her faded coat about her. The other women also began setting down their cups. There was a hub-bub of voices, and then Mrs. Kent from the window announced that the men were beginning to move out of the barnyard.

"Guess the sale's over." Mrs. Brown gathered up the bed-spread she had bought. "And where will you be going, Lina?" she asked, her pale face alight with curiosity. Mrs. Kent paused, her hands half way to straightening her hat. All eyes were upon Lina. She drew herself up, making the others feel tired, worn out.

"We have a homestead up north, near Bear Claw." And then with quick enthusiasm she went on, "It's a good land up there in the north. Real good pasture, and rain." She set down the coffee pot and put her hands on her broad hips, her face alight.

8

Mrs. Graham drew down the corners of her mouth. "It's no life for a woman, so Rod says, though God knows what he thinks this is."

"Farming's about the same most places." Lina gave the child the empty plates to take to the kitchen, smiling as though she had no worries.

"Abe says lots of folks get dried out in the north same as they do here." Mrs. Brown picked up her bundle again.

"And I suppose Sym will be waiting for you there?" Mrs. Kent asked, her hawk-like face sharply outlined against the window.

"He'll be with us real soon," Lina answered. Her lips smiled stiffly. "He's got the house and barn all ready."

Old Benjie came in, beating the dust from his broad-brimmed hat against his knee, and wiping the grit from his face with a red spotted handkerchief. He gave the women a toothless grimace as they crowded around, shaking hands, and went chatting out of the door. Helping himself to a noisy drink from the dipper, he peered through the window at the men loading up their wagons. Abe Brown walked carefully by with the gas lamp and the canary cage. Kent had Lady by the halter. He gave her a kick as she tried to pull into the barn again. Benjie turned away.

"Want a sandwich, Gramp?" the little girl asked, holding out the plate.

"No, Poppy, I ain't hungry. Come and sit down here by the door with me."

Lina went out with the other women, walking with them to the gate.

"Is it to-morrow you start?" Mrs. Brown inquired.

"Soon as we can get ready in the morning."

"Real western gal," remarked Abe Brown, handing the canary cage to his wife to hold. "When the little fellow sings, I'll think of you." He gave Lina a broad wink.

"You better get cranking." His wife sounded peevish.

Jed Carter tightened the cinch of the red saddle about his thin horse.

"You'll be remembering your neighbours when yer up there in the north, won't you?"

"Like as not," Lina laughed. "I'll be sending some of you a line to let you know when we make our fortune."

Brown cranked his Model T Ford desperately, sweat standing out on his forehead. At its sudden roar, Graham's old team reared up.

"Good-bye to a real lady." Abe held out a hard, earth-grimed hand. Rod stood grinning as he buckled the harness on his horses.

Mrs. Graham seized her husband's arm. "God in heaven, let's get going!"

At last all the wagons and horses had turned down their respective roads, and Lina thoughtfully watched them go. When she came back to the house, her face was calm and untroubled. She shut the door and a moment later began humming a tune as she swept the floor.

"We didn't make out so good, did we?" The old man got up and reached for his tobacco from a shelf.

The woman stood still, pushed back a loop of thick fair hair, and leaned on the broomstick.

"Not so bad, I think, Daddy. Course it ain't all figgered up yet; but considering how poor folks is, I reckon we didn't make out too bad."

Benjie sat down on an apple box and began to fill his pipe. He looked aged and weary. Poppy edged up to him, laying her gold head on his shoulder. The wind moaned around the house, lonely and forlorn. The woman spread a clean cloth over a little gate-legged table in the corner, and began laying a meal of bread and cheese, and generous portions of pie.

"It's good land we're going to," she said. "If anyone's a mind to work, they're bound to make out good. Now come on, everybody, supper's on."

As he sat at the table making a pretence to eat, Benjie remarked, "And Poppy will be going to school come fall."

"Don't want to go to school," Poppy answered resentfully.

"Course you want to go to school." Lina poured the child another glass of milk. "I don't want you to grow up to be somebody's work girl."

"Don't want no milk." Poppy turned down the corners of her mouth.

Her mother sighed. "Eat your supper like a good girl."

The old man gazed out of the curtainless window at the gloomy countryside.

"Lived round these parts goin' on thirty-two years," he said, leaning his chin in his hand. "Too bad Sym didn't like the place. We might ha' made out all right. I used to, when I was a younger man."

With some clatter, Lina began to gather up the dishes.

"Is Pop coming with us?" the child asked.

Her mother lit the one remaining lamp, and its flickering light brought out the lonely bareness of the room, the unsoftened outlines of the packing-cases, the broken plaster and the splintery floor.

"Is he?" the child persisted.

"Not just yet, Poppy. Not yet."

Benjie rummaged among their belongings and brought out a worn violin case. Opening it, he remarked with a sigh, "It ud brought a bit more money for us."

"Oh Daddy!" Lina cried. "Not your fiddle!"

"Play for us! Play for us, Gramp." The little girl danced about, smiling.

He tucked the instrument under his chin and began tuning the strings; and then the shack was filled with music, sad and infinitely sweet.

2

Outside, the wind threw up handfuls of gravel against the window panes. Swiftly the dark came. From far away could be heard the weird lonely howling of a coyote; and the thudding of hoofs sounded intermittently as though stumbling in the gloom.

3

In the early morning, Jim Kent and his wife saw them go. The wind was almost calm, the sky clear and the air fresh. Jim, with his eyes on the window, noisily sipped tea from a saucer.

"There's Benjie and Lina pulling out now."

His wife turned from the stove and the sizzling bacon to pull back the dingy curtain.

"They got Whisky and Rum pulling the load. There's the dog. Which horse is that black one, running free, Jim?"

"That's Queen." Jim got up for a closer look. "Well, dad burn it, they're taking their cow along too."

As the wagon moved on down the road, Mrs. Kent threw open the door, and she and her husband walked outside into the yard to wave. From their places on the spring seat of the wagon, Lina and Poppy waved back, and Benjie made an arc with his battered hat.

"Where is that place, Bear Claw?" Mrs. Kent asked, shading her eyes.

"'Bout three hundred miles north, and west some. Near Wandering River."

The wagon disappeared below a hill. Mrs. Kent dropped her hand, and they went back into the house.

"I figger I'd go too, if I was her." The woman turned her sharp face in the direction of the road.

"What'ye mean, you'd go too?" Jim muttered.

"Everybody talking about Sym going off like that and never coming back."

"Nobody's talking but a lot of fool women! He went north to get a place ready."

Mrs. Kent put a greasy platter of bacon on the table.

"But Flo says in all the letters as comes to the Post Office, none comes from Bear Claw after that one time."

Jim grunted with disgust. "A man buildin' a house has got no time for letter writin'."

"And Lina never talks about Sym."

"She's a decent woman what minds her own business."

Mrs. Kent sugared her tea in silence.

"We'll all be leavin' soon," Jim growled. "That is, if it don't rain."

"Whisky! Rum!" Lina shouted to the team, and slapped the lines against the dashboard. She grinned at Benjie, ruffled Poppy's hair. The ragged tarpaulin covering her possessions had gaping holes showing in places some of her pathetic, intimate belongings. A few hens in a box covered with wire netting moved uneasily under the spring seat. One hen caught her head in the wire, and set up a mad squawking.

Having rescued the hen, Benjie took out his pipe and began filling it.

"How long do you figger it'll take us to get there, Girl?"

"Can't tell. We can't go very fast on account of Queen and the cow."

"I wonder how much Sym got out of selling the car."

"Well, he never said in his letter. But the house and barn was getting built. Said he had a horse, too. He must have gambled some."

Benjie clamped his teeth on the pipe stem. "With luck, as usual."

In her blue denim overalls, and faded red coat, Poppy bounced up and down on the seat, pulling impatiently at the lines. Excitement had brought a faint tinge of pink to her milk-white skin.

"Let me! Let me!" she cried.

Benjie smoked contentedly. "If the weather stays this warm, we'll be settin' pretty."

"I've been figgering." The woman narrowed her eyes, looking far down the road. "I reckon we could put in a good garden this year, and we have our own milk. And we have the money to get some clearing done."

"We could get quite a mite of breakin' done," the old man said eagerly. "I'm a perty strong man yet."

On between the straggling barbed wire fences, along the hard rutted prairie trails, the wagon jolted, or moved with more muted sounds through the deep drifted soil that made the good team cough and plunge. The red and white cow plodded stolidly behind the wagon, her bell clanking with every step. Free of rope or halter, Queen followed, sometimes coming up beside Lina, sometimes dropping behind. She moved carefully for she was about to foal. The dog, soon tired from romping, trotted docilely beside the team. Thus they came to Randon, their nearest town, and pulled up in the lee of two stark grain elevators. At the general store Lina climbed down to buy supplies for their journey, while Benjie stayed outside with the horses, and his little grandchild explored the one street.

Duke Watson came up on horseback. He was approaching eighty, but his back was straight, his eyes keen-sighted.

"So you're leavin', Ben?" His white horse pawed the ground.

"I'd as soon stay, but it ain't fair to my girl." Benjie sighed, looking with longing at the ridge of rough hills from which they had come. His motionless horses stood with drooping heads, while the cow chewed deliberately. Gypsy lay flat underneath the wagon.

"We've had tough times," Duke remarked. "Stand still! She's had too many oats." The mare stood, tossing her head. "We've had tough times, Ben, but some day she's gotta rain again." Duke's far-sighted eyes in his brown lined face, scanned the horizon thoughtfully. "The land's good, if we could just git water. Some day, there'll be irrigation. Some day, Ben—"

"And in the meantime we all starve, or go on relief," Lina's voice broke in. She tossed a bag of groceries into the wagon, and swung Poppy in after them. "Well, I didn't mean it just like that." The woman's tone was kindlier as she looked up at the old man. "But Duke, it don't seem it'll be better for a good long time. And when you got a kid, you got to think of that too."

"Hate to see you folks go. Empty homes all over the hills. Think you'll make out?"

Lina stroked Queen's silky neck. "We'll make out, Duke. Some day I'll meet you at the Stampede with my prize stock."

"Well, Lina," Duke laughed gently. "Got to say good-bye to you folks."

"Nice seein' you," Benjie said.

"Good-bye!" Lina cried as she climbed up. Taking the lines, she whistled to the horses. The wagon moved forward while Duke called good wishes after them. For a long time they could see his white horse against the dull grey of the road as he loped homewards.

Lina's little procession passed prairie homes where women and children waved; passed blown-out fields and dried muck lands where the soil cracked gapingly; passed long weary stretches of prairie where cattle bones lay bleaching in the sun. Sometimes they stopped for water at the well of a neighbourly farmer, and sometimes they paused on the road to feed and rest the horses and snatch a hasty meal.

As night began to come on, they drew up at the gate of a grey farmhouse in which the lights were beginning to glimmer. Handing the lines to her father, Lina stepped down over the wheel. As she walked through the yard, her heart beat heavily, for it was hard to be asking favours of strangers. The door opened, revealing a short broad woman with iron grey hair done in a tight knob.

"I'm Mrs. Ashley." The light fell on Lina's strained face. "We're moving north, my father and me, and we was wondering— We have our own bedding. I wouldn't mind for myself, but Daddy is quite old, and then there's my little girl." She hesitated, smiling wanly. "But we wouldn't want to put you out."

"A little girl too!" The woman's voice was kind. "My dear, come in. I'll call my husband. I thought I seen a wagon coming down the road. No, just sit down, Mrs. Ashley, and I'll see to everything. Joe will look after the horses. Now you just sit down and have a cup of coffee."

"That's real kind of you."

"Our name is Peters," the other woman said. "There's Joe now talking to your father. I'll just go and bring them in."

Soon they all sat down to a generous meal. With his sandy brown hair standing on end, eyes peering under his shaggy brows, Joe poured coffee with a steady hand.

"We seen several families trekking north. They seem to get along all right, too." He looked admiringly at Lina.

She leaned forward at her place at the table, her face full of eagerness and courage.

"It's real thrilling, Joe. Like an adventure."

"That's right," the other woman broke in. "But I don't know but what I'd as soon stay home."

"Say!" Joe waved his fork in the air. "You could stop at Benton's just this side of Beaver Creek. They're friends of ours."

Poppy gazed about in shy silence.

"Eat your supper, dear," Lina whispered.

"She's tired," Mrs. Peters smiled sympathetically.

"Not tired!" The child's tone was hostile.

Benjie put his rough hand on her head, and she leaned against his shoulder.

When he woke her next morning, the night clouds were lifting, and grey light shrouded the prairie.

"Wake up, Poppy." He shook her gently by the shoulder. "Wake up, child, and come on out and see Queen's new colt."

"A colt!" She was wide awake in a moment, struggling up, groping for her clothes. "Gee, Gramp, a colt!"

At the barn, in the dim light, they could see Queen's great liquid eyes looking anxiously at them over the boards of the stall. In the straw the little fellow lay, knobbly, bewildered. Joe caressed the mare reassuringly.

"We can put the little tyke in the wagon box," Lina suggested. "We can make a bed of straw for him, and wrap him up good. Then he won't get tired."

The child bent over the colt. "What are we going to call him, Gramp?"

Benjie scratched his head. "How about Prince? He's the son of a queen!"

The three looked at each other, the old man, the child, the newborn colt. Whisky and Rum stood patiently in another stall with the wilted dog at their feet. Even in the half darkness, the beasts looked thin. The dusty road lay ahead, and days of toilsome travel in good weather or bad. Lina went outside into the misty light. Somewhere there was pasture and well-watered land.

Chapter II

In the darkening light of his one-roomed shop, Tudor Folkes sat with a saddle on his knee, his hands caressing the worn leather.

"It's been a mighty good one in its time, I'd say." Through a haze of pipe smoke, his shrewd blue eyes regarded his companion. "It's good now for a long while."

Tilting on the uncertain back legs of a chair, Sym Ashley inhaled deeply on a cigarette butt, before tossing it on the floor, to grind it out under his heel.

"It should be a good one." He came forward with a jerk, his eyes brilliant and dark, the whites extraordinarily white. "It belonged to my father-in-law, Benjie Farrel. He was a cow-puncher in the early days down in the south country. Well, and how much will this set me back?" Sym smiled with singular charm.

Tudor ran his fingers through his curly black hair.

"Well, considering how I rushed to do this, making other people wait—" He indicated with a glance the worn shoes, riding boots, and harness that lay in rows on the floor; and the shoes on his work table under the window; "—some of them walking bare-foot as it were—" Grinning, he held up a pair with gaping holes in the soles. "I'd say at least fifty bucks."

Sym shoved back his broad-brimmed hat and chuckled. From the hip pocket of his denim overalls, he took out an old wallet, handling it carefully, peering into its contents with a secretive look. Tudor removed the pipe from his mouth.

"Three and a half." He put the pipe down carefully on the table while Sym counted out the money.

"How about coming over for a beer, Tudor?" he suggested as he handed over three ragged bills and a shining half dollar.

Folkes took the money gingerly, wrinkling his nose in distaste. "The filthy bills that circulate round this place." Opening a little drawer in the table, he put the money away. "Smells," he growled, shutting the drawer, and then sniffing contentedly the wholesome, horsey, leathery smell of his shop. "Well, when is the wife coming?" He sat on the table, easing the saddle down beside him.

Sym poured some tobacco from a little cotton bag into a cigarette paper in the palm of his hand. With his teeth and free hand, he pulled tight the strings of the bag which he put into the breast pocket of his work shirt. "Should be coming soon now." Intent on the making of the cigarette, his face seemed full of gloom and brooding. "'Bout the middle of May, I guess." He wetted the flap of paper with his tongue, and finishing off the job, snapped at his lighter two or three times without success.

"Try mine," his friend suggested, handing him a bullet lighter.

"My little girl will be that excited." Sym shut off the flame and puffed contentedly. "Cute little kid." Tudor saw the affection in the other's face. "Not very often you see someone with fair hair and brown eyes."

Folkes looked thoughtfully at him. "Sym, if you're going away now, there might be a chance your wife will arrive when you're gone."

"Yes, I'm afraid she will, Tudor. I'm up a tree. You know that deal I got into with Vic Rex? He's so crooked he can't lay straight. Well, we fleeced old Robblee from Seven Corners. There's a chance he may let me work out what I owe him on his place. Or it might mean jail."

"Sym, a gambler's life can never be secure. You can't hope to win in the long run." Tudor relit his pipe. "There's your little girl to think of too."

"I know, I know. I been so lucky till now. I swear I'll never touch another card when I get through this. I'll make a clean start."

"Aren't you going to leave word?"

"How can I leave word that I might be in jail?"

"But will they be able to manage, alone?"

"Lina can manage anything." Sym stared out of the window. "She's really quite wonderful. She can do anything, Lina can." He got to his feet, buttoning his leather jacket. "You should meet Benjie; you'd like him."

"Awful dried out land, that south country." Tudor got up too. "No rain, no crops." The grey light from the window fell on his hard, angular face.

"Funny, the people that end up in this country here."

"Most of them make out all right, too." The older man's tone was comforting.

"Well, how about having a beer with me?"

Tudor was almost persuaded. He found himself loath to see the other man go, but he shook his head.

"Another time." He reached for the gas lamp that hung from a long hook in the ceiling. "Shoes to mend."

A moment later, the door clanged shut, its little bell ringing wildly, and Sym strode off, the heavy saddle under his arm. Thoughtfully, Tudor began pumping the gas lamp. Strange how homesick he sometimes felt for the prairie. Like to-night. It must have been from thinking of someone else's leaving it, pulling out for the north. Good country here. He looked out from under the boughs of an enormous hospitable spruce tree that towered above his shop. One or two lights were shining at the hotel and at the general store. Good country. But the prairie. . . . Being able to see for miles without any bush in the way!

Always he remembered that night when he had gone out to the chicken-house to watch for a weasel. In the moonlight, his dapple-grey horse, Freckles, came lumbering up to the water-hole, standing there with trembling legs, lowering his head, trying to find water where there was only dusty earth. God, what a place!

Tudor struck a match on the heater that glittered, even in the dimness. The gas lamp flared up, puffing. He picked up a pair of riding boots, noting the fine texture of the leather. A man got to be hungry for the sight of grass, and rain, and water. He went over to his work table, walking with a slight limp. Under the hard light, a long scar stood out white along his cheek. But his eyes were wise and kind. He began singing in a low voice:

> Cobbler, cobbler, mend my shoe;
> Weave a golden thread in so;
> Sparkling heel and buckle too,
> Milkmaids trip to the King's ball oh!
>
> With Lord Laney I would dance;
> Waltz and polka I would do;
> Lady May will look askance,
> Cobbler, cobbler, mend my shoe.

Chapter III

1

T hough the spring rains had not yet fallen on the vast lonely
bush country, the air had a sweet freshness, filled with
the tang of spruce and pine. Down the narrow roads that
led to Bear Claw, teams and wagons passed each other,
the drivers calling in French, Ukrainian, Cree, and English. Many
teams and saddle-ponies stood tied to hitching-posts in the village,
and a single automobile, sleek-looking in these surroundings, bumped
along the uneven road among shying horses. In the beer parlour of the
battered hotel building with its ragged Union Jack, men from far-away
lonely places in the bush gathered in little groups about the round
tables. Roughly dressed, most of them bearded, noisy, pounding their
fists in argument until the beer slopped over, they talked interminably
in a mixed jargon of accents and languages. Puddles of spilt beer,
cigarette stubs, and papers littered the floor, while layers of stale smoke
made the air thick and blue.

Gustav Hanson, the proprietor, a big man with sandy red hair,
sat alone. Silently he watched the door opening and closing with the
comings and goings of the men. A wizened little man named Brenner
scuttled about, slinging beer with an expert hand, keeping a shifty eye

on the big Swede. He heaved a sigh of relief when Gustav got to his feet, moving quietly out of the bar.

The good steamy smells of roasting meat and freshly made cakes filled the hot kitchen. On the huge black stove, with its blazing fire of spruce logs, stood great pots of soup, gravy, potatoes and other vegetables. Opening the oven, the cook began putting in fresh pies to bake. Heat pinked her plump good-natured face, and little beads of sweat stood out on her forehead under bright blond hair. A slim dark waitress tramped in from the dining-room, shouting orders and crashing dishes into the sink. Behind her, a young woman dressed in a vivid green skirt and a gold satin blouse, teetered along in the spike heels of her gold shoes. She was flushed with anger.

"You do as I say or you're fired!" She stamped about the disorderly room. "Tommy!" The back door opened and a boy with blond tousled hair staggered in under a great armful of wood. "Didn't I tell you to take hot water up to number eight? And you never picked up those crates out of the way of the trucks in the yard. And you never swept the waiting-room this morning, did you?"

The boy clattered the logs into the woodbox.

"But Molly, a minute ago you said—"

"There you go again! Who gave you leave to call me Molly?"

Tommy made a helpless gesture with his hands. "What'll I do first?"

"Get out there and take the crates away, and get hot water up to number eight, like I said."

"But I'm going to be late again for school!" His face quivered. "And teacher said—"

The waitress picked up a tray of food ready to be taken to the dining-room.

"You take my tips every time," she cried defiantly. "It isn't you de man tip, it's me! And I ain't goin' to skin my face asking for fifty cents for a meal like dat!"

The cook slammed the oven door.

"Shut up everybody!" Gustav came in, bringing silence with him. "Get off to school," he ordered, seeing the boy standing uncertainly in the middle of the kitchen. Tommy went on the run. After repairing her make-up before a swimmy mirror, the waitress disappeared with the tray. The cook fled to the pantry. Gustav faced his wife.

"Gus, can't you do something with Tommy?" she pouted. "He never minds me."

"Leave the kid to me."

"Fifty cents isn't too much for a hamburger dinner, is it?" she asked. "He had pie and coffee too. And everything's getting so high."

"The dining-room's your affair." Gus put a fresh cigarette into his mouth and walked towards the door. He stopped, looking belligerent. "But for Pete's sake, quit yelling in here."

As the door swung to, hiding the big man, the cook rushed out of the pantry to open the oven, from which smoke was rising. Molly stood counting money into a glass jar, but she looked up now and then to peek through the round hole in the door to the dining-room. Her face, with its row of curls on her forehead, was the object of a good many side-glances from the men, and disgusted looks from the loud-voiced women. A noisy crowd filled the room to-day, taking every seat around the four tables, while more hungry people waited in the vestibule.

She watched with amusement as Jim Nelson, who travelled in dry goods, winked at her over his menu, while his companion talked endlessly of politics. She had to move aside as the waitress came in, shouting: "Three ham sandwiches!"

Molly took a closer look at three strangers settling themselves at the small table in the far corner of the dining-room. An old man with round red bunchy cheeks and a sunken mouth removed a battered stetson from his grizzled head, and helped a little golden-haired girl out of her red coat. But it was the woman with them who took Molly's attention. A tall woman, well built, striking in spite of her shabby clothes. Towering above the man and the child, she looked strong and determined, with strongly marked brows and an almost aquiline nose. Her honey-coloured hair made a thick knot at the back of her head.

"Who are they, Greta?" Molly asked the waitress.

"Dey want to see Gus."

Molly swung open the door.

"Did you wish to see my husband?"

Lina glanced up sharply. She had not noticed the other woman's approach.

"Are you Mrs. Hanson?" she asked. "It's Gus Hanson we're wanting to see."

"Yeah, I'm Mrs. Hanson. You could tell me your name. You see, he's awful busy in the beer parlour."

"I'm Mrs. Ashley."

"O.K., I'll tell him Sym Ashley's wife is here to see him." She went off smiling to herself.

Lina stiffened. The waitress who had now come to wait on them, looked over the child, the old man, and Lina with undisguised curiosity. The noise of conversation and the clatter of dishes seemed to pause all around the room. Across the smudgy glasses, spotty table cloth, lazy clinging flies, the smells of food, horses, sweat, garlic, Lina spoke to Poppy.

"Have a drink of water, dear? Benjie, are you sure you don't want nothing but a sandwich?"

"Seems like she knows Sym," the old man said.

"But of course," Lina answered easily, "he said in his letter that Mr. and Mrs. Hanson kept the hotel." She swallowed a mouthful of water.

Greta brought them sandwiches and coffee, a glass of milk for the child. Poppy bit into a sandwich without interest, and put it down again. She leaned back in the chair, infinitely weary, her head lolling from side to side. Benjie poured coffee into his saucer and blew on it. Lina composedly drank her coffee, turning encouragingly to her family, looking up only to see if Gus had yet appeared.

He came at last, filling the doorway, his face half veiled behind the smoke of a cigar, his eyes narrowed as he searched the room. Everyone quietened down at his entrance. Even a young Ukrainian who was loudly settling a European problem, drawing dents in the table cloth with a knife, stopped suddenly with the knife poised.

"Gus," Molly said behind her husband, "this is Mrs. Ashley to see you. Maybe she's come to pay the twenty bucks Sym owes us."

Lina's large hands with their discoloured callouses suddenly clasped together on the table. Gustav pulled up a chair.

"Get into the bar and see to things," he growled.

His wife clattered off swiftly on her high heels.

Gustav sat down heavily and took the cigar from his mouth, looking warily at Lina.

"You want to see me?"

"Yes." She met his gaze with a challenge in her own. "I'm Mrs. Ashley, and this is my father, Mr. Farrel."

Gustav half rose. "Nice meeting you. It's good to see all the new folks coming in."

"My husband," Lina went on, "my husband was here a while back. He wrote to me that he knew you."

"Why, yes. We saw quite a little bit of Sym." Gustav puffed at his cigar.

Opening her worn leather purse, Lina took out some bills.

"He told me to pay you."

"Now Mrs. Ashley," the big Swede protested, "I'm not after you folks for money. Any time is all right with me."

"Sym told me to pay you, and I got to."

Gustav glanced at the old man who sat stiff and tense, and at the little girl, almost asleep with her head on the table.

"Now please, Mrs. Ashley, you keep your money." He ground out his cigar into the ash-tray.

"I'm paying my bills and then I'll strike out for the homestead."

He looked into her face with the lines of weariness upon it.

"You folks need to rest up. I got lots of room."

"I figgered you could maybe tell me where the place is so we could get there by night."

"Course, if you're bound to go, I'll tell you. But you would be welcome, Mrs. Ashley."

"Thanks, but we aim to go."

"Take the east road and follow it about nine miles till you get to a steel bridge. That's the crossing over Bear Claw Creek. You turn north there, and a piece up the road you'll find a log shack. That's where Jack Two Knives lives. He's a breed. You'll need him to take you the rest of the way. He knows. He helped build Ashley's place."

"East to a steel bridge," Lina repeated. "Well, thanks. I figger we can find it."

Greta came round to see if they wanted anything more. They paid the bill. Lina and Benjie put on their things, and helped Poppy into hers. Gustav got up, holding out the twenty dollars.

"I wish you didn't feel you had to do this. Well, I wish you luck, Mrs. Ashley."

She smiled. "I reckon we'll be seeing you again some time."

The Ukrainian interested in European affairs watched, nodding to himself.

"Look at dat nice good Gustav," he murmured to a companion at his table. "De nice, good gentleman, Gustav." His mouth drew into a sneer. "He know how to make a lady smile."

The wagon moved slowly down the rough road. The little colt lay in the wagon box with Poppy sleeping beside him. Benjie huddled on the wagon seat, bent and weary, while the figure of the woman drooped beside him.

"Lina," the old man said presently, "I thought you was goin' to ask him if he knew where Sym is."

His daughter gazed ahead.

"I don't trust him. Did you look when he came across the room to us? He's too short in his step. His steps don't match his size."

"Mebbe Sym don't owe him money. Mebbe that guy just gypped you." The old man looked worried.

"Sym always owed money." Lina's eyes were shrewd, her tone bitter. "When Sym owed someone money, the fellow might just as well write it on his belly and wipe it off with his shirt."

"Reckon he'll ever turn up again?"

"When he gets broke enough and sick of everything, he'll turn up. His kind does."

"Gustav said you didn't need to pay right now. Why didn't you wait awhile? We ain't got much money."

"Daddy, you know as well as I do that if you owe a fellow money, it gives him a hold on you. I aim to be free of such like."

Glancing at her profile, he said no more.

Whisky and Rum were stiff and trembling after the long trek. The cow plodded stolidly. The footsore dog trotted behind, his ears flattened to his head, his tail drooping. Queen seemed to have fared quite well, but her eyes were anxious. With their load and their animals, it was difficult for them to pass other wagons on the narrow road. Drivers, however, though they stared, always spoke with great friendliness, usually in broken English. The sky was clear and bright, but by late afternoon, a coolness seemed to sweep upon them out of the forest.

Spring was not very far advanced here; yet they noticed a pale but definite greenness in the trunks of the poplars, and a deepening of colour in the spruce.

"Well, dad burn it, there's the bridge," Benjie said at last, straightening up to look ahead. "Girl, we're gettin' there!"

Having crossed the new-looking steel bridge, Lina turned her team northwards. Then they seemed to have left behind them the last vestige of civilization, for beyond lay the trails of trappers, and roads hand-hewn by homesteaders. Jolting, lurching, the wagon wound about through spruce and rocks, through interlacing bushes not yet in leaf, and by great black stumps. At last they came upon a low log house, half hidden in the thick vegetation. At the sound of their wagon wheels, a large mongrel dog sprang up from the door step, growling and showing his teeth at Gypsy. A man came out, shouting in a strange lilting tongue, making the dog retreat out of sight. The man lifted his dark face and smiled.

Lina pulled in her tired horses. "Is this Jack Two Knives' place?" she asked.

"I'm Jack Two Knives."

"I'm Mrs. Ashley. You helped my husband build a house. Where is it from here?"

"You Mrs. Ashley? You come here to live?"

Friendliness and welcome were in his voice. He shouted something into the half open door, and from it tumbled a group of six children, four boys and two girls, ranging in age from about twelve to two years old, all dressed alike in denim overalls and buckskin moccasins. Their eyes shone under ragged black hair. Then Mrs. Two Knives, small and slim, her heavy black hair bound in shining braids about her head, came out on noiseless feet, talking kindly, though unintelligibly.

"She speak not much English," Jack said. "But she say, you stay? Have to eat? Then I take you."

"Thanks, we did eat."

Excitement and laughter awoke as the little colt struggled up in the wagon box and Queen made warning noises. Lina climbed down, and she and the big native reached up for the colt which Benjie lifted out to them. Poppy, now thoroughly awake, slid to the ground like an eel to watch with the other children while the colt was sucking.

"Sym he tell me you come very soon." Jack rubbed the mare's head. The white woman was rigidly silent.

"I'd sure like to get there before night."

"It gets dark." Jack looked at the sky. "But I come with you. I get my horse."

The children began running and shouting, tumbling about on the ground, Poppy too, as though she had always known them. Mrs. Two Knives beckoned the other woman into the clean, bare home, with its one large bed, its rusty stove and home-made table. From a birch-bark basket under the bed, she took a beautiful pair of beaded moccasins of Poppy's size.

"Make you welcome." She put them into the white woman's hands.

Chapter IV

1

It seemed unreal, that last long stretch of road down which Jack Two Knives led the way with such assurance. They forded bridgeless streams; they lurched over great stones that threatened to tear off the wagon wheels; they bumped and rattled through the quiet land. The constant movement and jolting had become a part of Lina; but her shoulders ached, and her whole body felt stiff and sore. Her leather gloves had worn through to the fingers. Benjie swayed with the motion of the wagon, his eyes half closed, his body infinitely weary. Through it all, the child slept. Almost imperceptibly, the land was darkening.

Jack turned and shouted something, pointing ahead. At the same moment, the team suddenly sank into oozing mud at their feet. They jerked from side to side, terrified. Lina jumped up, cracking the long ends of the lines over their heads, yelling in a voice that woke a thousand echoes in the silent forest. The cow bawled in fright. The horses plunged wildly, straining great muscles of shoulder and flank, their feet making sucking sounds. The wagon creaked and groaned, writhing like a snake as it wriggled forward, moved on, found dry land. Queen appeared beside the team, trembling and spattered with mud. Jack had turned his horse to one side, ploughing his way through with loud shouting. He rode past with the casual words, "Pretty soon now."

The woman sat down, exhausted. Her horses moved slowly along, sweating, stumbling with weariness. The journey seemed a nightmare. Lina had become a numbed mind within pain. Benjie grinned and spat.

"You're a great girl!" He looked at her with tired eyes.

Jack's horse stood across the road, blocking it.

"Here."

"Whoa!" Benjie shouted, and stood up, stiffly.

To their left in a clearing in the dense bush they saw a log house and a small, flat-topped barn. All about the place hung a silence that poured from the vacant windows and the half-open door of the barn. A gate of upright poles, with a tall pole in the middle, slanting down to smaller ones on each side, stood in front of the fenceless yard. Just such a gate Sym had made for their place on the prairie. For a few long moments Lina sat silent. At last she climbed clumsily down and hobbled slowly towards the home that Sym had built for them. The men got down too, and began to look after the animals.

Lina tried the door. It swung open easily. Inside, in the dim light, she saw two rooms. The large, airy kitchen had three windows, a stove at one side and table and benches made of slabs nailed to the floor. In the other room stood the skeleton outline of a bedstead and springs. She found beside it a small stub of candle on a jam-can lid. Taking it back to the kitchen, she lit the candle, looking curiously about her, noting the mud-plastered walls and the rough splintery floor. A china clock hung near the door, its hands pointing to the hour of two. Outside she could hear the chink of harness, and the heavy tread of the horses' feet as they passed on their way to the barn. She heard Poppy saying, "Princey, Princey."

"We need a bridge of some kind over that last piece of muskeg," Benjie remarked as he and Jack passed the window. The woman stood motionless, looking at the clock. Her face was gaunt and weary, her hair untidy. "A clock," she thought. "He always liked clocks. Said it wasn't a home if there wasn't a clock ticking." She put the candle down on the table, and hunted for the key. As soon as she had wound it, the clock began to chime. She started the pendulum, and a musical tick sounded in the quiet room.

Benjie appeared at the door with a large cardboard carton which he dumped down on a bench.

"Let's eat," he suggested, "and then get out the bedrolls. Jack's gonna help me unload the plough, but we can unpack in the morning." His eyes went about the room. "Looks like a snug place, Lina. There's a good well in behind the house, too."

"Ask Jack to dinner," she said, hiding her face from him as she bent over the box. "We should unpack the lamp. It's handy to get, right by the chicken pen."

"I'm hungry," Poppy wailed from the door.

Her grandfather put a comforting arm around her. "There's wood piled up in the barn, Lina. I'll make a fire. C'mon, Poppy, help me bring in some wood."

They sat at dinner in the quiet lamplight. Jack tore ravenously at the ham sandwiches, but Lina and Benjie leaned heavily against the table, eating little. The child wandered about the new home, a piece of bread and butter in her hand. As Jack gulped down the last of the strong black tea, the woman said to him,

"Come and work for me. I'll pay you."

The gaunt man lit a limp cigarette.

"I come. But Gustav want me soon."

He inhaled deeply, lazily, his whole attitude one of careless indifference.

"Next week?" Lina asked.

He nodded. A moment later, without a farewell word, he was gone. They heard his horse's hoofs trotting quickly away from the clearing.

The forest was everywhere. On the springy root-matted paths and by water holes were the print of deer and moose, and the broad, almost human track of bear. As their ears became attuned, the strangers noticed the forest sounds: the thrumming of partridge, the hooting of the deep-feathered owl, the scolding of chipmunks in the spruce, the chatter of the Canada jay, the songs of unknown birds, the wind making the branches creak and old trees groan. Wolves howled at night, deeply hidden. These were strange sounds to the ears of prairie folk. The only thing that sounded familiar was the clanking of the bell which the cow wore in her wanderings through the day. In this vast and lonely place it was easy to feel lost or hunted. The winding trails constantly needed to be cleared of fallen trees or fast-growing bush. Amid this maze of vegetation, the newcomers, used as they were to gazing across measureless miles of prairie, felt themselves shut in, imprisoned.

For the most part, the acres that Sym Ashley had staked off, lay beneath a covering of heavy brush and conifers. Here and there in the open places grass would soon grow, deep and green. To secure more grass, clearing was sufficient; but for a garden space, for just a small field of oats and of wheat, Lina began to tear at the land with bare hands. She was glad when Jack, riding by the house late one evening, came in to tell them that he would be there next day to help.

After breakfast there was no sign of the new helper. Benjie kept walking to the road, looking and waiting, while Lina, taking Poppy with her, worked on a fence of rails about the pasture. At last, towards noon, they all heard the unmistakable sounds of wagon wheels and horses. Benjie came to find his daughter, an incredible look on his face.

"He brung the wife and kids. They're pitching a tent in our yard."

"Kids?" Poppy cried in delight, scampering off ahead.

Lina threw down the rail that she was setting in place and followed.

There at the cabin door, the tent was spreading itself, and the children were already having a game of tag at the gate, while Mrs. Two Knives lighted a fire on the ground. Jack straightened up from where he was pounding in the tent pegs. They all looked so happy that Lina could not help smiling.

"Everybody came along, eh?"

Jack nodded. "We come to brush for you. My wife and boys, they help."

"I hadn't counted on feeding so many," Lina murmured to Benjie while the natives went on pitching camp. "I reckon Mrs. Two Knives can cook for the outfit. There's lots of bacon and beans."

"Jack says the boys will bring in some fish." Benjie looked worried. "A dollar a day is what the wages is here."

Lina's mouth went into a straight line. "We'll make out. Look at that kid of mine, would you! Running round like wild. There'll be no holding her now."

"Leave the kid be, girl. She's got to play sometimes."

3

But her chief concern had to be for the land. With Jack, she worked like a machine, scarcely stopping to straighten up or to rest. They wrenched out great stumps and roots, and prodigious rocks. Every inch of the rich soil must be fought for, with heaving of shoulders and backs, and straining of horses. Inch by inch Lina and Jack pushed back the forest, felling trees, ploughing, hauling away the stones. Day by day the spring was bringing the countryside to life. Grass grew green and thick by the roadside and in the cleared places. The poplars and the willows budded out into a haze of green, and then into full leaf. Benjie did the sowing, by hand. They would be late with their garden.

"I'll cut the oats green," Lina told her father one evening. "And Jack tells me that Sven Jensen does the thrashing around here. But we'll just have enough wheat to feed us through the winter and some left for seed. Jack won't stay much longer. We'll have to do for ourselves."

Looking at his daughter's sweat-stained clothes, and her face sharp under the grime, Benjie sighed.

"Wish I could get more done, Girl. Don't seem right, me just harnessing the team and drivin' around."

"Well, you got a nice rail fence put up, Daddy. Anyways the blame cow can't get away like she did at first. Where's the kid? We got to be getting to bed."

"She's out there with the rest of them, whoopin' it up."

Lina went to the door and listened. The children scampered about, playing in an ecstasy of happiness, their laughter gushing free, their shouts mingling with the barking of the dog.

"Poppy!" her mother called. "Come on in here!"

The native children stopped in their tracks, and the small figure of the little girl came slowly out of the shadows. Dirty, barefoot, clad only in her overalls, she appeared in the lighted kitchen.

"Wash your face now, and run along to bed. Hurry!" Lina poured warm water into the basin. "Use the soap. Don't rub off all the dirt on to the towel. Good gosh!" Lina exclaimed in horror as the child obediently bent to wash. "Daddy! Her head's fair crawling with lice! Come here, Poppy. For heaven sake stand still!"

But the child darted away from her, bursting into tears in a corner of the kitchen.

"We got to put some coal-oil on her hair." Benjie got up wearily, and went towards the little girl. "Come on, Baby, it won't hurt."

"What next!" Lina groaned. "I got an old piece of stocking that I could sew up the end and cover her head with!"

"Never mind." The old man rubbed oil vigorously into the heavy tangled hair. "She's getting tanned and tough anyways."

"I should of looked to the kid's hair. So much to think of—"

But it was good land. The day after Jack and his family had driven away, rain came, and they could rest for a little while. Grey and slanting, the rain seeped into the new-turned earth. What matter that their money was practically gone? They had almost forgotten what a slow steady rain was like. Everywhere, greenness rested the eyes. The croaking of frogs, the whistling of birds accompanied the music of falling rain. Lina could not stay inside, but dressed in old clothes and a slicker of Benjie's, she walked about, setting every available pail and pan to catch soft water. The next morning it was still raining as she rode along the trail on Queen with the colt following. She was taking time to explore, and to see what lay beyond the bend in the road. She thought of other springtimes she had known, with their blizzards of dust, and brown burnt prairie grass, and the few flowers blown to bits in storms. Now she rode through the grey sheets of rain, just to feel its cool sweet freshness. The trees lifted their leaves like faces to it, and every leaf was shining with moisture. Flowers she had never seen blossomed along the path, and every cup was filled. Queen slithered in the mud, but it did not matter. The woman did not care if she was covered with mud, or where she went, or if she were to come home drenched to the skin.

She came suddenly upon a low level stretch of land with just a scattering of brush. For the rest it was covered with grass, green and dripping.

"Wild hay!" Lina pulled her horse to a standstill. "Acres of it!" She feasted her eyes on the misty fields. And now she saw the gleam of water, and noticed a little lake with clumps of willows at its margin. Queen tossed her head as the colt moved restlessly about. Streams of water were running down the road under foot. The rain came in gusts, pattering on the leaves and soughing through the evergreens. The woman did not move. It was a long while before she turned back, becoming for the first time conscious of the wetness penetrating every part of her clothing.

5

That afternoon, Lina built up a good fire, and put on quantities of the soft water to get hot. Everyone, she announced, was to have a good wash and get cleaned up. She shampooed her own heavy honey-coloured hair, relishing the feeling of cleanliness. In a clean print dress and starched apron, she scrubbed Poppy in the wash-tub in front of the stove. The child was docile, submitting to the ministrations with good grace, talking all the while with a friendliness her mother rarely saw in her. She put on her clean overalls, and even gave in to wearing shoes and socks. Poppy's hair was shoulder-length, straight and thick, and pale gold in colour.

"We must get you a nice pretty dress to start school in," her mother said, brushing vigorously. "What colour would you like?"

"Pink, with frills." Poppy waited patiently for the ribbon to be tied. Lina's little hand sewing-machine and Benjie's fiddle were the two great family treasures.

"Have to get her a scribbler and pencil too." The old man buttoned his clean shirt before the mirror by the window. He grinned at his grandchild, his red cheeks shining.

"Bacon and beans for supper." Lina straightened up, while the little girl ran free, dancing about.

The grey afternoon soon darkened into evening, bringing with it a steady drizzle. Benjie lit the small coal-oil lamp which shed a dim but warm light, while the stove gave out a satisfactory heat.

Lina sat at the table, scrutinizing the shack with thoughtful eyes.

"Reckon we'll have to wait till winter to fix up the place."

"It's all right, Girl," Benjie murmured.

"Well, yes, but we need cupboards. And the bedroom, I figger we could partition that and make two rooms."

Benjie sat down by the fire, whittling a stick into the woodbox.

"Nice to see you just do nothing for a change."

"Play your fiddle, Gramp," the child pleaded, clinging to him.

It was the first time Benjie had taken out his instrument since they had left the prairie. He took a long time tuning it, and his eyes were sad; but when he played *Danny Boy* to them, a smile lit up his face. He played it over two or three times, while his daughter hummed it, seeming to forget for a moment her work and weariness, her driving determination. Poppy clasped her hands, enchanted.

Suddenly, Gypsy, lying just inside the door, sprang up with a sharp bark. There were the sounds of wheels and of voices outside.

"Down Gyp! Shut up!"

"Come here, boy!" Laying his fiddle aside, Benjie seized the dog by the scruff of the neck, ordering him into the bedroom. Opening the door, Lina looked out into the dripping night. A man stood on the threshold, and behind him a group of silent figures huddled in a wagon drawn by a team of scrubby horses. Two or three dogs slunk growling under the wagon.

"I was sure I heard a fiddle," the stranger said. His voice had a reedy tone, with something about the accent which told that Cree was his native tongue. "We're your neighbours. I'm Isaiah Waters."

"Won't you all come in?" Lina hesitated. "It's so wet."

Turning his head, the man said something she could not understand, and in the shadows, a group of people got down out of the wagon. Isaiah stood at the door with something wrapped in a flour sack under his arm. He was a thin, wiry man, dressed in a shabby blue suit and a clean plaid shirt, with three or four tie pins shining in his vivid red tie. Thick, matted black hair showed under a black hat tightened by a thong. His face, a dark greasy brown, beaten by every kind of weather, had deep lines about the eyes and mouth, which gave it, in repose, a remote sadness.

"My mother," he said, as an old woman with a wrinkled copper-coloured face and grey braided hair, huddling a blanket about her shoulders, appeared in the lamplight. A shrunken old man whose brown skin was full of thousands of fine lines, with more appearing at each word or smile or frown, followed her. This, Isaiah told them, was Bill Manydogs, the brother of his mother. They were duly introduced to Isaiah's wife, Martha, vivid in a red dress under a green coat and carrying a crying baby on her hip. She alone wore shoes, patent leather ones with high, wobbly heels.

"And this," said Isaiah finally, "is Jay." He had an affectionate hand on the shoulder of a dark-faced lad. They all trooped in, taking off their rubbers, walking with silent moccasined feet to the benches, and to the trunk which Benjie hospitably pulled forward for them to sit on. Lina shut the door, and immediately Gypsy stood beside it, growling menacingly, listening to the yapping of the dogs outside.

Isaiah sat down beside Benjie, taking a fiddle out of the flour sack.

"I heard you playing something, a new song. I never heard it before. How does that go?"

The poignant tune began again, and the three men leaned together. Old Mrs. Waters bent down to pick up her son's gloves from the floor where he had dropped them.

"Say them are some gloves. May I see them?" The white woman took them into her hands, studying the intricate beaded pattern on the backs and cuffs.

"Buckskin," Mrs. Waters said. "I make. Wear long time."

"How much for a pair like that?"

The shrewd blue eyes met the wise dark ones.

"A setting hen, and print for a dress, and fifty cents."

"Make me a pair."

Lina sat down on the edge of the wood-box and held out her hand while Mrs. Waters noted the length of her fingers, muttering to herself.

"Saturday I bring them."

Martha opened the front of her dress and began nursing the baby.

"I'll never get my little Sammy weaned. He cries all the time." Grey eyes in a dark face looked hopefully at Lina.

"Daddy says you should wean the baby at the change of the moon. We done that with Poppy and we never had no trouble at all."

"Nice yellow hair," the old woman remarked, looking at Poppy who had settled herself at the table with Jay. They had a piece of brown wrapping paper spread out before them, upon which the boy was drawing quick pencil sketches to amuse her.

"A reindeer!" the little girl demanded.

"All right, a deer." His voice had a sweet huskiness, a pathos rare in a boy of his age, and his mouth was fine and sensitive. With dense black hair, and large black eyes half hidden by drooping lids, he looked darker than he was beside the fairness of the golden-haired child.

"Does the little girl go to school?" Martha asked.

"She'll be starting in September." And then Lina was suddenly startled to hear Isaiah playing *Danny Boy* with a depth and tenderness that Benjie could not equal.

While Isaiah played, Bill Manydogs held Benjie's violin, touching it softly as though it were a live thing, looking at it with longing. His black snaky locks hung about his crafty eyes.

"Better hang on to your fiddle," Isaiah warned, as he finished with a flourish. "Some one stole Bill's." He handed the instrument back to its owner.

"You speak English real good," Benjie said admiringly.

Isaiah tightened his bow, and plucked at the strings of his fiddle with his fingers.

"I went to Mission School. My mother went to school once, too. She can still read." There was pride in her son's voice. "Play me another. What else do you know?"

"D'ye know this here hoe-down?" Benjie swung into some quick music which Isaiah soon joined, while Bill thundered out the calls of a square dance. The children laughed aloud over some drawings Poppy had made. The baby whined. The dogs within and without, snarled and barked. Martha talked volubly. The old woman filled her pipe. The close air of the little cabin reeked with the smells of wet dog, buckskin, strong body odours, and tobacco smoke. Lina got up, opening the window to let in the wind with its sprays of rain and fresh sweet air.

"Could you stay for a cup of coffee?" she asked. "The kettle is right on the boil."

"I sure would like to." Martha tossed her black mane with a look in Isaiah's direction.

The music went on and on as the three men played to each other and exchanged tunes. After the coffee, Lina began to feel weary, and hoped the guests would soon leave.

"Come with us," Isaiah urged Benjie.

"Where?"

"To the dance at the school. You can make five dollars, fiddling."

"Five dollars?" Benjie grinned at his daughter. She glanced at the battered alarm clock on the table which said eleven thirty.

"What time does it start?" she asked.

"It starts," Isaiah replied with dignity, "when I begin to play. You come too."

But she shook her head. "I've got to put the kid to bed."

He put his violin into the flour sack again, and stood up, looking questioningly at Benjie.

"Sure, I'll come," the old man declared. "Do they dance all night?"

"Till it gets light and the sun begins to shine."

The visitors quickly put on their things and gathered themselves together for their departure. As soon as the door opened, the dogs rushed viciously upon each other. Bill separated them forcibly. Lina grabbed Gypsy by the scruff of the neck. He growled and trembled while the group piled into the wagon. Benjie had gone into the bedroom to get a canvas to cover up with on the journey. Isaiah waited on the doorstep.

"I seen you this morning riding by the hay field."

The woman's hand tightened on the dog's ruff.

"Is it your land?" she asked.

"No. I live near."

"Whose land is it?"

Isaiah shrugged.

"Then who gets the hay?"

"Whoever gets there first."

Benjie came out of the bedroom carrying a piece of canvas and his violin case.

"See you in the morning, Girl."

The door closed on them with a draught that made the flame in the lamp flicker, blackening the glass chimney. After Poppy was in bed, her mother glanced over the paper on which the children had been drawing. There were the jagged scribblings of her own child, and about them marched many animals of the forest, deer, moose, rabbit, chipmunk. They were crudely done, but with amazing accuracy. She sat for a long time, looking at them, thinking deeply.

Chapter V

1

Early one August morning, the fire roared hot in the stove of the stifling kitchen while Lina fished out of the steaming wash-tub, quart and pint bottles of saskatoons and raspberries which she and Benjie and the unwilling Poppy had picked the day before. Poppy sat in the doorway, her mouth and fingers stained purple, purple stains marking the front of her coveralls. With her mouth turned down at the corners and her nose running, she cried endlessly, a wretched, irritating whine.

"Poppy!" With the back of her wrist, Lina pushed back the locks of loosened hair which clung damply to her forehead. "Stop that crying this minute!" She made as though she would shake the little girl.

"I wanna go with Gramp." Poppy got up and stamped her bare foot, but it struck sharply against a loose nail. The pain caused her to burst out into wild sobbing. Benjie drove up in the wagon from the barn, with Whisky and Rum impatient to be off.

"Whoa!" he shouted. "What's the matter now?"

Standing in the doorway, his daughter wiped her hands on a dish-towel, shaking her head, while the child rolled over and over on the ground.

"Good gosh, Daddy, anybody passing by would think I was killing the kid."

The old man got down from the wagon and took her into his arms. She clung to him, anguished.

"I can't let her go to town like that. She hasn't a clean thing to put on. I never even got time to comb her hair this morning, and she looks a sight."

Benjie still held Poppy. He hesitated. "It would take her off your hands."

"She's got the notion lately that she can get her own way by having tantrums."

"I'll see she don't get into no trouble. Something's wrong with a kid that keeps crying."

Lina saw a look on old Benjie's face that made her sigh with exasperation.

"All right then. Come in, Poppy, and get your face washed. You spoil her all to pieces."

"Why no, Girl. A little bit of loving don't spoil no kid. Need anything else besides the lumber and nails?"

"Coffee and sugar. I couldn't begin to comb out these snarls, it would take half an hour. Put your beret on. Where are your shoes? Oh, those raspberries should be coming out."

Poppy darted into the bedroom, coming out a moment later, quite presentable, her face shining and clean from its scrubbing.

"There's some pink broadcloth at Wong's," Lina said, tightening the screw top of the jar of hot fruit. "I was thinking to make Poppy a new dress to go to school in. She sure looks awful in them coveralls."

"An' a pencil-box, an' a book!" the little girl shrilled.

"You can pick those out yourself," old Benjie told her as he put her into the wagon box.

It was Hog Day in Bear Claw. Teams and wagons lined the two streets. The jingle of harness, the voices of men haggling in various languages, the squealing of pigs, the rumbling of wagon wheels, rose on the dusty air. Zachariah Olenski walked unsteadily down the main street on the hazardous board walks with their rotting planks mended with old auto license-plates of rusty reds and yellows. Many whiskered, rough-looking men spoke to him as he passed, but received only a sullen grunt in reply. His face was shadowed by an old felt hat with great patches of sweat on the lower part of the crown. From the hip pocket of his overalls, something bulged, giving his walk an ungainly appearance. As he approached Wong's, his steps became slower, and he finally leaned on the wall against a tobacco advertisement, the only sign of colour on the building. Here he struck a match, and practically hiding his face from view, relit a stub of cigarette which had gone dead in his mouth. But one squinty eye watched the street where Gustav, towering above most of the people about, came towards him with his quick small steps.

"Olenski, what about that hay?" The big Swede spoke quietly.

The other man turned his head aside to exhale a cloud of smoke. "De woman get dere before me."

"Full of moonshine, weren't you? Just like you are now."

"Gus!" someone bellowed from the hotel door. "You're wanted!"

"If you got no hay and no money, then by spring you got no farm," Gustav declared.

Watching him go, Olenski stepped to the side of the walk, spat defiantly and slouched into Wong's.

Ordering groceries for several neighbours who had hailed him on the way, Benjie kept close watch over Poppy who wandered about, blissfully chewing licorice. She looked wonderingly through the store, gazing with rapture at the enormous stockings hanging from the ceiling, feeling the slick feel of the rows of new boots, sniffing the leathery, horsey, grocery smell of the place. Wong smiled through his broken teeth as he helped her select a bright red pencil box and a scribbler on whose cover a cowboy roped a hapless calf.

"Velly nice, velly nice." Wong's eyes sparkled as he wrapped up her purchases.

"Got everything?" Benjie grinned at her.

"Pink stuff for my dress," she reminded him.

"Missy give you goods." Wong pointed across the store to where a neat Chinese girl was tidying up the bales of cloth. The old man and the little girl went over to her.

"Some pink stuff for a dress," Benjie ordered.

"How much?"

"Oh, enough to cover this here kid."

Miss Wong brought forward some pink broadcloth. "This is nice," she offered. "Won't fade either."

Benjie nodded his approval.

"Frills," Poppy demanded.

"We have some very nice white frilling," the Chinese girl began, looking doubtfully at Benjie out of her almond-shaped eyes.

"Sure, give the kid her frills."

Across the store, Wong shouted, "No! No! Olenski! You no pay, I give you notting!"

Olenski uttered a curse, banging the flat of his hand down on the counter.

"Come on, Zak," one of the men said, taking his arm; "let's go get a drink." Everyone stood aside as the two men went out, Olenski waving his arms and talking loudly and defiantly in his own language.

Tudor hammered busily, tacking on the loose sole of a shoe. His shop stood on a slight rise, facing the two streets of Bear Claw, so that he had a good view of all that went on in the town. The thick branches of the huge spruce beside the door, helped to keep the place cool on a hot day like this. There was a worse crowd than usual for Hog Day; good many strangers, too. Tudor paused in his hammering, taking several tacks out of his mouth. Through the window he could see an old man and a little girl coming up the slope. The child opened the screen, coming in to stare in wonder, while her grandfather bunched up his red cheeks, grinning at Folkes.

"Howdy." He shifted his pipe to the corner of his mouth.

Tudor nodded, standing straight and lean.

"Aren't you Benjie Farrel?" he asked, coming forward with his hand outstretched.

"Why, yes." The old man looked up in surprise at Tudor's thin tanned face that was not young, but had something in it that would never be old.

"Welcome to our city. I'm Tudor Folkes. I heard you people had come in. Here, sit down." He drew forward a dilapidated chair, testing it with his hands first, before offering it. "And what's this little girl's name, eh?"

"Mary Belle Ashley." Poppy moved over shyly to her grandfather, smiling slowly, showing her teeth stained with licorice. There was to Tudor something familiar about that smile. He sat down on the table, picking up his pipe and lighting it with great concentration.

"I've been looking out for you for some time."

"We don't git to town much. We been awful busy all summer. But," Benjie went on in a puzzled tone, "how in tarnation did you know who I was?"

"Oh, I keep count of all the strangers. I want to get a look at their shoes." Tudor drew his feet up on to the table, and leaning against the wall, sat hugging his knees. "There was a fellow I used to know," he said thoughtfully. "Lived down near Shingle Hills. He was quite a cattle man when I was in that country before the war. His name was Duke Watson. Did you happen to know him?"

"Duke Watson!" Benjie's face lit up. "Why him and me was pals in the East fifty years ago! We came west and rode the range together before we both went farming. He's down there still, waitin' for irrigation. And you knew him?"

Tudor grinned. "I was just out from England, and green as grass. Duke gave me plenty of good advice. He was a character all right."

"You do talk a little Englishy." Benjie drew the child on to his knee. "Why didn't you stay there?" the old man asked presently.

Tudor dangled one foot, hugging the other knee. "Well, after the war, I wasn't really strong enough to handle the farm. Oh, I hung on for a while, but it's dusty country, what?"

Benjie looked dreamily out at the expanse of bush beyond the town. "Oh, some years she's worse than others. Funny I never knew you," he said, his gaze coming back to the other's face. "Course, I was away East when the wife died, and then when I come back I pulled out of Shingle Hills. Been here long?"

"Going on ten years now." Tudor relit his pipe. "One place is as good as another, I guess."

"Well, sir, it's like seein' somebody from home to meet up with a friend of Duke's." Benjie beamed at him, putting the child off his knee and getting up. "He was like my older brother all this long time. I'd like to come in and spend the time of day with you now and then. And say, come out to our place some time."

"Well now, I'll try to do that." Tudor slowly put his feet to the floor. "What was it you wanted?"

"Do you have any harness buckles? Wong's clean out of them."

Folkes opened a wooden box on the table, and began sorting out a buckle or two from the odd mixture of shoe buttons, nails, and miscellaneous bits of metal.

"Here are three. I don't deal in them, you see. You can have them." He held the buckles out carefully as though they were treasures of great value.

Benjie dropped them into the pocket of his overalls. "Say, Folkes, did you ever happen across Sym Ashley?"

Tudor nodded. "He was in here the night before he went away."

"You wouldn't know where he went?"

"He said he was going to cinch some deal. I don't think he meant to be gone for long. Something must have happened."

Benjie puffed at his pipe. "Was he in any trouble?"

Tudor looked into Benjie's honest troubled face. "Not around here, as far as I know. Everyone seemed to like Sym Ashley."

The two men were silent for a while. Then they chatted about crops and the price of hogs until Poppy said suddenly, "Gramp, let's go home."

Benjie and Tudor shook hands. "It's been that good to see you," the old man said, his voice a little unsteady. Laughter lines creased the corners of Folkes' eyes as the child and her grandfather disappeared behind a wagon. He had forgotten to look at their shoes. He put some tacks between his lips. Where was Sym with his charming smile, he wondered, shaking his head.

4

The atmosphere of the bar was thick. Men crowded the little tables, talking with wild gesticulations, shouting, laughing and singing. Gustav moved among them calm and sober, helping Brenner eject any particularly tough customer. Olenski, watching from a far corner, sucked the beer from his ragged moustache.

"It's always tough on Hog Day," Jim Nelson told Norris who travelled in hardware. An old man with tobacco juice and beer running out of the corners of his mouth was shoved outside.

"Git!" Brenner panted. "And don't come back!"

Sitting near the door, Pete Panachuk roared loudly at some vile joke. Sven Jensen who sat with him, flushed a deep red, sputtering, "But—but will you take her? There's no place for her to go!"

Pete pushed his greasy cap back on his head and tossed off a glass of beer.

"Sure, Mr. Chairman," he replied, smacking his lips. "I take her. We got ten in de house already, and de wife getting one soon. She can board for twenty dollars de mont, and cheap at de price. Teacher of Tiger Lily School, she got to go someplace." He grinned, nodding towards the door. "Dere's Gustav's new wife." He said knowingly, "She brought good business waiting tables. Now she's hooked, she can't walk out on him."

Exchanging winks and snickers, the men in the bar watched Molly. Among the dark unshaven faces, hers looked fragile, almost beautiful. A vicious snarl sounded above the din of the room.

"Women!" shouted Olenski. "It's always de women dat make de trouble!" He got up from his place in the corner, knocking over a chair as he did so. "Women!" he clenched his fists, and lurched forward, his hat falling off, bringing to view his shaggy head with its tufts of unkempt black hair. Molly went white, uncertain whether to go to the door or to Gus. There was a curious quiet. The men stopped their singing and talk and watched with drunken interest. Brenner touched Olenski's shoulder.

"Come on, Olenski, you better go home." He spoke cajolingly as though to a child. "Come on, old man, we don't want no trouble here."

"Go on, Zak," Gustav said from the other side of the room.

Olenski twisted around to look at him. His mouth was frothing as he burst forth in a stream of filth and curses.

"Zak," Brenner spoke again.

"He ain't gonna take my farm! I'll rip—his—guts!"

The bar was suddenly in an uproar. Everyone crowded to the sidelines. In a mad rush, Olenski overturned tables and chairs, which went down with wooden thuds and the crash of breaking glasses. Streams of beer trickled across the floor. Jim Nelson pulled Molly outside. Brenner tried to grab Olenski by the back of his greasy shirt.

"Look out, Gus! He's got a knife!" Brenner cried, as Olenski raised his right hand menacingly, and a long knife blade gleamed through the gaze.

"I'll slit his guts!" he cried.

Gustav seized the upraised arm, and the knife went clattering over the bare boards. The men were both big, though Gus was by far the stronger. Charging at him, Olenski sobbed aloud, cursing frenziedly. Gustav landed a blow in the other man's face that knocked him to the floor where he lay, motionless.

"Take him outside," the big Swede said, wiping the sweat from his face with the back of his hand.

Some of the men carried the unconscious man from the bar.

"Come on, let's have another drink!" someone shouted.

The men crowded to the chairs again, and life in the beer parlour went on as though nothing had happened.

Benjie had put Poppy into the wagon, and was untying his team from the hitching-post, when he saw Isaiah coming towards them on horseback, superbly at ease in the saddle, straight and still. Under his black hat, his hair was plastered wetly to his head.

"Get through haying?" Isaiah asked, getting down at Benjie's side.

"We got done. Jack Two Knives borried us a hay-rack and rake from Sven Jensen. Thanks for the use of your mower."

"That's all right. So long you feed Jay's horse and Mother's team through the winter."

Benjie lit his pipe.

"Olenski been around your place?" Isaiah asked finally.

"Ain't seen him. Why?"

"He always got the hay. For five years he fed horses for Gus on the hay." The dark-faced man stroked Buck's neck.

"Gramp, let's go home," Poppy said from the wagon.

Isaiah looked up at her, his face softening. "How you going to send her to school?" he asked.

Benjie shrugged. "I got the lumber here to build a cutter for winter. But it's a long way for a little girl to walk right now when we're so busy."

"She could go with Jay. Buck's a good horse, gentle."

"I'll talk it over with her mother," Benjie said. "Lina'll want to take her the first day, I reckon. Mighty nice of you."

Isaiah had his foot in the stirrup. "Got to go. Working over at Jensen's." He rode gracefully off.

"Am I going to school with Jay?" Poppy asked her grandfather as he climbed into the wagon.

"Could be."

"Will Jack Two Knives' kids be there?"

"Freddie and Johnnie will be. They'll stay with Joe Poudre."

The child hugged herself with excitement, while her grandfather backed the horses into the road. Crossing directly in front of them was a group of men, carrying a limp form. An ugly boy of about fifteen had just joined them.

"Where's the wallet?" he asked.

"Here." One of the men gave it to him. The boy stood still, looking into it, not seeing the coming team, so that Benjie shouted to him in alarm.

"Not a damn cent left!" the boy cried, jumping to the side of the road.

"Where'll we put him, Mike?" someone asked.

"There," with a dirty thumb, Mike indicated the wagon nearest them. "Not a damn cent left after all that work with them hogs!" He flung the wallet after his father, and went to untie the horses.

"Can you handle him, kid?" asked Brenner.

"Yeah," he answered, climbing up.

A moan came from the wagon box.

"Oh shut up!" the boy muttered.

Chapter VI

I'll drive you this time," Lina said. "I'll be going by the school anyhow on my way to town. You can come home with Jay. And mind you put on your coveralls over that dress when you ride the horse. What's wrong, child?"

Poppy hunched herself against the breakfast table before her untouched toast and honey, a forlorn little figure in spite of her new pink dress with the frills. Though her thick hair was brushed till it shone golden, her expression was mournful. She gave her grandfather a look of silent appeal.

"You'll like school real well, honey," he said smiling.

"Come on, Poppy," her mother urged. "Eat your breakfast. I've 'most got the lunch packed. I've put in some nice little tarts, raspberry." Lina put the lid on the syrup tin which was to serve as a lunch-pail, and laid it beside the gay new scribbler and red pencil-box. Then she saw that the tears streamed down the child's cheeks as she wept silently and bitterly.

"Oh, Poppy don't cry," she pleaded. "Mother must go out and harness the horses. There's nothing to cry about. Daddy, can't you do something with her?"

As soon as Lina had disappeared outside, Benjie had the little girl on his knee, and let her sob against his shoulder.

"It's going to be all right, sweet," he murmured. "And when you come home, you can tell us all about it. And Jay'll be there. I bet Jay ain't cryin'."

Poppy hastily swallowed her sobs. "Have you got a hanky, Gramp?"

By the time her mother drove up from the barn, she had eaten her breakfast and, much subdued, but composed, she stood in the doorway holding her belongings. Benjie swung her up on to the wagon seat beside her mother, and she waved to him until the wagon rounded a corner and she could no longer see him. Lina struck the dashboard with the lines.

"C'mon Whisky! Get going, Rum!"

In the beautiful September weather, clear and hot, the leaves were beginning to turn on either side of the thickly bushed trail. The smell of autumn tanged the air. Along the rough trail with its great rocks and stumps, over rickety bridges and broken culverts, the wagon rattled. Whisky and Rum, sleek after a summer of rich pasture, were full of spirit. Lina held the horses with a firm hand, smiling as though she enjoyed the stubborn struggle between herself and them. The child remained silent, sad, gazing straight ahead.

"Poppy," Lina said, slowing the team to a walk.

"Yes."

"C'mon now, buck up. No cry-baby stuff. You're a big girl now."

"Yes."

Through the trees, they could see the schoolhouse, hear the shouts of some children playing ball. The horses pricked up their ears, and a saddle pony in the yard answered Rum's neighing.

"Poppy— Oh well, you'll be all right. Here we are."

They stopped at the gate where a group of little girls with shining faces and crisply starched dresses talked intimately together. Poppy eyed them with hauteur, jumping lightly down over the wheel.

"Be a good girl," her mother cautioned, handing her the coveralls. "Don't be no trouble to teacher."

Lina whistled, and the horses were off. The wagon disappeared in a cloud of dust, leaving the little girl very much alone. Clutching her lunch-pail in one hand and her scribbler, pencil-box and rolled-up coveralls awkwardly under the other arm, she moved towards the girls who had now ceased talking and were all staring at her. A smiling youngster, her brown hair cut in long jagged bangs, came up beside her.

"Are you Mrs. Ashley's little girl?"

"Oh Laura, isn't she cute!" whispered a thin one with long dark braids.

Poppy nodded mutely to the question.

"What's your name?" asked the girl called Laura.

"Mary Belle Ashley."

"How old are you?"

"Seven."

"Ever been to school before?"

"No."

"You better be careful old Goggle-Eyes don't give you the strap."

"Gee, don't scare the poor kid, Laura," the girl with the braids said.

"Oh shut up, Olga!" Laura replied rudely, tossing her bangs. The others giggled, nudging and pushing each other. "Is that a new pencil-box?" Laura went on. "Let's see it." She made a dive for it, but the child squirmed away, almost sobbing.

"Baby!" the tormentor jeered. "Keep the old thing!"

Just then a ball struck the ground near by and rolled to the gate. A boy came tearing after it, swift on moccasined feet, his forelock of black hair standing upright. Poppy cried out in relief: "Jay! Jay!" Someone in the crowd mimicked her: "J-a-y! J-a-y!" The lad stopped dead, taking in the situation with a swift glance, his face clouding with anger. There was a silence.

"Look, Jay, I got a new pencil-box," the child said.

Jay slowly unclenched his fists and Poppy smiled her lovely smile. The school bell rang.

From every corner of the yard, and from the barn and from the trails leading to the school, children began running towards the door where the teacher swung the bell in her hand. Only Poppy and Jay stood still, the little girl frightened and uneasy, the boy looking down at her with a kind of tender reassurance.

"Come on, Poppy." He put a hand on her shoulder. "You're a school kid now."

They were the last to enter. The indefinable, unforgettable school smell engulfed them. At the back of the room, youngsters flung caps and sweaters onto nails, piled their lunch pails in a corner by the unlighted stove, and scrambled for the back seats. The room seemed to shrink in size, holding the thirty pupils, many of them big boys, almost like men. They muttered low in strange accents, poked and shoved, and looked sideways at the teacher. Poppy walked slowly into this new world, bewildered but fascinated. She also glanced at the teacher who replaced the bell on her own home-made table.

"It's a cow-bell!" Poppy whispered to Jay. "A cow-bell on a stick!" He suppressed a grin. Across the room, Freddy and Johnny Two Knives waved to her. Jay put her lunch with the others and hung up his own cap.

"You stay here with Johnny Two Knives," he suggested. "He's just starting too. Teacher will look after you."

Noisily, the pupils filled up the rows of rough, homemade seats and desks, two at each place. From Indian, Slavic and Teutonic faces, thirty pairs of eyes fixed themselves ruthlessly upon the new teacher. They saw with the brutal honesty of children her plain clothes, her homely face, her thick straight hair pinned into an untidy bun. Sullenly, they regarded the blackboard, covered with arithmetic of varying difficulty. The teacher straightened her silver-rimmed glasses as she called the roll, her nimble tongue struggling valiantly with the foreign names.

"Neils Christiansen." A large clumsy red-haired boy at the back lifted a hairy hand. "Eugene Desjarlais." Shifty black eyes confronted her, belonging to a lean little boy who could never sit still. When called, Emil Ek smiled pleasantly. His hair was ash blond and curly, his cheeks pink, his eyes sky-blue. Laura Peterson grinned and said, "Present," tossing her long bangs with a characteristic movement and sniff. Freddy Two Knives had an appealing look in his pinched face, with his large quivering mouth and hungry dark eyes. Ole Olafson shifted uncomfortably in the largest seat the room afforded. In desperation he put his big feet out into the aisle, and ran his fingers through his greasy blond "pomp." Mike Olenski grunted finally when his neighbour gave him a sharp poke and told him that his name had been said. He looked ugly and dirty; his brown hair had a dead look about it. Felix, Max, Peter, Olga and Zinnia Panachuk nodded quick dark heads and blinked fast their darting slanting black eyes. Bessie Poudre, a coarse-looking squaw-like girl, paused in her placid chewing to say, "Here." Kost Poduasauki gave a beatific smile. His hair was black and shining, his eyes pale blue under thick black lashes. On down the list the teacher called through the noisy restlessness of the class. "Vic Revere . . . Ann Schmitt . . . Marie Setezanka. . . ." Finished at last, she got to business.

"Now boys and girls, I'm Miss Hughes; I hope we'll all be friends." There was not much friendliness on some of the faces. "Do as much of this arithmetic as you can while I look after the little ones. If you're good, I'll read you a story after recess."

The older pupils exchanged sly looks as she walked smilingly to the two beginners who stood rooted to the spot at the back of the room.

"And what are your names, children?"

"Mary Belle Ashley," said Poppy.

The other child hung his head and grunted. Freddy whispered something loudly in Cree, but the little boy only grinned, showing gaping places where his front teeth were missing.

"He's Johnny Two Knives, my brother," Freddy spoke up timidly. All heads turned towards the beginners.

"There are two places in that little front desk where you can sit." The teacher pointed, and without a word, the children marched to their places where they sat down to await further developments. Poppy looked about, searching among the rows for Jay. She found him sitting quite near her, alone in the double desk, intent upon his arithmetic. Then she remembered she was not to sit with any of the Two Knives children because they all had lice. Gramp had told her not to. Very quietly she went down the aisle and slipped into the empty place beside Jay.

"May I sharpen my pencil?" asked Mike Olenski, tousling his hair with dirty fingers.

"May I sharpen mine?" asked Laura.

"Me too. Me too," spoke up other voices.

"One at a time," Miss Hughes said quietly, as she closed the door and hung up some scattered garments.

"Then how the heck can we do our arithmetic?"

Mike clattered noisily to the pencil-sharpener, and on the way back, struck the head of each seated pupil in the row with the sharp point. At the confusion of outraged cries, giggles, and talk, the new teacher said nothing at all. She walked very calmly to where Mike had sat down, and catching the offender by the shoulders, gave him such a shaking that the dirty shirt was practically pulled off. He sat gasping with amazement with no ready sally on his tongue, while an awed and respectful silence fell over the whole room.

Jay watched these proceedings with half-closed eyes and little interest, his mind on a partly-solved problem. But when he happened to look at Poppy, he saw that she had gone quite white with fright.

"I'll draw you a picture," he murmured. Tearing a double sheet from the middle of his scribbler, he drew the outline of a dog. The little girl watched with absorbed interest. He shaded in tattered ears and a shaggy coat.

"It's Gypsy!"

"That's right." A light seemed to have turned on behind the boy's eyes. "Look, I'll write it. That says 'Gypsy.'"

They did not notice until too late the teacher coming up the aisle, looking over the scribblers.

"You shouldn't be drawing; you should be doing your arithmetic," her cold voice said. "And Mary Belle Ashley, what are you sitting here for?"

Some of the big boys in the back seats laughed.

"I am doing it. I'm on the fourth question." Jay showed his book with his neat figuring. Poppy was shaking beside him.

"What's your name?"

"Jay Baptiste." He lowered his eyes, not sulky or defiant, but dignified and very distant.

"This is nicely done." Miss Hughes handed back the scribbler. "But Mary Belle, I want you to sit up at the front with Johnny so that I can teach you both the numbers one to ten."

Poppy sat still and mute, her face white and strained.

"She's scairt." Jay had his gaze on the blackboard while the deep colour stained his olive cheeks as a loud stage whisper came from behind: "Jay's got a girl."

"Very well then, she may stay here, as long as you get your work done, Jay." The teacher bent over to make some large figures across the top of the first page of Poppy's scribbler.

The morning passed swiftly while the children were being tested in spelling, geography, and reading. Poppy spent the recess standing in the doorway dividing her attention between watching the older boys playing ball, and trying to get up courage to talk to Olga who cleaned off the boards for Teacher. After recess, Miss Hughes read to them for a while from *Tom Sawyer* until Johnny Two Knives' snores interrupted her and she had to stop and shake him awake where he leaned with his head on the desk. The school fairly shook with raucous laughter. By eleven thirty, the sun was streaming in the windows, making the room unbearably hot. The boys who had played ball went more and more often to the pail at the back of the room where they fought over the cup, and threw water on each other. It was a difficult morning. The teacher let them go early for lunch.

With a great clatter of pails, the children went off in little groups. The bigger girls clung to Miss Hughes, touching her hands, her watch, her hair, gazing at her shyly as she sat at her table, daintily eating green pickle sandwiches. Olga put her arm around Poppy where she was trying to get her pail, being shoved and pushed by some of the boys.

"Let's eat our lunch under the trees," suggested Olga as they went outside. Poppy felt suddenly very hungry, and her mouth watered for the tarts. She struggled with the lid of her pail, but as it spranged loose and tinkled to the ground, her lips quivered and the tears came into her eyes.

"Somebody ate my lunch! There's just the crusts left!" Her voice had become a wail. Some of the others gathered to witness the emptiness of the pail with its litter of crusts at the bottom.

"You can have my cookie," Olga whispered, glaring back at Mike who was tweaking her long braids. "Cut that out, you pig!"

"Never mind, Poppy," said Jay behind him. "You can have some of my lunch." And he offered her a piece of soggy bannock spread thickly with lard.

Laura snorted. "The breeds always steal lunches. They never have nothing but bannock." She gave Jay a meaning look. The boy flushed with anger.

"Just imagine," Mike sneered, "he gets a girl and then eats her lunch. Nice goin'."

"Hold this." Jay put his food into the hands of Freddy Two Knives. His own fists were ready. Mike swallowed a sandwich he had just stuffed into his mouth, and set down his newspaper-wrapped, jam-soaked package.

"Want a fight, eh? I'll show you, you dirty thief of a half-breed! You and your old Isaiah stealing my Dad's hay, too. I'll smash your gut!"

Jay was only twelve, and thin, but with a wiry strength. Mike was all of fifteen, heavy and clumsy, pasty faced and pimpled. He backed up a little, moving his fists slowly, squinting at the distance between them, as though gauging a blow; and then, without warning, he kicked the other boy cruelly on the shin with the toe of his thick-soled boot. For a moment Jay doubled up with the unexpected pain, and then swiftly he smashed into Mike's face with hard brown knuckles. Poppy looked on with tears, but Olga, with braids flying, ran to tell Teacher. The others shouted hoarse encouragements, according to their loyalties.

"Come on, Paleface! Lick the Redskin!"

"Atta boy, Jay! Make his nose bleed!"

By the time Miss Hughes came to stop the unequal battle, Jay was rolling over and over in the dust with a blackening eye and a swollen lip, while Mike held a filthy rag to his own bleeding nose. Most of the others quickly scattered.

"You two boys must eat your lunches in the school-house for a week," the teacher told them. "I won't have this fighting." She led Mike away to stop the gushing blood. Jay got up giddily and poked Freddy.

"Where's my lunch?"

Freddy swallowed hard, looked at the ground, at his brother Johnny, and at Olga and Poppy who stood around.

"Did you eat it?" The husky voice was not angry.

Freddy's large mouth quivered.

"Every bit of it?"

"I was so hungry." He could only whisper it, his whole face pleading.

The recent warrior rubbed his shin. "Next time you got no grub at home, don't come to school. It makes you too hungry."

"We wanted to see the new teacher." The Two Knives boys were ditto marks of hang-dog abjection.

Jay grinned crookedly with his swollen lips. "Where's the ball? Let's knock out flies." He limped off with Johnny at his heels while Freddy searched among the tall grass for the ball and bat which he had secreted there against the tyranny of the older boys. Olga dried the little girl's tears.

"Come on, Mary Belle, you can have some of my sandwiches."

Poppy put the lid back on her pail and composed herself bravely. "No," she said. "I ain't hungry. Let's sit on the swings."

"Jay is sure a nice boy," Olga declared, taking her hand. "He's the nicest boy in this here school."

Poppy swung to and fro on the creaking swing, feeling somehow very comforted, bearing her hunger like a martyr. Having eaten her fill, Olga swung high, her braids flying.

"You'll have to come and stay over night with me some time, Mary Belle." Olga's voice was now far, now near. "We always got good grub now Teacher lives with us."

Poppy stopped swinging and leaned her head against the rope, feeling sick. "School's OK, Olga. I like it fine."

At three-thirty they were all dismissed, going off shouting on horseback or on foot. She put on her coveralls over her dress, and climbing on the gate, got on Buck's back behind Jay, holding in her hand her empty pail and a treasured drawing of a yellow chicken to show Gramp. Mike passed them, cutting off on foot through the bush, his nose red and swollen in his white face.

"Just you wait, you dirty breed!" he shouted from a safe distance.

"We'll get back at you. Next year there won't be no hay for nobody. Just you wait!"

But the children seemed not to hear as Buck dawdled off, nipping occasionally at a tempting bush. The afternoon was hot and clear and windless. Poppy soon felt the horse sweat soaking through to her legs, irritating, itching.

"Like the teacher?" the boy asked, rattling his pail at Buck's ear.

"Yes, I think so."

"She's good," Jay had a judicious air. "She'll step on old Mike. We never had a woman before, but she'll do. Look Poppy! Choke-cherries! Want some?"

Ahead of them a bush loaded with ripe purple berries leaned into the road. The children slipped to the ground, where they were soon feeding hungrily, while Buck wandered off to a patch of green grass. After a time, Poppy took off her shoes and socks, wriggled her toes delightedly in the warm grey dust.

"You better put your shoes on again." The boy lay flat on his stomach, dipping his head into the creek, and shaking himself off like a puppy. He helped her scrub the berry juice off her face, and then heaved her up on the pony's back, jumping on himself afterwards while they both shrieked with laughter. Poppy's mouth was all puckered and queer, and she felt a little dizzy, but very happy. School was going to be all right. She wanted to get home to show Gramp her picture.

Chapter VII

L ina stood in front of a little cracked mirror, tidying her heavy hair. The light of the jam-can oil lamp revealed the room under the sloping roof: the rickety-bed, a wash-stand cut roughly from logs, shelves covered by a faded curtain. A curtain also served as a door, and at one side, Poppy's head appeared.

"Will you tie my bow?" Wonderingly she surveyed this unfamiliar Lina in her polished shoes, decent black dress, and pretty brooch, her hair smoothed, her face unharried and softened in the warm light.

"Ready yet?" Benjie asked, coming into the kitchen from outside. "Team's waitin'."

"Put on your things, child."

The little girl danced up and down, bouncing her frills, laughing while Benjie went after her with her hated red reefer. Lina blew out the light in the bedroom and came out with a flour-sack dish towel which she folded around her chocolate cake in its large tin.

"It'll be crowded, huh?" she asked.

"You bet." The old man helped Poppy put her frills carefully into the coat sleeves. "And I hope they leave their moonshine at home so Sven don't have to get tough with them." He looked about, found his fiddle and hat, lowered the wick in the lamp on the table. "Come on, gang." Blowing out the flame, he led the way outside where Whisky and Rum tossed their heads by the fence. "Gonna rain," he remarked, sniffing the air, and glancing up at the starless sky. "We better bring the tarp along."

The woman lifted Poppy into the wagon box, handing up the cake carefully.

"Let me drive," the little girl demanded when Benjie flung in the canvas and settled the violin case from the wheel. When he climbed in, he let her hold the lines in front of his hands.

As they lurched steadily on over rocks that stuck up in the ruts, or rumbled over the smoother stretches, Lina leaned against the wagon box, breathing deeply the cool night air with its damp earthy scent.

"Be nice to have a little visit with the neighbours," she remarked. "Didn't have time to get acquainted much yet."

"Likely Olenski'll be there," Benjie warned. "He's still mad about the hay."

."Too bad about him!"

"Well, I reckon he always counted on it, Lina."

"I got to count on something too. Had enough of seeing cows dying, feeding horses putrid old straw."

"The stock's lookin' good, I must say."

"You must say them two big stacks sure look good."

Light shone brightly from the school windows; and as they neared the yard, into the quiet evening came sounds of many voices, and laughter, the creak of wheels, the chink of harness. A lantern blinked welcomingly at the barn door, and men shouted friendly greetings to each other as they stabled the horses. Benjie began to unhitch by the barn, when the team ahead balked. A man came out, cursing wildly, brandishing a pitch-fork.

"Git in there! Git goin'!"

He raised the pitch-fork again and again. One of the horses reared, knocking off the flimsy door; the other floundered painfully. Men swore, and heavy hoofs stamped. Young Mike Olenski suddenly appeared, got hold of the excited team and led them quietly into the barn.

"Lamed his horse," Benjie muttered.

"Olenski," whispered Lina. "Full of moonshine."

"Think I'll tie Whisky and Rum outside. There's a clear space over there. I'll bring down some feed, and they'll stand quiet." The old man chirruped to his horses.

"Come on, Poppy, we'll go in." Lina had her cake ready, and took the little girl by the hand.

A good crowd of many nationalities had already gathered, every face sharply etched under the glare of the gas lamps. Young women with babies. Old women, wrinkled and dirty; and young girls plastered with lipstick, bashful. The men dumped the school desks out of an open window, and set up benches, boards stretched between empty nail kegs. Here, babies suckled brown breasts, and children dozed. The men far out-numbered the women, swaggering or aloof and shy, dark, ugly faces among blond Teutonic types. They spoke to each other in their own languages, or in broken English. More people kept appearing, pushing their way in, crowding the small low-roofed schoolhouse. A fire burned in the rusty stove, on which a huge pot of water had been set to boil for coffee. In spite of the open windows, the heat of the room was stifling.

Lina took her cake to Mrs. Olenski who piled up the food at the teacher's desk at one side. She was a tiny woman, enveloped in a huge old coat and poke bonnet, out of which her peaked little face with its red-rimmed eyes peered curiously. Mrs. Poudre, a huge squaw dressed in a black-fringed shawl, stood nearby, looking hungrily at the piles of cakes and the mounds of sandwiches. Her black hair hung in braids to her waist; she carried her bulk with a grace that a white woman would envy. She grinned widely at Poppy, and the little girl smiled back, holding tightly to her mother's hand.

Lina turned towards a bench where the teacher sat, looking very prim.

"Pleased to meet you, Miss Hughes. I'm Mrs. Ashley."

"Mary Belle's mother? How do you do?" Nervously, she touched some shining glass cherries pinned at the throat of her white silk blouse. She had curled her hair too, Poppy noticed, and tied it with a ribbon. Her little hand went unconsciously to the bow on the side of her own head.

"Quite a crowd, isn't it?" The teacher's eyes strayed across the room to where Sven Jensen, in his best catalogue suit, his face pink and shining, his butter-coloured hair carefully brushed, argued with Pete Panachuk. The hubbub drowned their voices.

"Mrs. Ashley! You come to de dance?" Mrs. Panachuk cried, swooping down upon them, swiftly, for all her size. "You meet Miss Hughes?" She tucked some frizzled pieces of hair under a green beret as she spoke. Lina secretly admired the fine cross-stitch embroidery on the high neck of Mrs. Panachuk's blouse under her blue coat. "Teacher, you come wit me, and I introduce you."

At last, Benjie and Isaiah, holding high their violins, threaded their way through the noisy room, and sat down on an improvised platform at the front. There, a third man joined them, holding a guitar, a hunch-backed fellow with a swarthy face under his black hair. After a preliminary plucking of strings, the tune of *The West, a Nest and You* wailed from the fiddles. Pete Panachuk managed the crowd, pushing them back to the doorway, the window-ledges, the benches, clearing a small space for dancing. Bill Manydogs boomed forth: "Get your pardners for a waltz!" and couples began getting up to dance, stumbling on the rough, uneven floor, singing lustily with the music.

Poppy hung her coat on a nail beside Lina's and smoothed down her frills. By the stove, Mrs. Panachuk struggled alone with a large carton of heavy china cups. Lina touched the child on the shoulder.

"You sit down and keep out of the way. I got to help Mrs. Pana-chuk."

After standing quietly against the wall for a few minutes, the little girl wormed her way along a bench, pushing past other children who sprawled on the floor or amused themselves trying to trip the dancers. She found herself at last at the front, where she crawled up beside Benjie. The musicians paused while the dancers circled the floor, clapping loudly, calling: "More!" The guitar player looked down at the child with sad grey eyes in his Indian face, handing her a stick of gum from his pocket. Poppy took the proffered gift, favouring him with her smile.

Benjie prodded Sven on the shoulder with his bow as he passed.

"How's Olenski doin'?"

"Snoring over by the door. Mike's looking after him."

The music started up again. Poppy sat hugging her knees and chewing her gum, enjoying the horsey smell of the men, and the fragrance of their tobacco, and the quick movements of their fingers. Johnny Two Knives came by and tagged her, darting away to start a game with her. She would have followed, but Benjie stopped fiddling and caught her by the shoulder.

"The kid's got a louse in his hair prit near the size a kernel of wheat. You stay put, little girl."

At last she saw Jay dancing a jig near one of the benches at the side, while his old grandmother watched him delightedly. Poppy scrambled down from her place, making her way through the crowd towards him. She touched him shyly on the sleeve.

"Teach me."

"You want to learn to dance?" the boy asked. He had stopped jigging, and laughed with sheer joy. "Come on, Poppy. Like this." She skipped about in wild imitation, her ruffles bouncing, her gold hair flying, while couples crowded and stumbled beside them.

Mrs. Panachuk measured out coffee into the boiling water.

"Your little Poppy, she dance too," she told Lina. "Jay, he is good, good."

Lina glanced across at the children.

"He's a breed. Good little worker in the hayfield, though."

"You got lotsa hay, Mrs. Ashley, yes?"

"Enough."

"Look, look, Mrs. Ashley. Teacher, she dance with Sven again."

"She's a good enough teacher, I guess," Lina remarked.

"Yes, yes. Mike Olenski, she tear de shirt right off. De kids dey tell me."

"Get your pardners for a two-step!" Bill Manydogs bellowed. "Pardners for a two-step!"

"Mrs. Ashley, can I have this dance? You are Mrs. Ashley, aren't you?"

Lina was taken by surprise, and Sven Jensen had her arm before she could protest. Mrs. Panachuk laughed after them.

"I hear you got the hay by Lilly Lake," Sven remarked with admiration in his tone, as he guided her skilfully about the densely packed dance floor.

She smiled, looking into his fine clean face. "News sure does travel."

"I thought I better tell you something." He became grave as they paused to let a wildly dancing pair pass them. "You better watch that Isaiah Waters don't steal your hay to feed his horses. He done that every year on Olenski." They danced on. "Isaiah's a tough customer."

"I've made a deal with Isaiah."

They linked arms and circled the floor, clapping with the others who were shouting, "More! More!"

"You're doing all right!"

The music started up again. After the second round, Bill Manydogs called, "Tag! Everybody tag!" in a thunderous voice.

"By the way," Sven began. Pete Panachuk slapped his shoulder, winking knowingly at him. But when Lina had danced a few steps with Pete, and he would have made some remark, Sven tagged her back, and danced with her swiftly to the other side of the room.

"What I was going to say," he went on, "is that I need a cook real bad on my threshing outfit. I had a man, but he broke his leg yesterday. Fell out of the hayloft. I can't get a cook nowhere. What about you?"

They stopped dancing and went over to the sidelines where they leaned against a wall. Lina folded her arms. Her foot beat time to the wild music.

"Well, I got a little field of wheat of my own that's got to be harvested some way. I got to have flour for the winter."

"I'll guarantee it gets done. I'm paying five bucks a day."

Isaiah scratched the strings on his fiddle with the bow, making a wild discord, silencing the music. Couples broke up, looking for new partners.

"I'll do it," Lina said calmly. "As soon as this rain gets over. I'll have to fix things at home. But I'll come."

"It's a bargain," Sven grinned at her, and then went off to say something to Bill Manydogs.

"Nice boy friend you got," Mrs. Panachuk snickered from beside the stove.

"Very," Lina agreed amiably. "How's the coffee coming?"

Presently Bill announced the supper waltz and the older married women looked after the food so that the young folks could have supper partners and enjoy themselves. Panachuk passed Benjie's old hat around while everyone drank coffee, a cup between two.

"Olenski, wake up!" Panachuk prodded the snoring figure. "Time to pay!" Mike stepped up in front of his father, scowling down at him. Mrs. Olenski moved over beside her husband, and sitting down on a box, said something to him in their own language. The music started up again now, and people getting to their feet, fell against the two figures.

"Two more couples!" Bill shouted as he arranged sets for a square dance.

The music became quick and wild. Dust rose up out of the floor from the pounding feet. Bill's deep voice called against the din: "Promenade! . . . Give her a swing! Swing your pardner! . . . Down the centre, cut off two! . . ." Round and round the dusty little room, the couples swung, eyes following them from all sides. The watchers pressed back against the wall to escape the flying feet.

Lina pulled a great tub of cups out of the way, and set them down behind the stove. Olenski stared at her intently. Then he wet his mouth from something in a strong-smelling bottle which he had hidden in his ragged sweater. Mrs. Panachuk pushed her way through the dancers, holding Benjie's hat in her hands.

"No cake, no sandwich left!" she exclaimed jubilantly. "Let's count de money. Over dere on de bench!" Lina wiped her hands on a dish towel and followed Mrs. Panachuk. Olenski lay down again, his wife and Mike watching over him on either side.

After they had counted the money, Lina tied it up in a large red handkerchief.

"That'll pay the orchestra and five bucks towards the Christmas Tree," she declared. "Some of these guys went outside when the hat was going round. I see they're back now."

"Look, dere's Sven and de teacher," Mrs. Panachuk whispered behind her hand, giving Lina a very apparent nudge.

Lina looked about anxiously for Poppy, spying her at last up on the platform with her head on Benjie's knee. Sound asleep, probably. It was getting light now, and through the windows, she could see fat squaws swinging on the children's swings, while their tall men friends slid down the ropes, shouting. She dozed a little there on the bench, amid the dancing and the confusion, coming to with a start as Benjie began the tune of "Home Sweet Home." The dance broke up in short order.

The men went outside to harness their teams, while the women searched for cake tins, and gathered in little groups talking. Olenski still slept. Lina shook Poppy half awake and put her into her coat. Mike came in and spoke to his father, and Mrs. Olenski talked loudly in Ukrainian, shaking her husband by the arm. He lifted his head at last, and got up, staggering about.

"I'm going to Bridgeville today," he shouted to Panachuk who came in to collect his family. "Yup, to Bridgeville." He looked about, vacantly.

Benjie came in for his hat and his fiddle, and Lina picked up her sleeping child. Miss Hughes waved to Sven who was taking down the gas lamps. Mike had his father by the arm, urging him to the wagon. Outside, a light rain was falling. In the misty greyness, teams and wagons jogged homewards on the winding bush trails.

"That was a real nice dance," Lina said as they stopped at their own door. "I don't feel tired at all." She carried Poppy into the house and deposited her on the bed in the kitchen. When Benjie came in after having put the team away, he found Lina putting on her overalls and slicker, and a scarf on her head.

"Where you goin', Lina?"

"A day's journey," she replied, the light of adventure in her eyes. "I won't be back till late." She put a package of sandwiches in her pocket, and without waiting for him to answer, went outside.

He found her saddling Queen at the pasture gate.

"Where you goin', Lina?"

She chuckled, slipping the bridle over the mare's head.

"To Bridgeville."

"Why to Bridgeville?"

Lina threw the blanket and saddle on Queen's back.

"That's where Olenski's figgering to go. Only his horse is lame, and he's dead drunk, and it's raining."

Benjie tightened the cinch for her.

"What would Olenski want in Bridgeville?"

"He's after the hayland, I'll bet my bottom dollar." Lina laughed, throwing the reins about the horse's neck. "He's aiming to cancel the claim on that land, I figger. Well, I'll get there first. My tracks will wash out in the rain, and no one will know I went."

"Get your horse some feed at Bridgeville," he warned her.

Putting her foot in the stirrup, she heaved herself up, waving to him as Queen went off at a brave trot. The sky was darkening with heavy clouds. Grey rain slanted down through the needles of the spruce trees. Soon the rhythm of Queen's hoofs died away, leaving a silence broken only by the gentle sound of falling rain. Benjie shrugged and spat, going wearily towards the house.

Chapter VIII

1

Yes, winter's coming fast," Tudor Folkes said. He opened the heater to put in a green poplar log and two spruce logs. The orange flames licked eagerly at the wood as he jammed down the lid. "I lose a good deal of my boot trade in the winter. Nearly everyone goes into moccasins as soon as the snow flies."

"What do you do then?" Benjie asked. He was baking himself by the heater, his cheeks like two red apples.

"Oh, I don't worry about it too much. I've got some land in England, you know. And then I usually get some marriages and murders to handle." He grinned, reaching for his pipe. "And I've got my luxury trade. Look, I'll show you." Limping across the room, he took down a wide leather riding belt hanging on the wall by the window. He put it into Benjie's hands.

"Ain't that something!" the old man exclaimed, admiring the beautiful pattern tooled into the fine leather.

Tudor lit his pipe.

"Now some poor devil of a breed will start saving his money, and coming in here to see if the thing is sold yet, and coming back, and asking for credit. And finally he'll get the belt, and have to tighten it because there won't be anything in his insides but wind pudding. Vile trade I have, what?" He carefully hung his treasure on the wall again. "Obadiah Poudre has been gazing at this thing for three weeks already. I've got the cuffs to match it too." Tudor sat down on the edge of the table, lit his pipe again, flinging the burnt-out match to the floor under the heater.

Benjie tilted back on the chair, making its old legs groan dangerously. "Well sir, this is the first time I ever heard tell of Lina wishin' winter ud come on the run. She's waitin' for them roads to block up with drifts high to the horses' bellies."

"How much more time has Gus?" Tudor asked, looking thoughtfully across the room through the pipe smoke.

"Well now," Benjie began, settling his old fur hat more comfortably, "she cancelled the claim first week in September, and they give him ninety days from then to do somethin' on that land. If he doesn't do nothin', she's got thirty days to file the claim at Bridgeville, and the land's hers."

"Why, it's as thrilling as those Western shows they have at Bridgeville," Tudor laughed, ruffling his shaggy curls. "The villain of the piece has less than a month left. And he has so many irons in the fire. So much land all over the country."

Benjie lifted the lid of the heater, knocking his pipe gently on the nickel, blinking against the heat.

"Lina sure was plumb shocked when she got to Bridgeville and found out big Gus had the claim on the hayland. He done nothing on it the years he's had it."

"It'll be his turn to get a shock now."

"You know, Folkes, I don't know as Lina done right to grab that land. Suppose she wins over Gus, what about Olenski?"

Tudor drew his feet up on to the table, and sat as usual, hugging his knees. "Well, it's a question if that fellow would make out anywhere no matter what he had. I don't know. It's a hard thing to know what's right in a case like this."

"He won't have nothing to pay his rent with," the old man reflected worriedly. "For five years he fed stock for Gus with the hay."

The fire made a comfortable roaring sound. Outside, the branches of the tall spruce at the door moved in a chilly wind. The sky was grey. Benjie looked out at it as he put on his old sheepskin jacket again.

"It's all rather tough on young Mike Olenski," Tudor remarked suddenly. "He doesn't get much of a chance."

"That's right," Benjie agreed. "The kid had to quit school and work on Sven's threshing crew. He did all right, too. Even helped with our stuff."

Tudor slid his feet down from the table.

"I don't think we should underrate Gus. Maybe he still has plans."

Benjie shook his head. "But Lina's got Isaiah Waters and Jack Two Knives on her side. She's got Isaiah that excited I believe he'd put a knife in Gustav's back if that big Swede showed up in the hayland."

"Isaiah hates Gus on his own," Tudor put in quickly. "Always did for some reason."

Benjie looked troubled. "We never done them things in the old days. We had tough times, but we didn't go cuttin' a neighbour's throat."

As the old man trudged off into the cheerless November weather, Tudor took down a new piece of leather which was hanging on the wall, handling it as though it could feel his touch. "She'll win out," he thought. "She'll get her hayland. Well, who can blame her? She's practically alone, and a woman."

2

The sky was dark and starless when Lina got through the milking. She came up from the barn with the heavy pail of milk, holding the lantern before her in her free hand to light the way to the house. How cold and raw it was, the wind making a lonely moaning in the blackness of the trees. When she went in, the warmth of the cabin wrapped her round with its comfortable odours of burning spruce logs and baked potatoes. Poppy sat on the bed, reading aloud in a highly pitched voice, while Gypsy lay at her feet with his head resting over her ankle.

"'Not-I-said-the-pig-not-I-said-the-dog-not-I-said-the-cat. Then-I-will-said-the-little-red-hen-and-so-she-did.'"

She stopped for a moment, watching her mother strain the milk through a clean flour sack. She was dressed in moccasins, heavy woollen slacks, and a bright red sweater. Her cheeks glowed pink in the light of the oil lamp.

"Did you hear Gramp coming?" she asked.

"Not yet. It'll be a cold ride home for him, too."

After a moment the child sighed. "Oh, I wish he'd come!"

"Read the one about Chicken Little," Lina suggested, as she took off her jacket.

"OK," Poppy put down the tattered book she had been reading, and leaned over the bed to pick up another, moving carefully so as not to disturb Gypsy. He looked at her sleepily. Lina opened the oven door and pinched her baking potatoes gently with her fingers.

"'So Goosey Loosey, and Turkey Lurkey, and Chicken Little ran to tell the king that the sky was falling,'" Poppy read on, in a breathless rapid recitation. The clock on the wall suddenly gave seven musical notes. And then Gypsy went tense, growled, sprang from his place, barking.

"Quiet, Gyp!" Lina said sternly, while the child stopped reading, and they all listened intently for a moment. Then the woman opened the door, looking out into the darkness. She heard hoofs moving slowly along the trail before her gate, and a man's voice saying: "Hullo! Say, what place is this?"

79

"Ashley's." Lina spoke quietly, trying to identify the voice. "Are you lost? Who is it?"

Gypsy slunk past her, almost snake-low, to bark at the stranger. The man muttered what sounded like a curse under his breath. The dog stood in the light from the doorway, quivering, with a growl deep in his throat.

"Bring me the lantern, Poppy," her mother whispered.

"Say, could you put us up for the night?" the man asked out of the dark.

"Sure, just a minute. I'll be right with you." She put on a jacket as she spoke.

At the gate, she held the lantern high. Outside on the trail were two horses, the one mounted by a small boy, while the rider of the other struggled with the pole which fastened the gate. He raised his head at her approach, the light falling directly on his face.

"Hello Mr. Hanson!" Lina exclaimed as she drew back the pole. "You're just in time for supper. I kep' it back on account of Benjie's went to town today."

"I hope this won't be putting you out, Mrs. Ashley. My horse stepped in a hole back there, and the kid's tired. I'll pay you for the night's stay for the kid here, and me." He looked huge by lantern-light, in a dark fur cap and a thick sheepskin jacket. His big horse moved restlessly, pulling at the reins which Gustav held in a firm grip.

"That's OK, I don't need no pay," Lina answered him. "I ain't turned nobody from my door yet, and I don't aim to start now. The barn is over there. You can put your horses in. There's feed." She handed him the lantern. When the two strangers had passed into the yard, she went out into the dark road to listen for Benjie's coming, shivering in the raw, penetrating cold. From far away, came the sound of hoofs beating on the hard trail. But it might be Isaiah, or Jay, or Jack Two Knives. Benjie usually rode more slowly than that. She listened again. It sounded more like two horses. She returned to the yard, putting the pole of the gate back in place, watching the glow of light from the lantern move to the door of the barn and pass within.

"Who is it?" Poppy asked in excitement when her mother came into the house.

"Mr. Hanson and a boy. They're staying here tonight." Lina took off her coat, and washed quickly at the wash-stand. When she had finished, she poured fresh hot water into the basin for her visitors, and found a clean towel in the trunk. She brought out a pretty table-cloth also, embroidered with bright flowers.

"Come on, Poppy. Don't sit reading. Help me lay the table. Put on that little jug that was in the cereal, the other day."

"Is Gramp coming?" the little girl asked, putting down her book.

"He'll be home real soon, and we won't eat without him. But I don't want Mr. Hanson to think supper's a long time off." Drawing the trunk up to the table, she covered it neatly with a quilt. "That'll hold him. He's quite a big-sized man."

A knock thumped on the door, and at Lina's "Come in!" Gustav and the boy and the dog trooped in. Gypsy wagged his tail, fawning on the company. Gustav stamped his feet in their big high boots, and rubbed his numb fingers, holding his store-bought gloves under one arm. When he had taken off his outer clothing, he washed noisily at the wash-stand. Lina scrutinized his companion, a boy of eleven, tall for his age, with large steady grey eyes in a brown face, and blond hair not trained to lie in any particular direction. He had an attractive lopsided grin. Gypsy jumped up on him, licking his cheek.

"Miserable night to be out in," Lina remarked cheerfully from the stove where she fried smoked fish. "Too bad there's no Northern Lights tonight like we been having so much. But tonight, she's black!"

Gustav rubbed his face ruddy on the rough towel. "These trails seem different than when I was here 'bout six years ago. Most of my land lies west of town, so I don't come this way much." He turned to the boy. "Hurry up, Tommy. Get washed."

"Easy enough to get lost." Lina spoke above the sizzle of the frying fish. "Sit down, Mr. Hanson. There at the end. You'd never find your way in the dark."

"A person doesn't want to stay at most of these places," the big Swede remarked, seating himself with his back to the table. "Full of bugs."

"Put the plates round, Poppy," her mother said to the child, who stood in the middle of the room, staring. "What's the boy's name?" she asked Gustav.

"Tommy." He gave his young companion a stern look.

"Take off your things, Tommy, and sit down," the woman suggested.

Gypsy ran barking to the door.

"Go see if that's Daddy," Lina told the little girl.

Poppy ran to do as she was bidden, letting the dog out into the cold night, while she called, "Is that you, Gramp?"

"Hello darlin'!" he hailed her from the darkness. She could hear him shutting the gate. "Supper ready?"

"Take him the lantern, Poppy. It's so dark out there, and he won't know there'll be other horses in the barn. Here, put a coat on."

Lina bustled about, sending the child outside, efficiently tending to her dinner, and giving her table the last minute touches. In spite of its tin plates and aluminum table ware, it looked very attractive with a dish of preserved saskatoons, some home-made mustard pickles, fresh brown buns, a slab of yellow butter, and a pitcher of thick cream. She put a large baked potato on each plate, and drew the frying pan to one side of the stove. An appetizing odour of coffee came from the tall grey coffee pot. Gustav watched the woman's every move with his sleepy eyes. Her cheeks were flushed with heat, and short ends of hair curled damply on her forehead.

Poppy and Benjie came in, carrying a knobbly sack between them, letting the dog worry a fraying end of the sack. Benjie's face was almost purple with the cold.

"Howdy," he said to Gustav.

The little girl looked from the visitor to her grandfather with a look that said, "I told you so."

"Have a good trip, Daddy?" Lina asked.

"Kinda cold on the way home." Benjie took off his things, hanging them neatly on the nail by the door. "How do you like our country?" he asked Gus as he got a dipperful of hot water from the reservoir on the stove.

"You need a highway in here," the big man replied.

"See anybody you know?" Lina asked as she served the fish.

"Rode a piece with Jack Two Knives on the way home." Benjie spoke from the depths of the towel.

"Jack Two Knives?" Gus was suddenly on the alert. "Where'd he go?"

"Don't rightly know where he's goin'. Times he goes to his grand-father's when he wants tobacco. Times he goes to see Isaiah Waters." Benjie flung the towel on a nail, smiling at Poppy.

"Where's that devil been all fall?" Gustav turned around on the trunk to face the table. He looked angry.

"Come on, supper's ready," Lina said in blithe tones. "Tommy, will you sit on that little bench with Poppy? Poppy, are your hands clean? Quick! Go wash them! Daddy, will you sit at this end?"

"Jack Two Knives was threshing with Sven's outfit this fall," Benjie answered calmly as he sat down.

"Where's he been since then?" Gus growled.

"Him and Isaiah worked up at the saw-mill." Benjie liberally but-tered a bun. His daughter flashed him a warning look. "Them breeds made good money up there this fall."

"They're always poor, though," his daughter broke in. "If they had a thousand dollars a month, they'd still be broke before the end. And hungry? You dasn't turn your back a minute on a single egg in the hen-house."

"This your little boy, Mr. Hanson?" The old man looked at the youngster with kind eyes.

"That's my Tommy."

Gus attacked the dinner with hearty appetite.

"How'd you make out with your garden and crop?" he asked, turning to Lina.

"We done all right, Mr. Hanson. We got plenty of potatoes, and flour, and round three hundred quarts of stuff in sealers. One thing about this country, there's plenty of wood. Never need to worry about keeping warm so long as one of us can manage the axe."

"Terrible hard work for a woman, this homesteading."

"Oh, my days are easy now," she assured him. "Why, I got time to knit socks, and piece a couple of quilts."

"Lots of dances coming up, too." Benjie grinned to himself.

"I can dance, can you?" Poppy asked the boy.

He smiled shyly, shaking his head.

"Know what we're going to get?" she went on, sociably. "A pig. That's what we're getting."

"Shh! Don't talk so much," her mother cautioned her.

"Good money in hogs these days," Gustav remarked.

"Well, this is just a sow Sven promised me for part of my wages."

They had just finished dinner when Jay came. He opened the door very softly, and was standing inside before anyone had realized he was there. Beside the stove, the dog lifted one ear and yawned.

"Could you give us a little milk, Mrs. Ashley?" the boy asked, holding out a lard pail.

"Why yes, I could give you a little. Had supper?"

Jay took off his cap. He did not answer the question, but looked hungrily at the table.

"Who's he?" It was the first time Tommy had said anything. He spoke to Poppy out of the side of his mouth.

"That's Jay." She said this as though she thought anybody would know that.

"Sit in and have something," Lina invited, taking his pail. "There's still a potato, and you can have some berries and a bun."

The boy ate ravenously, at the same time, taking in every detail of the appearance of the two strangers and of the talk going on around him.

When every crumb had vanished from the table, Lina got up yawning.

"Well—dishes."

The men pushed the trunk back to the wall and sat smoking. Tommy and Jay remained silent at the table, while the little girl dried the tin plates.

"Got something for you," Benjie said to his grandchild. "When you're done helpin', you kin have it." He pointed mysteriously to the sack. Poppy could hardly wait. Tommy shared her excitement. Jay stared resentfully at the white boy. As soon as Poppy laid down the last dish, Benjie put his hand into the sack, drawing out a bright red rubber ball which he bounced across the room. The child raced after it with shrieks of delight, while Jay scrambled off the bench, and sat down at the opposite end of the room.

"Come on, Poppy! A game! Bounce it across to me in two bounces!"

"Let Tommy play too," said Lina as she wiped out the dish-pan.

Jay sulkily ignored the white boy. But Tommy got up quickly and caught the ball with one hand as it flew across the kitchen.

"Come on, Jay, he can play too," Poppy pleaded.

"All right, throw it to Gypsy!"

The four of them rolled about after the ball which shot up and down, a streak of red. Benjie smiled contentedly over his pipe, while Gustav enjoyed a cigarette. Lina sat near the lamp, knitting on a sock with great energy.

When the clock chimed a single note at half past nine, she put down her work.

"Come on, Poppy. Bed time. Better go home now, Jay."

"One more bounce," the little girl pleaded, sending the ball an inch past Gustav's cigarette. She put her hand over her mouth, half in horror, but her eyes danced. The boys smothered giggles.

"That's enough," her mother said. "Good night, Jay. Don't forget the milk. There it is on the window-ledge. Mr. Hanson, do you think you and the kid could share the bed-roll? It's a fair size. I'll lay it out here by the stove."

As she lowered the lamp wick and bade him good-night, she saw his smile of admiration. He looked significantly into her eyes. Quickly she retired behind the curtain, leaving him in Benjie's company.

3

Several days after Gustav's visit, Poppy and Jay jogged home from school, riding bareback on the buckskin horse. Jay held the ends of the rope bridle carelessly in one hand, while he rattled two lunch pails at the pony's ear with the other. Under a shapeless nondescript hat, a lock of black hair clung to his forehead. His jacket and denim overalls hung loosely on his thin body. He wore moccasins and rubbers, and his gloves were of buckskin. Poppy clutched him tightly about the waist, her face pale, lips blue with cold. The sky above them was grey and gloomy, but as yet no snow had fallen. The poplars stood naked and colourless, their leafless branches outlined starkly against the dark evergreens and sombre sky. Dead leaves, brown and frosted, clung here and there to the thick green boughs of the spruce and scattered everywhere on the forest paths. Mist hung in pockets throughout the trees, while the breaths of the children and the buckskin drifted behind them as they cantered along. The sound of the hoofs on the hard frozen ground carried backwards and forwards in the loneliness, while the noise of a breaking branch cracked like a pistol shot.

Since Lina and Benjie had gone to Jensen's to bring home the new sow, Poppy had been instructed to go home with Jay until supper time; the children therefore did not stop until they reached Isaiah's cabin. It stood in a bare space just off the trail, with a few spruce trees rising about it, a low log house with smoke curling in wisps from the chimney, and the sound of voices coming from within. Poppy slid to the ground. Her teeth chattered.

The boy turned his horse to the flat-roofed log barn.

"Go on in, Poppy."

The house was spotlessly clean, with bare mudded walls and three beds, each in a different corner, boxes neatly pushed underneath them. On one bed lay Martha's baby, crying peevishly, kicking up his little moccasined feet, while his mother bent over him, talking softly, her thick dark hair hanging about her face. An open fireplace made of stones, glowed with embers. Beside it on the floor sat old Mrs. Waters in a bright mauve print dress, smoking a strong-smelling pipe. Her grey hair twined in many braids about her head, its colour contrasting strangely with the deep copper colour of her seamed, leathery face. Her dark claw-like hands worked over some rabbit skins but she often looked up to talk to Isaiah and Bill Manydogs playing cards at the table under the window. With intense concentration, the men dealt and redealt the greasy pack, their dark faces bent, their brown cigarettes hanging limply from their lips. They spoke softly to each other, and Bill laughed sometimes when he thought he had triumphed, or threw down a card with an oath when his luck was bad. Isaiah showed no feeling, except that his eyes grew eloquent as he quietly played his last card. Bill sank over the table with a groan. The door opened and Poppy came in silently on moccasined feet, going directly to the stove to warm herself.

For a moment they all paused, looking at her, while she smiled slowly, holding her hands over the heat. Martha picked up some wood from behind the stove to replenish the fire. Then, taking off the little girl's red toque, she smoothed the fair hair.

"Can I see Sammy?" Poppy whispered, pulling off her coat.

Mrs. Waters said in Cree, "How much did you lose, Bill?"

Bill twisted his fingers in his long black locks. "My saddle-blanket, and bridle, and my spurs."

"You have no horse, anyhow." Isaiah swiftly shuffled the cards.

"But some day I was going to win a horse." The old man grinned, his eyes almost disappearing in the network of lines around them.

Isaiah relit a half-smoked cigarette, inhaling deeply. A flicker of a smile showed in his face. "I give it all back to you so we can have another game." He dealt the cards with expert hands. Bill drew up close to the table, laughing like an excited child.

While Martha sat on the bed, sewing, Poppy began helping Sammy to walk, holding his tiny hands as he staggered uncertainly across the room to his grandmother, where the little girl sat down, holding him in her arms.

"What are you making?"

Mrs. Waters smiled, and taking the pipe from her mouth, touched the golden hair as Martha had done. "It is a rabbit robe for Isaiah when he goes to trap."

The hides of many rabbits had been cut circular-wise and twisted and pulled as they dried. Now they were stretched on a sort of frame, like so many grey furry ropes, through which the old woman wove others. As Mrs. Waters resumed her smoking and her work, the fair child sat quiet and happy, the dark head of the infant against her cheek, while the heat of the fire brought a bright colour into her face. In a few minutes Jay came in, banging the lunch pails noisily on the floor, flinging his coat and hat on a nail. The children smiled at one another.

"There was a team on the road." The boy spoke in Cree to the men.

"An ace! an ace!" Bill exclaimed in great glee.

"Whose team was it?" Isaiah asked, suddenly on the alert, while Bill became anxious. "Did it go near the hayland?"

"I don't know. It went into the bush, suddenly, far down the road."

Isaiah looked at the cards in his hands, glanced at those down on the table. Bill peered out of the window into the greyness of the afternoon.

"It is only Jack Two Knives who goes to see his old grandfather in the bush." He turned back to his game, the delighted expression on his face returning.

His companion put his cards face down on the table.

"We should look." He rose with a swift silent motion.

"You are losing!" the old man cried in vexation. And as Isaiah took his hat and went outside, Bill reached forward to see the cards of his opponent. "Losing!" he repeated. Nevertheless, he soon followed into the mistiness.

"'Grandmother, will you make me a rabbit robe too?" Jay asked, taking the baby from Poppy, and tossing him up in the air.

"When you go on the trap line with Isaiah."

"Put him down, Jay. He'll get the tummy ache," Martha protested, coming up to rescue her son.

Jay scowled, digging his hands deep into his pockets. Then his face lighted.

"I've got a new game." With a piece of chalk, he drew a small circle on the floor. From his pocket, he took a handful of brightly coloured agates and marbles, which he began arranging carefully inside and outside the circle. Poppy knelt beside him her eyes shining, her cheeks flushed. Martha watched them, the baby on her hip.

"My, they're pretty. Where did you get them, Jay?"

"I won them at school," he said. "With this little goldie one I borrowed from Emil, I won all the others out of the ring. Then I won the goldie in the next game. See, like this." With his thumb and forefinger, he shot the gold-coloured agate, knocking three marbles out of the ring at once. "Poppy, you can use the goldie; and Martha can have the red, and I'll take the blue." His dark face lighted as though by a lamp inside. The little house filled with the sounds of their laughter. Mrs. Waters stopped her work for a while, watching with wise old eyes as they scrambled about on the floor.

Suddenly the door burst open.

"The gun! The gun!" Bill shouted, coming in so quickly that he nearly fell over the crawling baby.

"What are you going to shoot?" the boy asked, longing in his voice.

"There's a moose in the trees at the other end of the hayfield." The old man took the gun down from the peg on the back of the door. "A—a moose!"

"Let me come!" Jay pleaded, scattering marbles in every direction as he jumped up from the floor.

Bill put a firm hand on the boy's shoulder. "Not this time. You might get hurt. Now you stay home with grandmother." An understanding look passed between the two older people, and the woman said, "Stay with me this time, my little boy."

Terribly disappointed, he went to the window, but he could see nothing through the trees except Bill's retreating figure.

"What did he say?" Poppy asked, coming up to him, for she had not understood their talk. "Where is Bill going with the gun?"

"There's a moose," Jay replied glumly. "And he told me to stay home."

Presently they returned to their game, but the boy let the girls win all the marbles. As they were beginning again with fresh spoils, a shot sounded, followed by the shouts of men.

"Wonder if they got him." Jay walked about impatiently.

"We need some wood," Martha suggested.

Mrs. Waters shook a warning finger. "Stay close to the house."

The boy was gone in a moment. But outside he could see nothing of the excitement. Added to the mistiness, the greyness of the late afternoon was deepening. Beyond the hayfield, the trees were but a blur. It was very cold. As he gathered up an armful of split poplar and spruce logs, he listened intently, sometimes hearing a shout. He went two or three times for more wood; and at last, when he dumped the last armful on the floor, and brushed himself off with his hand, he heard voices outside. A moment later, Isaiah and Bill came in, bringing Olenski with them.

Olenski's face twisted with pain, his mouth drawn up in a grimace. On his bare head, his hair stood up in uncombed locks. He held his right arm with his left hand. Blood dripped from the arm onto the floor, and a great blood-soaked patch showed on the sleeve of his jacket. Isaiah supported the wounded man on his left side, while Bill walked behind him, carrying the heavy gun. Olenski sat on a bench at the table, bowing his head over his injured arm. Mrs. Waters silently rose from the floor, and spread an old coat of Isaiah's on one of the beds. Drawing out a box from under the bed, she brought out some rags which she tore into strips. Meanwhile, Martha bombarded the men with questions.

"What happened?" she cried in Cree, shaking at the sight of the blood. "Did you miss the moose? Will he ever stop bleeding? Tell us what happened!"

Bill hung the gun on the door again before he answered. Then he took her gently over to the bed where she had been sewing.

"It is so bad," he moaned, speaking in English. "I think I see a moose in the trees. I shoot. It is Olenski." He rubbed his lined face with knotted fingers, with a look of such misery about him that the girl grasped his arm reassuringly.

"Isaiah's mother will fix it," she whispered. "He will be all right."

Jay took Poppy over to the fireplace. Both children watched wide-eyed as Mrs. Waters helped Olenski out of his coat, and Isaiah got him to lie down on the bed where they bathed his arm in a basin of water. The baby rolled on the floor, forgotten, stuffing his mouth with marbles, until Martha, with a gasp of horror, ran to him, expelling the marbles by holding him upside down. The children could not help laughing. Hearing them, Olenski cursed furiously from the bed. Such a stream of filthy language flowed from his twisted lips that Martha began to talk to Jay with great energy.

"You must take Poppy home now," she told him in Cree. "Her mother will be back from Jensen's. You stay for supper there; they have lots to eat. And bring me some milk in this pail."

Jay nodded.

"She says to get your things on, Poppy. Your mother will be home now."

"Don't take the horse, Jay," warned Isaiah, who was holding the basin. "I need him. I must go up to see Jack Two Knives."

Bill put on his beaded buckskin coat.

"I take your team home, Olenski. I tell your woman you get shot." He went out hurriedly with the children. Olenski cursed more violently, trying to get up from the bed. Bill put his head in the door.

"I get you some moonshine!"

"It is a bad wound," the old woman said in Cree to her son as she emptied the red-stained water and poured fresh into the basin.

Isaiah spoke soothing words to his irascible neighbour. "You stay here. We have moonshine and cards. You get better soon."

"I lose de money from Gustav for working on de hayland!" Olenski shouted.

"You get drink with money. We give you drink here."

"It is a bad arm," Mrs. Waters repeated, but her patient could not understand.

Bill closed the door on the scene, pulling his fur cap over his long black hair as he passed Jay and Poppy.

The little girl shivered.

"He was bleeding awful."

Jay took her hand, hurrying her along the darkening road.

"Bill thought he was a moose. Funny looking moose, isn't he?" They laughed at the thought.

"First to hear a chickadee, it's their chickadee," Poppy sang out.

They listened intently, walking softly among the dead leaves.

"Chickadee!" they both shouted together, as the unmistakable notes sounded from some trees near them.

"Whose is it?" the boy asked.

"It's our chickadee," Poppy declared.

After a time, Jay remarked sniffing the air, "It's going to snow."

"Mother says the roads will be bad when it snows." The child panted in her efforts to keep up the brisk walk.

"Yes, it will be deep snow everywhere. You can only go to town on horseback. There's a light on at your place. Let's run."

They shouted as they ran, the boy pretending to let his companion win an easy race.

"Something smells good," he said wistfully, as they came up to the gate.

Lina opened the door, making a block of warm light in the dark bulk of the house.

"There you are," she called cheerily. "Did you bring your lunch pail?"

The child's steps slowed instantly. Her voice was faint.

"But Mrs. Ashley!" the boy cried excitedly from behind his friend. "You don't know what happened! Bill thought he saw a moose, and he shot, and what do you think? It was Olenski. Full of blood, wasn't he, Poppy?"

"All bleeding!"

Lina was silent for a moment. "Olenski? Well, don't stand out there, children. It's beginning to snow, I do believe."

"What was that about Olenski?" Benjie called from within.

"Come on, Jay. Come to supper."

They went into the warm, lighted house, full of eager talk.

Outside, a slight wind made a chill sighing through the trees. Fine snow was beginning to fall.

Chapter IX

1

On New Year's Eve, Benjie lay on his bed in one corner of the kitchen in the half dark cabin. A hacking cough tore at his chest. He was alone, for Lina had taken Poppy up to Panachuk's to break the monotony of the Christmas holidays. Though the cabin glowed with warmth, and he did not mind being alone, yet, huddled beneath the patchwork quilt, he felt a heavy depression over his heart. After a fit of coughing, he sat up to pour out a spoonful of a dark liquid from a bottle on the chair beside him, swallowing the dose with a grimace of distaste. He had refused Lina's suggestion that he go to bed like a really sick man, but he had consented to take the odious medicine that Mrs. Waters mixed up for him. When he lay down again, he felt his throat and chest eased, and a peaceful lethargy came over him.

Some time later, half asleep and half awake, he became aware of someone walking softly about the dark room with shuffling footsteps.

"Who is it?" he asked, drowsily.

After a pause, he heard the word, "Sick?"

Benjie recognized the voice of Bill Manydogs, and forced himself to alertness. "Yeah, would you light the lamp?"

A match scraped on the stove, and Bill guarded the flame carefully with his hand while he took it to the lamp on the table. The sick man watched his visitor put the chimney carefully in place and turn up the wick. He had a beaded buckskin jacket on his bowed back, and his fur cap on his head, under which his uncut hair hung down in snaky locks. The skin seemed tightly drawn over his high cheek bones and prominent nose, as though he had been hungry for a long time. From sunken eye sockets, his eyes glittered, and moved about quick as a bird's.

"Come to visit me?" Benjie asked, sitting up and trying to shake off the blackness that swam about him.

"Come to borrow fiddle for New Year's dance," Bill answered.

"I missed all the holiday dances," Benjie remarked thoughtfully. "I ain't made no money. Tell you what, Bill, I'll sell my fiddle to you."

The old native sat down on the edge of the wood-box.

"How much?"

"Ten dollars."

"I got five here." Bill produced a greasy wallet from some dark inner pocket. He licked his fingers, counting over five ragged bills. "Won it last night with cards." He grinned, showing long brown teeth, and a thousand lines in his face.

Benjie lay down again. "Ten dollars is my price."

Bill glided silently to the bedside. "I get five dollars tonight, playing, if you lend the fiddle. I bring the money tomorrow."

While the other man watched him craftily, Benjie coughed, fighting the pain in his chest. Then he got up and walked steadily into the bedroom, reappearing a moment later with the violin case in his hand. Bill trembled with excitement.

"Gimme your five bucks," Benjie ordered. ". . . OK. Now gimme your buckskin coat. You can have it tomorrow when you bring the rest of the money."

Bill stared blankly for a moment, running his fingers lovingly over the rich beaded designs of his coat.

"You get it back tomorrow when I get the money." Benjie put the fiddle on the bed, pouring himself another spoonful of medicine. Bill tore off his coat at last, flinging it on the chair without looking back at it. With knotted, twisted fingers, he opened the violin case, took out the instrument, plucked at the strings, tightened the bow.

"Tomorrow I bring money," he said in his softest voice; and gathering up his treasure, he went out into the night. Benjie staggered over to the chair to pick up the coat. Lina would call him a fool to trust Bill Manydogs; she must not know. The thing smelled horribly, but the hide was heavy, the beading really beautiful, done in rich colours in designs of horse-heads on the sleeves, and roses down the fronts and the middle of the back. The old man put the garment under the patchwork quilt, and hid the money beneath the mattress. Then he lay down again, feeling a terrible weakness.

He knew nothing more until he woke to broad daylight. Not wanting to disturb him when she came home the night before, Lina had covered him with a robe. Poppy danced lightly about on moccasined feet. An appetizing odour of frying bacon and bubbling coffee filled the kitchen.

"What time is it?" Benjie asked hoarsely.

Lina came over to him at once, stirring something in a cup. "Have a good sleep, Daddy?"

"Slep' all right," Benjie muttered. "Folks gone by from the dance yet?"

"Oh they must have went by long ago," Lina told him. "It's almost afternoon now." She went back to the stove.

"Don't you feel good, Gramp?" Poppy rubbed her cheeks against his hand.

"Nothing extry."

Lina flung the tin plates on the table.

"They sure was having a wild time at the dance last night. We could hear old Bill Manydogs yelling clear out to the road when we was passing."

"Someone at the door!" Poppy cried. "Come on in!"

Mrs. Waters in her shawl and blanket stepped inside, shutting the door behind her. Light snow powdered her clothes, and her face was pleasantly ruddy with cold.

"Bill said to get his coat. He leave it here last night."

Lina had the frying pan with the sizzling bacon in her hand.

"Bill's coat?"

"He leave it here."

"Did Bill leave his coat here, Daddy?" Lina asked, turning her searching gaze on her father.

Benjie put his arm over his eyes and nodded.

"Whatever for?"

"He was to bring me five bucks this morning, for my fiddle." His voice rasped as he spoke. They gathered round him.

"You sold your fiddle for five dollars?" Lina demanded.

Mrs. Waters clasped her dark hands.

"He owe you five dollars?"

"He gave me five bucks last night, and he said he'd bring me five more after the dance," the old man answered.

"But Daddy, why did you do it?" His daughter turned away to put down the frying-pan.

He lifted his aching head. "To git the land, Lina. You got to have ten dollars to file, and you got to git there by tomorrow or you lose it."

"He owe you the money? For land?" Mrs. Waters folded her blanket tightly about her shoulders, and went silently to the door. "I bring money," she said nodding.

When she had gone, Lina sat down heavily on the foot of the bed.

"But you thought it was a crooked deal. You swore no money of yours was going into it."

"I know." His voice was weak. "But I got to thinkin'. You can't git along without the hayland, I kin see that. It's like Tudor says. Hard knowin' what's right. And now you've went so far in the deal, better finish."

"But it's no use, Daddy. The time's run out. You see, I didn't have the money. I kep' waiting, hoping I'd get it some way, and I waited too long. I could still be first for the hay every summer," she declared.

"The time ain't run out, Girl. You look it over again. You got till January second at five o'clock."

Lina opened the trunk and took out some papers, studying them with great concentration. Poppy wandered forlornly to the wood-box where she sat kicking her moccasined heels.

"You're right!" the woman exclaimed. "Horseback," she decided, walking up and down the kitchen. "A team and sleigh could never make it past Olenski's. I'll get to Two Knives' tonight, and ride into Bear Claw tomorrow."

"Better git Martha to come over," her father suggested.

"Yes, after we eat." She opened the stove and flung in some wood. "I'll have to try to catch a ride from Bear Claw if I can. Oh, I'll make out." Her face glowed in the light of the flames.

"Feed your horse plenty oats, and see you dress up warm," her father advised from his bed.

Lina banged the lid on the stove. "My God, I hope she brings the money. I saved up four bucks other than what I gotta lay out for grub. But even with that, your five bucks won't swing it."

They ate a hurried meal, and while her mother washed the dishes, Poppy scraped the frost from the window, to announce the first sign of anyone's coming. After a long while, Bill himself appeared at the door, shivering and demanding his coat.

"Here's the money," he wheezed, exuding a powerful odour of alcohol as he spoke, and thrusting a bill into Lina's hand. "Gimme my buckskin!"

"Is that Martha in the sleigh?" the woman asked, looking out at the one-horse conveyance. "Martha!" she called. "Will you come and stay while I go to town?"

The girl got out of the sleigh, and came up to the house, holding her baby wrapped in a blanket.

"I don't mind if I do, Mrs. Ashley," she answered, sniffing hungrily. "I was just going to Poudre's to visit. I'll stay if you like." Her grey eyes in her thin face darted to the food shelves.

Bill had put on his coat; he went reeling into the snow. "See you after my card game, Benjie!" he shouted, jumping into the sleigh. "Git goin', Buck!"

2

The short winter day was already darkening as Lina tramped up to the door with Queen to say good-bye. The door opened just a few inches, but the steam and warmth of the house rushed out in a hoary cloud.

"Them iron stirrups are sure cold," Martha said, shivering as she retreated within.

"Never mind, I'll be warm enough. They won't know what's coming when they see me." Lina grinned down at herself in Benjie's overshoes, her own overalls and shabby coat with the ratty fur collar. She had borrowed Martha's fur-lined mitts, and tied Poppy's scarf around her head, hiding the heavy coil of honey-coloured hair. Hearing Benjie coughing, she warned, "Keep up the fires, Martha, and do the chores. The chicken feed is behind the manger. You can get what you like for meals."

"Sure."

"Be a good girl, Poppy." The child's white face appeared for a moment as Lina struggled into the saddle. "Shut up the door quick now. The heat's all going for the crows." A chorus of farewells sounded as the woman turned her horse to the gate.

Through the bare branches of the trees, the sky showed grey and cheerless. Ice lay on the trail under the fresh fall of snow; and Queen, who was unshod, with difficulty kept her footing. Lina urged her on with encouraging words, for the afternoon was almost spent. They wound through the snow-covered spruce, the scarring black stumps, the deep drifts piled up in the brush. As far as the schoolhouse, the way was well worn and not too difficult, but beyond that, it became untracked and treacherous. Sometimes Lina would dismount and lead the horse to bring the feeling back to her own numb feet. On a good stretch, she would ride again and make time. But before she had gone four miles from home, a light shone far off in the distance, and the bitter winter night was almost upon her. The paralyzing cold seemed to close in with the darkness.

Fine snow sifted down, and it seemed to Lina that her face was being frozen into a stiff mould, eyes shut, lips drawn back from her teeth in a leer. But it would be worth anything to get the hayland. Gradually, she could build up a herd of cows and send cream to town. Sally, the red and white cow, would calve in the spring, and that would be a start. In time she could raise more horses. There would always be feed for them all. Besides, she wanted that land. She wanted to be able to look over those acres and know that they were hers. She put a hand up to wipe the snow from her eyes. The trail was growing dim, but she knew it by heart and felt no fear. And there would be high school for Poppy when the time came. She was a smart little thing, learning to read in no time at all, even spelling out the newspapers and catalogues. How like Sym she was, sitting by the fire chafing her hands, that discouraged, peaked look about her. Lina shook off the thought. And Benjie. He always had those terrible chest colds in winter. This one seemed worse than most. But he would perk up and look forward to spring when the hayland was once hers. No more watching beasts starve on putrid straw four years old.

The horse floundered beneath her. Good God, maybe she had better get off and walk a piece again. Every joint was stiffened, her whole body felt stone cold. She climbed clumsily down. There in the grey light, the woman bent against the stinging wind, slapping her sides and legs with her free hand, pulling on the reins of the big horse with the other. Slowly they progressed through the unbroken drifts beside the bare poplars with their cracking branches, and heavily laden spruce trees. The woman mounted again, numbly, crouching in the saddle. Somewhere a lone chickadee uttered a few notes and was silent. The night had come, black and starless.

Mrs. Two Knives' children were all asleep in the one large, home-made bed. She herself sat by the stove, stitching a new pair of moc-casins for the littlest, while her husband, at the other side of the stove, sharpened his skinning knife on a flint. The small oil lamp lit the single room of their house, its light falling on the sleeping faces of the children, on Mrs. Two Knives' shining black braids of hair, and on Jack's gaunt face. Suddenly the mongrel dog which had been sleeping in a corner, opened his eyes and lifted one sharp ear. He rose, growling. Jack got up and opened the door a little, peering out. The dog rushed past him, barking, and a woman's voice called out, "Hullo, Jack!"

"Lina!" Jack spoke excitedly to his wife in Cree. "Go in, Lina. I look after horse. Where you goin'?"

"Bear Claw, tomorrow."

Lina came in, taking off her outer clothes, and beating the snow from them. Even before the roaring fire, she thought she would never be warm again. Mrs. Two Knives, unintelligible, but kind, poured her a scalding drink of muskeg tea, and spread out a deer-hide bedroll near the stove.

"Had supper?" Jack asked, bringing the winter night with him as he came in, stamping his feet, the dog at his heels.

Lina nodded, swallowing the hot drink from the thick, handleless cup.

"That warms you." He picked up the lamp. "We sleep now."

Taking off her shoes, Lina crawled into the bedroll, shivering. The light was out. She could not sleep. The draughts of the stove glowed redly, while the good spruce logs burning within sent forth a warm pungent odour. The dog scratched his fleas, shook his hide, and lay down again. It seemed that everyone was snoring, each in a different key. The woman lay there, shaking with cold. She would never sleep. Now she could feel the motion of the horse again along the tortured miles she had come. Queen floundered, and Lina's body jerked nervously in the sweaty bed-roll. The visitor's bed; it was probably full of lice. If so, she was too chilled to notice. Sym had slept here once. The thought disturbed her. Would she never sleep? Her head throbbed; her feet were icy cold. Against the hard floor, her back ached intolerably. She turned over; in a short time, the whole side of her body felt numb. She lay on her back again, staring into the dark, shivering. The dog gave little whines in his sleep, his feet twitching on the bare floor. Everyone except Lina was deep in slumber.

She was wakened by the sound of fresh dry wood crackling in the stove. Grey light filled the log house and Lina knew it was no longer early, and she must get up. Mrs. Two Knives was busy about the breakfast, while the children, thoroughly awake and tousled, ran about in every direction in some wild game of their own. Lina sat up, gradually pulling herself out of her coverings, shaking out her crumpled dress. Her shoulders hurt even to touch, and her whole back seemed bruised from her sleep on the floor. She put on her shoes with an effort, for stiffness seemed to have affected every muscle. She thought she had never been so tired in her life. Her head ached dully, and her eyes were heavy. She drove out of her mind the thought of the coming journey. Mrs. Two Knives smiled, talking softly in Cree.

After a breakfast of saltless bread spread with lard, Jack brought the horse around, and Lina started out for Bear Claw. The nine miles seemed to take an eternity, but it was light, and the sharp wind with its stinging sleet had gone down. The cold air cleared her head, while the ride gradually took the stiffness out of her body. Lina tried to plan how she would manage the twenty-five miles from Bear Claw to Bridgeville. Obviously, the beer parlour was the best place to find someone who might be going on the road, only Gustav would be there. Various teams and cutters passed her, and she hailed their strange drivers. Her spirits rose in spite of the difficulties which she felt lay ahead.

She rode Queen to the livery barn, where for fifteen cents a horse could shelter all day. An old Rumanian, muffled up in a sheepskin jacket, took the mare.

"Know of anyone going to Bridgeville?" Lina asked him.

"I seen the old car at the hotel pointing that way." He spoke from the depths of a stall. "Ask Gustav."

The few people who were in town huddled about Wong's stove, their coat collars turned up, caps pulled down until only their frost-bitten noses showed. At the hotel stood a decrepit old auto of the open type with flapping curtains. Above the raised hood, the wizened face of Brenner appeared.

"Would you be going to Bridgeville by any chance?" Lina asked him.

"You bet." He jammed down the hood. "I gotta get a keg of beer on account of this one's gone dry, and it's expensive to open bottles and pour into glasses. Got to get some repairs for my old bus, too."

He looked at her thoughtfully, turning a wad of tobacco about in his mouth. "You wanna come?"

"That's right."

"I'll be goin' in about half an hour if you want to wait."

She must go into the hotel, she decided, as it was the only place where she could get a meal. In the dining room, she took off her scarf and mitts, ordering coffee and pie. As the waitress brought the order, piping hot, Molly clattered in from the kitchen, and stood over Lina with a slight sneer about her red lips.

"Hullo, Molly," the big woman said coolly.

"'Lo Lina." The long lashes dropped. "Haven't seen you for a long time." She sat down carelessly on a vacant chair. "Heard from Sym lately?"

A sudden confusion of shouts in the kitchen interrupted her, and she left, her face tightening in anger.

Lina finished her lunch quickly, and putting on her things, went into the waiting room. Looking through the window, she saw that Brenner was filling the radiator of the old car with hot water from a kettle.

"Hop in," he called, as she opened the door. "I'll be right back."

He came out of the hotel with a huge coat draped around his thin shoulders, and a shovel in his mittened hands. As he climbed into the front seat, the big head of Gustav Hanson showed at the door. Lina turned the other way, pulling up her coat-collar.

"Brenner!" Gustav shouted. "Mind you bring them hams! And don't pay too much!" The motor roared, the rattling old vehicle shook, groaned, and leapt forward.

Twenty-five miles to Bridgeville. They had started at one. After they had covered ten miles, the car stopped dead. The man got out, patient, efficient. The woman sat silent, stiff, her eyes half closed against the dismal scene. The motor started up again, and they moved on. The man chewed steadily, his gaze on the road with its icy ruts. But further on there were drifts, and they had to shovel. Lina set her shoulder to the back of the car.

At a quarter to five, she walked into a little office where a greyish man sat at a desk. The warm air of the place smelled of dust and horses. A fellow in a buffalo coat was arguing volubly about a lease, but he finished at last. Lina placed the papers and her ten dollars on the desk.

"I've come to file my homestead."

The grey man went on making notations in a book. After a moment, he glanced over the papers. He said condescendingly,

"Well, you're too late. That thing ran out two days ago."

He went on making marks in his book. But a woman's furious shouting filled the room. "You count them days over, you damn blockhead!"

The eyes of the grey man widened. He saw before him a big woman, almost grotesquely dressed, her eyelids red-rimmed by the cold, her face coarsened by wind and weather. With blazing eyes and clenched fists she bent over the desk. The papers shook in his hand as he studied them again, carefully, making figures on a pad. At five minutes to five, he said humbly, "I beg your pardon, Madam. You are on time after all. Would you kindly sign here?"

While Brenner finished his business, Lina spent a precious fifty cents on a good supper, and another fifty on candy and ginger-snaps for Mrs. Two Knives.

"Weather's gittin' colder," Brenner announced as they started up for Bear Claw. "Gonna be a bad spell."

The woman smiled grimly. "Bad spell? You haven't seen nothing. Spring's coming. Didn't you know?"

With the baby on her hip, Martha scraped some of the frost off the south window with her free hand, and peered out anxiously. Her face looked drawn and terrified. Benjie lay on his bed, very still, so still that she wondered if he still breathed. Poppy whimpered, rocking herself miserably on a bench.

"Your mother's coming!" Martha cried from the window, her voice full of relief.

The little girl came running to look. Martha put the baby down on the floor, and snatching up a coat, went outside. Queen pranced with eagerness, and Lina waved, sitting stiffly in the saddle.

"Didn't get froze up, eh?" She had stopped, and was trying to dismount.

"I thought you'd never come."

The woman clambered wearily down. "Well, I made it."

"Go on in, Lina. I'll take the horse."

"I sure am wore out."

Martha took the reins. "Lina . . . Benjie, he's worse. He looks bad to me."

The woman looked into the girl's frightened face.

"Take the horse," she said quietly. "I'll look after Daddy." As she turned towards the house, Poppy came running out, bareheaded.

"Mummie, Gramp wants you!" she cried.

Lina pulled her inside, feeling ready to drop with weariness. Taking off her coat and mitts, she sat down at Benjie's side, feeling his pulse and silently chafing his hands. When Martha came in, Lina said, without looking up, "I'll have to go for Mrs. Waters."

"Isaiah's mother is up at Olenski's." The girl picked up her crying baby and sat down on the rocking chair. "I was going to go, but I didn't want to leave them all alone."

"I guess Olenski's pretty sick again, but I got to get Mrs. Waters just the same." Lina put on her coat.

"I'll harness up the team." Martha laid the infant in the bedroom and poured a cup of coffee for Lina before she went out. Poppy, who had been wandering about, forgotten, resumed her rocking and whimpering.

"Stop that crying this minute!" her mother scolded. She drank the coffee, beside the mound of unwashed dishes on the table. "Couldn't even do up a few chores!"

Along the five miles up to Olenski's, the trail was broken and the team fresh, so that they went along at a good clip. The woman felt almost devoid of thought, as though the cold had numbed her mind as well as her body. Wrapped in a horsehide robe, she sat still in a kind of apathy until she pulled up at last at the log shack half hidden in brush and snow. In answer to her knock, Mrs. Olenski, looking smaller and more peaked than ever, opened the door and beckoned her to come in.

In the tiny one-roomed house, with its single window, dull now with coatings of frost, the bed occupied half the space. Here Olenski lay, tossing with fever, his arm in dirty bandages. As the door closed, the cabin seemed very dark, and Lina could just make out the forms of Mike and his elder, half-wit brother, outlined against the window. They sprawled over the table on which were cluttered unwashed dishes and the remains of the last meal; two orange cats were licking up the scraps. Mike sat up rigidly when he recognized the visitor. On the floor in one corner a hen clucked noisily, her feathers fluffed out against the cold. Filthy, smelly garments hung from the rafters, and among them Mrs. Olenski moved, taking bread out of the oven of a little stove. When her eyes became accustomed to the gloom, Lina found Mrs. Waters sitting on a large rock that protruded from the dirt floor. She puffed contentedly at a strong pipe.

"Oh, you got to come, Mrs. Waters. Daddy's worse. He looks awful."

The old woman knocked out her pipe without a word, and got up, tying on her red shawl over her grey braided hair, and wrapping herself in a heavy blanket. She moved to Olenski's side, putting her hand on his forehead.

"He is all right by tomorrow."

Again the cold drive. Long and monotonous the trail seemed. It was getting dark now, but the horses trotted eagerly in the direction of home. A light shone from the window. While the old woman made her way to the house, Lina fumbled about, putting the team in, bedding down the animals for the night, moving slowly and mechanically.

When she entered the cabin, it seemed terribly silent. Martha shivered beside the stove, pale and frightened. From the bedside, Mrs. Waters looked into Lina's haggard face.

"Old man dead."

"Yes."

Poppy lay curled up asleep on the foot of the bed, her face tear-stained and dirty. Mrs. Waters put a gnarled hand tenderly in the golden hair, her fathomless eyes on the child's mother.

"Little girl not feel so good."

The white woman straightened, towering above them all.

"It'll be a cold day to put him in his grave," she whispered.

Chapter X

1

While the child still slept, the three women moved Benjie into the bedroom, covering his peaceful face, and darkening the room, drawing the curtains over the window and the door. Putting the sleeping baby beside the little girl, Martha built up the fire and made coffee, while Lina, completely exhausted, still in her outer clothes, sat on the trunk, leaning against the wall. Mrs. Waters, having laid aside her own blanket and shawl, untied the scarf from Lina's head.

"Could you take Poppy home with you?" the white woman asked, gazing fixedly ahead of her. "I don't want the kid to see him."

"I take her," the old woman nodded. "But take off the coat, and you must rest."

Lina took off her things with slow, tired motions. Everything seemed unreal: Mrs. Waters, her mauve print dress and unadorned moccasins, her leathery face and grey bands of hair, Martha putting strips of bacon into the frying pan, setting the table, moving softly in her brightly embroidered moccasins, averting her frightened eyes, letting her thick dark hair hang about her face, the children, one pale and golden, the other dark, lying side by side on the foot of the bed under the patchwork quilt with its gay pieces, the clock ticking on, as though hurrying.

Already the house was darkening, each window grey and colourless. Outside, the dog, Gypsy, raised his pointed nose to the dull sky, and howled despairingly. Somehow the place seemed cold; Martha was not a good firemaker. Feeling an almost appalling weariness, Lina arose, walking heavily to the stove to stir the logs. Immediately she had shaken the grates, poked at the wood and put on more fuel, the fire began to roar. Mrs. Waters lighted the lamp, setting it on the table beside a great mound of bread. Gently she cajoled Lina into eating some bread and meat, and drinking quantities of hot coffee.

"Jay bring Sven tomorrow," she said. "Sven, he tells you what to do."

Lina leaned her cheek against her hand. Her heavy fair hair was dulled, coming out in loops from the thick coil at the back. Her face was drawn and greyish. She looked old about the eyes.

"You want to stay alone?" Martha asked, helping herself to another large slice of bread.

"Yes. I want nobody with me." The white woman roused herself, straightening her shoulders. "I got to get the kid's clothes out. I'll fix her a lunch for school tomorrow."

Shortly after the women had washed the accumulation of dirty dishes, Poppy suddenly awoke, sitting up blinking in the light.

"Where's Gramp?" was her first question.

"Shh!" Martha warned. "He's sleeping, and you mustn't wake him up." She sat down on the bed, putting her arm about the child. "You're coming on a visit to our place to stay all night."

Poppy rubbed her eyes, scarcely awake.

"Come and wash," her mother said quietly, as she poured hot water into the wash-basin.

Martha wrapped the sleeping baby in his blanket, while the little girl got ready for the unexpected visit. The house seemed unnaturally quiet. Mrs. Waters sat on the edge of the wood-box before the stove, peacefully smoking her pipe, watching Lina brushing Poppy's hair.

"Is it school tomorrow?" the child asked, pulling on her red sweater.

"Yes. There's your lunch." Her mother put the lunch-pail on the table. "There's your coat and toque, and your mitts are behind the stove."

While the others were getting ready, Lina wrapped up some bread and cheese and a few cookies.

"You can eat this when you get there." She handed the package to Poppy. "And give some to Jay."

She watched them go off into the cold night, Martha carrying the baby, Mrs. Waters huddling into her blanket, Poppy trailing after them, their shoulders hunched against the cold as they disappeared into the darkness. They would hurry down the snowy trail, she knew. And soon, before the blazing fire, the children would eat the lunch she had made for them, while Martha told them wild stories about wolves, and Mrs. Waters sat on the floor beside them, smoking interminably, and Bill played solitaire, and perhaps had a drink of moonshine and a bite or two of bread and cheese.

Lina called to the dog. She could just see his dark form against the snow by the gate. But he trotted off. How cold it was! She closed the door, and stood with her back to the stove, chilled through, worn out, and terribly alone. Outside, the dog howled in low, heart-breaking tones.

When she looked back later, the days that followed always seemed
somewhat vague in her mind, the events confused. She could
remember the mist and the grey morning when Sven appeared, driving
a team of impatient black horses on the snowy trail. In his heavy dark
mackinaw and fur hat, his enormous fur mitts with cuffs to the elbow,
he stood up in the low sleigh holding in the lively blacks. Even then she
noticed how red his cheeks were, as he shouted to Gypsy who barked
furiously upon his arrival, stiff and angry inside the yard. And later,
Sven sat drinking coffee, his bright yellow hair vivid in the cheerless
little house. She was wan and colourless, dressed in overalls and an
unbecoming black sweater. Her hands outstretched on the table,
were chapped and work-worn. She felt so tired that she could scarcely
follow what he was saying about the arrangements for the funeral.
His foreman was a carpenter and would make the coffin. There was
a burying plot down the road from his place where several of the old
people who had died in the district were buried. Word must be sent to
Tudor.

And then suddenly, he stopped talking about these details, and
came to sit beside her on the bench at the table. She thought how
pleasantly he smelled, of tobacco and soap.

"Divorce him, and marry me," Sven said.

She looked at him, bewildered.

"He's gone and left you. How does he think a woman lives in this
country, alone?"

"Sym?"

"Yes, Sym."

"Lina—"

She shook her head, wearily. "No, Sven. I've had all I want of men."

"D'you think I'd treat you like this? Leaving you all alone to get
along how you could?"

"Maybe you wouldn't."

"It's tough country, Lina, even for a man. And for you alone—why, it would take all the woman out of you. But you and me, we could do anything!"

She had a distinct remembrance of those words, and of his fine vivid face as he said them. She put her head down on the table.

"Oh, I'm so tired, so tired."

She had complete confidence in him that he would take care of everything, as he did. She remembered watching him drive away, taking her dead with him. The black horses, the strong figure of the man driving them, the sleigh, the burden it held, moved through the bleak, leafless trees, rounded the bend in the road, and was out of sight.

She remembered that the day of the funeral was colder than any she had ever known. A bitter wind blew sleet into the faces of the people where they stood at the open grave. She looked about, dazedly, at the small respectful crowd. Pete Panachuk. And his wife, white and weak from a recent confinement. Sven Jensen. Jack Two Knives. Mrs. Waters and Bill Manydogs, and some other neighbours whom she scarcely knew. Tudor Folkes. And Constable Trevors from Bridgeville. The men took off their hats while Tudor read from a small Bible:

"I am the resurrection and the life. . . ." His shaggy dark curls blew about in the wind. His face was gaunt and thin. The young mountie burrowed down into the collar of his buffalo coat.

Sven filled in the grave. In his buckskin coat and fur cap, Bill Manydogs watched him, his head bowed low.

"My heart is sore, so sore," he said. "And the fiddle gone too, in a poker game."

When it was over, Tudor pulled up his parka hood over his cap. He shook hands with Lina, with a sad compassionate expression.

"I am glad to have met you, Mrs. Ashley. He was a good old man. They don't come much better. Drop in to see me when spring comes. He would have liked that."

And when she went to settle with Sven, he shook his head. "Fifteen dollars, to pay the carpenter any time you got it, Lina." Panachuk was waiting to drive her in his cutter. Sven shouldered the shovel. "It will be so lonely for a woman. We could start over, you and me."

She gave a bitter laugh. "No use talking about that again!"

About them, teams and sleighs were departing through the deep snow in the bush trails. Mrs. Panachuk had settled herself for the drive, while Pete took the blankets off the horses. Sven turned away. She remembered watching him leap into his cutter, shouting to his fine black horses.

At Panachuk's, she got her own team out of the barn. Poppy, in her red toque and coat, came slowly out of the house where she had been staying with Olga during the burial.

Her mother helped her up.

"Come on, child. Let's get going."

"Olga says I won't see Gramp no more."

Lina started her horses.

"No, he's gone, Poppy." She looked sharply at the child. The little girl buried her white peaked face in the robe, closing her eyes as though to sleep on the cold trip home.

Chapter XI

1

A gentle wind blew over the silent land; and the breath of the wind was tender for the first time in long months. The new warmth brought a soft shade of blue-grey to the clouds, and tinted the shadows in the snow. The wind stirred the tree-tops where bird cries and whistling and twittering were like the happy exchanging of greetings of friends who have been snow-bound and now set free to meet and gossip and exclaim. Deeply hidden, the horned owl hooted in low throbbing tones. And then the wild geese passed over. The sky was alive with the beat of their wings and the noise of their honking. Their voices called into the quiet forest with waking thrilling cries as though bringing great news.

With his rifle in his hand, Isaiah emerged from the depths of his trapper shack half under ground and mounded over with snow. Far away he could hear the weird clamour of the geese, and his keen eyes probed the sky above the trees. A team of dogs pulling a toboggan appeared from out of the bush, and presently the gaunt figure of Jack Two Knives. Still watching the sky, Isaiah went towards them. At a shout from their owner, the dogs stopped, lying down in disorder in the snow, their long red tongues hanging out, their slanting eyes half closed. The men moved slowly together, and when they were near enough, conversed in low tones, sometimes making signs with their hands, laughing at jokes but half implied. They smoked, luxuriating in each puff, wafting a fragrance of tobacco smoke into the air about them.

"He come back," Jack said again. "A long time he is gone."

They meditated on these words in silence. Then the honking of the geese came closer, and above their heads, a flock of the great birds came into sight. The men looked up, roused out of their indolence. Jack made excited gestures. Among the haunting cries of living creatures, sounded the short crack of a rifle, and then another, while the birds rose in terror, clamouring over the forest, leaving their dead behind them.

2

Pete Panachuk stood up in his low sled, holding in horses that were eager to dash along the last two miles from town. When he saw Ek bringing Emil in the cutter home from school, he pulled in his team sharply, stopping to let Ek come abreast of him on the narrow road.

"De geese, dey go over." Pete blinked up at the sky.

"Feels like spring," said Ek.

"It is spring," the boy piped up. "It's the first day of spring. Teacher said."

"What's new in town?" Ek asked, reaching for his tobacco pouch.

"Whoa!" Pete shouted, pulling on the lines as his team moved restlessly. "Lucky Strike, he's back."

The men were silent for a moment. Ek struck a match on the sole of his boot.

"He's in town?"

"Won a horse off Cy."

Ek shook his head. "Still lucky, eh? What will *she* say, I wonder?"

Pete's team refused to stand, and the sleds swung off in different directions. Just past the school, Pete slowed to let Olga and the boys jump on.

"Did you see the geese go over?" Olga cried with shining eyes.

"The geese! the geese!" the boys shouted, each trying to tell his story at the same time.

"I tink I got geese right here," Pete said good-naturedly.

"There's Sven Jensen stopping at the school," Olga exclaimed as the sled passed behind a clump of trees that blocked her view.

At the sound of footsteps, Miss Hughes glanced up from her stack of exercise books. She flushed when she saw Sven, and her look was warm with welcome. He flung his fur hat and leather mitts on a desk at the back of the room and came up to her with an armful of mail.

"Oh it's good to see you. With all that mail, I mean," she added with a quick laugh.

He sat down before her, leafing through a text-book, squeezing himself uncomfortably into the small seat, his great frame seeming larger by contrast.

"I thought this letter would never get here," Ethel remarked, turning over one of the envelopes and looking thoughtfully at it. "So much of a woman's life is spent in waiting."

He shot her a swift look. But she glanced through the other pieces of mail, handling each with an interest that was almost emotion.

"Did you hear the geese go over?" she asked. "I could hardly get the children to stay in school for the rest of the afternoon."

He threw down the book. "It's like spring today."

Ethel looked out of the window at the soft greyed tints of the land-scape. "It'll be good to see it at last."

"You wouldn't want to go through another winter like that?" he asked anxiously. "You don't like our country?"

Ethel tore the wrapper from a magazine and straightened her glasses with a chalk-greyed hand.

"I like your country, Sven. I like it." She paused, pushing a set of arithmetic books aside. "It's good to be—well, building up something worth while."

"Just why I like to be doing the breaking," Sven said, gripping a pencil in his big hand. "Ethel, you know me pretty well now."

The colour flooded her cheeks, bringing a flash of beauty to her plain face. She sat silent, her eyes on his bright bent head. At the sound of the muted beating of hoofs, they both glanced up at the window. A rider on a bay mare went by.

"He's a stranger, isn't he?" Ethel asked, watching the rider go on down the road.

But Sven turned quickly away with some hardness in his look.

"I got to be honest with you, Ethel," he said. "I asked Lina first because I thought you wouldn't like to get stuck up here in the bush. With all your education and everything. I'm only telling you, Ethel, so she won't be able to throw it up to you, and you not knowing."

He looked into her face, his eyes desperately pleading.

"I never got much education. I never got time. I had to go and work. But I'm not so dumb; I read. Ethel, it's so God-awful lonely for a man. And I'd be good to a woman."

She looked on him with compassion, but with a great sadness.

"I was a fool, Ethel," he muttered.

She put her hand on his forehead, pushing back the bright hair as though he were a child. Faintly they could hear the honking of geese far away in the forest.

Sym Ashley heard them too as he rode down the wooded trail on the bay mare. He slumped in the saddle as though he were very weary, and his face revealed tired lines about the eyes and mouth. He climbed down stiffly at the gate he had made himself, looking about curiously at the rail fences, and at the well tramped snow in the yard. After he had put the horse in the barn, he walked around to the door of the house, running his hands over the logs as he went, trying the chinking with his fingers to see how it held.

Quietly, he opened the door, and his step with the jingle of riding spurs sounded on the bare boards. Poppy sat on the wood-box, reading by the stove with the dog at her feet. The kitchen smelled warm and sweet as though it held the fragrance of many bakings of good things. The clock ticked musically on the wall by the window. But at the sound of Sym's coming, the dog sprang up with a low bark. Staring at the stranger, the child dropped her book. Suddenly, Gypsy leaped upon him, barking and whimpering in glad recognition.

"Down, boy!" Sym cried. "Don't you know me, Poppy?" His old gay laugh rang out. Whirling his hat on to the trunk in the corner, he came towards her with his jingling hearty walk, bending down, holding out his arms, while the dog jumped playfully about him.

"Sym!" the little girl said wonderingly. And then she ran to him, crying "Daddy! Daddy!" and flung her arms about his neck.

"Where's your mother?" he asked presently, as he sat with Poppy on his knee.

She slid her hand up and down the shoulder of his leather jacket.

"Jay and me forgot to shut the gate, and the horses got out. Mother went to get them."

He smiled. His hard frost-bitten face had a charm about it.

"Was she mad at you?"

"Yes." But the child looked radiant. "Are you home for keeps now, Daddy?"

"Hm. Do you want to see what I brought for you, Poppy? A plumb gentle horse all your own to ride to school."

She jumped down, eager and excited, her cheeks nearly matching her red sweater. "Let me see. Let me see."

She ran happily by his side as he strode to the barn. He lifted her onto the mare's back in the chilly gloom.

"Well, how is it? Her name's Big-Enough-Girl. Like her?"

Poppy wound her hands in the thick mane, and slid to the ground. The horse rubbed a velvet nose on the child's shoulder.

"Will she take oats out of my hand?"

"She sure enough will."

Back at the house, Sym built up the dying fire while the little girl laid the table for supper. The house began to darken, while through the window, the trees were black outlines against the grey-blue sky. The wind was rising. Then the work horses plunged through the yard with a great pounding of hoofs. Lina, in overalls and an old sweater, followed on foot leading Queen with the yearling close behind.

While the horses gathered at the water trough, the woman went to the barn to unsaddle Queen. She stopped short at the sight of the new mare, for a moment, and then went on with her work. When Lina had uncinched, strong hands took the heavy saddle from her, and she felt the lightness of a burden eased. In the murkiness of the barn, she turned to find herself face to face with Sym.

He threw the saddle down, and she caught the gleam of his eyes.

"Lina, I've come back."

There was a strained unnatural silence between them as they stood near each other, and the horses moved about, waiting to be fed.

"You've been in and seen the kid?" Lina asked at length.

"Of course. I wanted to see her."

"Had supper?" There was a coldness in her tone as though she spoke to a benighted stranger.

"No." He touched her shoulder.

"We could have a talk when the kid's in bed," she told him, reaching for the pitchfork. But he took it from her.

"I'll do up the chores, Lina."

She turned her face away. "I'd be glad. I'm that tired."

4

Ten musical notes sounded from the china clock. Lina sat knitting by the pool of light from the coal-oil lamp on the table. The light made her hair gleam a dull gold, but tired shadows showed about her eyes. Her face was thin and sharp.

"I guess I got no right to say I couldn't help it." Sym sat on the trunk, a cloud of cigarette smoke about his head. "I got pulled into a deal that turned out to be crooked. And I owed money and didn't have none. Believe me, Lina, I had to do what I did. I had to work for that fellow and square things up. If I hadn't, it might of meant jail."

"You and your deals," Lina sighed.

"That's right. I shouldn't of got into it in the first place. But holy bald-headed, we needed cash so bad."

"It wouldn't of mattered so much about the deal, Sym," Lina declared, tugging out some wool from the tight grey ball. "But what gets me is you never let us know nothing where you was. You might of been dead for all I know."

Sym watched her, brooding behind the smoke.

"I didn't want to write a long story of how I was in trouble. I wanted to get square first. If I wrote, you might not believe me then."

The woman put down her knitting, holding up her free needle as though she held a weapon.

"But you left me just when everything was tough. Just like you didn't care what happened to me and the kid. I had to fight for that hayland like I was a man, and leave Benjie dying." Her voice broke. "Now everything's easier, you come back."

He leaned forward tossing his cigarette butt into the stove. "Is everything so easy? Lina, you need me bad. And there's the kid too."

"What about that woman, Molly?" Lina burst out. "I want to know what was between you and that woman."

"There was nothing between us!" Sym growled angrily. "She likes to think every man is crazy about her. Didn't you hear she ran off with Jim Nelson a couple of weeks ago?"

"Ran off?"

"That's right. Gus didn't even go after her. She'll never come back." Lina began knitting again.

"Oh, I don't know, Sym. You let me down so bad. And everybody knows. People feels sorry for me. Sven Jensen, he wanted to marry me." She spoke rather defiantly.

Sym smiled, looking at her with admiring eyes.

"Just goes to show he knows a good article when he sees it."

"You and your fine words," she scoffed.

But he seemed surer of himself now.

"I'm all squared up, Lina, and I could start right."

"There's the drink and the gambling," the woman said wearily.

"But we're far from town. And Lina, I'm trying. Honest. I never had a drink since New Year's. And now I'm on the homestead, I swear I won't touch another card."

He came and sat beside her, looking into her face for some sign of relenting.

"You're too good to lose. I know a good article too."

"If I thought there'd be a chance! Oh Sym, it's been that hard fighting alone!"

"And I got good news, too," Sym told her with sudden eagerness. "I been South. Duke wants to buy Benjie's old place. He'll give a dollar an acre. Thinks he'll make good on some irrigation scheme down there. Just needs your say-so."

"Sym Ashley! And you sat there all the time, and never breathed a word that I've as good as got eight hundred bucks!"

"I only wanted you to need me bad before you knew about the money."

"Where in tarnation does Duke get all the cash from?"

He saw in her eyes a look of new hope, and plans. She got up, and began walking about the room.

"If we could only work together now, Sym, we could get some-wheres."

"Give me a chance."

"The land's all right, and there's hay."

He caught her hand. "Lina, you're—you're good."

They became aware of the wind moaning through the trees.

The woman lifted her head, listening.

"Spring's coming fast. Won't be long till we can get on the land."

"Did you hear the geese go over?" he asked.

5

Outside, the warm wind tossed about through the forest, while the land beneath the snow seemed to be gathering a mighty strength to free itself. And in the night, the gurgling and dripping sound of running water began.

Chapter XII

1

S ym walked down the trail towards home, driving the harnessed horses before him in the cool of the evening. From behind the leafing trees, yellowish grey smoke from a bush-fire rolled up in billows, rising to the sky, making vivid colours in the clouds of the setting sun. The man moved wearily, his clothes grimed with earth, his face a black mask in which the whites of his eyes gleamed and his mouth showed red, set in a dour expression. He looked moodily at the greenness of the grass, and at the budding of flowers. The latest quarrel was heavy on his mind.

Always things seemed to begin with the child. That morning when Sym brought Big-Enough-Girl round to the door, and Poppy came rushing out from breakfast with her book and her lunch, Lina called from the kitchen,

"You're not riding that horse to school, Poppy!"

"Yes I am!" the little girl cried out. She stood beside the big horse, her pink dress hastily tucked into her overalls, her bare feet deep in the dust. Her mother appeared at the door,

"Put on your sneakers, and run along. Jay'll catch you up with Buck."

Holding the rope bridle, Sym sent his wife a pleading look. With a loud wail and a gush of tears, Poppy threw down her things.

"Honest, Lina, she's plumb gentle," Sym remonstrated, patting the neck of the mare, who looked around at them all patient but questioning.

"Did you know the kid got throwed last night?" Lina asked, coming out and grasping the child by the shoulder. "Her and Jay will race, and this critter shied at a rock. The kid only hurt her knee, but next time it might be her neck! She'll have to wait till she's old enough to take care of herself."

Still scolding, she took Poppy back into the house. Sym picked up the pail and book and set them on the doorstep. He turned the horse out into the pasture, leaning for a few minutes on the fence, watching the mares and the colt grazing. The air was beautiful and birds sang, but the man stood lashing a fence-post with a switch. He could hear the child still crying when she started off for school.

"Lina." He came quietly into the kitchen. "A fall or two won't hurt the kid. She'll learn soon enough." He looked sombrely at her across the bare room where she worked swiftly at her dishes.

"She'll learn with a broken leg, maybe. She's getting so darn spoilt, a person can't hardly speak to her."

"I don't like her always with that Indian. Perhaps I could trade the mare off for a shetland pony. Fellow out near town has a couple. I could maybe make a deal tomorrow." Sym took a drink from the dipper, clanging it back into the pail when he was done.

"Sym." Lina wiped her hands on the dish towel and picked up the broom. "Will you be done seeding that field today?"

He paused in the doorway, quietly on the defensive. "I figure to be done."

"I been thinking." Lina began to sweep methodically. "Olenski don't seem to be putting in any crop. Seems like they been doing nothing round there this spring, and Gus wants Mike to go into town and work for him. What do you say we get that land? The lease is due. But we could maybe buy. You could see Gus tomorrow."

Sym stared at her, pushing back his old bashed-in hat. There were bitter lines in his face.

"I say no!" he told her harshly. "Olenski don't work on account of his arm. He's sick. And he's sick because he got shot at, down by the hayland. We done enough to him already."

"Wasn't my fault he got shot," Lina declared, gripping the broom handle. "And they'll never make out now. Better they should go to town."

"I tell you, it's not right," Sym answered. "And they can make out. Mike did quite a bit of trapping this winter, and I know he got seed potatoes from Jensen."

They faced each other with hard stubborn faces.

"I s'pose you think your deals are all so square!" Lina flashed at him. "Where'd you get Big-Enough-Girl? Didn't you win her off some poor devil in a poker game?"

"That's different!"

"Sure is different," she affirmed vehemently. "This here's a decent deal."

Sym squatted down by the door, rolling a cigarette with shaking hands. He urged in a calmer tone, "But, Lina, we got enough to do right here. I figure to get some clearing and breaking done."

"But there's land up there broke already. It's a sight easier than what I went through last year." She stopped in her work, glaring at him.

"I won't do it, Lina," he declared quietly, lighting his cigarette, and getting to his feet. "It just don't seem decent to me. Going behind another fellow's back and taking his land. How do you know? Maybe he don't want to go to town, nor the boy neither."

"If we don't take it, somebody else will!" the woman cried in stubborn exasperation. "Can't you use your head? Olenski's no good to pay. And we can pay and make money on it too."

He pulled on his worn leather work gloves and turned to the door.

"I won't do it, Lina. We can make out."

He went to the barn, while she sent stinging words after him.

She spoke little at noon, and they did not refer to the quarrel. Yet the strain between them was worse than bickering. And now, after his long day's work in the field, Sym looked up apprehensively as he neared the house. But he saw its closed door and the barn shut up too, while the cow bawled forlornly at the pasture gate. Even the dog had disappeared. Sym looked after the horses and did the chores in the coolness of the twilight. The house had that empty waiting look inside which a house has when the woman who belongs in it has been away for a while.

The man washed at the tin basin on the wash-stand, his skin burning, his eyes red-rimmed. He cut himself hunks of bread. Against the whiteness of the loaf, his long hands were grimed with earth, hard blackened cracks on every finger. Over a hot crackling fire, he brewed himself a cup of strong black tea. He ate and drank mechanically, sometimes getting up with a piece of bread in his hand to look out and listen into the stillness of the night, hearing only the ordinary night sounds. The far-off barking of a dog, the night birds calling, horses chomping grass. A hazy slice of moon hung in the light sky.

He was sitting on the trunk, smoking, when he heard wheels and harness and hoof-beats, and rose stiffly to open the gate. Lina drove the light two-wheeled cart Sym had made, Queen prancing between the shafts. The woman got down, carrying parcels to the house, while Sym took the horse to the barn. They did not speak. When he came in, she had lighted the coal-oil lamp, and was having a cup of tea, watching for him, a determined look about her. Yet she began carefully.

"Poppy in bed?"

He started.

"No! She isn't here. I thought she'd be with you, or else you'd at least know where she's at."

"I left at noon." Lina grew anxious. "She gets in trouble when she don't come right home." She had grown a little pale.

"She must be at Waters'." Sym stood still and thoughtful. "But I didn't see anybody pass on the trail. Not even Jay."

"Jay didn't pass this morning." Lina got up distractedly. "The kid must of walked all the way. Maybe she went home with Olga."

"You didn't happen to see her when you went past the school?"

"The kids was all in."

Sym went to the door and stood looking out. "I think—I think I'll just ride over to Panachuk's to be sure. That rotten old bridge over the creek—a kid could easy slip. And that fire Ek started when he was clearing, spreading through the brush. . . ."

"Sym for God's sake don't talk like that! She must of went home with Olga!"

He looked into her tired pale face. "I want to be sure."

Lina clenched her hands. "Good God! Nothing could of happened to her. It just couldn't!"

"I'm not trying to frighten you, Lina. But Poppy went to school crying this morning. You're too hard on her. You are, Lina. She's not much more'n a baby, and you treat her rough. I'm afraid for her. Lina, why are you so hard? You didn't used to be like this. You're changed, Lina."

She looked down at her hands. "I don't mean to be hard," she said miserably. "Daddy used to say that too. You and him, you put everything on me. I got everything on my mind."

He softened at that. "But, Lina, you don't need to. Can't you leave some things to me? You don't need to always be worrying. We'll make out."

"Oh yes, we'll make out!" she cried. "Just leave the deals to you!

So I got to ride to town in dead winter to fight for a piece of hayland. And I got to go to town today to make a deal you're too weak-kneed to handle!"

His look stopped her.

"So you made that deal!" He turned away and went outside.

"Where are you going?" she cried.

"To look for the kid," she heard him say, indistinctly in the night.

Her triumphant anger gone, her shoulders sagged. Then a new anxiety came into her face, and she rushed out after him. He caught Big-Enough-Girl and brought her into the yard, throwing Benjie's old saddle on her back.

"Going to Panachuk's?" she asked him, shivering.

He struggled with the mare to get the bit between her teeth.

"I'll go to Waters' first and see if maybe she went down there and didn't go to school at all, when we was inside, talking."

"Sym, if it's really my fault, I never meant no harm to the child. I was trying to do my best for her. Sym, you got to believe me."

"Yes, I know, Lina," he answered, with a roughness in his voice. "She'll be all right, but we got to find her."

"Come back from Waters' right away and tell me," Lina implored him, backing away as he put his foot in the stirrup.

"I'll be right back," he assured her.

She opened the gate for him, watching him out of sight. He came back very soon, with a thud of hoofs.

"Nobody home at all," he informed her, dismounting and leading the mare to the fence. "Lina, I think you'd better take Queen and the cart, and go up to Panachuk's. I'll hit into the bush."

She could see the whites of his eyes gleaming under his hat brim, and the bulky outlines of his broad shoulders against the lightness of the sky. Big-Enough-Girl chafed at the bit, tossing her head, her sides heaving quickly.

"Where'll you hit for?" she asked, doggedly.

"You know them breeds from the north, went through here yesterday? They're camped by Little Bear Creek. Waters might of went over and took the kid along."

"Yes, that's more'n likely," Lina said thoughtfully. "I know they *was* home. They must of passed this afternoon when I was gone. Sym, you'll come right back and tell me?"

He leaned over the fence and patted her shoulder.

"Sure I will. You better get going right away."

He leapt into the saddle and rode quickly into the bush.

2

The night had become brilliantly lighted with a wide, greenish-white, quivering path of northern lights spanning the whole sky from west to east. The white tents of the Indian encampment showed starkly against the spruce and the dark swirl of water. From across the creek, deep behind the big trees, came the dull roar of the bush fire. Now and then blood-coloured flames shot up high, a mile distant. Before each tent smouldered a low-burning camp-fire, round which huddled dark figures, with firelight playing upon the faces. Voices murmured low, and the tramp of horse-hoofs dragged through the grass. The trees with their sticky leaves, the spikelike tips of evergreens, a horse with lifted head, were silhouetted on the sky.

Sym tethered Big-Enough-Girl at the edge of the bush, and walked slowly, with the wet grass catching at his feet. As he neared the first tent, he heard, above the murmur of voices, a man's low sweet singing within. Fresh kindling crackled brightly at one of the fires, and a figure bent, holding a shallow drum over the flames, pounding it rapidly with a stick, sending out resonant beats into the night. Suddenly, the singer came out of the tent, wailing a high, shrill, wordless song. A man on horseback approached and took up the song as he unsaddled. The drummer had the drum close to his face, holding it by the crossing of two thongs on the under side, beating with quick fierce strokes, and keeping time with movements of his whole body. People began getting to their feet and heaping the fire high. The song ended, and the beating ceased, while excited laughter and the quick rush of talk took its place. The white man advanced casually to the fire, spreading his hands to the blaze. Among the strangers, Isaiah, Bill Manydogs, and Mrs. Waters welcomed him with expansive friendliness.

"You come to the dance?" Isaiah asked him. "Indian dance. Biggeman got a son, just born." He pointed to the drummer who warmed his drum over the flames, his fine Indian face well lighted, and gleaming with sweat.

"I'm looking for Poppy," Sym replied anxiously. "Did you see her, Isaiah?"

The native looked up with a dark secret smile. Bill Manydogs laughed, shaking his black locks, and pointing to the tent beyond.

"Poppy come with us. Have fun."

"She's here?"

Sym left the crowd as the beating of the drums began again, and the weird monotonous chant rose, high and sweet. A few long steps brought him to the smouldering campfire where several native children lay on the ground, deeply asleep under ragged bits of canvas. Jay sat awake, poking at the dying embers with a stick. A bit of flame came alive, dancing brightly among the ashes. The white man could see the pale face of his own child by Jay's elbow. She slept peacefully beside Martha's little Sammy, under the same covering.

"Hello," the man said quietly.

Jay looked up, startled. "Hello."

Sym knelt down beside the children. The song grew louder now, and a second drummer helped to pound out the rhythmic beat. Men and women began to dance about the fire, in twos, holding hands, old squaws, and old men, and young men, and young girls, about twelve of them in the ring, while others stood watching. Sym did not move, following with his eyes the weird shuffling steps of the gay, shouting dancers.

Martha came out of the tent, buttoning a sweater about her.

"Hello, Sym," she said shyly.

He glanced up. "How'd Poppy get here?"

"We saw her, after school. We come, in the wagon." Martha shrugged her slight shoulders, making an expressive gesture with her hands. She looked away from him, and moved to the crowd.

The singers tired, ending on a low minor note, and the dancers broke away from the fire to select new partners.

"Look!" Bill Manydogs cried, coming up to Sym. "New moccasins!" He offered the gift to the white man to examine.

"Pretty nice," Sym nodded, giving them back.

"You come and dance too?" Bill stuffed the new moccasins into his pocket.

Sym shook his head. "I got nothing to give away this time."

Bill capered away at the sound of the resonant banging of the drums over the flames. The boy Jay looked into the dying embers with half-closed eyes. Sym roused his sleeping child. She sat up in bewilderment, but gave a sigh of content upon seeing him.

"Coming home now?" he asked her.

Her head sank against his shoulder. The monotonous beating and the wailing song started up again with greater intensity. The white man watched with a kind of fascination the free primitive movements, the firelight playing on happy faces, the long fantastic shadows, the bright sparks bursting upwards to the silent shooting lights of the sky. He carried the child, with her head and one arm hanging limply over his shoulder. With one last look at the group in the warm light, he cut off through the field of wet grass to the spot where he had left the horse.

But the strange beating and singing pursued him into the silent forest. With Poppy on the saddle before him, he made the mare stand while he listened intently. Under all, the bush fire roared dully in the distance like a coming wind, and tongues of flames and a reddish glow marked the place. Overhead, the northern lights faded to thin nervous greenish fingers. He turned Big-Enough-Girl sharply into the path, and holding the sleeping child, slouched wearily in the saddle. Like a hypnotic chant, the Indian song penetrated far beyond the sight of the encampment. And as the dawn came in with haggard greyness, there was a look in Sym's eyes that had not been there before.

Chapter XIII

1

It seemed as though he had never stopped riding, that he rode on into the hot noon sunlight, his shirt wringing wet with sweat where the child clung to him, that the night had been replaced by day, of which the morning was a heavy dream.

Lina had fallen asleep with her head on the table, but she awoke with a start when Sym came in, carrying Poppy. Greyish light in the house, made familiar objects recognizable. The blackened lamp chimney, the oil burned out, told of the long night of waiting. The man laid the child gently on the bed in the kitchen, and stood looking down at her.

"Gave me a fright, I can tell you." Lina rose to put a blanket over the little girl. "Was it like you said?"

"There was an Indian Tea Dance." Sym sat down on the edge of the bed. "A fellow can hear the drums and the singing the longest ways."

She looked at him with a doubtful expression.

"It *was* Isaiah's outfit took the kid along?"

He nodded, pressing his hand against his forehead.

"I'll get us something to eat." The woman rattled things about the

135

stove. "We'll knock off a bit today, and just do up the chores. I reckon there's time yet."

He got up suddenly, slouching off to unsaddle the mare. When they had finished breakfast, the light brightened in the kitchen.

"Reckon we could do with some rain," Lina remarked from the window. The colour had come back into her face, and she had tidied her hair. She looked as though the night's ordeal had not touched her. Sym, sitting at the table, leaning his head in his hands, dishevelled, had dark circles round his eyes, and hard weary lines about his mouth.

"I'll be going today, Lina." He spoke in a muffled tone.

"Going!" She left the window and whirled upon him. "Where'll you be going?"

"I'm going away from here." He looked up at her steadily.

She sat down to face him.

"You would," she said bitterly. "You would! Oh, you're no good, Sym. I've tried and tried." Her tone was hard and grating.

"I know," he said sadly. "Lina, I don't want no words with you. It's just that we can't live together peaceable. It's no good. I'm not the kind of a man you want me to be. I'm thinking I'll go to town and get a job. I'll send you money."

His charm, his gaiety, seemed to be dead, and his eyes had a far-away look that maddened her.

"You would pull out now, just when we could get someplace! The tom-toms must of got into your blood," she said scornfully.

"When I get to feel like I envy an Indian, I know I got to go." He spoke without anger. "You can't tell somebody what they're going to do with their life, Lina. Like deciding what Olenskis will do. It might be all wrong for them, even though it looks good to you."

"I got to do the best I know how," she shot back.

"For me too," he went on in the same quiet voice, "I can't stand it."

"A person has got to use their head!" she cried. "If you won't, some-body in this house has got to."

"Well, I'll be going today."

"Well, why don't you go, then?" Lina got up, fairly throwing the dirty dishes into a pile. "If you're going, go now while the kid's asleep. You don't seem to think what she'll be like, finding you're gone, again!"

"It's the only thing to do." He got up stiffly from the table. "But I won't just leave her like this. I'll take her along on the horse to school on my way."

"Take the kid's horse and all!" Lina muttered sarcastically, as she poured hot water into the dishpan.

"I'll send it back from town," he returned mildly. "I'll let Poppy sleep for the morning while I do the chores, and take her for the afternoon lessons."

2

The warm noon sun beat down on the dusty trail. When they reached the school, the other children had already been called in. Poppy seemed to have cried herself out by that time. He set her down, and she stood alone in the empty school yard, white and mute, watching him go away with clouds of dust churned up by the horse's hoofs billowing about him as he went.

Chapter XIV

1

I t was breathlessly hot. Lina wore a handkerchief on her head, and she had tied up the legs of her overalls at the ankles. Yet the sandflies, swarming round her in dark clouds while she hoed the stunted potato plants, bit her cruelly on the neck and hands. The perspiration ran down her flushed face. She felt tired. More than tired. Her body seemed weighted down at the shoulders, while the hands and arms felt lifeless. A caterpillar dropped from an overhanging tree onto her arm, and lay, wriggling, trying to gain a foot-hold on her shirt sleeve. She shook it off, straightening up to look about her. The trees were bare and leafless, their trunks and branches alive with greenish striped caterpillars. It seemed strange to see the sky through bare branches in the middle of June. She started, thinking one of the loathsome creatures had gone down her neck, but it was a great bead of sweat she had felt. Wiping her forehead with the back of her hand, she began to hoe again, crushing caterpillars into the earth, the sandflies darting at her face, and mosquitoes singing in her ears.

The rumble of wheels roused her a few minutes later as an Indian family in a wagon passed on the trail. The man stood to drive, while the woman in her scarlet kerchief and the children with ragged unkempt black locks sat in the back. Behind them, trailed three large wolfish dogs. Gypsy, who had been sleeping peacefully on the doorstep, started up, barking at the strangers. Lina watched him advance, stiff-legged, wagging his plume of a tail. And then, suddenly, without a sound, the Indian's dogs, slinking under the lowest fence-rail, closed in upon him. Growling, squealing, snapping, snarling, the animals fought, rolling over and over, advancing, retreating, tangling. Forgetting her weariness, Lina ran to them, shouting, with up-raised hoe. From the wagon, the Indian yelled something in Cree as he disappeared around the bend in the trail.

At the woman's approach, the strange dogs fled, leaving Gypsy to stagger to his feet, matted with blood and dust, blood dripping from his torn throat. He began to cough, looking up at Lina, with old, strained, blood-shot eyes. "I'll have to shoot him," she thought. "He can't suffer like this. I'll have to get Sym's old gun and shoot him."

Caterpillars almost covered the screen door. She scraped them off wholesale with the hoe. The sight of their soft, squashed bodies at her feet nauseated her. With rasping breaths, the dog stood beside her, his tail feebly wagging. She knew she could not shoot him. "I'll have to get Jay to do it when he comes home," she thought. "How late the children are." Her head throbbed; her throat ached. Gypsy had been Benjie's dog. A horrible stench came from his mouth and from his dusty body.

"Come, Gyp." She led him, with encouraging words, to the shady side of the barn where he dragged himself to a clump of grass. She brought him a shallow dish of water. Lifting his head, he lapped painfully once or twice, and then lay down and stretched out stiffly with glazed eyes. He was dead. He would have to be buried. But she had no strength. Dizzily she leaned against a tree-trunk. How hot it was! Strange bluish-grey clouds were piling up in the west, and the sun blazed down with a merciless heat. Something warm and heavyish fell on her neck. With earthy fingers, she scraped it off. A caterpillar wriggled and squashed in her hand. And then, suddenly, there beside the barn, she was violently sick into a clump of pestilence-laden willows.

2

School had been out for some time when Pete Panachuk with his wife and his neighbour, Mrs. Ek, drove past the schoolhouse in the wagon. Not far ahead, they could see Miss Hughes with Poppy and Olga each clinging to a hand, while Jay walked a little apart, leading his buckskin, which took the opportunity now and then to snatch a bite of tall grass. When he overtook the group, Pete pulled in his horses at the side of the road under some of the strangely leafless trees.

"Heard de news, Teacher?" he asked, while the fine dust which his wagon wheels had stirred up, began settling on them all. "Olenski, he is dead in de town, and dat crazy boy sent to Ponoke."

"Oh dear, how dreadful! Poor Mrs. Olenski. And Mike too!"

"Want a ride, teacher?"

"Oh no, thank you. I'm going to hang my curtains today. And I won't be home for supper either." Miss Hughes held up her hand to shade her eyes from the sun, face flushed with the heat.

"Your face so red, teacher," tittered Mrs. Panachuk. Above the din of the wailing of her six months' old child whom she held on her knee, the woman went on, "You get Sven de dinner to-night? Plenty time when you marry wit him to be de cook."

Unknown to her, a striped caterpillar toiled stickily across the back of her green beret. But Poppy and Jay saw the creature, and began to snicker, so that she thought she had made a good joke. Plump blond Mrs. Ek smiled pleasantly, not wishing to offend either party.

"Come, Olga," Pete ordered. "You come home quick wit us."

"Aw hell, Pa, I wanna walk with Teacher," Olga wailed.

Her mother interposed here with a stream of Ukrainian talk, lost to the girl as Pete gathered up the lines and shouted to the horses.

"Dat teacher!" Mrs. Panachuk gossiped as the wagon moved off down the trail. "All de men in de country been by my house to get her to marry wit dem. She wait, wait for de best one, you bet! Pete, already he got fifty more peoples dat want de job."

Miss Hughes continued to walk slowly through the dust with the children.

"How unnaturally hot it is," she remarked. "Is it going to rain, Jay? Look at those funny clouds up there."

"Flies are awful thick." The boy sniffed the air. "Might be a thunder-storm coming."

"You never coming back no more?" Poppy asked, trotting along beside her, clinging to her hand.

"Why no, Mary Belle. I'm going to marry Mr. Jensen. But I won't be so very far away."

The two little girls burst into tears. Jay looked uncomfortable, jerking Buck away from a tempting clump of green grass. They had come to the side road in the trail where Miss Hughes would leave them. Through the bare branches of the poplars, they could see the outlines of a huge barn, the largest one in the country, and also of a neat white house, the only painted building in the community.

"Olga." Miss Hughes wiped her eyes under the silver-rimmed glasses with a startlingly white handkerchief. "Don't ever give up going to school. You've done so well. Come to me any time you want to, will you?" Olga wiped her own eyes with a grimy hand. Miss Hughes took a caterpillar out of her pupil's long black braids. "And another thing," she went on, "try to stop using such filthy language. It certainly isn't becoming to a nice girl." She tucked a loosened strand of her own untidy hair into her bun. "And Jay." He looked at the ground, kicking at a toadstool in the grass. "Learn everything you can whenever you're not away brushing." He swallowed a hot lump in his throat when she touched his shoulder. The sandflies swarmed about them. The children scratched their legs which were bitten until the blood ran. "Mary Belle." Miss Hughes put back the hair from the child's hot forehead. "How I shall miss you. Oh children, I mustn't keep you here with the flies getting so bad. Good-bye for now. There'll be a nice new teacher there on Monday, and I'll be seeing you ever so often!"

They watched her going off down the road. Olga wiped her face on her cotton dress. Jay slapped a vicious horse-fly on Buck's rump.

"C'mon, Poppy. We'll be late, and your mother will wonder what's happened." He heaved her up on to the horse's back. Olga began walking slowly along a short-cut through the bush. But huge mosquitoes attacked her on the damp path, so that she ran madly through the caterpillar infested trees. Buck trotted stolidly in the dust, great patches of sweat appearing on his neck and flanks, while the children on his back were wet through.

When Lina came up from the barn, she saw them at the gate.

"Jay," she called, "will you come here?" She scraped a few more caterpillars from the screen with the hoe before going in, pressing her hands against her aching forehead. "How the children reek of the smell of horses," she thought, when the two entered the stifling kitchen. She began opening the windows to get a cross breeze.

"Jay, will you do up the chores?" she asked. "The heat has got me sick. It's near milking time, and the cows are in the pasture."

She sat down on the bed, still with the same feeling of dragging weariness. The boy and girl stood silently by the door, looking at her. There were large holes in the canvas of Jay's running shoes, showing parts of his bare dirty feet. His red plaid shirt was unbuttoned down the front, revealing the sandfly bites, raw and sore, on his body. Under his greyish-white cotton cap, the sweat ran down his dark face. He nodded when Lina asked him to do the chores, set down his lunch pails, and went silently outside.

"Poppy, for heaven sake, take off them overalls. They smell terrible. And if you want something to eat, wash your hands first."

Lina lay down, watching Poppy take off her slacks, bringing to view her grubby cotton dress and insect-bitten brown legs.

"What was you doing so long?" she asked.

"Saying good-bye to Teacher. Pete talked to us. Olenski's dead in town, he says."

Lina closed her eyes.

She could hear the little girl dutifully washing herself at the wash-basin, could smell the strong disinfectant soap. From the distance came the sounds of the cow-bells. "Anyway," she thought, "I never gypped Olenski on the deal—getting them two cows when he moved to town."

Opening the bread-box, Poppy took out a loaf from which she hacked herself a thick slice, spreading it liberally with peanut-butter.

"Take it to the door, Poppy," Lina said weakly. "The smell of it makes me sick." She thought how filthy the child looked, her pale gold hair full of dust and hanging in lank locks, dirt streaking her arm and cheek.

Jay came in at the gate with the cows, banging the pole into place. The animals mooed forlornly. When the boy came in for the milk pails, Poppy gave him what was left of her bread. Lina watched him take it into his dirty hands and stuff it hungrily into his mouth.

"Wash your hands before you milk, Jay," she scolded. "And Poppy, go gather the eggs, will you? In that old pail there by the window."

When her child had gone, the woman talked quietly while Jay washed with the strong-smelling soap.

"The dog got killed today," she told him. "Will you bury him after supper? He's out behind the barn. Don't tell the kid; she'll take on so."

Jay picked up the clean shining pails. "Say, will you bring me a pail of water from the well, Jay? The water here is 'most warm, and I'm that thirsty for a cold drink."

He brought it to her, not telling her that he had scooped out a couple of caterpillars from the water with his hand just before he came in. He set it beside her, and she drank a dipperful, slowly, gratefully. Caterpillars crawled on the screen again. She could see them black against the sky. Poppy came in, bringing the eggs, slamming the screen, not in the least dislodging the caterpillars, which clung tenaciously to their positions.

"You'll have to get supper, Poppy. We won't light a fire, it's so hot; I'll tell you what to get." The thought of food made her quite ill again.

Jay finished milking, and worked the separator manfully. Lina listened to the feeble tingling of the bell.

"Harder!" she exclaimed impatiently, wishing she had the strength to get up and take the handle from him.

After he had done his best with the separator, he washed again, with Lina's eye upon him. The children ate hungrily, helping themselves generously to cold meat, pickles, bread and butter, radishes, preserves, and cookies and quantities of fresh milk. While they ate, the breeze, fanning in through the open windows, seemed to turn noticeably cooler and fresher. Through the screen and the caterpillars, Lina could see that the clouds were gathering, hiding the sun, while thunder sounded, a low rumbling far away.

"I better get the pigs fed." Jay wiped his mouth with the back of his hand.

"The chickens, too, Jay. Just pile the dishes, Poppy. I'll wash them when I get hot water."

"Here's Martha." The boy opened the screen, talking in Cree to the newcomer before he disappeared to finish the work.

Martha was stockingless, her bare feet thrust into running shoes, wet with perspiration along the soles. Her shapeless print dress did nothing to hide her condition, for her second child would be born any time now. Her thin face looked pathetically young. She sat down, panting and uncomfortable.

"You sick, Lina?"

"It's the heat." The white woman lifted her face to try to catch the coolness of the breeze that was blowing into the room. "Is it really going to rain?"

"Might blow over," Martha answered. "A worm!" she exclaimed, putting out her foot to step on a caterpillar which had somehow found its way into the house. "They're everyplace." She scraped her shoe on the floor.

Lina lay back, putting her hand over her mouth.

"Had supper?" she asked faintly. "There's fresh milk and cookies."

Martha leisurely downed three cups of milk and several cookies, talking all the while. At last she said, "I wish Jay would hurry. We're going to the dance tonight. These are awful good cookies." She helped herself to another.

The wind was rising, making the curtains flap wildly. A terrific burst of thunder crashed overhead, seeming to shake the earth. Gusts of wind full of rain hit against the panes, and soaked the ends of the curtains. Poppy, who had been sitting at the crumby table with her head on her arms, ran to close the windows.

"Jay must have went home!" she cried, as a flash of lightning cut through the grey clouds.

"Better close the door," her mother suggested.

Martha paused in her munching. "Jay never went home," she told Poppy. "He told me he was going to bury the dead dog."

The little girl stared from one to the other, her face white. Before anyone could stop her, she had run out into the storm. Another peal of thunder sounded, followed by a downpour of rain. It soaked into her thin dress and canvas shoes, ran down her face, and wet her heavy hair. Some instinct led her to the place where Jay was covering the animal's body in a shallow hole in the ground.

"Go home, Poppy, you'll get wet!" The rain beat on his cotton cap and red shirt.

"It's Gypsy!"

"Yes." He began shovelling earth very fast.

"What happened to him?"

"Some dogs killed him, I guess."

The child sobbed bitterly. "Everything's dyin'." She stood looking about at the leafless trees, her tears mingling with the rain.

Jay quickly finished filling in the grave.

"C'mon, Poppy. You're wet."

She sobbed uncontrollably, refusing to move, her hair dripping, plastered to her head. He leaned the shovel against the barn wall.

"The leaves will grow on again after a while. And I'll get you a new dog. One of Isaiah's puppies. He'll be a fighter with big teeth!" He made a fierce grimace, growling and pretending to snap dangerously. Taking her hand, he led her back to the house through the beating rain. Already on the path, large puddles of water had formed in which lay the bodies of many caterpillars, wriggling, or drowned.

The heavy storm cleared the air and settled the dust, but it did not last long. Presently it dwindled to a light sprinkle, while rays from the sun shone brightly through the clouds, making a rainbow right across the sky. Jay called Poppy to see it, but she did not answer. In the bed-room, she sobbed brokenly.

"Come on, Jay. We can go now," Martha said. "It's about over."

When they had gone, Lina lay listening to the sobs, and to the light patter of rain. She breathed deeply of the fresh reviving air. She thought of Martha walking awkwardly with her heavy burden, along the rough path. And going to the dance, and being jostled by the careless crowd. How could she! There was something almost unchild-like in the sounds of weeping that frightened Lina. She dragged herself into the bedroom where Poppy lay in a damp little heap on the bed. She longed for old Benjie at that moment, not for the child's sake only. She had thought she was a strong woman who could endure anything; but now strangely, she felt the need of comfort.

She took off the child's wet things, and wrapped the little girl in a quilt, feeling a great tenderness for her. How she was growing! Last year's dress came far above her knees. Lina lay down beside her. The sobs quietened. Lightning flashed and still another growl of thunder rumbled in the distance. Near the house, a vesper sparrow sang his high piping notes. One of the horses was cropping grass close to the open window, while the angry clucking of fighting chickens came from the pen, and the clanking of cow-bells in the pasture. How her head throbbed! The things that she had most loved, the garden and the hay-ing, and the harvest to come—she hated to think of them. Where did she get this listlessness, she wondered? She who had never known a day's sickness in her life, except of course when Poppy was on the way.

Realization came upon her at last.

Chapter XV

Out of the intensely blue sky, the sun shone down upon a cold white world. Columns of white smoke rose from the chimneys at Bear Claw; and frost whitened every tree, and post, and wire. Through the glistening front windows of Wong's General Store, the welcome sunbeams slanted in upon dusty merchandise. Wong himself, picking his gold-filled teeth with a straw from a new broom, sat smiling on the counter, listening to the talk of the two men who lounged near the roaring stove, which was red with heat. Sitting on a keg of nails near it, Pete Panachuk, in his sheepskin coat, smoked a cigarette.

"You're late to go to de shop, Folkes." He knocked some ashes to the floor.

Tudor relaxed against a great mound of men's overalls piled up on top of a crate of breakfast cereal. His face was almost hidden by the flaps of an enormous fur hat, and by the smoke of his pipe. He opened his heavy parka jacket, showing two or three sweaters underneath.

"You don't even get home at night," he retorted.

"A man he got to go away from de wife and de kids," Panachuk shook his dark head sadly. "I sell a little cream, I drink a little beer, I play a little pool, I feel better." He gave a wide yawn, and rubbed his hand over his puffy eyelids.

"How are the roads?" Tudor asked.

"Some places she's not so bad; some places—" Pete indicated drifts with a motion of his hand.

Tudor touched a match to the top of the stove. Flame hissed up in a sudden flare.

"How is Mrs. Ashley making out?" he asked, as he lit his pipe.

Pete leaned forward on the nail keg, his face red in the heat.

"Mrs. Ashley, she makes out. Her garden, she is wormy like de odder gardens, but she gets de potatoes, she gets de carrot and stuff. Her hay, she comes up good, and her wheat and oats comes up good. She got de money to pay for to put de hay into de stack, and she got de money for de harvest. Everyone, dey tink Lina is de Lady." Here Pete spat accurately into a spittoon six feet away. "But no! Lina, she gets de baby." He flung out his hands in an expression of disgust.

Tudor thrust his hat back and took his pipe from his mouth.

"No!"

"But no, yes!" Pete cried. "No one see Lina from de Christmas Tree at de school. She is anyway de big woman, and she sits on de bench. No one know anyting. Jay, he brings de cream to de school in de cutter; I take de cream to town and bring de sugar, de coffee, de bacon, like her note says. I take dem to de school, and Jay, he take dem home. No one see Lina, but she gets de baby." He stood up, collecting his hat of sheepskin hide, and his leather mitts, from the top of a large box of onions with flaky brown skins. "My wife, she go to see Lina, and she say Lina, she gets de baby dis mont. You see!" Pete snapped shut the harness buckles down the front of his coat. "Ohhhhhhh," he moaned, "de kids dey yell, de wife she yell, de teacher cry. A man, he got to get way from de wife and de kids sometime." Going to the door, he put on his hat and mitts, stopping for a moment to give Wong and Tudor a wink with a swollen eye before going out into the cold.

Folkes' pipe had gone out, but he did not light it again. He stood holding it in his hand, looking thoughtfully at Wong's large black cat, which came slinking up from the basement to leap gracefully on·to the window-ledge and curl himself up in the sunlight among some dusty electrical appliances. From outside came the beat of hoofs, the jingle of harness, and the sound of sled-runners on the hard-packed snow. Tudor roused himself. Lifting the cover of the heater, he knocked his pipe out into the fire, and nodding to Wong, went outside. The sunlight on the snow dazzled his eyes. Finely patterned flakes of hoar frost blew gently down from the electric wires above the walk. The forest beyond was etched like white lace against the blue sky, with its arc of delicate rainbow on each side of the sun. Tudor fastened his coat, taking his mitts from a large pocket. With a half smile on his face under the huge fur hat, he scrunched through the snow on the way to his shop.

"Hey, Folkes!" Gustav hailed him from the door of the Hotel. He made a stop gesture with his hand, coming down the steps and cross-ing the street.

"What's this trouble about the kids in town?" he asked in a low tone when the two men were together. "I hear Constable Trevors is in from Bridgeville talking to parents."

"Well, several of the boys have been raiding the candy at Wong's for some time now. They got caught with the goods on them."

Gustav pulled down the ear-flaps of his light-coloured cap, his face massive and heavy under it.

"Tommy mixed up in it?"

"No, Tommy's all right."

"If that brat gets caught and has a police record, I'll warm his pants."

"The boy is all right, Gus," Tudor said mildly. "You're not going to be so hard on him as to suspect trouble when there isn't any?"

"I'm not so sure."

"Don't worry. Tommy often comes to talk to me. He listens." Tudor nodded, moving off, while Gus continued on his way to Wong's.

When Folkes reached his own shop, he took a pasteboard sign from a drawer in the work table, and hanging it on the outside of the door, locked up and went off. Anyone coming to see him that day would be met with the words, COME AGAIN TOMORROW. The town seemed practically empty as he limped down the walk past the power house and the second-hand store to the livery barn. Only Panachuk hailed him, driving by at a fast clip with a team of lively horses. At the door of the barn, a young lad smoking a limp cigarette, sourly watched him come.

"Hello, Romeo," Tudor said.

The boy sniffed, catching his lower lip with long foreteeth. A greasy lock of hair hung down under his cap into his eyes.

"Got a team of horses I can hire?"

Romeo looked over the newcomer suspiciously.

"Have to ask the old man."

Within the murkiness of the barn, the old toothless Roumanian in his sheepskin coat, gave permission for the loan of the team, and of a low, closed-in sled or caboose which stood frozen into the ice behind the building. Romeo helped Tudor to harness up, and at the sight of a brightly-shining fifty-cent piece, brought him some khaki-coloured feather quilts which smelled strongly of horses, and with an axe chopped at the ice about the runners. He also built a fire in the tiny stove inside the sleigh. There was a door at the back of the box-like enclosure, and small windows with glass panes on all sides, with an open one at the front for the lines to pass through. Seating himself on the driver's backless seat within, Tudor gathered up the lines, and clucking to the horses, started off with a jerk as the sled came free of the ice.

The first nine miles to the Bear Claw bridge were smooth and swift, the horses eager and fresh, the road hard and good like a narrow ribbon through the lacy trees. Tudor smoked a pipe or two, watching the blue shadow of the caboose with the shadow puffs of smoke coming from the chimney, and the bright glistening of the frosted forest. After the bridge, however, the road became more difficult, and he got out to walk beside the team to keep the treacherous sleigh from overturning, rejoicing in the brilliant beauty of the day. The ugly black stumps and the bare branches of poplar, balm of Gilead, and birch, had put on white garments that shone with tiny stars. The needles of the evergreens clustered in white clumps, icily accentuated. Blue and mauve shadows of long bare trunks of trees, and deeper shades from stumps and drifts fell upon the trail, marked as it was by the passing of sled-runners. Tudor's coming sent loud echoes into the silence. A frightened white rabbit hopped across the road to disappear into the bush. A jay scolded from a high tree, and intrepid chickadees called from far and near.

Quickly the shadows lengthened, the cold becoming more intense. When the traveller passed the school at last, vaguely he heard a lesson being carried on in a unison of voices. Various cutters waited emptily in the yard, while on the snow-covered ball field was a hard-packed ring where the children played Fox and Geese. Smoke poured from the chimney in a straight column of greyish white against the deepening blue of the sky. Tudor walked again outside his caboose, guiding the horses over the churned-up snow of the cross-roads. He had never been to the Ashley place before, but he knew it lay along the only trail going north from the school, a well broken trail, where Jay drove daily. Yet it seemed the loneliest Tudor had ever seen, narrow, and densely wooded on both sides, with no relieving broad field or sign of human habitation along its route. The whitely frosted trees stood silent, blue-shadowed, sparkling only in their tops where the slanting rays of the afternoon sun shone upon them; Tudor got back into his shelter, grateful for its warmth as the team trotted briskly, taking the strange, house-like sled with its smoking chimney, ever deeper into the wintry forest.

He knew the place by its gate of poles, which had been described to him by every native who had seen it. The log house, half buried in snow, looked lost and lonely in the immensity of the white bush country which surrounded it. Smoke rose in a straight column from the chimney. As Tudor passed the heavily frosted window, taking his horses to the barn, he heard the whining of a dog within. Otherwise the place seemed deserted. About the water trough, Whisky, Rum, and Queen with her colt, huddled together, their heavy coats whitely frosted. They nuzzled around him as he broke the ice with the axe. When he opened the barn door, the horses crowded past him into shelter. Some hens fluttered down from the mangers, clucking noisily. Beyond them, Lina's three cows stared, silent, chewing placidly.

Having cared for the horses, he tramped back to the house, his footsteps creaking on the hard-packed snow. It seemed colder still with longer and deeper shadows, and less of sparkling sunlight. He pounded the door in an almost primitive desire for warmth. He heard the dog bark sharply, and a woman's voice saying,

"Come in."

Inside, he leaned against the closed door, blinking a little, coming from the whiteness into the quiet dimness of the kitchen. He pulled off his huge fur hat, white around the edges from his frozen breath, as were his lashes, the stubble on his chin, and his coat collar. His face was stiff with cold, cruelly reddened. Taking off his cow-hide mitts, he slapped them together, dropping them into a corner with his hat. "Drab," thought Tudor, looking about at the rough board floor, unpainted furniture, and mudded walls. The wood-box stared emptily. Lina sat in a chair, looking heavy, dragged out, infinitely weary, her face thin and worn. Her hair seemed lifeless, coming out in untidy wisps from the heavy coil. She leaned her chin on her hand, staring rather dazedly at her visitor.

"Good day, Mrs. Ashley." He bowed slightly.

"Tudor! I was wondering who it could be."

As she spoke, a clumsy young dog of husky variety, came from behind the chair, and advancing upon Tudor with wagging tail, began to lick his hands.

"Quite a cold spell," he remarked, patting the dog's head.

"Do sit down, Mr. Folkes." Lina moved as though she would get up.

"No, no. Sit still, Lina, I'll find my way to a chair."

He pushed the dog aside, limping across the room in his frosted overshoes. "Shall I build up your fire?" he asked, stopping at the stove and lifting a lid. "It's going down." He glanced round at her, catching the strained look that had come over her face. She rocked herself back and forth.

"Jay's been doing my chores," she replied. "The kids will soon be home."

"You need some wood." He shook the grates. She watched his efficient movements as though from a great distance. "I'll just go and bring some in." He went to the corner, gathering up his hat and mitts.

"Tudor."

With his hand on the door-knob, he paused.

"What are you doing out in this neck of the woods?"

"I heard about Benjie's grandson, and I just wanted to make sure he has a Christian birth." He smiled whimsically. "I'm taking you out to town tomorrow. That is, if you'll come peaceably."

She waited until he had built up the fire and filled the wood-box to overflowing with freshly-split wood, before she said anything. Then, as the cheerful fire roared, and he curled himself up on the trunk, a cloud of pipe smoke about his shaggy dark head, his hands clasped about his knees, she said to him,

"But I wasn't aiming to go to no town, nor doctor either. Mrs. Waters looks after the women round here."

"You're no native woman, to stand her methods."

"And Panachuk looks after his wife at home, every time."

"Would you care for him as a midwife?" Tudor asked, striking a match. He held it to the bowl of his pipe for a moment, the flames reflecting in his eyes. "Lina, you've got your little girl to think of. Supposing something were to happen to you? Something that could have been avoided if you'd had the right care?"

"But I got to look after my own troubles. I don't want nobody putting themselves out for me." She pushed back her untidy hair.

Tudor dropped the burnt-out match, and lit another.

"Woman!" he said impatiently, "don't talk like that. Besides, I'm here already, and I've got to go back. It wouldn't make any difference to me to have you along. And I've a personal interest in seeing that Benjie's grandson comes properly into the world." He puffed contentedly at his pipe.

"You seem mighty sure it's going to be a boy." The colour had come into Lina's pale cheeks. "And I'm certain of a girl." She rocked herself, gently.

"There are some friends of mine in Bridgeville where you can stay until the time comes," Tudor went on. "Do you good to get away from the place for a while. You'll get bushed stuck out here forever."

She took refuge in a helpless silence. The smell of the pipe smoke, and the presence of this man with his young-old face and gentle hands which touched things as though they were alive and had feeling, somehow made her think of Benjie.

"Soon there'll be another person in your life, to grow up and keep you from getting lonely." Tudor looked about the shadowed room as though visualizing the child to come.

"Soon? Seems like waiting forever for this baby to get born," Lina said bitterly. "Shouldn't never of been born at all. I got enough trouble to raise one kid, here like I am, let alone two."

"Now, Lina, don't say that. I shouldn't be surprised if this child turns out to be the greatest blessing of your life. When your girl is grown and gone, you'll still have him. You'll see, he'll be a great comfort to you."

"She'll be little for ever so long," the woman retorted impatiently. "It'll be years before she'll be able to help. Crying and fussing when I got to work."

He grinned, the shrewd lines appearing about his eyes.

"The time will go so fast, he'll be to your elbow before you know it. And then to your shoulders." He stood up, indicating with his hand the height of the child yet unborn. Lina could not help smiling, though rather wanly.

"That's better," he said, limping over to the stove. "Shall I put on the kettle?"

"I'm that sorry." Lina leaned forward in her chair. "I never offered you nothing. After your cold drive, too."

They heard the sound of voices, and presently of a horse and sleigh. The woman looked up.

"That's the kids."

"What are you going to do with the little girl while you're away?" Tudor asked, filling the kettle with water from a bucket.

"I wasn't going away, so I didn't plan nothing."

"What about Panachuk's?"

She shook her head. "They just got the one bedroom, and all the boys sleep in one bed, and the girls in another, teacher too."

"Come on, Buck!" Poppy shouted shrilly outside. The sound of heavy hoofs on hard snow moved slowly by the window.

"There's Mrs. Sven," Tudor suggested. "She's a good woman. She'd be good to the little girl."

Lina looked at the floor.

"I'll take her up there tonight, if you like. Can you get someone to stay with you? I don't like leaving you alone."

"Martha would come. Her and Jay could stay and eat off what's here, and do up the chores, while I'm gone, and keep fires going so the potatoes and stuff don't freeze." She drummed her fingers on the arm of her chair. "I'd leave Poppy with Martha," she went on, "but the kid wouldn't even be washed or fed right. Not much of a housekeeper, Martha isn't."

The dog moved clumsily to the door, whining with eagerness, and Poppy and Jay burst into the kitchen, their faces glowing with the cold. They were both in buckskin parkas with fur-edged hoods which they now pushed back with mittened hands. Lunch-pails and groceries tumbled to the floor.

"Hello, my hearties!" Tudor barked out, grinning across at them.

Sudden delighted laughter bubbled up in Poppy. The boy leaned against the wash-stand, inspecting the stranger carefully.

"Nice day at school?" Lina asked tiredly from her chair.

"Yes." Her daughter began taking off her things, dumping them on top of her lunch-pail on the floor, where the dog pawed them.

"Freddy Two Knives seen you passing," she told Tudor. "Teacher made him stand in the cloak-room for squirting ink, and he peeked through the cracks."

"Want some bread and jam?" her mother asked.

Poppy ripped off her red sweater over her head, making her locks of fair hair stand on end. A glance passed between her and Jay before she answered.

"Yes," she said, "Yes."

"Then wash. And get Bruin away from them things."

Jay bent down over the animal, talking to him in Cree. He pointed to the space behind the stove, and the dog shuffled off to it with drooping tail and bent head. Something in the boy's manner, his movements, struck Tudor as being oddly familiar, reminding him vaguely of someone he knew. He studied the dark face, the sleepy eyes with their

157

sooty lashes, the sensitive line of the mouth. But the feeling of recognition had gone almost as soon as it had come. His interest roused, Tudor watched the boy. Jay took off his parka and washed. He looked lanky, loosely knit, but not awkward. He carried himself very straight, and moved with grace. When they all sat down at the table for a hot drink and a bite to eat, the white man noticed Jay's finely shaped hands. The youngster had a kind of beauty all his own.

Tudor became increasingly aware, too, of the understanding between the children. He had noticed it first when Lina inquired if Poppy would like something to eat. An unspoken question and answer had passed between the boy and girl. It was as if she had asked, "Are you hungry?" And he had answered, "Very hungry." It was almost uncanny, the silent messages they flashed across at each other. Something unchildlike in their understanding of one another, Tudor thought. And Poppy had grown. She had lost her babyish roundness, and seemed all arms and legs. Her face was thinner, and her hair rather unmanageable. It pained Tudor to see a hint of the tragic in her dark eyes.

"I'm thinking to send you to visit Mrs. Sven for awhile," Lina told Poppy, as she moved heavily away from the table. "Mr. Folkes is taking me to town for a few days. Jay, could you ask Martha to come over tonight, and stay while I'm gone? You and her could do the chores."

Poppy looked across at Jay.

"I could stay here with Martha," she declared, rebelliously.

"Too much work for Martha. She's got her babies to see to, you know." Lina sighed, holding her head in her hands. The children glanced at each other with disappointment. Then their faces cleared as though they had agreed on some resolution. Watching them, Tudor thought, "A mighty good thing there is to be another child in Poppy's life. I wonder if Lina knows."

When Jay had put on his parka, the dog came out from behind

the stove, whining expectantly. Again the boy pointed, and once more Tudor had the impression of recognition.

"Whose child is Jay?" he asked Lina, when the boy had gone.

"Nobody knows," Lina answered in the shadows. "Old Mrs. Waters has raised a lot of kids not her own. He was just some homeless kid, I guess."

"Strange." Tudor stirred his coffee thoughtfully.

"Just some breed's kid," the woman said wearily. "Poppy, get the lamp, will you?"

"Well," Tudor remarked, getting up a moment later, "if this young lady will do the dishes while I milk, we'll be able to make an early start."

The girl smiled at him. There was promise of beauty and charm in that smile, he thought. He went out into the cold, pulling his big fur hat over his ears, calling up faces to mind, and finding that Jay bore likeness to none of them.

Chapter XVI

By the time Lina returned to the homestead, the weather had changed. A sweet mildness from a chinook wind miles away softened the knife-like cold, and the snow showed wet and dark at the dint of footsteps.

"Lucky she turned warm when I was to come home," the woman remarked, looking out of the window fast clearing of frost. "Too soon yet for spring, though."

They were at breakfast, she and Poppy, with the winter morning light slanting greyly on them. Lina's eyes had a look now of watchfulness, and at times, briefly, of tenderness. New tired lines had appeared about them. She looked gaunt, her strong frame hunched somewhat as she leaned her elbows on the table. But the hollows of the child's face seemed to have filled out, and her hair shone sleekly.

"Do I have to go to school today?" she pleaded. "Can't I stay home and mind the baby?"

Her mother glanced about the untidy room with its stack of unwashed dishes on the cupboard shelf, the unswept floor, the pile of soiled laundry in one corner. She sighed.

"You better get along to school, Poppy. I'll get things straightened up. My God, what that woman's done to the place! A person just can't trust them breeds."

"I could help," Poppy protested.

"There's lots for you to do anyways. I got to go out now and milk. Do up these dishes of ours. Leave them others, they'll take soaking. Make the beds; give the scraps to Bruin."

Wearily, Lina rose from the table and went over to a home-made crib by the stove. With a piece of buttered toast in her hand, Poppy scampered after her.

"Is he still asleep?" she asked, peeking shyly under her mother's arm at the little wrinkled face of the tiny baby.

"He sure sleeps fine." For a moment, Lina's eyes were anxious, wondering. "Never cries, neither." With a big work-worn hand, she touched the light down on the baby's head.

"He's much nicer'n Martha's babies," Poppy breathed rapturously. "Amos was black, black, when he was born."

Lina smiled a little, looking down at the infant.

"He's sure good, this one is."

"What's his name going to be?" Poppy asked, munching her toast.

The woman straightened up, a sadness in her face.

"Benjamin. Like Daddy. We can call him Benny for short."

"Benny. I like that name."

"Well, I better be getting along now. He'll sleep for awhile yet, and then I can feed him. Get going right away, Poppy, so you won't be late for school."

The little girl hurried over the dishes, her sweater sleeves pushed up, her hard little hands working deftly in the dishpan. She had to stand tip-toe to reach inside. The morning lightened, meanwhile, and a brightness shone through the window. At the sound of a familiar whistle, Poppy threw open the door. Jay had tethered his horse to the fence, and leaping over, came running lightly to the house.

"Ready?" he asked, looking curiously beyond her into the kitchen.

"I'm doing the dishes. D'you want to see my baby brother?"

Poppy brought the boy in, and closing the door, went softly to the crib. Jay followed, ill at ease and sulky, his hands deep in his pockets.

"His name's Benny," the little girl told him eagerly.

"Babies! They cry all the time." Jay shook his head. "They're no fun." He looked distrustfully at the sleeping babe.

"Benny don't cry at all," Poppy declared, carefully rearranging a pink blanket. "He's good."

The boy shrugged.

"Coming to school?" he asked.

"Yes, when I get my work done. Jay, Mother brought my pony home. Big-Enough-Girl! She was in town all this time. She's going to have a colt in spring."

"Gonna ride her to school?" Jay asked, seating himself on the edge of the wood-box while Poppy dried dishes.

"Yes, Mother says I can."

The door opened and Lina came in with a pail of milk.

"Jay." She set down her pail, frowning at him. "Poppy will be going to school on her own pony from now on, so you won't need to be calling for her. The mare's in foal, so I don't want you kids to be riding together and racing." Her tone was cold. "You know what happened last spring when you raced. Better you should ride on ahead. The kid's got her dishes to do."

Black-eyed, silent, hostile, Jay looked at the woman. Hearing her mother's words, Poppy tried to telegraph Jay a look, but he moved out of the house like a shadow and was gone. She set down a dish with trembling hands.

"Poppy." Lina sat down at the table. The child went on working. A curious whiteness had appeared about her lips. "Listen, Poppy," Lina told her wearily. "You got a little brother of your own now. You got a horse of your own too. And I had enough trouble getting Big-Enough-Girl back for you from that fellow Sym left her with. I done all that for you. Now I want you to be a good girl."

"Can't I ride to school with Jay no more?" Poppy asked, distantly.

"Child, you heard what I said about you and Jay racing. It's for your own good. You don't want nothing to happen to your pony, do you? Or to you, neither? Good gosh, pretty soon you'll have a colt, and me a baby to look after."

"We won't race." The child looked up guardedly, her little face set.

"Now Poppy, just do like I tell you. And come straight home from school. I'll be needing you. And that Jay, he hangs around so long with the boys. Why Poppy, he's near a man now. Another couple of years and he'll be out on the trap-line all winter with the other breeds. And you've got your little brother now. Are you listening to me, Poppy?"

"Yes, Mother." The little girl piled up burnt crusts and porridge scrapings on a tin plate and took it outside.

"You got to get broken in to learn to do a few things," Lina told her when she came back. "I'll be starting to raise hogs soon, and it'll be a heap of work. You can help. You'll be all of nine years old in a few weeks. You must of lazed round some at Mrs. Sven's. Anyways, they put some weight on you."

The child's lips quivered.

"I worked good for Mrs. Sven. Fed chickens, an' got eggs, an' dried dishes, an'—"

"Well, for gosh sake don't start bawling. My baby don't go howling around." She stopped at the crib on her way out. "Hurry up, then. You can come out and get your horse from the barn when you're done."

Alone, Poppy hastily dried her hands on the dish-towel, and choking back a sob, began making her mother's bed. When she had made a rather lumpy job of each bed, she put on her parka and picked up her lunch-pail from the table. A slight movement and noise in the crib made her advance cautiously towards the baby. From his little face, great dark blue eyes looked up at her. With a kind of awe, Poppy put out her finger, and a tiny hand closed tightly round it.

"He likes me," she whispered in the lonely kitchen. "Benny likes me!"

Lina was pitching manure from the barn into a big steamy heap by the door when Poppy came out.

"The baby's awake," the child said, smiling. "He ain't crying. Just sort of cheeping, like he's hungry."

"Guess I got to go feed him." The woman leaned the pitchfork against the wall. "Can you put the bridle on yourself?" she asked, taking off her glove and pressing a hand against her forehead. "I don't trust that mare without a bridle."

The little girl stood on the edge of the manger, breathing on the bit to warm it.

"I can do it."

"All right, then. See you come right home. And no racing or waiting around for Jay."

High on Big-Enough-Girl, Poppy rode through the slush to school, bareback on the tall horse. She kept looking beyond each bend, trying to find Jay, though she knew he must be far ahead. She did not catch up to him, and barely got to school on time. She rode through the gate while the bell was ringing. In the school barn, pushing aside another horse, she tied her mare beside Buck.

Jay did not talk to her at all during school hours, but the girls did. She had much to tell, to whisper, and to write notes about, though while they were at lunch, Olga sniffed.

"A brother? They're the worst!"

"But he never cries," Poppy insisted, disappointed.

Olga hugged her. "Oh well, never mind. He'll be a nice kid like you."

When school was dismissed, Poppy trudged alone to the barn for her horse, looking anxiously at a knot of big boys wrestling by the swings. Standing on the rail to which the horses were tied, she fought stubbornly, but she could not get the bit into the mouth of the mare. Big-Enough-Girl tossed her head, closing her strong teeth. When Jay came in for Buck, he undid his piece of ragged rope without looking up.

"She won't take the bit!" the little girl wailed.

"Go tell teacher," Laura Petersen suggested, dragging a wicked-looking cayuse to the door by the reins.

"I'll do it," the boy muttered. "Hold Buck for me."

Poppy jumped down and took Buck's rope.

"I done it this morning all right."

"There. Now get on, and I'll lead her out."

They trotted their horses side by side on their homeward trail for a few minutes in silence. Then, with his face averted, Jay remarked,

"Gonna freeze again. Getting colder." He did up his parka. "Hold in your horse, Poppy. I'm going ahead."

"Wait, Jay," she pleaded piteously. "Don't leave me all alone."

"Lina said not to ride with you." The boy's face was sullen.

"That's silly!" Poppy broke out in sudden rebellion. "Nobody goes down this trail but us, and I can't hold Big-Enough-Girl if you go ahead."

Jay considered this, flicking Buck's ear with the rope bridle.

"I can ride with you down to the gully every day," he suggested thoughtfully. "Then I'll cut through the bush. Lina won't know."

He turned his dark face towards her and smiled. Comforted, they trotted their horses side by side.

Chapter XVII

1

Hog day in Bear Claw had been more crowded than usual, and very hot and dusty, but evening brought coolness and a peaceful quiet. Surprising, the number of people who rattled over the wagon roads to town at haying time, Tudor thought, surveying the numerous pairs of dusty, broken-down shoes on his counter. With his back to the window, he held up a paper and began reading the news by the light of the summer evening. Presently the bell over the door tinkled, and he looked up to see the tall figure of a man enter.

"Why, Sym Ashley!" Tudor threw down his paper, limping forward to shake hands. "I heard you were coming back, Sym. Gus told me."

"Got a ride with a truck from Bridgeville. You know I've come to take over the pool room?"

"So Gus was telling me. Here, sit down. Have you had supper?"

"Sure, I had a bite to eat at Bridgeville. Well, it's sure good to see you, Tudor."

Sym took off his hat, seating himself on the proffered chair. Threads of grey showed in his thick dark hair, and deep lines furrowed his hard weather-beaten face.

"I'll be closing up after a bit," Tudor said cheerily. "We'll go over to the house and have a good hot cup of tea."

"I need a good long drink of something," Sym grunted. "Getting old, I guess."

"Oh, no!" Folkes ran his hands through his shaggy dark hair. "I used to think fifty was ancient. Now I don't consider a man is old till he's over eighty."

"Seems like an age since I was here." Sym stared moodily out of the window. "Don't know what Lina will think when she hears. Tudor, I was going Outside and make good, and send Lina plenty to help out. I sent her some, when I heard about the baby. And a bit since. But it's tight as a drum Outside to get a job. I was bumming round Edmonton when I run into Brenner, and he told me Yakes was pulling out from the pool room."

Thoughtfully, Tudor filled his pipe.

"It'll be nice having you round, Sym. I'm glad to see you."

"So much I'd like to talk over. But seems like you're going to have company. Who's this coming?"

Folkes took a quick look through the window.

"Don't rush off, Sym. That's just young Tommy Hanson and Pete Dizzon. Sit down again, and I'll see that they don't stay long."

"Hello, Tudor."

Tommy breezed in at the tinkle of the bell. "Dizzy's got one of those Insurance things. He asked me to read it for him." Tommy handed the letter over to Folkes. He was a fine squarely-built lad, blond and clean-looking, his sun-bleached hair lighter than his tanned face. His clear steady grey eyes had a frank coolness. Behind him, Dizzon slouched in, dark and furtive, a broken-peaked cap pulled down over a big hooked nose. Large dirty hands hung aimlessly at his sides, or passed nervously over his unshaven face.

"Remember Sym Ashley, Tommy?" Tudor asked, taking the letter.

"Oh, sure." The boy's face was attractive and friendly.

"But you was just a little lad when I seen you last." Sym looked him up and down. "You're growing up fast."

"This letter just says that if you'd like a Life Insurance policy, the above company will gladly oblige," Tudor told Dizzon. "You're not keen on it, are you?"

"Cost money?" Dizzon asked, rubbing his nose.

"Yes. They won't let you get away with that for nothing. The sales-man will be in town next week, and will gladly see you. Better take my advice and keep away from him."

"And that's all it is?"

"That's all."

"No kind of trouble?"

Tudor grinned. "Sorry. Not this time. Get through haying?" he asked, turning to the boy.

"We got through down to the Corner. Dad wants me to go over to Bentley's tomorrow, and keep an eye on things there."

"Hm. Gus will miss you when you go off to school in Edmonton this winter."

"He'll get along," the boy answered.

"You going to run the pool room?" Dizzon asked Sym.

"A fellow has to make a living some place."

"Yup. Pigs as turn up their noses never gets fat." Dizzon wiped his forehead with the back of his hand.

Tommy looked questioningly from Sym to Tudor.

"Well, guess we'd better be going. Thanks, Tudor." Reluctantly, Diz-zon followed the boy out of the door.

"Dizzon's one of Bear Claw's latest characters," Folkes remarked. "You're likely to see a good deal of him in your business."

"I can't get over how that kid has grown. Course, he must be round fifteen now. Is he a friend of the dizzy character?"

"Oh, no! Tommy's a fine lad. Quite a protégé of mine, as a matter of fact. I began taking an interest in him when that awful Molly woman appeared on the scene. Remember her? She used to push the boy around so much, I decided to be his Dutch uncle."

"Tudor, what about my little Poppy? How is she?"

"She's coming on fine. Pretty little thing."

"I feel like I can never face Lina again the way things turned out. When I heard about that baby—" Sym bowed his head, twirling his hat in his hands. "What kind of a kid is he?"

Tudor looked across at his friend with kind eyes.

"Benny is the loveliest little boy you'd ever want to see. He's round and rosy-cheeked, with tight gold curls all over his head, and eyes as blue as old Benjie's used to be."

"Let's see, he'd be about two and a half years old now. Well, I'll never have any of that kid." Sym shook his head. "That's the way life goes. I played a rotten hand. Reckon I'll never see Poppy unless I just happen to meet her in town. But how's Lina making out, Tudor?"

"She's prospering. She makes good money in hogs and calves. Lina's doing all right."

"I reckon the money I did send her seemed like small potatoes to her."

"Every bit helps on a farm, Sym."

"I'd like to see Poppy."

Tudor puffed thoughtfully at his pipe.

"She has a bit of a lonely look, that child. But I think having a little brother has been wonderful for her. She's very fond of young Benny."

"Lina was tough with the little girl," Sym said.

"Well, Poppy has a very good friend in Olga Panachuk. You remember that youngster with the long braids. She's bright as a button and has plenty of common sense. She's growing like a weed these days. Poppy too."

"Is that breed boy still around? You know the one I mean, Jay Baptiste?"

"He's practically a man now, going out on the trap-line with the men. He turned out to be a rather handsome lad."

"So Poppy has a lonesome look, eh? Well, I don't know what's worse. To grow up lonely, or to see a fight going on in the house every day."

"Come and have a cup of tea with me, won't you? I'll try to get you caught up in the gossip of the district. Did you know Sven Jensen's had a son, and now a girl, born just the other day? Of course you knew Olenski died, and Mike works here in town for Gus. I'll just lock up. My, it's good to see you, Sym."

2

Under the blazing sun of late afternoon, Jay raked the mown hay. Flattened red-top and deep slough grass lay mingled with fading cut flowers, Michaelmas daisies white to pale blue to deep violet, yellow hawk weed, golden rod, and purple fire weed. The heat brought out the smell of the grass and flowers, and of the bruised wild mint. Jay's grey work shirt had dark wet patches on it, and perspiration streamed down his dark face under a broad-brimmed straw hat. He shouted to the sweating horses as the hay-rake rattled clear of a windrow. Beyond the field, Lilly Lake glimmered a cool blue through the willows. There, ducks flew up quacking, circling into the woods.

A light rig appeared from the trail in the bush, and stopped at the edge of the field. Poppy jumped quickly to the ground, and put the baby on a blanket out of the sun. Lina climbed out, and reaching into the back of the rig, began lifting down large boxes and bundles. Jay let the team stand and walked slowly to the camping place. From a shady spot under a tree, he picked up a large vinegar jar tied round with wet sacking. Lifting it high, he took a long drink of the cool water, delicious to his thirst.

Lina looked sharply over the deserted field, the idle hay-rake and team, the few straggling windrows, and the small hump of the beginnings of a stack.

"Where's everybody?" she demanded, her mouth tightening into a hard line.

Jay put down the jar, leaning indolently against a tree.

"Isaiah went bear hunting."

Lina dropped a box heavily on the ground.

"Good gosh! Martha too?"

"I don't know."

"Where's all that grub I sent over yesterday?" She looked about her at the dead ashes of a campfire. "You breeds sure got your nerve. D'you figger you can eat off me and not work?"

"I am working. I been raking."

"Isaiah and Martha was going to help. With Olga we was going to be done in no time flat!" Behind her, Poppy listened tensely. "You'll get just how much hay you work for, no more," Lina went on angrily.

He looked at her with half-closed eyes, his face expressionless. The woman began to unhitch her team.

"Poppy, get wood to make a fire. After a while you can put the kettle on to boil and get the grub ready when I tell you. I'm going to start pitching. For God's sake, look after the kid!"

Benny had toddled off the blanket, and crowing and chattering, trotted down a path into the bush. Poppy scampered after him.

"When's that Olga going to show up?" Lina muttered, glancing at the trail. "Well—" she glared at Jay who stood unmoving by his tree. "Maybe we better get going."

He lifted his hot face to cool it, his nostrils quivering.

"I'm going to take my Grandfather's team home," he said, avoiding her gaze. "I'm going hunting too."

"Holy bald-headed! How d'you figger to feed your team all winter? No work, no hay! Now, I'm telling you straight!"

"I'm going hunting," he insisted.

"Take your damn team and get out of my way, then!"

The boy plodded over the hot field to unhitch his horses from the rake, while Lina led Whisky and Rum to take their places. Holding Benny's hand, Poppy watched them from the camp. Presently Jay came by, taking his horses down the trail towards home.

"Jay!" the girl called to him. "Wait, Jay!"

Stopping his weary horses, the boy squatted on the ground, drawing lines in the dust with a stick, while Poppy came along with the tiny boy toddling beside her.

"Where're you going, Jay?" she asked anxiously.

"Hunting."

"Ain't you coming back no more to hay?"

"No."

"Oh, Jay."

"I'm only going hunting." He took the tiny boy's shoulders in his dark hands. "I'll be coming back some time, won't I, Benny?" He stood up, swinging the child high in his arms. Benny laughed aloud with delight. Jay set the little boy down again, suddenly alert. "I'm going hunting." He picked up the lines, clucking to the horses.

Olga came on the gallop, riding bareback on a clumsy work-horse.

"Hi, Poppy!" she called, pulling on the rope bridle and slowing to a trot. "Whoa! Whoa!" Olga slid to the ground, big and awkward beside the two children. "Gee, we got so many chores to do when Pop goes to town. I came fast, like mad! Where's Lina?"

"Raking and pitching, I guess."

"I tie up Caesar good, you bet! Then I better go see what Lina wants me to do."

Poppy brightened as Olga swung her dark braids, swearing heartily at the big horse.

"There! Now try to get away!" she exclaimed, leaving him in the shade where grass grew deep. "C'mon Poppy, let's all go out across the desert." She took Benny's other hand, and the three of them trudged to the stack where Lina pitched hay with a kind of furious vigour.

"So you got here at last!" The woman paused, the perspiration running down her flushed face.

"Pop went to town, and we got chores, chores!"

"Well, Olga, them breeds left me flat, team and all. Isaiah knows damn well I can't stand by and see a horse starve. He figgers he'll get his hay anyways. And I can't stay out here with a shotgun all winter. What a blasted outfit!" She looked down at the chubby face of her little son. "My God! Will I be glad when this one's big enough to take over. Think you can rake, Olga?"

"Sure, Lina, I can rake."

"All right, then. There's your team fresh and waiting."

Olga beamed. "OK. Me, I like working with horses."

"We'll work on into evening. It'll soon be cool now. Did you get that wood, Poppy?"

"I'm just going to."

"Say, Olga, did Pete bring me my groceries from town?"

"I dropped them at the house. Lina, Pop says Sym's in town now, running the pool room."

The woman turned a shocked furious look on the big awkward youngster. Her mouth tightened.

"Poppy! Get that baby out of the sun this minute!"

Almost frightened, the girls started quickly away. Lina picked up the pitch-fork, plunging it savagely into the hay.

Chapter XVIII

1

Harvesting was done, and once more the leaves were flying. Nine seasons she had seen in this country, Lina was thinking, holding back the new horses, Racer and Sal, as they went swiftly over the trail from Bear Claw. Now winter would soon be upon them again. But it had no terrors for her, and at present her mind was full of plans. The back of the wagon was piled high with her purchases; new linoleum, beaver-board, pipes and fixtures. She was going to have real comfort in the wilderness, a home that she could be proud of.

The Indian summer was prolonged and warm, every day borrowed time from winter. Benny was six now, and starting school, while Poppy had begun grade nine, the highest grade in the Tiger Lily School. She must plan ahead for Poppy too, Lina thought, pulling to the side of the road as another team and wagon passed her. It was Ek, shouting a good day to her. Young Emil had started in the new Bear Claw high school this fall. But that would not do for Poppy; not with Sym in the pool hall. Lina's mouth tightened to a hard line. Edmonton was the place. If Gus could send young Tommy there—.

Racer shied at a black stump by the side of the road, frightening

Sal, and both horses rushed ahead while the woman pulled on the lines with all her strength. They rounded a bend, coming into view of the bridge over Bear Claw Creek; and ahead, approaching the bridge from the other side was Panachuk's team of greys and his wagon. She had her horses under control now, but she did not attempt to slow them down. Both drivers raced ahead to try to reach the narrow bridge first. The wheels of Panachuk's wagon had turned once upon it when the hoofs of Lina's nervous horses struck it on the other side. The woman saw Panachuk's furious look, heard him shouting while the greys reared, backed off before her oncoming horses, turning the wagon off the road to hang precariously on the edge of the creek bank. Triumphantly, Lina drove past, lifting her hand to wave a friendly greeting.

"Beat you that time, Panachuk!" she cried with laughter in her voice.

The rattle of her wagon drowned out his words, and its dust soon hid him from her sight. She was making time to-day. She grinned to herself, thinking of Panachuk. After all, who were these foreigners to hog the roads! A fellow like Pete who sent his kid to school in his own old clothes. Poor Olga, what chance would she ever have? But it must be Edmonton for Poppy next year. Lina decided she must think it out, find a way.

2

Pete Panachuk put his hands on his hips, surveying the neat little log shack just outside the school grounds.

"Ten years I board de teacher, and cheap at de price. And now—" He spat emphatically.

Fritz Lieman picked up a cardboard carton full of groceries from the ground where Pete had dumped them. He was a big, fair-haired young man with mild eyes behind rimless glasses. Somewhat above medium height, he had slightly stooped shoulders as though his length made him self-conscious.

"Won't you come in?" he asked pleasantly.

"Even I bring de eatings to de teacher."

"Awfully good of you, Pete." Fritz patted his shoulder. "Sit down and have a smoke. I have a little time before recess is over." He drew forward the one chair, and handed his visitor a box of cigarettes. He himself relaxed on the hard narrow cot with his feet against the wood-box. A table with some dishes and a frying-pan face downwards on it, a small radio on a crude shelf, a stove, and a couple of suitcases completed his furnishings. Through the window and the rapidly baring trees, he could keep an eye on his pupils who had three ball games going at once. The batting, running, pitching, and shouting made quite a din outside.

"Even de kids is different," Pete went on with a sniff. "I put my Olga to work for Mrs. Sven, and what she do? Work one year." He held up one finger expressively. "And den go to de school. Work a liddle, and for no money, and go to de school."

"But surely, you won't make Olga quit now?"

"I not stop her," Pete answered with a shrug. "But she get no cloes from de catalogue; but de pants and de shirt of de old man."

Fritz smiled. "She doesn't mind. Well, Pete, what's new in town? Who's been ruffling your feathers?"

"Notting new in de town. It's de woman on de road made me mad, by heck!" Pete scowled. "Lina Ashley. She tink she de fine lady. I hit de bridge first, going to de town. She see me, coming home, she was. She hit de bridge and come straight for on; I no can pass. She no can pass. My team scairy is, and back, back, back. I got to go to de ditch. And dat Lina, she pass me and laugh!"

"Oh well, Pete, that's the way a gentleman must act with these women."

"Dat Lina!" Pete's black eyes snapped angrily. "I tell you, she got de land and de hay and de cow, yes. But Lina big fool. She let her Poppy run wit' a breed."

"Pete! She's just a kid."

"By heck, Ek see dem on de road. Jay and Poppy. After de school is out. Lina, she should get Poppy tight in de fist like de land and de hay."

Fritz did not answer. He took out his watch, winding it conspicuously before putting it back into his pocket.

"She is time to go." Pete got up, nodding. "De kids dey run wild, and she is time to go." Together, he and Fritz shuffled through the dry leaves to the wagon.

When the school bell rang, fifty-five pupils trooped into the small school room. Balls bounced into corners, bats banged to the floor, and caps and jackets hung in disorderly mounds on shaky nails. The children jumped, climbed, and crawled to their places in the seats which were crammed together with two narrow aisles separating them into three groups. In a surprisingly short time, there was complete silence among them.

"We will pull down the tables," Fritz said in his quiet voice.

Quickly the narrow aisles disappeared as the children shoved the desks back to the very walls, and a couple of the bigger boys let down from the ceiling two table tops arranged on pulleys. On these the pupils had set out their work. With great good humour and co-operation, they made the best of the crowded situation, taking turns in cutting, pasting, drawing, and looking through the ancient volumes on the long book shelf at the back of the room. The thirteen beginners, crushed up to the very front near the blackboard, stayed in their places modelling animals with plasticine. Some of them could not yet speak English, but they managed to understand each other by means of signs and grunts. Fritz now turned his attention to the older group.

"Grades seven and eight." Fritz spoke through the buzz of orderly conversation of the other forty-four pupils in the room. "You will prepare yourselves for a quiz in science on Monday. If there is any question, I'll reserve some time for you before the afternoon is over. Now grade nine, we will go on with our discussion in Social Studies."

He considered the three of them. Big Olga Panachuk in the ragged cast-off clothes of a man, her black braids swinging, her dark eyes full of life and intelligence, her mouth sweetly shaped, showing her fine white teeth in a smile. Theodore Setezanka, lanky and bashful, with dark hair and light grey eyes, and large clumsy feet. And Poppy. Pale gold hair catching the light; dark moody eyes. With new anxiety, he wondered about her.

"Tell us about Russia, will you, Mr. Lieman?" Olga asked eagerly.

Fritz smiled. "I'll do my best. At least, I'll tell you all I know. I wish I knew more. You know, Olga, I feel every year as though I knew less than the last year."

She beamed at him, waiting expectantly. That was like Olga, he thought. Straightforward and frank, she said all the things she thought about, wondering out loud. She was the best student of the three, with a flair for history and current events. Theodore, too, was alert and eager to learn. But to Poppy, school was simply, the inevitable. While he taught the lesson on Russia, Fritz thought about Poppy.

He wished he could know her, but strangely, she had that kind of reserve which belongs to most native children, holding herself aloof, her thoughts secret. He felt her intense awareness, her almost adult perception in her appraisal of others. Too bad she seemed so oblivious of Theodore who obviously worshipped her. Then perhaps it was true that the girl's heart was already taken. Fritz frowned, thinking of Poppy at the Harvest Dance the week before, dancing with Jay Baptiste. It had seemed to Fritz, watching them, that there was some deep under-standing between them, no mere boy-girl affair. Yet they had danced very little with each other, he remembered. Surely the whole affair was gossip, cooked up by Ek and Pete and his wife. And Jay would soon be going away trapping again.

With an effort, Fritz brought his thoughts back to Russia, talking earnestly to the three. There were dreams in Poppy's eyes. She heard nothing, he knew. A girl's mother ought to know these things. But Lina was so hard! No, he could not think of talking to Lina about Jay, and Pete's gossip. "I should do something about Poppy," he thought. "Someone must. If I could only get her interested. Perhaps Mrs. Sven. Now there is an idea."

"Draw a map of Russia," he said to his class finally, "and see what you can find out about the industries and products. Now I shall deal with the science questions."

Poppy opened a backless geography book with torn pages, and maps heavily scored with pencil marks. She flipped absently through the pages, looking across the crowded room at Benny, who sat with the beginners, modelling a grotesque monster supposed to represent a deer. He and Amos Waters, the smallest children in the school, sat side by side, their chins just coming above the smallest desk. They rolled out their plasticine against the legs of their overalls. Benny was pink-cheeked and blond, his hair tightly curling, his eyes vivid blue. Amos had great black eyes, straight black hair in ragged locks, and a wide grin showing a gap where two teeth were missing in front. Benny held up his shapeless deer for his sister to see. On the desk stood Amos's model of a horse, crude, but definitely recognizable. The girl smiled at the children. But when Fritz caught this look, she became again aloof and distant, her head bent over her book.

"Can you come over for a while after school?" Olga whispered, turning around. "Just for a little while?"

Poppy glanced up with a look of warm gratitude. "A little while," she murmured.

"That's not Russia, that's Germany." Olga laughed noiselessly. "Russia's further back." She began leafing over the dog-eared pages.

Theodore poked Poppy in the back. "I got a real good outline map of Russia," he told her. "You can use it if you like." She really did not want his map, but she would not hurt his feelings by telling him so. "Trace it up at the window," he suggested.

At the window, she tired, facing the dazzling light, and her arms ached from holding up the two sheets of paper against the pane. She was glad when the big boys pulled the tables up to the ceiling again, and Fritz dismissed them all.

"We're making sauerkraut," Olga told her as they put their books away. "But come over and talk to me for a while. Mrs. Sven likes you to come."

"I mustn't stay too long," Poppy said. "Benny and me have got lots of chores to do."

"Don't I know what it's like though?"

They stood aside while the younger children burst out of the door with glad shouts as though they could no longer contain themselves.

"Gee, I like Russia," Olga said dreamily. "I'm going to look up Mrs. Sven's good map tonight."

"I'm glad it's Friday." Poppy threw the old geography book untidily on the shelf.

Fritz Lieman who was starting to put things to rights, shook his head sadly.

3

"This is really the nicest time of the year, don't you think so, girls?" At the hot stove, Mrs. Sven stirred her mustard pickles with a long-handled wooden spoon. "All the heavy work is done, and we have just the little things left to do."

The sun's slanting rays flooded through the sparkling windows of her large bright kitchen. Olga shredded cabbage with long rhythmic strokes over the blades, while Poppy worked at the table, cutting up the vegetables into chunks with a big knife.

"We're getting our house all fixed up. The men'll be working for some time yet," she said.

"Are you getting a sink?" Olga asked eagerly.

"A sink, new linoleum, and the roof fixed."

"My, it's upsetting for a woman to have her kitchen being done over," Mrs. Sven remarked. "I remember when I was having mine done. Men tramping in every minute."

"Not even room to do homework." Poppy smiled shyly. "No wonder I can't get my geometry done."

"Did you get those questions we had in school today?" Olga asked.

"No. I can't do that darn geometry."

"I think you'll get it in time," Mrs. Sven assured her. "Here, taste this, Olga, and tell me if you think it's sweet enough."

Olga licked the spoon.

"Mr. Lieman is a good teacher."

"So they say. Sweet enough, is it? Well, I hope he'll be here when my little Neils starts school."

"There, I've cut them all up, Olga. I should be going soon now." Poppy piled up the chunks of cabbage, and wiped her hands on a towel.

"Must you rush off, dear?" Mrs. Sven asked. "But you will try a little harder on your geometry, won't you? You know, I'm so proud of my pupils who go ahead in school like this. And now they have that new high school room opened at Bear Claw, you girls will be able to go right along. Theodore too."

Poppy hesitated. "I—I don't know as I want to go on after this year, though."

Mrs. Sven looked kindly at the girl from behind her silver-rimmed glasses.

"What do you want to do, Poppy? You'll be only sixteen in the spring."

"I don't know. I just don't know."

"Of course, I'm all for education myself." The woman drew the big pan of steaming pickles aside on the stove. "I'd like to see all these children get a chance, the native children too. Look at a boy like Jay. It seems such a pity."

Poppy was silent, withdrawn into herself.

"You know," said Mrs. Sven thoughtfully, "I think that Jay—"

A loud noise of squealing and shouting arose in the yard outside.

"That must be Benny!" Poppy exclaimed. "He's so crazy over little pigs, he's always playing round with them."

"Dear, dear, they'll wake up Margaret Ann just as I've got her to sleep. She's been fussing around all day." Mrs. Sven rushed to the door. "Boys, boys, you really must not. Neils, come here, will you please?"

As she spoke, the two little boys scrambled out of the pig-pen and began walking slowly towards the house. Benny hung down his head, but his blue eyes twinkled. Neils was the blonder of the two, a rather plump, solemn child of five.

"All right, son." His mother took some bits of straw from his hair. "Get me an armful of wood, please."

"Well, we got to go, Mrs. Sven." Poppy came out beside her, buttoning on her jacket.

"I'll bring the horse around!" Benny cried, scampering off to the fence where Big-Enough-Girl was tethered.

"Do come again, Poppy," the woman said kindly. "Couldn't you come some Sunday when you're all through house-fixing? And bring Benny."

She stood at the door watching them, until the horse trotted off down the road.

"I wish," she sighed, coming back to her work, "I wish I could keep that child by me for a time, I do indeed."

Olga swung her braids.

"Well, I guess Poppy's a pretty good worker. She can cook better than me, I know that much."

"My dear, I wasn't thinking of that. You're as good a worker as I'll ever want. It's just that—"

Olga chewed a bit of cabbage.

"You needn't worry about Jay, Mrs. Sven. He's all right. You know, Poppy isn't like some of the girls, boy-crazy. Like Laura. It's different about her and Jay."

"Yes, I know. That's what worries me. Jay's good in many ways, and I like him. But natives are different from us. Please don't mention it to her, Olga. But I am worried about that child; I'm very worried about her."

4

Lina looked at the clock. It was going on five, and there was no sign of Big-Enough-Girl. Jack Two Knives and Mr. Carson, a carpenter from Bear Claw, were clearing up in the kitchen for the day. As she mixed feed for the pigs in the barn-yard, Lina's exasperation grew. She felt she must be a fool, working and planning for Poppy's future, when the girl would not even come home and do her share of the chores. Little Benny at six was more to be depended upon. Lina looked down the road again. No sign of the children. The woman lifted a heavy pail in each hand. Where could they have gone? She saw Jack hitching up his team.

"If you see them kids of mine, tell them to get a leg on!" she shouted to him.

"I tell them."

She heard his words, slow and indolent. With an exclamation of disgust, she turned to the hog-pens.

Big-Enough-Girl slowed to a walk, her hoofs making a rustling among the new-fallen leaves. A whistle sounded from the side of the road. Poppy answered it, pulling in her horse.

"I think that mare must be getting old," Jay said, jumping out onto the road. "My horse Buck never took that long to come home from school."

Poppy slid down to the ground. "Buck didn't go visiting."

He took the reins from her hands. "Let's go back in there and sit by the creek. Stay where you are, Benny. I'll see you don't fall off."

"I can't stay long," the girl murmured. "I was over at Sven's already, and I got to be getting back."

"Why are you feeling like this?" he asked as they threaded their way through the bush.

"Oh, I can't do my geometry any good."

He tied the horse to a poplar tree and swung Benny down.

"See that spruce tree there, Benny?" he said, pointing to a tall one near them. "If you climb to the top of that tree, you can see Snakeshead Hill."

"Gee whizz!" The little boy ran off and began climbing up the strong branches like a cat. Poppy and Jay sat down at the edge of the creek. Gold leaves floated on the brown water. The sun was warm on their backs, but there was a chill in the air.

"I want a piece of Snakeshead Hill," Jay said, skimming a flat stone down the stream. His dark face was sombre.

"What will you do with it?"

"Live there."

"I see Snakeshead Hill," Benny called out. "Gee, big timber!"

"When are you going away?" Poppy asked, hugging her knees.

"Pretty soon now. I'm going to work awhile before I go on the trapline. I'll see you in the spring when the fish are running." Jay took off his hat and stretched out on the sun-warmed ground, watching some birds darting above the tree-tops.

"What's wrong?" she asked, looking down at him.

"I wish I could have got to go to school," he said huskily. "I know some things. I can speak Chyp and French quite good now. But I wish I could tell them off sometimes, when I'm out working."

They fell into a troubled silence. Then Benny came rushing past them.

"I betcha I can make a splash!" he shouted, flinging a rock into the stream. "There she is! Pretty good splash, eh?" He scurried about, looking for another stone.

"Won't you—won't you tell me about what you've been doing?" Poppy asked.

"What I've been doing?" Jay leaned his head on his hand. "Not about the harvesting!"

"Tell us about the wolf that got away," Benny cried, dropping a rock and throwing himself on the ground beside him.

"The wolf with the track as big as my hand without the fingers?" Jay laughed. "All right, I'll tell you."

He began to talk then, freely, as though it were a release to his spirit, telling them stories about his experiences with wolves. And he told them what it was like, trapping out in the forest, and sleeping outside in the snow. And how he played cards all night with the game warden, far away, in the dead of winter. The stream beside them murmured soothingly, while the golden leaves fell upon the water. Big-Enough-Girl nibbled brown grass, moving slowly with heavy muted steps.

They were roused by the sounds of a wagon rattling over the road beyond.

"It's late!" Poppy cried, jumping up. "We got to go!"

"You'll still be here by spring, won't you?" he asked.

"Sure, Lina won't be moving."

With a run and springing jump, the girl flung herself upon the horse's back. Jay put Benny on behind her. There was a feeling of deep happiness among them.

"Benny, don't you tell we saw Jay." Poppy prodded the mare with her heels as they reached the road.

"Why?" he asked, holding her tightly around the waist.

"Because. School kids don't tell things. You're not a baby staying home no more. You're a school kid. And a school kid's got to learn to keep a secret. You won't tell, will you?" She looked around at him as they rode along. "We was at Sven's the whole time."

He stared at her with his wide, innocent blue eyes.

"Heck, I won't tell. Honest, Poppy."

"Gee, we're late! Hang on, Benny, we're going to tear."

Big-Enough-Girl carried them on a swift exhilarating ride.

Benny laughed and shouted. Near home, however, Poppy pulled the horse to a trot. With a pail in each hand, Lina walked through the yard towards the house.

"Fine time to be getting home!" she shouted, when she saw the children coming. "Where was you?"

Poppy slid down and opened the gate, leading the horse behind her.

"We was at Sven's. Mrs. Sven wanted me to come."

"Mrs. Sven knows you got chores! Didn't I tell you to be here at five to feed them pigs?"

"I forgot the time, Mother."

"I'll learn you to forget. You won't be going to Sven's no more if you can't keep your mind on the time. Here I got to do all your chores and my own. Got your horse all sweated up, too!"

Poppy stood twisting the ends of the reins in her hands, her eyes on the ground, while Benny jumped down beside her.

"Well, don't stand there!" Lina exclaimed. "Take your pony and go get the cows. Bring in the lunch-pails, Benny."

At the door, Lina watched Poppy ride off. So they had been at Sven's. She supposed that was all right. They could get into a lot worse company. Oh, Mrs. Sven could sit around handing out tea; she had her man to do the heavy work. But Mrs. Sven was too soft. She would spoil a girl like Poppy. It seemed a mighty long visit, Lina reflected. Mrs. Sven was not a fool to keep the girl from her chores. A sharp suspicion thrust itself into her mind.

"Where was you all this time?" she asked Benny.

His eyes grew round.

"Over to Sven's. Me and Neils played with the little pigs."

"Hm. Better you should play with my pigs. With a pail of swill, I mean." She rubbed his curls in a rough caress. "Go gather the eggs, will you?"

Chapter XIX

1

School had been dismissed when Lina pulled up her team at the gate under the budding trees. Children came flying out of the building, running and shouting as they scattered in various directions through the bush, or went to the barn for their horses. She spotted Benny among a group of small boys who bounded from the doorway to the shade of the school, wrestling and boxing with each other.

"Tell that Benny I want him!" she exclaimed to Theodore Setezanka who was leading his horse up from the barn.

"Benny!" the boy bawled out, making a cup with his hands. "Yer maw!"

Lina's son disentangled himself with beating fists, and seeing Lina, came scampering across the yard to her, barefoot, with bits of grass and wood chips clinging to his clothes and hair.

"Where's your shoes?" his mother demanded, looking down severely from the seat of the wagon.

He grinned, showing his teeth, purplish from chewing an indelible pencil. "They're over there by the fence." He pointed to a clump of greening willow.

"Hurry up and go get them, and come on home with me." She watched him go, noticing the stains of green on the elbows of his clean blue shirt, shaking her head in tolerant amusement. "Where's Poppy?" she asked, as he shinned up over the wheel and plumped himself down beside her. "Don't see her no place around."

"Poppy went." He wriggled on the spring seat, rubbing her shoulder with his curly head. "She went just a minute ago to see Olga at Mrs. Sven's." He looked up at her innocently with round blue eyes. "It was geom'try." He wrinkled his snub nose over the difficult word. The purple stains were everywhere on his freckled face.

"You look a sight," his mother told him. "What does Poppy have to see Olga for? Teacher's right here. She shouldn't go bothering Olga, keeping her from her work. Come on, Racer! Sal, git going!" The wagon lurched forward.

Lina pulled over sharply to the right as another team appeared on the trail, coming from the opposite direction.

"Howdy, Mr. Ek!" she called, as the driver came abreast.

"Woah!" he shouted to his horses. "Hello, Miz Ashley."

They both stopped, each team pointing in a different way, blocking the trail. Ek sat high on a load of rails, smooth and well packed, with thin swaying ends. He shoved back his hat on his grizzled head, a dreamy expression in his large eyes.

"Still aiming to buy my weeder?" he asked amiably.

"Not at that price. Knock off twenty-five dollars, and the thing's sold."

He smiled at the big woman with her uncovered head of heavy hair, and her stern profile, and at the gamin-faced little boy peeking past her.

"Twenty-five dollars is a lot of money," he said mildly. "Cost a lot of money keeping my son in school in town." There was a hint of pride in his voice.

"You're telling me twenty-five dollars is a lot of money." She began

189

gathering up the lines; but he sat quite still, reclining indolently on top of his rails.

"Coming to the ball game and dance tonight?" he asked.

"Reckon the kids'll want to go."

"I'll talk to Hilda and see what she thinks. Maybe we can come to some agreement tonight."

"OK, Henry. Be seeing you tonight." She whistled to the horses, and drove off smiling to herself. "If it wasn't for poor Hilda, there wouldn't be no town school for Emil," she remarked as the swaying ends of the poles disappeared slowly into the bush. "Git up, Racer!"

The sun warmed their backs, and a summery breeze full of fragrance, blew in their faces, gently moving the branches of the greening trees about them. Patches of green grass showed between the wagon ruts and along the sides of the trail.

"The fish sure must be running good," Lina remarked as they came in sight of the bridge over Crooked Creek. "There's Mrs. Waters and the whole family."

She waved to Martha who stood on the bank with a fishing-pole in her hand. In rolled-up slacks and a red shirt of Isaiah's, her black hair bound back, her feet bare, she looked little more than a slip of a girl. Her two small boys grinned at Benny. With trouser-legs rolled up high, they paddled knee deep in the shallow water, each with a pole poised and ready. Farther up the bank, on the pebbly ground among some willows, a tent was pitched, and near it, Mrs. Waters knelt before a smoking fire, cleaning fish, and putting them to be smoked on a rack of slim green poles.

"How's the fishing going?" Lina shouted, as the hoofs of the horses clattered on the wooden bridge.

"I was just saying," Martha said, coming closer, "that a while ago the kids was taking them out with their hands, they was so thick. We'll get enough fish to last for quite a bit."

"Be worth while to take a day off and go fishing," Lina observed, leaning over to look down into the water. "I can see them from here. Big fellows, too."

"Let's get going." Benny bounced impatiently on the seat.

"What's the matter with you?"

He squirmed. "Another wagon might come, and it wouldn't be able to pass us on the bridge."

She gave him a good-natured cuff on the ear. "Stop your noise."

"It's lovely weather," Martha remarked, adjusting the wire loop on the end of the pole with great care.

"How many did you get?" Lina asked with interest.

"About forty this afternoon, and they're still thick. Sammy! What are you doing?"

Her young son was leaning forward, his pole out of sight under the bridge.

"Fish in here," he said, rolling his dark eyes upwards from under his ragged black locks.

"Come away from there!" His mother began sliding down the bank after him. "Aren't kids awful?" she said, appealing to Lina. "There's broken glass under there. He'll get his feet cut."

"Mom, I'm hungry. Let's get going." Benny rolled from side to side.

"How long did it take?" Lina asked Martha who was wading into the water.

"We come just after dinner." She seized Sammy by his cotton shirt between the shoulders, dragging him away from the bridge, while he kicked and splashed with his feet. Amos watched, giggling.

"Let's go," Benny said again.

"Land sakes, child, be still! You said a mouthful when you said kids is awful," Lina declared. "And boys above all." She slapped Racer's rump lightly with the end of the line. "Git along, you old mule!"

"Why don't *we* go fishing?" Benny demanded as they continued down the trail.

"We will, come Sunday. But what I want to know is, why don't you behave? I can't even stop to talk to a neighbour in peace, you're getting that spoilt."

Benny grinned at her, certain of forgiveness.

"And if Poppy don't come home soon to help with chores, there'll be no ball game for you and her both," Lina went on. "I can see Ek any old time."

"It was geometry," Benny insisted.

"She better not fail her exams," the woman said grimly.

2

The wheels made a hollow rumble on the wooden bridge, and then, the noise of the horses and wagon getting farther away, there was just the sound of the lapping water sliding smoothly over large rocks and water-logged trees. Under the bridge, Jay and Poppy listened, motionless, knee deep in water, holding their fishing-poles upright. The green shadowed water moved lazily by their bare legs, where sometimes fish, swimming languidly with the slow current, touched them briefly. Bright lines of sunlight, coming through the cracks in the boards of the bridge, fell across their faces. A damp, fishy, earthy odour hung about them.

"Nearly in the trap," Jay's dark eyes gleamed with mischief, as he lowered his pole and adjusted the snare at the end of it. "Wait till I get that Sammy!"

"I got to go home right away. I didn't know Mother was going to town today." Poppy waded slowly into the sunshine.

"You're a bad girl," Martha laughingly scolded her from the bank. "If your mother got to know you was standing under that bridge!" She gave Sammy a playful push. "Playing hookey and all."

Poppy trailed her pole into the water, wriggling her toes in the mud beside Amos. She had a blue silk kerchief tied over her fair hair, and blue cotton slacks rolled up above her knees. There was a warm colour in her cheeks. She watched Jay who stood very still, his snare poised, his eyes following the motions of a fish. Suddenly the pole bent, the struggling sucker with the wire tightening about its body was jerked into the air and flung to the bank. Jay splashed ashore to loosen the snare. The victim flopped helplessly in the grass, opening its wide mouth, and finally lay still. Disturbed by the noise, other frightened fish darted swiftly into cool dark hiding places behind submerged logs and stones. The flowing water, with its low soothing murmur, sparkled in the sunlight. Amos combed the water aimlessly with his snare.

"You really got to go?" Jay asked, leaning carelessly against the bank.

"Yes, I got to," the girl replied, making no move to go, fascinated by the play of light reflected on his face from the glint of sunlight on water. He wore his black hat on the back of his head, the thong loose about his chin. His grey cotton shirt was open down the front, the sleeves rolled up. Lazily, he watched the two little boys splashing water on each other, and Martha taking the latest catch to Mrs. Waters. The warm breeze lifted the acrid scent of the woodsmoke to them.

"Your horse in the school barn?" he asked.

"Yes." She tossed her pole onto the grass above.

"I'll come with you."

They sprang out of the water, leaping barefoot up the steep bank, hand in hand.

"We got to be careful," Poppy said, "so Fritzy won't see us."

3

The sun was down. The clear blue sky, deepening in colour, still glowed in the west with a ruddy hue. It was still quite light, though the trees were beginning to look blackly outlined in the distance. The ball game between the men of the Tiger Lily district, and those of Crooked Creek, was in the first half of the last inning. A long line of wagons stood up against the school yard fence, tethered teams guzzling in oat bags, or nibbling bundles. Squaws in bright blankets, and other women of various nationalities, in gaily coloured dresses, yelled from the wagons, stood and sat in clusters behind the home plate and along the side lines with the men who were not taking part, to heckle the opposing teams. Small boys dodged about, getting in the way, and adding to the general din. Tiger Lily had the field, with Jay pitching, Freddy Two Knives on first base, and Fritz Lieman, his mild bespectacled face well caged, catching. Sven Jensen, bending forward with his hands on his knees, his hair yellow as ripe wheat, stood behind the dark-faced pitcher, an efficient umpire. Gene Rivière was up to bat.

"Strike one!" Sven called, as the ball sailed over the plate.

Loud yells of protest went up from the wagons of Crooked Creek.

"He can't hit nothing! Baby-face Gene! Baby-face, baby-face!" came the howls of derision from Tiger Lily fans. "Crooks! Crooks!"

"That's the fellow Laura Petersen's getting married to," Lina told Poppy as they watched from their wagon. "He sure shows the breed, useless bum."

"Strike two!" Sven called.

A great uproar of heckling and yelling arose from both sides. Gene bent his great frame low, gripping the bat tightly, kicking out dirt from under his feet. Jay caught the ball neatly, holding it speculatively for a moment, the whites of his eyes gleaming in his brown face.

"Come on, Crooked Creek! Drown the lilies! Look at that pitcher! Look at that smart-faced guy!"

"Strike three and you're out!" Sven called, jerking his thumb up, as Gene struck wildly at a low ball, missing it by a foot. Deafening cheers and loud boos resounded. The batter flung his bat angrily to the ground, directing a flow of abusive language to the umpire. Sven remained calm, a smile on his pink-cheeked face.

"Batter up!"

Flip Brown, a tall blond youngster of seventeen, picked up the dusty bat.

"There's Olga," said Poppy, watching the big girl bending over the score-keeper near third base. "Olga!" She took the kerchief from her head, waving it. "What's the score?" The yelling all around them drowned her voice. Suddenly, a beautiful fly ball sailed over the diamond, while Flip ran swiftly, bat in hand.

"Get it! Get it! Miss it! Miss it!" were the hoarse cries.

Freddy Two Knives, on first base, howled, nearly weeping, to Emil Ek, dreaming out in field.

"Emil! Emil!" Jay shouted. But the ball bounced into a willow bush, causing the fielder to wake with a start. He tore frantically at the grass at the foot of the willows like one possessed, giving Flip time to run easily round the diamond, scoring a home run. Groans sounded from the Tiger Lily wagons, while the Crooked Creek fans shouted and jumped joyfully up and down.

"What's that Emil think he's doing?" Lina exclaimed in disgust. "I s'pose he's home for the week end from town. Where's Henry and Hilda, I wonder?"

"Here comes Olga now." Poppy leaned over the side of the wagon. "Come on up here, Olga."

"It sure is close," Olga said, eagerly, swinging her long legs over the side of the wagon box.

"What's the score?"

"It was five-five, but that home run made it six-five for the Crooks."

"Seen my kid around any place?" Lina asked.

"Benny? He's right down there with my brother. There!" she cried, as a cheer went up. "It's three down. Now we can make some runs."

Lina looked the girl up and down speculatively.

"We don't see much of you any more, Olga."

"Well, I'm working, you know, for Mrs. Sven, so I can get to school in Bear Claw this fall."

"How are you going to manage that?"

Olga sat down on a corner of the wagon-box. "Well, I'm going to raise a garden this summer. I can stay in town with Mrs. Howe if I do the cooking and cleaning up, and pay the rest with vegetables and a little money. Pop fixed it for me."

"That's the way to hit! Atta boy, Jay! Beat the Crooks!" the fans shouted as the ball disappeared far beyond the fielders, and the captain of the Tiger Lily team scored a home run.

"Them breeds sure can play ball," Lina remarked. "'Bout all they are good for. Say, Olga, did you hear Laura's marrying Gene Rivière?"

"It's true," Poppy broke in. "She told me. I saw her when I was coming home from school yesterday."

"What's her mother thinking of?"

"Laura got in trouble, I guess," Olga answered matter-of-factly. "Oh hell! Freddy Two Knives went out!"

"It's getting dark, and they can't see the ball so good," said Poppy. "Gee, it's chilly. Where's my sweater?"

Olga clapped her hand over her mouth. "Did I say 'hell' again?" She held out her hand. "Hit me hard, Poppy! That's right! Oh dear!"

"What's come over you?" Lina asked, as both girls shook their stinging fingers.

"Mrs. Sven is learning me my manners," Olga replied. "Shall I show you?"

The woman hesitated, surprised.

"Sure, go ahead."

Olga was in ragged denim slacks, and a worn shirt of her father's tucked in at the collar. Shaking back her long braids, she bent her head a little, making a pleasing gesture with her hand.

"How do you do, Mrs. Ashley. I do hope you are enjoying the ball game. It's a lovely evening, isn't it?" Her voice was rather high-pitched, but musical. She spoke with just a hint of an accent, scarcely definable. There in the wagon-box, she stood smiling, gracious, her face alight, while round her the swearing, yelling crowd shouted and heckled in the most abusive language as Fritz came tearing in from third base, and Gene missed the ball in the catcher's box. Poppy went into fits of laughter, but Lina looked at Olga with a curious new admiration mingled with envy.

"Well, Mrs. Sven ought to know her manners, being a teacher and all," she remarked.

"There goes Emil out on first, the silly old—!" Olga cried, coming out of her pose. "Oh, Poppy, there I go again! Hit me hard!"

The ball game ended then, and the players came in from their positions out in field. A fight started almost immediately between Gene Rivière and Freddy Two Knives. They rushed at each other, going down in a rolling heap. One of the Whitefish boys ran to Freddy's assistance, while several men from Crooked Creek clenched their fists. What looked as though it might become a general free-for-all was swiftly checked when Sven and Fritz separated the combatants forcibly. Cries of, "Three cheers for Tiger Lily!" roared from the wagons of the district. "Hip-hip—!"

"Three cheers for Crooked Creek! Hip-hip—!"

"Three cheers for Tiger Lily!" Benny shrilled as the cheers died down. He looked up adoringly at Jay, who ruffled the little boy's curls with his dark hands.

Lina climbed down out of the wagon.

"Hand me that box of sandwiches, will you, Poppy? I want to see Emil and ask him where his old man is."

When they came up to the building where the ball players had gathered, arguing loudly with Sven, Poppy and Olga dropped behind a step, following Lina through the crowd. Jay and Poppy exchanged glances. She held up three fingers. His eyes flickered a smile.

In the vague grey light of early morning, teams and wagons pulled out from the side of the road, crowded and noisy as they rattled off. Pale light shone from the windows of the school where a few loiterers still talked together.

"I want to go to sleep," Benny murmured, rubbing his eyes. He curled up in a quilt on the bottom of the wagon. Poppy stood beside him, leaning against the back of the wagon-box, chewing a straw and humming the home waltz. Lina climbed in, gathering the lines.

"Just a minute," she muttered. "I think—" She looked over at the school with its lighted windows. "I think maybe—I'll be right back. I just want to talk to Ek for a moment. If I come up five bucks—" She gave a short laugh, jumping down to the ground again.

It was that time of the morning when everything seems grey and shadowless, outlines indistinct, and faces weirdly pale. The fresh air was crisply cool, full of scents of pine, and drenched grass, and damp earth. Young birds were cheeping sleepily in the trees. A team and wagon slowly passed with Isaiah driving, sitting on the spring seat with Martha beside him. She held his fiddle carefully aloft, guarding it from the wild scuffling of the crowd in the back where the little boys, Freddy Two Knives and several of his cronies, and old Bill Manydogs, were having a hilarious time of it. A sudden loud creaking of wood brought them to a stop.

"Something break?" Freddy asked, leaning over precariously.

Jay appeared from behind them, walking. He inspected the axles and peered underneath, while everyone in the wagon waited hopefully, craning their necks.

"It's OK," he announced. He stood in the trail as they drove off, Bill singing lustily, Freddy holding a screaming, wriggling Sammy head downwards over the side of the wagon.

"That's all they got to do," Lina thought disgustedly. "No matter about chores. Milk the cow any old time. Ruin the horses; let the wagon fall to bits." She shook her head.

Henry Ek and Emil had hitched up their horses at the barn when Lina called to them. She could see the top of Hilda's flowery hat bobbing at the school door.

"I say, Ek!"

He looked up.

"'Bout that weeder." She stood, arms folded, staring him down. "If I come up five bucks, will you sell?"

Ek looked thoughtfully at the ground.

"That's still twenty dollars less than what it's worth," Emil protested.

"Oh well," said Lina turning away, "take it or leave it."

Ek looked about, lost, for his wife. She was still chatting to Mrs. Panachuk by the school, and Lina seemed to have made up her mind.

"Tell you what—" Ek began, "I guess that price would be OK. If you come up five bucks—"

"Well, that's just fine, Henry! Shall we call it a deal then?" The woman spoke with finality. "I'll be over tomorrow."

She moved off just as Mrs. Ek, calling a laughing good-bye to Mrs. Panachuk, came hurrying to the waiting wagon, and Henry.

Lina came out of the school-yard with Fritz who carried an unlit gas-lamp in each hand.

"Very successful evening," he said. "We'll soon have enough money for a dandy school picnic."

Lina watched a wagon pass them and go off down the road.

"That Henry Ek is sure pig-headed, but he come down some for me."

"Well, good morning, Mrs. Ashley. Going to be another nice day, isn't it?" Fritz turned off in the direction of his little shack among the trees.

Poppy no longer stood where her mother had left her. Probably gone to sleep beside Benny, Lina thought. She walked quietly through the short wet grass, feeling pleased with herself. The night was gone, and a bird sang. The sky was somewhat lighter now. It would be about time to milk when they got home. They could catch up on some sleep in the afternoon when—.

She saw them when she came around to the other side of the wagon. Jay and Poppy. They did not hear her come. For a moment Lina stood speechless.

"Poppy!" she cried out. The girl turned swiftly, shrinking back against the wagon. Jay stood with his hand on Poppy's shoulder. "So this is what you're up to!" the woman stormed. "The minute you think my back is turned, you're in the arms of a dirty half-breed!"

"Mother!" the girl gasped. She looked like a ghost in the grey light.

"Get into the wagon, you piece of misery!"

Her daughter did not move.

"You dare defy me!"

"Leave her alone," Jay said, very low. "It wasn't her fault, Lina. It was mine."

"You! The number of times I fed you at my door. I might better of fed a stray dog."

His face quivered. "There are dogs better than you." He walked away, then, into the coming light of the morning.

"Never mind him. He'll get drunk and feel fine," Lina said to her daughter. "Now get into the wagon! There'll be no more running around for you, my girl. I'll not trust you out of my sight."

As they took the rough homeward trail, the woman cracked the long lines over the horses' heads. Flecks of foam flew back to her from their mouths. Behind her in the jolting wagon-box, Poppy sat limply, holding Benny's curly head in her lap. The miracle of the day was breaking over them as a line of scarlet appeared in the east, and the trees about them seemed to emerge from greyness, sharply distinct and colourful as though they were waking and stretching themselves. Cool and fresh the breeze blew, sighing in the branches.

When they drove into their own yard, the girl shook the sleeping child partially awake. She climbed down over the wheel, her foot slipping on the metal rim. Benny jumped down to her, sleepily. Lina did not look at them at all. She had unharnessed the horses when Poppy came outside again.

"Where are you going?" her mother called.

"To get the cows," she said tonelessly.

"Come here. I want to talk to you."

Poppy came slowly along the path, seating herself on a log near the barn door.

"You're going to school this fall. To Edmonton." The woman opened the pasture gate, standing aside for the horses to go through. "I've been planning it for quite some time. There's good money in hogs now." She fastened the stiff wire gate with expert hands. "And what's more—" She turned back to the girl. But Poppy had got up from the log and faced her.

"I won't go!" she cried. "I won't get on the train. I won't go, and you can't make me. I'll run away, I'll go to Sym!" Her face was white, but unmistakably determined.

"You'll do as you're told," Lina said. "Go get the cows."

"I won't go to Edmonton!" the girl flung out as she went off into the bush.

The sky was dappled pink in the east, and rays of sun straggled through the tree-tops.

"Someone's got to talk turkey to you," Lina said, sitting on an upturned pail, milking the red and white cow. "You don't know what you're doing."

Poppy was silent, pressing her forehead against Bessy's warm black thigh. The milk foamed into her pail in steady rhythmic sounds.

"Jay Baptiste's just another of them breeds. Got no folks. Nobody

201

knows who he is or where he come from. Born under some spruce tree more'n likely. Drinks up his money. No more reliable than a hen trotting round without its head. Put him in the hayfield, and he'll leave you flat if he happens to smell a moose in the wind. Jay's a mongrel breed."

The girl said nothing.

"You can't just stick around after this year," her mother went on. "School's the best place for you. At Edmonton you'd meet someone decent. Well, what do you think of it, eh? Poppy!" Lina got up, kicking away her stool, and emptying the heavy pail of milk into a cream-can. "Don't sit there and sulk. Say something!" She came over to the girl. "Poppy!"

The girl turned her pale face to her mother, leaning her cheek on the cow's black hide.

"I'll go to school with Olga, at Bear Claw," she answered desperately.

The woman was silent at this, staring at her daughter. Bossy chewed placidly while the streams of milk beat monotonously into the pail. A grey cat and an orange one stood near, mewing expectantly. Polly, the black and white cow, mooed plaintively. Lina went to her.

"But there's Sym. The Bear Claw pool room is no place for a young girl."

"I want to be with Olga at Mrs. Howe's." Poppy moved to empty her pail of milk.

"Go along and get breakfast, will you?"

So this was the way the wind blew, Lina thought, watching Poppy enter the house. While the woman milked, the purring cats rubbed themselves against her. She pushed them roughly aside. Her anger was subsiding now, but it was replaced by a calculating hardness. She saw clearly that it would do no good to insist that her daughter go to Edmonton. Like Sym, the girl would run away. But Lina knew how to hold the whip-hand over Poppy.

"Bear Claw," she mused. "OK, my girl!"

While Poppy was frying flap-jacks, Benny came out of his room, rubbing his eyes sleepily.

"I'm hungry," he announced, sitting down at the table before his empty plate. "Poppy, Benny's hungry." He rubbed his tangled hair with a grubby fist. But his sister did not answer. She kept her back to him in a strained unnatural silence. He could not endure it, but ran to her, looking up into her face.

"What's the matter, Poppy?"

She turned the sizzling flap-jack without answering.

"Look, Poppy." He dug into his pocket. "You can have my biggest gopher-tail. It's lots bigger'n Sammy's. You can have it." He slipped the treasure into the pocket of her blue jeans. She pressed his head against her side.

"Go tell Jay—" She looked apprehensively at the door, "Tell Jay *I* don't think he's a dog. And tell him I got to go to school at Bear Claw after thrashing. Will you tell him that?"

"Yes." He hugged her hard around the waist.

"When?" she persisted.

"Tomorrow, when me and Sammy and Amos goes gopher-trapping."

"It's a secret. Cross your heart and hope to die if you tell."

He stood back, looking solemn. "Cross my heart, Poppy, I won't tell."

Chapter XX

1

Lina slapped the lines on the dash-board, hurrying the horses. "See you get good meals. Don't let her cheat you. She's a hard dame, but she'll see you toe the line. Just as well in that Bear Claw dump."

Olga and Poppy sat beside her on the spring seat of the wagon. It was a day in the middle of October, their first day at high school. The weather was bright and crisp, but about them, dry leaves fluttered from the trees, blanketing the forest paths. Olga wore Mrs. Sven's fawn skirt and jacket made over, and brightened by an orange blouse. Poppy had a smart red and navy outfit which her mother had made for her.

"Guess it's all right to wear slacks and moccasins when the weather gets cold," Lina remarked. "But if you're going any place, you've got decent clothes; and see you wear them."

"There's the grain elevators. Gee, we're nearly there. Pinch me, Poppy. I think I'm dreaming." In spite of the jolts of the wagon, Olga gazed raptly ahead, clutching a large worn loose-leaf note-book under her arm.

"Mrs. Howe's won't be no dream," Lina warned her, casting a quick look into the back of the wagon where two large sacks of vegetables and an old suitcase shook around on the floor. "But you'll have enough to do there so you won't have no time for monkeying round."

"We better go right to school, Mother." Poppy looked rather frightened, her hair wind-blown under her little round hat. "We're late now."

Lina slowed the horses at the railway line, pulling them in expertly. They bumped over the rough crossing, spanking down the main road.

"I'll let you off at the hotel. I'll go see the Mrs. myself. Out you get then! I'll be in for you on Friday."

Stopping only long enough for the girls to climb out, Lina drove on down the long street to the post-office. Inside, by the wicket, she came upon Mrs. Howe.

"I was on my way to see you," she greeted.

Mrs. Howe glanced up from a letter she was reading. She had a thin-lipped, sharp-featured face with two deep lines between her brows.

"Brought the girls in, did you?" she asked.

"That's right. Their stuff's out in the wagon."

"I hope they've a mind to work," Mrs. Howe remarked sourly, pocketing her letter. "Most of the girls in this town do nothing but tramp round. Just tramp round. And this town's full of sin."

"I'd like to ask you not to let my girl tramp round," Lina said quietly. "I've spoke to Poppy and told her she's got to get permission from you wherever she goes."

Mrs. Howe sighed.

"I'm no hand at bringing up someone else's girls," she snapped. "Flighty things that age."

"I've spoke to Poppy," Lina repeated. "One complaint from you, and home she goes. It's all right, a school party with the teacher and the others, but no tramping round."

"Well, if I've got the say-so, it's fair enough. But they better have a mind to work."

"They'll work." Lina picked up her mail. "Shall I give you a lift home? Then I can bring their things over."

2

"What time is it?" Poppy asked nervously, as Lina drove off, leaving them beside the hotel.

Olga brushed some straw from her jacket. "Let's look in here," she said, craning to peer through the window of the hotel waiting-room. "Doesn't seem to be no clock."

Romeo came up the street, mooching along with his sloppy walk, his cap at a rakish angle over one ear.

"Wanna drink?" he asked, grinning, making his long teeth conspicuous.

Olga drew herself up. "We were only looking to see the time."

"Time? It's day-time." He went off with a loud laugh.

"Let's get going," Poppy suggested. "Anyway, we know we're late."

They set off through the alley between the hotel and the pool room, to a wide field where the school stood, the tall girl with her dark braids wound round her head, and her smaller companion in her red cap and jacket. A chilly breeze blew in their faces, nodding the dry brown weeds of the field, fluttering the Union Jack on its tall pole beside the school-house.

"Do you think we should knock?" Poppy asked.

"Yes." Olga's fingers tightened on her notebook.

"Olga. Let's stick together."

"OK, Poppy. I'll do anything for you, if you'll do anything for me."

They took hands, standing for a moment in the October sunshine.

"Don't be afraid! It'll be new, anyway. It'll be different." Olga flung back her head with her quick spontaneous laughter. "Well, let's bang the old door down, and see what happens next."

They approached shyly, going up the steps as quietly as possible in their stiff new shoes. Olga rapped sharply with her knuckles, her eyes alight with daring. Poppy waited tensely, her hands in her pockets. They heard the quick clicking of heels, and then the door opened, revealing the teacher in her new blue tailored school dress with its immaculate white silk collar.

"Good morning," she said, playing with the chalk in her hand. She had a pleasant face with delicate features and grey-blue eyes. Her voice was rather thin.

"Good morning," Olga answered, thoroughly awed. Poppy only stared.

"Are you new pupils?"

"Yes, yes!" Olga remembered her manners in a rush. "We are Olga Panachuk, and Mary Belle Ashley from Tiger Lily School. We have our report cards." She opened her notebook.

"Come in, come in. The wind is cold this morning."

As the door closed upon them in the dark little cloakroom, Poppy had a feeling of panic. Through the half-open door of the class-room, she heard the whispers, the snickers, and scraping of feet of the students there; the noise of a pencil-sharpener, the slapping of a ruler on a desk. She clenched her hands deep in her pockets.

"You may take off your things here," the teacher told them. "You are in grade ten, I suppose? Olga and Mary Belle, was it? I'm Miss Walker."

"Pleased to meet you," Olga said, sliding off her jacket and beaming with smiles. "Come on, Poppy," she whispered. "Take off your coat."

They went into the crowded, sunny class-room of forty students who looked around at them in curiosity. At the back of the room were some desks piled up on top of each other. When Miss Walker went to these, put her hand on the top one looking helpless, Jim Holberg, a tall gangling youth with thick glasses and large red hands, came to her rescue. Somehow he managed to settle two desks and seats near the stove, in the only remaining space, and the new girls sat down. Poppy took a folded piece of paper and a stub of pencil out of her skirt pocket, while Olga opened her large notebook with a business-like air.

A complicated time-table and a map of Europe covered the side black-board. Miss Walker began to explain a difficult-looking geometry diagram on the front board. Olga looked at it with shrewd comprehension, Poppy with desperate agony. It was very hot so near the stove. The room smelled of lunches and apples. A few seats ahead of them, Theodore turned around, smiling. Emil Ek, suddenly grown out of all recognition, sat with the grade eleven group, flushing very red and refusing to look at the two who had just come in. On the whole, the class worked industriously. Several of the girls looked as though they would be nice, Poppy thought. But, sitting a couple of rows over, she saw Viola Brown, the daughter of the post-master and Rosalee Trent, whose father was the station agent. Poppy disliked them both instantly. Viola was a little blond thing, with round blue eyes and curling eyelashes and a wide smiling mouth. Rosalee's dark waving hair was plastered almost over one side of her painted face. Staring at Poppy and Olga, she whispered something to Viola behind her hand, and they both giggled.

"And therefore," Miss Walker ended triumphantly, "AB is greater than DG. Take Theorem Eight for homework."

She moved to the desk, giving a little jingle on a silvery bell. Recess, and the class could relax. Olga wrote on the first clean sheet of her loose-leaf note-book. "Homework—Theorem Eight." The teacher beckoned to the new pupils.

"Come up here," she said, "and we'll arrange for your courses and your books."

"Hurry up, Viola," said Rosalee from the doorway. "Got to get away from the wife and the kids!"

Olga turned scarlet, but she marched up to the front. Poppy followed, holding her piece of ragged paper.

"You will be a bit behind for a while," Miss Walker told them when they were duly registered. "You will have to work to catch up. Perhaps you could borrow someone's notes from the grade ten class."

"I will work very, very hard!" Olga exclaimed with enthusiasm. "It is so wonderful, Miss Walker."

"Agnes, would you lend these girls your notes?" the teacher asked, turning to a plump, red-haired girl who was writing on the black-board. "And show the girls the library. I'll send out for your books on the morning train."

Agnes gave them a wide friendly smile. "They're not so good," she told them, as she led the way to her cluttered desk. "But they'll give you some idea. I'm glad you're here." There was an earnest expression on her freckled face. "Most of the kids are awfully nice."

"Thanks, thanks." Olga towered above her, awkwardly tucking her orange blouse into her skirt. "We'll be real careful of them."

"The library's back here." Agnes went to a door behind the stove. "There's not so many good books, only one or two by Zane Grey." She almost tripped over the long legs of Jim Holberg who was talking solemnly to Emil.

"Of course, Cyrus has no modern counterpart." His eyes roved weirdly behind his spectacles. "He seems to stand alone in history."

Olga listened, staring, while Jim struggled to get his feet into the small space under his desk to let her pass. Agnes opened the door, and took them into a tiny room containing three or four shelves untidily piled with old books and out-dated magazines. On a table stood a dusty globe and some atlases. Olga drew a long breath.

"I'm going to read every one of them!"

"I can't get through half of them," Agnes admitted, grinning. "There's some nice pictures in these here *Geographics*."

"Where's Zane Grey?" Poppy asked.

Miss Walker hunched at her desk, her head almost hidden by a great pile of exercise books on which she worked rapidly while her pupils sat in little groups talking, or played outside with a base-ball.

"Theodore Setezanka," she said in exasperation, "how many times must I tell you to write your compositions in ink?"

Theodore looked sheepish.

"Miss Walker, can I be the librarian?"

She looked up sharply. That great awkward girl who had just become a new pupil in her already overflowing class-room, stood above her. "What's that?"

"The library. Can I look after it?"

"Yes, certainly. Go ahead; I'd be only too glad. It's always in a mess. Agnes, ring the bell, will you?"

Poppy thought that the morning crawled by. She felt desperately hungry when finally class was dismissed for the noon hour.

"We'll have to hurry," Olga whispered. "We're supposed to help with getting dinner."

They walked quickly across the field, passing groups of loitering pupils. As they cut through the alley, Agnes waved.

"Teacher's nice too," Olga breathed rapturously.

"I don't like her."

"All those books! I can hardly wait."

When they came up on to the walk, they nearly collided with Sym who had just stepped out of the pool-room.

"Why Poppy!" he exclaimed. "I wondered if you'd ever show up to come to high school. Where have you been all my life?"

"There was harvest," she said shyly, feeling drawn to him as to a warm comforting hearth. "We had to wait till we was through."

"And Olga too! Look, you two must come over and see me some-time. Some Sunday night. Won't you?"

Beneath his flashing smile, Poppy saw his look of entreaty.

"We've got to hurry," Olga said, suddenly.

"Liking school?" Sym asked.

"It's wonderful!" Olga answered for them. "Are you coming, Poppy?"

As they hurried on, Poppy felt bewildered. Sym made her shy, but she longed to be with him. Her memory of him was somehow all confused with thoughts of Benjie and of Jay. She fell into a silence on the way to their new home, hardly hearing Olga's enthusiastic comments about school, and geometry, and Teacher. There was a dull ache within her.

Mrs. Howe's place stood a little off the beaten track, a log weatherworn building fenced off with rails. A bright orange truck stood at the gate when the girls arrived, and they could hear a shrill voice raised in argument. The front door opened into a small room with a counter and rows of shelves covered with tinned food. The truck driver, with his cap shoved back, and a pencil behind his ear, waved his hands, trying vainly to stop the stream of talk of the woman who confronted him, arms akimbo.

"I don't want the eggs. You can tell the old man he can sit on them and hatch them, for all I care! Take them away! I never ordered no eggs. They're practically ready to walk away themselves. They were ready to cluck when they got here. Take them out of my store!"

The truck driver shrugged resignedly, and swiftly carried off a large crate from the counter.

"The idea," Mrs. Howe muttered, her head bent over some bills.

The door of the truck slammed. The engine roared to a start. Mrs. Howe looked up and saw the girls for the first time.

"Why didn't you get here sooner?" she snapped. "You're supposed to get dinner ready, and here it's quarter to one right now. It'll have to be cold sandwiches at this rate."

"We stopped to talk to my father," Poppy answered, trembling.

"It can't be that late!" Olga cried defiantly. "We just got out of school."

"Well, glory be!" Mrs. Howe looked at a bent-up alarm clock that ticked loudly on a shelf among the cans of pork and beans. "I clean forgot. I put it ahead a half hour last night to get me up early. This'll be your room here." She lifted a curtain to one side of the store. "There's a table where you can study."

The girls looked in, noting the slanting roof of the lean-to, the lumpy Winnipeg couch on which their dusty suit-case had been tossed, the wash-stand made of apple-boxes, the one chair and tiny table, the swimmy mirror in which they could see their faces, distorted, from the doorway.

"Isn't there any heater?" Poppy asked, shivering a little.

"There's a stove in the basement," Mrs. Howe replied, crossly. "The heat comes up into the store, and you can leave the curtain up for it to come in here."

"The kitchen is back there?" Olga pointed to another curtain behind the counter. "I better get dinner ready."

"Go ahead. I got to see to them bills." Their landlady bent over the counter again, mumbling figures, occasionally making impatient exclamations to herself.

The kitchen seemed incredibly small and full. There was a good-sized stove with a table near it. A large barrel of water filled one corner. A couple of chairs stood in the small floor space, like naughty children in the way. The walls were lined with narrow shelves full of odd plates too wide for them, and pots and pans with their handles jabbing outwards, and bottles and jars with their contents running down their sides. Dirty plates, sticky with jam, and cups dribbling the dregs of coffee, were piled up on the table. Another curtained doorway led into a second bedroom.

"I'll get a cold lunch for today," Olga whispered. "How about cabbage salad? I'll clean up this mess tonight after school." She looked around hopelessly for a place to put her jacket.

"Give it to me," Poppy suggested. "I'll put them in our room."

"And another thing!" Mrs. Howe looked up from her bills as Poppy came out of the lean-to, and crossed the see-saw floor. "You cannot go running the streets at night. There'll be some high school parties you can go to where the teacher is, but no others." She shook her finger at the quaking girl. "This town's that full of sin. I've been telling your mother, and she's laid down the law."

"We got plenty studying to do," Olga cried, rattling the dishes in the next room. "Poppy, will you bring me a cabbage from the cellar?"

The woman stooped, seizing a small ring, and lifting a part of the floor, making a yawning hole from which came an earthy odour.

"Down there," she said.

3

"So your little girl has come in to town to go to high school?" Tudor spoke above the whirr of his sewing machine on which he was busily stitching the torn uppers of an oxford. "Where is she staying?"

"Her and Olga are over at Mrs. Howe's." Sym tossed his cigarette stub into the heater. "Hope that woman won't be too hard on the kid."

"Maybe it's just as well, in a way." Tudor stopped working for a moment to look through his window. He watched Mike Olenski and Pete Dizzon disappear into Wong's. "Though of course, the woman has an awful tongue."

"I'd like to get to see the kid, but I don't suppose Lina would approve. She hardly knows me any more," Sym said moodily.

Tudor tossed the shoe lightly onto his table. "She has a lonely look about her, that child has. Tell you what, I'll invite you all over to supper some night. Genteel and proper." Sym shot him an appreciative glance. "Here comes friend Olga now."

The bell tinkled as the tall girl came in.

"Oh, Mr. Folkes! Hello, Sym. Mr. Folkes, could you ease out these oxfords? I got blisters big as peas on both my heels, and I can't wear these running shoes to school here in town." Yet she smiled, her dark eyes shining with happiness.

He took the new-looking black shoes out of her hands. "I'll do the best I can. Where do they hurt? Just the heels? If you come around tonight, I think I could have them stretched out a bit. How do you like school?"

"Oh, Mr. Folkes, it seems like I'm dreaming to be here, in town, and going to school."

"Like the teacher?"

"Well, she—we don't know her very well yet. But there's books."

"Where's Poppy?" Sym asked.

"She's gone over at Mrs. Howe's. And I've got to go too!"

"I say, Olga." Tudor felt over one of her shoes with searching fingers. "If you should ever want more books, just come along to my place. I've a book or two there, and I'd be glad if you'd like to borrow one at any time."

"Thank you so much, Mr. Folkes. Do you know—" she came back, leaning towards him confidentially. "It's just like Mrs. Sven says. When you take the first step, opportunities just follow." She was radiant. "But I've got to go. I left Poppy all alone with the dishes and the mess." She went off, as though on winged feet.

"Poor child!" Tudor looked down at the big shoes in his hands.

"She'll be a fine-looking woman some day," Sym commented. He struck a light for a fresh cigarette. "Not a patch on my Poppy, though."

"You're prejudiced."

"Coming for a beer?" Sym asked, stretching.

"Another time, Sym. Shoes to mend, you know."

He hummed softly to himself, watching dead leaves scuttle before the wind.

4

Winter set in early. Morning after morning, the girls wakened at the sound of Mrs. Howe's shrill call to the pitch blackness of seven A.M., hating to put back the warm quilts and bear the chill while they dressed. The logs of the house cracked with the cold. They were allowed a candle in the morning, and by this light they sleepily groped for warm clothes and moccasins, broke the ice in the basin to wash, tidied their hair with numb fingers, and put everything in order in their room. While their landlady went back to sleep, the girls made mush and coffee for breakfast, washed up the dishes afterwards, and took turn about in scrubbing the kitchen floor and preparing the vegetables. Their hands were always rough and red, their feet tortured with chilblains.

At school they could get thoroughly warm, sitting beside the stove, though the heat woke the agony in their sore feet. During the lunch hour, the two friends rushed home, got the meal ready, ate very fast, and washed the dishes before hurrying back to school. Classes were dismissed at three-thirty, but they stayed at school as long as possible, long after the teacher had gone, reading and doing homework under the dull electric lights. Olga fell hungrily upon the books of the inadequate library, devouring whatever she found. She made the little book room a model of neatness, mended book covers, catalogued magazines, and pasted loose maps back into atlases. The globe shone. She read antiquated texts and dusty volumes of Shakespeare's plays and neglected works of Dickens and Scott. But Poppy sat dreaming and brooding.

At five, they must go to their boarding-house and prepare supper. Olga trudged home happily, her arms loaded with books. Poppy dreaded the evening most, sitting huddled on the bed under a quilt, reading by the light of a little coal-oil lamp in the bitter chill of the room, while Mrs. Howe entertained friends out in the kitchen, or put the radio on full blast with some comic program.

"This room feels mighty cold," Lina remarked to Poppy one Friday afternoon when she came for the girls.

"It's all right."

"Well, don't ever belly-ache to me about it. In Edmonton you could of got a nice place. Here, you got to work so you won't be monkeying round."

"I'm not belly-aching," Poppy answered doggedly.

Her mother shrugged. She was wondering what went on in the mind of this quiet little thing, her daughter. It was only Olga who knew the depths of homesickness that Poppy suffered; for Lina would have been angered had she known.

"What are you thinking about?" Olga asked one night. Poppy was curled up on the foot of the bed, holding her geometry book open, and making criss-cross lines on a sheet of paper. Olga sat on the one chair. She had been reading from a heavy volume of history under the light of the coal-oil lamp at their little table. Her dark braids hung down her back. She sniffed continually. Both girls wore heavy slacks and sweaters. From the kitchen came the blaring noise of a hockey game being broadcast on the radio.

"I was thinking how nice it would be to be home," Poppy answered. "I could be reading to Benny by the heater." She sat up, rubbing her cold hands together. Her face looked rather wan, framed in her light hair. "Gee, Olga, don't you ever wish you was home?"

"Oh, I miss the kids sometimes, but gosh, our place is that noisy, a person can't hear themselves think. It's quiet here." She fell into a kind of dream, looking contentedly round the crowded little room with its crude uncomfortable furniture. The announcer's voice, recording the game, and the applause, seemed lost on her.

"Are we going to the school dance next week?" Poppy asked presently, drawing the quilt about her shoulders.

Olga sighed. "I never get to have a dance."

"Let's stay home."

"We could wait till Christmas and have fun at our own dances at Tiger Lily." Olga beat a tattoo on the floor with her moccasined heels.

"What day is it today?" Poppy asked, idly, bending her fair head over her geometry book.

"Tuesday."

"I wish it would be Friday."

"What the hell are you waiting for?" Olga asked mildly, turning a page. "I mean, good gracious, why do you always want the days to go so fast?"

The radio was suddenly switched off, and the silence fairly rang in their ears, until they heard the quick step of Mrs. Howe.

"Well, I'm off to the whist drive," she told them, standing in the doorway by the pushed-back curtain. Bundled up in her ancient black fur coat, with her blue scarf tied over her head, she glared at them as though they had defied her. "I've brought in the wood you can burn for the evening, and don't take a stick more. If anyone knocks, tell them the store's closed."

The girls sat tensely while her footsteps trotted out to the kitchen and the back door banged. Then Olga stood up, taking the lamp in a steady hand.

"Come on, Poppy. The kitchen stove! Fire, heat!"

Over the slanting floor she led the way, scuffing her feet in her moccasins, the moving light falling upon the rows of tinned goods on the shelves, and on the scales and cardboard crates. Poppy followed, carrying their books. In the kitchen, they put their things on the oil-cloth covered table before the open oven door of the stove. Lifting the stove lid, and taking a cautious look, Poppy remarked, "My mother would say that's a very poor fire. And if you're a poor fire-maker, your lover don't love you."

"Let's have heat while we can!" cried Olga, reaching for some hunks of wood. "If we run out, I'll go chop down the nearest tree." She made up the fire, flinging her dark braids around with a great show of defiance. "Let 'er rip, let 'er roar!" She opened the draughts and made a mock bow with the stove-lifter in her hand. "Now Romeo, where art thou?"

"He's likely in the pool room," Poppy snickered. "What made you go for him? Jay says he looks like a husky dog." She sobered suddenly, opening her geometry book. "I can't understand this stuff about parallel lines." She hunched herself over the table, her chin in her hands.

"I'll show you," Olga offered, drawing up a chair. "Now look, I'll make the diagram." She sat down, her glowing face bent over the sheet of paper. "Now." She held out the work, her dark eyes bright. "You know from last year, that parallel lines never meet."

"Never meet?"

"That's right. No matter how far you produce them, they never meet."

"I hate the whole thing!" Poppy declared suddenly. "School, and geometry and those catty dames. Don't you?"

"There are only two or three who are catty. And I like the school, and the books, and the geometry and history." Olga deepened the lines of the diagram with a chewed-up pencil.

"What's the use of it all?"

"I don't know," Olga replied, dreamily. "Mrs. Sven says that at University there's more books yet, and lots of people who like to read them. I'd like that." She got up to shut off the draughts, for the flames were roaring up the chimney.

"But what for?" Poppy looked wonderingly at her tall friend.

"I don't know."

"What day is it?"

"Tuesday."

"Only Tuesday?"

Olga sat down beside her again. "I'll show you. That is, if you like."

"Yes, show me, please."

"AD is a transversal cutting the two parallel lines AC and BD—"

"Christmas is still a long time away, isn't it? It'll never be spring."

"That makes the alternate angles equal. It'll come real fast, Poppy. The whole thing goes too fast for me. It'll soon be time to plow again."

After the week's slaving with hogs and milk cows, it annoyed Lina to see Poppy come home moody, irritable.

"Why do you look so thin and poorly?" her mother demanded. "All you got to do is sit on your fanny the whole day long. What's eating you?"

"Nothing."

"Olga's looking good. She don't come home sulking. She's lending a hand the minute she's in the gate. *Must* you stand there doing nothing?"

Chapter XXI

1

A person don't need to get religion, but they should have some notion about church and things like that." Lina pushed back her chair from the table, glancing round at Mrs. Howe, Olga, and Poppy. "There's never been no Sunday school close enough for my kids to go to. This seems like a chance to learn something."

"Brother Conrad talks real good," Mrs. Howe declared, refilling the tea-pot with hot water. "If it wasn't for my rheumatism, I'd go this Sunday too. But I got to sit by the fire and ease the aches." She sniffed defiantly, jamming the cosy back on the tea-pot.

Poppy and Olga were silent, sleepy after the long drive in the cold.

"You might as well go," Lina prodded them. "Pete and myself are pretty strict, I know. But you kids can go to church, such as it is. That's respectable. You don't need to be saying you can't go no place in this town."

"Anybody that's anybody in Bear Claw goes," Mrs. Howe put in. "And Brother Conrad sure does tell them off plenty now, and no mistake."

"The singing is supposed to be real good," Olga ventured.

"Well, change into your decent clothes, Poppy," Lina said, looking severe as her daughter yawned, "and run along. Going to church now and again never hurt nobody."

2

In the cheerless hotel lobby, lit by a single small electric light bulb screwed into a socket in the dingy white of the ceiling, lukewarm heat came from a small register in the streaky wall. Several chairs stood about, much the worse for wear, and on the walls hung two or three fly-speckled calendars, each proclaiming a different year and a different month. Propped up on the counter, an eye-blearing red and black sign read:

CHURCH TONIGHT IN THE TOWN HALL
BROTHER CONRAD WILL SPEAK ON:
"BE SAVED NOW!"

Wearing a clean white woollen sweater buttoned up to the throat, Tudor sat in one of the deep arm-chairs whose springs sagged nearly to the floor. He lolled his head comfortably on the stained leather chair-back, and rested his feet over the edge of a tarnished brass spittoon.

His pipe had gone out, but he held the stem clamped between his teeth. Beside him, on an equally comfortable chair, his knees nearly touching his chin, sat Brother Conrad, a plump figure in a severely black suit and coat, and a stiff black hat.

Brother Conrad spoke impressively.

"Brother Folkes, a man in your position, a Justice of the Peace, a *Marriage Commissioner*, should set the example. This town is full of corruption and sin, and you know it!" He shook his fist in the direction of the window, through which could be seen the lights of the town glimmering through falling snow. His sharp eyes moved restlessly, as though trying to ferret out the secrets of this den of corruption. As though in answer to his unspoken desire, a young native girl appeared, teetering down the narrow dark staircase on spike-heeled shoes. Her painted lips resembled a wound in her sallow, heart-shaped face. A well-dressed white man lurched after her, opening the door with difficulty. When it closed upon the pair, the girl laughed shrilly.

"Brother Folkes! The unsaved! What will the Lord say to sinners like these on Judgment Day? When *in due season* they shall reap what they now sow?" He spoke in a dramatic whisper. "Brother Folkes, let your own heart answer."

"Well," Tudor replied, taking his pipe from his mouth, and holding the bowl cupped in his hand, "I fancy that when a poor girl like that one comes before the Lord, He'll probably say, 'My little one, you didn't do too badly considering the brains you didn't have.'"

Brother Conrad started. Tudor went on in a calm, unaffected voice, his eyes sad, "And no doubt when you and I come before the Lord, Brother Conrad, and other so-called righteous people like us, He'll say, 'What a miserable mess you made of things, for all your conceit. Think of the opportunities to be kind that you missed.'" Tudor reached in his pocket for a match, and leaning forward struck it on the sole of his boot, carefully steadying the flame.

"You blaspheme!" Brother Conrad choked out. "Oh repent, Brother Folkes, and come, and *be saved!* Perhaps the Lord will move you to come. I must leave you in His hands." Turning up the collar of his coat, he shot his companion a last glittering glance, before going off to his meeting, banging the door behind him.

The door to the dining-room opened a few inches.

"So our brother's gone, has he?" a voice asked.

"Yes, Tommy, he's gone." Tudor dropped the match into the spittoon as the flame burnt his finger. "Got your lighter there?"

The young man came in, smiling.

"Here it is. . . . I didn't like to interrupt the saving of your soul, you know." He stood looking out of the window, young, clean, with steady eyes, steady hands, his hair tawny in the dull light.

Tudor lit his pipe, making a cloud of smoke about his head.

"Poor Brother Conrad. He does the best he can with us sinners. Going to the meeting?"

Tommy returned the lighter to his pocket. "Sure. The singing's great. Why don't you come? I guess a person shouldn't say so, but really, Brother Conrad's meeting is as good as a show."

"Oh, I've got to see a man about a horse, if he ever gets here," Tudor answered lazily.

"Well, Brother, until the Lord moves you." Tommy went off with a salute to the old soldier.

3

Through the falling snow, dull light shone from the high windows of the hall, a big, unpainted barn of a place, thrown together hastily with just enough construction to keep it up. Near the door, Mike Olenski lounged with Pete Dizzon.

"C'mon in," Mike urged.

Dizzon shook his head emphatically.

"I'd do a heap for you, Mike, but getting saved ain't in my line."

"You don't have to be saved. You can find a nice little girl to hold hands with in the dark when they show the slides."

"Women!" Dizzon sniffed.

"Well, nuts to you! I'm going!"

"Oh, there's daddy's little boy, Tommy Hanson," muttered Dizzon. "Why don't you go hold his hand?"

Mike beat the snow from the front of his wind-breaker.

"Aw, shut up!"

Several ancient autos stood in a row outside the door, while not far off, teams and wagons waited in the dark. Loud, chattering groups of people constantly entered the place, or left it. Within, a large crowd had gathered, sitting row upon row on backless benches of boards placed precariously across saw-horses. Benches stretched along the side walls also, while many people stood along the back, or around the low stove which gave out a blistering heat into its immediate vicinity. Here, Tommy moved in to warm himself. In the middle of the hall, a projecting machine and boxes of slides stood on a small table. At the front, on the platform, Brother Conrad leaned on the piano, conferring with his orchestra, a fiddler, banjo-player, and pianist. Behind him on the wall, hung a white sheet.

Now Brother Conrad moved to the edge of the platform, his chin thrust forward, his large white hands holding a heavy hymn book. A shock of dark hair stood straight up all over his head. His mouth was large and pliant, his voice sonorous.

"Friends, Brothers, Sisters, we'll start tonight by singing Hymn 282, 'Washed in the Blood.'"

While the congregation leafed through the paper-bound books provided, the orchestra swung into the well-known hymn, giving it a quick, exciting tempo. Once again the door opened, and Mike Olenski shoved his way through the crowd around the stove, looking up and down at the people on the rows of benches, the children, mothers with babies in their arms, groups of men, rows of high-school youngsters, young people of many nationalities, dark and blond, dressed in catalogue clothes, in the old world style, or in buckskin coats and moccasins. Near the machine was a space on the end of a bench, and next to it, Mike recognized someone. Disregarding arms, legs, feet, bundles of coats, sleeping babies, that seemed everywhere in his way, he ploughed through to the bench, while all about him, rousing voices were raised in song. He slid into the empty place.

"Hello, Poppy."

The girl looked up nervously from the hymn book. She wore a neat grey coat that Lina had made for her, with bright red mitts sticking out of one of the pockets. Her feet felt icy cold in her shining black oxfords. Recognizing Mike, she turned coldly away, moving as close as possible to Olga who sat on the other side of her, singing in a sweet voice full of pathos.

At the end of the chorus, Brother Conrad suddenly shouted,

"Sing that chorus again! Everybody! Sing!"

"Why, I knew you since you was a kid," Mike protested, under cover of the thunderous response. "Don't go stuck up on me." She thrust her hymn book into his hands, turning her back on him to look on with Olga. "Have you found the Lord?" he asked. "Didn't know He was lost, myself."

"'Washed in the blood,'" Olga sang. And then stopping abruptly, "What's wrong?" she asked, peering past her friend to the intruder. Olga looked her worst, for, unlike Poppy, she had not changed her clothes after driving into town from the farm. She wore heavy slacks and a man's windbreaker, with a black shawl tied, peasant fashion, over her braided hair. Her nose was very red. Mike gave her a disgusted look.

"All right, friends, all right!" boomed Brother Conrad, holding up his hands for silence. "Now we'll have, 'Yield not to temptation.' Hymn 568. Hymn 568. Oh Brothers, Sisters, this is the one to sing! Now everybody clap your hands, and swing from side to side, and sing!" He started them off with a fine bass, "'Yield not to temptation, for yielding is sin—'"

The building fairly shook as feet stamped, hands clapped, and the swaying, enthusiastic congregation sang lustily. Poppy found herself pushed against Mike and back against Olga in time to the music. But somehow, for the moment, her feeling of hostility broke down as she sang and clapped with the rest. On the platform, Brother Conrad made mighty gestures, seeming to hold the crowd in hypnotic power. For half an hour, the singing of hymns continued, sometimes with the people standing, sometimes with the company sitting down and swaying together. Then, removing his coat, Brother Conrad plunged into a long prayer for the souls of sinners in general, and more particularly for those in the vicinity of Bear Claw. While his head was bent, some members of the congregation craned their necks, looking about to see who was present, and others got up to leave, their interest being over once the singing was concluded. Newcomers took their places, eagerly awaiting the showing of the slides. Brother Philip, a long lean individual with rimless glasses and thinning red hair, had sorted them out.

After his long prayer, and many shouts of "Alleluia!" "Amen!" from those who were "saved," Brother Conrad stood to one side of the sheet at the back of the platform, and ordered the lights to be put out. Brother Philip came forward to do his task. In the sudden darkness, a square of white light glimmered on the sheet, reflecting eerily on the faces of the people. Then flashed on the screen a highly coloured picture representing Eve, coyly hiding behind a large rock, and Adam waist deep in reeds and bush, gazing at her in adoration.

"Here, Brothers, Sisters, here was Paradise."

In the darkness, only the plump hand of the Preacher could be seen stretched out in the light towards the sheet.

"Why don't she come away from that rock?" asked a deep voice at the back of the hall.

"But man has sinned, man has sinned; and we come to call sinners to repentance."

Mike reached out roughly, taking Poppy's hand in his. She snatched it away. Somewhere near them, a man gulped a quick drink from a strong-smelling bottle. Mike laughed, low in his throat. Meanwhile, the sermon went on at a wild pitch, as slide after slide was shown, each dealing with some phase of Biblical history, and each explained in fierce terms as part of the history of sin in man. The voice of Brother Conrad boomed, raved, whispered, sobbed. People came and went, smoked, quietly chatted about many matters, made rude comments aloud. The air of the place was fetid with moonshine, buckskin, people.

Finally a slide appeared depicting a girl busy making up her face at a mirror. In one corner of the picture, a heart was drawn, covered with cobwebs. A short whistle pierced the hall.

"Lemme at her!" someone shouted.

"This," said the preacher in a trembling voice, "this shows us the heart of one bent on worldly pleasures and ambitions. What a fate for a sister! Her heart forgotten of the Lord!"

Mike seized Poppy's hand, right under the very nose of Brother Philip.

"Leave me alone," she muttered, desperately freeing herself.

"Well, you dirty little snip! Lina Ashley's Poppy. I heard you was stuck up."

The lights went on, revealing Brother Conrad on the platform. He had loosened his black tie, and the perspiration streamed down his face. Mopping his brow with a varicoloured handkerchief, he bent forward impressively.

"Brothers, Sisters! God is not mocked. Whatsoever a man soweth, that shall he also reap! All have sowed sin. But that sin, though it be as scarlet, the Lord can wash it away, *white as snow!* Brothers, Sisters, who among you will come forward this night—and—be—*saved!*"

The dull lights in the lamps dimmed.

"Now pray God the power plant holds for sinners to be saved!" Brother Conrad entreated, raising his eyes heavenward.

"Amen! God save us! Alleluia!" murmured voices from various parts of the hall.

The light brightened.

"Who are you to treat me like this?" Mike muttered, leaning towards Poppy.

"Olga, let's go. Come on!" the girl whispered.

"Where?" Olga asked dreamily, her eyes fixed on the platform. But seeing Poppy get up, she rose too.

"You can't get rid of me so easy," Mike declared angrily, following them as they pushed through the jovial crowd.

When they neared the door, Poppy turned back, and seeing the big hulking fellow coming after them, she stopped short.

"Leave us alone!" she exclaimed in a hoarse whisper. "Go away, please!"

"So that's how it is, eh?" Mike asked in a nasty tone.

"Having trouble?"

Poppy looked up to see Tommy leaning against the wall.

"Keep out of this!" Mike snarled. "Mind your own business!"

"How do you know it isn't my business?" Tommy asked pleasantly. "This is a friend of mine, as it happens."

Mike glared at him.

"Oh, sinners, we call upon you now! May God have mercy on you!" Brother Conrad boomed.

"Alleluia! Amen!" murmured a pious, meek-looking little man by the stove. Mike elbowed him roughly aside.

Olga seized Poppy's arm.

"We got to get out of here, Poppy! There'll be a fight next."

"He's too yellow to fight!" Mike sneered, grabbing the door as the girls opened it.

"That so?" Tommy followed, and the four of them stood out in the dark snowy street.

"OK, Brother, go mind your own business before I have to mess up your pretty face," Mike challenged.

"Say, that you, Mike?" A dark figure loomed up beside them. "For Pete's sake, leave everything! I tell you I got to see you, Mike." It was Dizzon, shouldering his crony away from the others. "There's plenty trouble, Mike. Let women alone for now. I got to see you."

"Trouble? What are you talking about?"

"C'mon, get out of this!"

"That does for him," Tommy remarked, watching the men go off.

"It was swell of you," Olga said shyly.

"That's OK. I say, aren't you Poppy?" he asked the other girl. "I think we should know each other. I'm Tommy Hanson."

"Yes. Yes, I guess we should," Poppy replied uncertainly. "And this is Olga Panachuk."

"Well, girls, let's not stand here. How about coming over to Wo Ling's for a coke?"

Poppy looked up at Olga inquiringly.

"Well," the big girl said, "if we go home to Mrs. Howe's, Poppy, you know it'll be cold. And it's too early to go to bed yet."

"All right then. We'd—we'd like to."

They found a booth in the crowded confectionery store with its slippery dark oiled floor and wobbly tables covered with cracked oil-cloth. Tommy watched Poppy brushing the snow from her coat with her red mitts, while snowflakes melted into her fair hair. Olga removed the shawl from her head, shaking back her long dark braids. When they had seated themselves, in the home-made booth with its rough, unpainted boards, Wo Ling, the Chinese proprietor, came to serve them.

Tommy gave him a friendly smile.

"Three cokes."

Wo Ling nodded.

"Do you remember, Poppy, when we came out to your place once, Dad and I?" Tommy asked.

Poppy frowned a little.

"Seems like I should know you, somehow."

"We played with a red ball—and a dog, it seems to me. There was another boy there too, Jay Baptiste, wasn't it? I see him around town sometimes."

The girl swallowed hard.

"Yes, yes, he was there."

"Jay's a darn good trapper now," Olga put in.

"I knew you right off," Tommy said to Poppy. "Funny I didn't see you round before, but of course I've been out to Edmonton taking a course on machinery."

Wo Ling brought their drinks and some pink and blue straws. Conversations in broken English drifted to them from the other two booths. The door opened and closed, heavy feet tramped about, as Wo Ling did a running business in cigarettes, cokes, and gum. Poppy fell silent.

"I think I'm going back." Olga set down her empty bottle.

"Where?" Tommy asked, sipping at a pink straw.

"Meeting." She clasped her big hands, looking absently above and beyond Tommy's tawny head. "I think I'll go and be saved."

"If you feel like that, you should go ahead." Tommy finished his coke, looking at her with kind tolerance.

"You said at supper you didn't think there was anything in it," Poppy protested.

"I know. Maybe there isn't; but if there is, I'll be on the safe side."

"In front of all them people? Tomorrow you'd hear about it. Viola and Rosalee'd give you no peace." Under the table, Poppy gently jogged Olga's knee with her own.

"Oh well, another time would do." Olga pinched and flattened her straw with her fingers. "Let's go home then, and warm ourselves over a candle like Bob Cratchit." She tied the unbecoming shawl over her head.

"Let me see you home," Tommy suggested. "The streets are dark down your way."

As they passed the hotel, Folkes and Constable Hicks came out together. In the dim light of the open door, the young people recognized Tudor's white sweater and the big burly figure of the young mountie. The sleek police car was parked at the foot of the hotel steps.

"I wonder who's in trouble." Olga sounded anxious.

"Some poor breed, likely," Tommy answered. "By the way, are you coming to the dance on Friday night?"

"I don't know," Poppy replied.

"It's a school dance, a Valentine party, isn't it?"

Olga said nothing, and Poppy went on hesitatingly.

"I don't know as my mother would want me to go."

Olga turned to her.

"You could ask. She'll be still in there gabbing to Mrs. Howe."

"Let me ask her," Tommy pleaded as they came to the gate of the girls' boarding-place.

"Come right in," Olga invited hospitably.

They shook the snow from their clothes at the back door and went into the kitchen. Mrs. Howe and Lina sat in front of the stove, empty tea-cups still before them on the table.

"You're early," Lina remarked.

"Well, it's school to-morrow." Poppy brushed some snow from her hair. "Mother, do you remember Tommy Hanson? He's brought us home."

"Why sure, Tommy. I thought you was out to Edmonton?"

"Just for a couple of months."

Olga spread her hands expansively. "Machinery."

Lina looked the boy over critically.

"Mrs. Ashley," he began, "would it be all right with you if—. Well, there's a Valentine dance on next Friday, a school dance. Could Poppy come with Olga and me?"

Lina put a hand on her hip and looked at the boy with new interest. She smiled, but her eyes were shrewd.

"Why, sure thing. Pete will be in Saturday, and the girls can come home with him. Save me a trip." She nodded to Poppy.

"But Mother, we'd be a day late then. I couldn't do much to help with the chores."

"That's all right for just this once," Lina declared. "It's real nice of Tommy to ask you. And you got that new dress I just finished; it'll be just the thing. She can go, Tommy, and much obliged."

The boy was suddenly thoughtful. He turned to Poppy, shyly.

"You really want to come?" he asked. "If you'd really rather go home, why, it's all right with me. Only I thought—"

She looked up, pale and shy.

"That's fine, Tommy. We'll be coming, Olga and me."

"Nice enough fellow, that Tommy," Lina commented when the boy had gone, and the girls were taking off their wet things in the bedroom.

"All the folks like Tommy," Mrs. Howe snapped. "There'll be plenty coming to him when the old man goes. Mebbe my rent'll go down when the land passes to the young man."

Lina buttoned her coat and picked up her heavy mitts.

"I always figgered Poppy should of gone to Edmonton to school," she said thoughtfully. "But I don't know but what this way's better. She's near enough to home so as I can keep an eye on her. This school year is doing her good. Well, I guess I'll shove along to the hotel. Got to pull out early tomorrow."

Chapter XXII

1

It was bitterly cold at Bear Claw. Bands of quivering Northern Lights among far-distant stars, gave the early night a greenish twilight. Sounds echoed in the sharp, frosty, stinging air. Yellowish light shone dully from heavily frosted windows of Wong's General Store, Wo Ling's Confectionery, the hotel, and the pool hall; and dark hooded figures passed and repassed the buildings, tramping the hard-packed snow, their breath in foggy clouds about their heads. Sleigh bells jingled on the road as teams of horses, whitely frosted, with steaming breath, drew closed-in sleds with smoking chimneys, in the direction of the livery barn.

In the pool-room, Sym piled logs into the roaring fire of the heater, his face lit by the ruddy flames. The place was crowded. At the two tables, under the green-shaded lights, wild, angry games were in progress, while loungers stood around the stove or sat on the benches along the side walls.

"What a time to sewer!" Tommy cried. He stood aside, sliding his hand lightly up and down his cue, watching Romeo shoot. Tommy had taken off his suit-coat, and in a white shirt, he looked startlingly clean among the other men in their heavy dark work clothes.

"Hell!" Romeo growled, straightening up. "Nothing but squares!" He bit his lower lip with his long front teeth.

Pete Panachuk squinted down his cue.

"If I couldn't put more on de draw dan dat, I'd quit de game!"

Romeo looked savage, a lock of lank black hair falling into his eyes from under his cap.

"Try a little chalk!" Tommy suggested, as the cue ball rolled but a few inches, and Pete cursed his luck, stamping round the crowded table, shoving Romeo aside.

"Hey! Look out!" Romeo trod heavily on a moccasined foot behind him. "Obadiah!" He looked around, staring at his victim who was sitting on a bench. "Get lots of jack for your catch?"

Obadiah grinned, touching the pocket of his buckskin coat with a protecting hand.

"Good going!" Romeo moved off to follow the game more closely. "How many ways have you got?" he shouted to Tommy.

Obadiah watched silently, seemingly fascinated by the fast movement of the brightly coloured balls on the green tables. With his beaded buckskin gloves on his knee, he smoked leisurely, his eyes narrow in his flat brown face blinking against the heat of the nearby stove. The air of the place was foul, smelling of horses, woollen clothes damp with sweat, alcoholic breath, and buckskin. Across the room, Mike Olenski watched Obadiah through the layers of stale tobacco smoke.

"If we get caught, we'll need jack," he muttered to Dizzon beside him. "We'll need plenty jack."

"Where do we get it?" Dizzon glared round, sniffing loudly, rubbing his large hooked nose with a filthy forefinger.

"I got an idea." Mike struck a light for his cigarette. "Let me handle this."

Dizzy rubbed a nervous hand over his bald head. "Mebbe we don't get caught."

The confusion of curses, clashing balls, tramping feet drowned their voices. Obadiah smoked on, grinning happily to himself. Mike bit his fingernails, letting his cigarette burn itself out in his free hand.

"What a robber!" Romeo shouted, brandishing his cue.

Near the door, Emil Ek and Jim Holberg, in their best clothes, talked soberly together.

"The democracies have been sleeping," Jim twisted his large red hands, shaking his head with heavy sadness.

"Isolationism is a thing of the past." Emil stared into space, forgetting for a moment his embarrassment about his good suit, which he had suddenly outgrown, so that it showed a pathetic length of wrist and ankle.

Heavy footsteps scrunched outside, and then the door, thickly coated with frost on lock and hinges, screeched open, letting in an icy blast of bitterly cold air, and the figure of Constable Hicks enormous in his fur hat and buffalo coat. As he crashed the door shut behind him, constraint fell upon all. Dizzy huddled down on a bench, trying to make himself unnoticeable, while Mike's cigarette burned his fingers. He did not feel it, sitting motionless, hardly breathing. The players stopped cursing, and paused in their game, not noticing a cue ball following an odd ball into a pocket. Constable Hicks had the whole roomful covered as though with a loaded gun.

"Ashley," he said, in a pleasant voice, as he pushed his hat up above his ears, "we want you over at the hotel."

Sym nodded. Telling Romeo to see to things while he was gone, he reached for his coat. Everyone relaxed again. The players resumed their games. The young mountie stood watching and listening. One of his large red ears drooped downwards as though to attend to all near and imminent sounds, while the other cupped outwards to catch unsuspected clues from the background. There was little conversation until he and Sym were safely out of the place, when the wild cursing in various languages began again.

Under cover of the noise and confusion, Mike went over to Obadiah, sitting beside him in a friendly manner.

"How about a game of vingt-et-un?" he whispered.

Obadiah's eye-lids flickered. He took a long drag on a cigarette he had just finished making. Finally he shook his head, looking away from Mike to the balls sliding about the tables.

"I've got a bottle," Mike murmured very low.

The dark-faced man turned towards him, and Mike touched a slight bulge that showed in the front of his leather jacket.

"In the dive." The white man got up slowly, wandering off nonchalantly to a door in the shadows at the back of the room. Obadiah smoked furiously for a few seconds, waiting for Romeo to turn his back and bend low over the table with his cue.

"Dat's de fourt' ball you fluked!" Panachuk laughed jeeringly, watching the cue ball race between the five and the three. Romeo cursed, glaring through his hair at Pete. Tommy looked on with amusement. The men at the other tables were having a hot argument, helped on by watchers from various sides. The door at the back clicked softly.

"Have a drink," Mike invited, taking a flat bottle from an inside pocket.

He and Obadiah seated themselves opposite each other at a little table in the small room lit by a dull electric light bulb that glowed in the side of an unpainted wall. Along one side of the room stood a narrow cot where Sym slept. His clothes hung on nails in the rough boards at the foot of the bed. Behind the two men three or four steps led up to the door to the pool room. Tilting back his head with its thick uncombed locks of black hair, Obadiah took a long drink, swallowing noisily, setting down the bottle with wet mouth and bright eyes, while Mike shuffled a pack of greasy dog-eared cards. His companion reached into his pocket, bringing out a wad of bills. Pieces of brown hair fell out of Mike's pompadour in greasy points about his colourless face. He made a fan with the pack on the table. The bottle stood between them. Obadiah took a card with one hand, reaching for the bottle with the other. Through the flimsy door came the sounds of the pool room.

"How many ways have you got?" Panachuk shouted to Tommy.

"Six." Tommy was putting on his suit-coat, straightening his tie.

"Come on, have another game!" Removing his cap, Romeo shoved back his hair, jammed on his cap again to start afresh.

"I'm going to the dance," Tommy answered.

"She don't start yet," one of the men told him.

"It's that homely little wash-out-looking dame he's going after." Sourly, Romeo showed his fang-like teeth.

With a foxy expression on his face, Panachuk watched Gus Hanson's son depart.

"Lina, she got everything tight in de fist," he declared. "Tommy and Poppy too, you see, you see. Lina, she get de land, she get de hay, and now she get Gustav's Tommy for Poppy."

Dizzon rubbed his bald head.

"The breed'll get her yet."

"Go 'way wit you! Lina, she get what she want. Get everyting tight in de fist. Lina, she tink she get me, even, tight in de fist!" he finished angrily.

Fresh in his mind, and rankling there, was the remembrance of Lina's visit to him the Monday before.

"Reckon you can pick the kids up on Saturday," she told him, suddenly opening the kitchen door and putting her head in. The cold swirled in with her. Even the cat retired behind the stove, shivering. "Olga and Poppy are staying in Friday night for a Valentine party."

"Valentine party?" Pete straightened up from his beet soup, looking uncomprehendingly at Lina.

"Come in, Lina, come in," his wife urged, advancing to the door. "Cold it is. Have some soup."

Lina looked distastefully at the small, noisy, ill-clad children about the table.

"I got no time for visiting," she answered. "Wouldn't wonder if that Matt Poudre down at my place hasn't got the cows milked even. I just come to tell you about Saturday."

"But Olga, I want her home for chores," Pete protested. "I figger you bring Olga home like you say, and I go to town for my bizniz."

Lina laughed.

"You don't need to worry, Pete. I gave my permission."

"Olga, she asks not to home if she can go to a Valentines party." He looked at his wife as if she were to blame. Mrs. Panachuk went on feeding the children without looking up.

"They just got invited," Lina said, her hand on the door-knob. "They're going with young Tommy Hanson. They'll be all right with him; he's a good lad." To Pete's look of protest she replied, "Well, I count on you to bring them home Saturday." The door banged and she was gone.

At the pool table, Pete was silent, thinking of Lina.

"Jay Baptiste, he gets that Poppy," Dizzon insisted.

"Shake 'em out, high pea breaks!" Romeo yelled.

2

The dull light in the "dive" dimmed, brightened, and dimmed again. The bottle had disappeared from the table; some bills were piled up in its place. Obadiah held the pack clumsily in his dark hands. Upturned before him lay a three of spades. His head wavered from side to side.

"Hit me." Mike pointed to his own two up-turned cards, the ten of hearts, and the ten of diamonds. As though his fingers were two inches thick, the native put a card face down on each, and one on his own.

The white man put his right hand protectingly about his cards, turning up the ones just dealt, with his left. On the ten of hearts, he turned up the ace of clubs; on the ten of diamonds, the five of spades. Obadiah looked gloomily at his deuce of hearts on the three.

"Hit me again."

On the five, Mike turned up another five, and reached for the money.

"Nuther game," Obadiah muttered thickly, feeling in his pocket. He took out a lone five dollar bill, looking at it with drunken interest as he put it beside Mike's money, and the other man shuffled the cards.

"Lemme play for Obadiah, jusht thish one game." Mike whirled in his chair; Sym stood on the top step, smoking a cigarette, looking down at them. He lurched down the steps and crowded the native off the chair.

"C'mon, Obie, I'll win lotsa money for you." His hand with the cigarette moved uncertainly. Obadiah staggered to the cot where he leaned back, his face twisted with pain. Mike grinned as he made a fan with the pack.

"Go ahead, draw."

Sym drew the king of hearts, Mike the nine of clubs. Sym took the pack into his hands, burying the top one. He dealt a card to Mike, one to himself. Craftily, Mike glanced at his, laid it down. Sym gave him another card. Mike was about to make the same protective movement with his hand as he had done with Obadiah. Quick as lightning, Sym grabbed his wrist, forcing back his arm. An ace dropped out of the sleeve of Mike's leather jacket.

"Now we'll play vingt-et-un," said Sym in a cold sober voice. "And we'll use my deck." He took a new pack from his pocket, breaking the seal. White with rage, Mike sat still while the fan of shining new cards spread out before him. He drew his card.

On the cot, Obadiah smoked a cigarette. Sweat ran down his dark face. He rocked about, moaning. The dull light brightened, dimmed, brightened. From the pool room came the noise of tramping feet, dashing balls, and curses.

"Shake 'em out, high pea breaks!" Romeo shouted again.

The front door opened and slammed shut. The door of the heater banged as more logs were shoved in, and the fire roared. In the little back room it was cold and quiet. The snickering of the cards, and the groans of Obadiah were the only sounds. Sym kept adding to a pile of bills at his side, until Mike turned his empty pockets inside out, and the game was over. Mike was silent, but raging. He stumbled up, out of the room, closing the door behind him.

"C'mon," Sym said to Obadiah who had staggered to his feet. "I got to get you safe home with your money."

3

Under the dull lights in the big draughty hall, red and white streamers drifted from the rafters, and large red hearts hung along the edges of the platform and the benches. The girls wore red ribbons in their hair to show that they had contributed something to the lunch, while tiny red hearts were pinned to the lapels of the boys and men as they paid at the door. In spite of cold, people had come from all the surrounding districts, some even from Bridgeville. Five Ukrainian lads on the platform played by ear their cow-boy tunes, old-time music and square-dance hoe-downs on two fiddles, a guitar, a mandolin, and a drum with cymbals.

Between dances, the men crowded to the back of the hall. Tommy brought Olga back to a bench just as Theodore left Poppy and asked Rosalee Trent for the next dance.

"Poppy, will you have this one with me?" Tommy asked.

The tune of *When I Grow Too Old To Dream* wailed from the fiddles. "I'll be back," Poppy murmured to Olga, squeezing her hand.

240

The big girl watched them dance off together. How pretty Poppy looked in her blue dress, the full skirt swinging as she moved in perfect time to the music. And there was Teacher dancing with a slick travelling salesman. Olga wondered what "line" he was stringing her as he smiled, swinging her round a corner. They looked well together, being of an equal height and both excellent dancers. Olga tucked her large feet in their heavy brogues well under the bench. Rosalee and Viola looked pityingly at her as they passed. Not far off, Jim Holberg and Emil Ek leaned sprawlingly against the wall.

"The European situation is certainly serious," she heard Jim say. "We're on a steep down-grade now, sliding towards an abyss." His eyes rolled behind his thick glasses. She could not hear Emil's reply, but she longed to talk to these two. At last the crash of the cymbals indicated that the waltz was over.

"Get your partners for a square dance!" the drummer called, coming down from the platform.

"Won't you have it with me?" Tommy pleaded, taking Poppy's arm.

"I promised Olga to go back."

"Oh, please." He led her to the first set at the front of the hall.

Tudor Folkes joined Jim and Emil, and with his foot up on a bench, listened to their political views. Olga wished she had the nerve to go and talk to them. She saw Mike Olenski and Dizzy deep in conversation at the other side of the room. About her the young people laughed and chatted, joining the sets being formed on the floor. And then, suddenly, she saw Jay. It was impossible to mistake him as he threaded his way through the crowd at the door. Many heads turned in his direction, as people gazed curiously at his beautiful white duffle-cloth jacket, embroidered with bright flowers up the front and on the hood, which he had thrown back. Against the white cloth, his face looked dark and striking. He wore knee-high mukluks, richly embroidered with red roses.

"Two more couples!" the drummer shouted, rolling up his

shirt-sleeves, and pushing back his shock of dark hair, while the fiddlers warmed up to a quick hoe-down.

Jay saw Olga immediately as she sat conspicuously alone on the bench. He flashed her a quick smile of recognition, coming over at once to sit beside her.

"When did you get in?" she demanded.

"This afternoon."

She thought he looked tired and very much older than she remembered. He was smoking a brown cigarette, looking around with half-closed eyes as though uninterested and aloof.

"Aren't you going to dance this one?" he asked huskily.

"Nobody asked me this time."

"One more couple!" the drummer called.

Jay ground out his cigarette on the bench beside him. "Come on, Olga." He took her hand. They filled in the last place of the set.

The music started up, fast and wild, and the drummer's voice, calling the dance, was all but lost amid the noise of the pounding feet and the shouts of the dancers. As they swung together, Jay said to Olga,

"Where's Poppy?"

"Way up front, dancing with Tommy Hanson."

"That coyote!"

As she and Jay went down the centre to "cut" the circle, Olga explained, "He asked her mother. I wanted her to come too." As they swung together again, she went on, "It was Lina said to come with him."

His face lighted. How well he danced! Red and black tassels flying about, his feet seemed scarcely to touch the floor. Olga flushed with pleasure, breathless and happy. Even Tudor and his young companions turned to watch the tall couple.

"Nice girl, that Olga," Tudor remarked. "I'll bet she could tell you something about affairs. She's no fool."

Jim hummed and hawed in embarrassment.

It was getting hot in the hall, and already the smell of the coffee heating on the stove at the back began to tease the appetite. After the first half, Jay took off his coat and hung it on a nail. The dark red colour had come into his olive skin. He stood very still, looking searchingly at the people as they milled about the room. Yet Poppy saw him before he saw her.

"You dance better than any girl in this room," Tommy told her, leaning against a large valentine below the fiddlers. He looked immaculate in his white shirt, his tie a rainbow of colour.

"Don't believe a word of it," Miss Walker's slick traveller said, taking the teacher's arm.

Miss Walker, in a wonderful red dress with shining sequins, smiled at her pupil, but Poppy gazed fixedly across the room. As they slowly took their places on the floor again, Jay's eyes met hers in a long look. A wordless message flashed between them. To Poppy, though she became suddenly exhilarated and full of life, the second half of the square dance seemed endless. As soon as it was over, she slipped away from Tommy, disappearing along the side, past the benches, to the back of the hall where her coat hung. Behind the broad backs of several men, she put it on, tied her scarf over her head, and took her mitts from her pockets.

Outside, the intense cold made her catch her breath. She stood shivering in the cloud of white fog that had rushed out into the night when the door had opened. A moment later, Jay appeared beside her, fastening his coat, and pulling the hood over his head. He led her down the walk a little way, and into the darkness beside the blacksmith's shop. Their feet scrunched in the snow, and Poppy's became numb with cold in her low shoes.

"I shouldn't take you out here with me," he said dejectedly.

"You didn't. I came."

"You know what I mean."

"Yes."

"There'd be trouble if your mother found out."

They stood together in the bitter cold, drawing comfort from each other's presence. Above them, great gashes of greenish light tore into the blackness of the sky. Along the horizon, the green merged into pinkish white, against which the myriad tips of spruce trees were blackly etched. Stars shone cold and pale, blue tinted. From the hall came the high sweet notes of the fiddles, while near them, footsteps scrunched past on the walk.

"Why are you here?" Poppy asked at length.

"Bill's in trouble with the police, so I came. The old man wouldn't know what to do, and he might need money. I sold some wolf pelts."

"How did you know?"

"Moccasin telegraph. Freddy Two Knives heard it in town, and he told some Indians coming out our way. Obadiah's with me."

On the walk, the tall figure of a man walked slowly up and down, sometimes stopping for a moment, and then moving on. She rubbed her cheek against his sleeve.

"That's a lovely coat. Where did you get it?"

He drew away from her. "A woman in the north made it for me. Poppy, we can never see each other again. It only brings trouble."

"Will you be at Treaty?" she asked desperately.

"I don't think so. And if I am, we can't see each other. You know it's no use."

The man on the walk stepped into the shadows, standing a little way off from them.

"Is that you, Jay?" he asked.

Poppy gasped. It was Sym's voice.

"Jay, you're wanted. Obadiah's awful sick. Looks like poisoning."

"Obadiah?" Jay and Poppy moved over to Sym. "But I saw him a while ago tonight. He was with me. He was all right."

"I know. I saw him a couple of hours ago myself. He was a bit tight, but I didn't think anything. Tudor's gone over there now."

Jay went off without a word, leaving the girl and her father together.

"Romeo told me you and Jay were out somewhere," Sym said. "Be better to meet him inside the hall, Poppy. Then folks can't say things."

They went back to the walk. In the strange greenish light, he looked down at her, pulling his collar up higher, and stamping his feet.

"Come on, let's go back to the dance," he suggested, taking her arm.

She went with him, feeling cold to the very marrow. The music had stopped, and as they entered, refreshments were being served to the crowd who mobbed the benches on the sidelines. Sym found Poppy an inconspicuous place near the stove, where she sat very pale and silent. While she drank the hot coffee he brought her, Tommy stopped beside her.

"Where have you been?" he asked anxiously.

"She's been out with her poor old dad," Sym replied, warming his hands over the hot stove.

Tommy offered her a sandwich.

"Olga's being a diplomat with Holberg and Ek." He sat down beside Poppy. " Life is dull without you," he told her.

"So Obadiah's sick?" Romeo asked Sym as he opened the stove to put on a huge log.

"Maybe he's been drinking extract," Sym suggested.

They felt a draught of cold air as Mike and Dizzy clumped outside, leaving the door ajar until someone slammed it shut.

"I been framed," Mike said despairingly, his feet crunching the snow in the shadowed alley. He took a bottle from his inside pocket, and removing the top, smelt the contents, feeling only the stinging cold in his nostrils. "Something was bad in it!"

"Poisoned?" Dizzy asked, taking a sniff himself.

"I been framed!" was all Mike could answer, looking up with fear into the strangely bright, silent sky.

Chapter XXIII

1

At the R.C.M.P. Detachment No. 1, Bridgeville, a few nights later, Constable Hicks' burly figure loomed up from the grey twilight. It was still bitterly cold, and steam poured forth from every chimney in the town. The young mountie watched the road for any sign of headlights, his breath surrounding his head in a steamy cloud, his feet making squeaking sounds at the slightest move. Seeing nothing, he opened the door, ducking his head to accommodate his height.

The court-room was a bare, masculine one with a dark oiled floor, a large desk with orderly piles of papers, some hard-looking chairs set in a row against the wall, and shelves with neatly tabulated files and books. At the back of the room from a large construction of black bars, issued the sounds of heavy snoring. A fire roared in the large heater that stood beside the door, and the redness of flames showed through a hole in the black stove-pipe. The room was hot in the upper regions, with a heat bearing the scent of burning poplar; yet about the floor crept an Arctic cold, seemingly coming from the keyhole and from the frosted crack all along the door.

As Constable Hicks was taking off his shaggy buffalo coat and fur hat, Corporal Ross came in from the next room.

"You're late," he said heartily. "What happened?"

"Engine trouble again," Hicks replied briefly. "Walked from the point. Never saw so much snow. Right up to the knees."

"Had supper?"

"No such luck. No time now, either."

Ross glanced at a large clock that ticked matter-of-factly on the wall above their heads.

"Almost seven, eh?"

He was the older of the two, and his face was the kindlier, with a whimsical smile and a friendly twinkle in his eyes. He was not very tall for a mountie, so that Hicks seemed to tower above him by contrast. Hicks had a relentlessness about him and a grim young face.

"Hope they get here on time."

He hung up his things and stood by the stove, rubbing his rather prominent red ears. Ross wandered over to the desk, sorting through the papers.

"Tudor will get them here."

"How do you think this thing will come out?" Hicks asked.

"The way Tudor always does things," Ross answered, grinning. "The guy who can pay will pay through the nose, and the underdog will get off easy."

"He's too easy. We could clean things up much more quickly if he'd be a bit tough with them. Make an example of this fellow, for instance." Hicks pointed to the "pen" with a jerk of his thumb. The snores had softened to deep regular breathing.

"Guess I'd better let poor Bill out now. If he's going to be Court witness, he'd better be in good shape. And by the way, will you bring in those beaver pelts? Cover them up with a sack for the present." Ross produced a bunch of keys from the drawer of the desk, and selecting a large crookedly shaped one, went over to the door of the cell.

Bill Manydogs limped out sleepily. He looked thinner than ever, with the high cheek bones prominent, under tightly stretched brown skin. His eyes were black pools of tragedy, pathetic and pleading. There was a greyish tinge to his colouring, and he moved stiffly like a very old man. He paid no attention to Hicks who covered a bundle with a sack under the desk, but lifted his head in a listening attitude.

"Hear something, Bill?" Ross asked kindly, jingling his keys.

"Just wants us to open the door," Hicks said grimly. Bill cowered like a hunted creature.

"A truck!" The Corporal glanced up at the clock which was on the stroke of seven. "Sit down and take it easy, Bill. They'll soon be here."

The old man did not sit down. He stood listening a few feet from the door, his back bowed, his lank locks hanging about his face, while the distant groaning of a truck came closer, and finally wheezed to a stop just outside. There were the voices of men, and the crunching of footsteps in the hard snow, and then the door squealed open. Tudor came in, pushing back the hood of his parka, behind him a group of men, while a blast of icy air chilled the room.

"Congratulations, Judge!" Ross exclaimed. "You're right to the minute."

Romeo and Sym, Dizzon and Mike crowded in, dressed in heavy dark clothes and frozen overshoes that squeaked on the oiled floor. Then at the steamy entrance, Jay came, straight and silent in his white coat and bright mukluks, closing the door softly, looking around with a kind of dignity. At the sight of the old native, his face changed. He caught Bill's arm, talking to him huskily in Cree, while the old man's face lit up with a child-like delight.

"He's all right, Jay," Ross said. "We didn't keep him locked up all the time, but he tried to run away."

Jay regarded Bill's hollow eyes and cheeks with an almost maternal anxiety.

"He's been off his grub, too," Ross went on. "But he'll be all right."

"If everybody will please sit down, we'll be able to start," Hicks was saying. "You may as well take off your coats. We'll be here for some time." He stood powerfully above them. "Where's Gus?" he demanded.

"Not in my truck," Romeo growled, twisting his mouth so that the tips of his teeth showed in a sneering grin.

"He'll get here, I guess," Sym said. "We're just unusual coming so soon." He smiled at Ross who was urging the men to sit down.

"Who does he think he is!" Hicks said irritably. "Now everyone has to sit around and wait for him!"

"Give Bear Claw a ring, and see if he's left," the Corporal suggested.

Tudor sat down at the desk and began filling his pipe. Dizzon's bald head turned and turned, catching the light. Beside him, Mike's face was white and puffy. Hicks gave the telephone a loud jangling ring, turning the handle with quick angry twists.

"Hello, Bear Claw? Hello!" he shouted.

Sym sat back nonchalantly, smoking, looking with a bit of an amused grin at the young mountie's back. Romeo shed a greasy-looking navy blue parka, and narrowed his yellow eyes at the "pen" at the back of the room. Jay and Bill were a little apart from the rest, talking swiftly in Cree. The old man's childlike glee at seeing his young friend had changed to grief. He held his head in his hands and moaned, rocking himself in his chair.

"What's wrong?" Ross asked, holding a large log over the mouth of the heater, where tongues of flame leapt up intermittently.

"Obadiah was Bill's friend," Jay answered. "I had to tell him."

Ross let the log down, slammed the lid back on the stove, and stood with his back to the heat.

"Is he round town? Did he leave for Bridgeville?" Hicks was shouting. "—OK—OK."

"Well," Tudor asked, as the young constable hung up the receiver.

"On his way. Left ages ago." He sat down on the edge of the desk, drumming his fingers impatiently. Tudor leaned back, pipe smoke about his shaggy head, as he watched each face in turn. The men talked quietly in pairs. The burning logs crackled and roared, but still the invisible cold could not be shut out. At last, they all heard the faint roar of a motor, and in a few minutes, a second truck drew up in the yard. Gustav pounded at the door.

His face was almost buried in the immense collar of a sheepskin coat and a pulled-down fur hat, showing the end of his nose faintly purple. He stood in the doorway, with the warm steam and the light streaming out upon him, until Hicks stalked over to him.

"Little trouble with the truck," Gus said pleasantly. "Got to stay in town and get her fixed." He seemed to crowd the room as he discarded outer garments.

"Must be catching," Ross remarked with a grin for Hicks, whose face relaxed a little.

Gus sat down on the only remaining chair, beside Jay. The big Swede and the young native gazed straight ahead in an effort to ignore each other. Tudor straightened up now, laying his pipe carefully on the ash tray, and drawing paper and pen towards him. But his attention was caught by the sight of these two men, so strikingly different. Gus with his sandy hair, his sleepy blue eyes and thick bull neck, and Jay with his dark face, so absorbed and remote in expression. Yet the thought startled Tudor that there was about these two, something alike. Something in the set of the shoulders, the carriage of the head, the eyes, the characteristic of holding apart as a disinterested observer. Each had a kind of presence about him, Jay to a more intensified degree. And both leaned forward with the same half indolent, half watchful air.

Corporal Ross opened court, and Tudor called his thoughts back to the business in hand. But it was strange, he thought, while taking down notes in a crabbed black handwriting regarding the charging of Gustav Hanson and of Mike Olenski with the taking of beaver out of season and without a licence, it was strange how two men so utterly different could look so much alike. Each in his own way was powerful too. He got a fresh piece of paper to take down the evidence of Constable Hicks.

"It was on the night of the 8th of February. I found Bill Manydogs going into the Bear Claw poolroom garage with five beaver pelts on his toboggan."

The old native fidgeted in his chair, as though he would bolt. Jay laid a reassuring hand on his arm.

"The said Bill Manydogs having been arrested and tried, pleaded guilty, confessed, and was held for Court witness. On the night of February thirteenth, being the night mentioned by Manydogs as that on which pelts were to be trucked out of Bear Claw, I was coming by car on the road behind the truck owned by Gustav Hanson, driven by Mike Olenski."

Gus smoked calmly with a great show of indifference, while Mike bit his fingernails nervously. A half smile flickered over Jay's face. Tudor's pen travelled swiftly back and forth over the page with a scratching and spattering of ink.

"The truck stopped," Hicks continued, standing straight and grim. "There was a deep drift in which it had stalled. Since I was coming behind, I got out to see if I could help the driver. We shovelled around the back wheel, but it kept spinning. I reached into the truck and got an empty beer keg to place behind the wheel. The truck lurched back upon it, splintering the keg. Inside were two beaver pelts."

Sym and Romeo exchanged glances. Hicks looked at them, stopping to let Tudor finish writing the last sentence. Amused, Ross tilted back his chair.

"Upon searching the truck, I found forty pelts. They are here," he added, bending to pull the pile out from under the desk, and removing the sack. "Exhibit A."

Tudor duly examined the pelts with the keen eyes of the trappers upon him. Bill looked at them sadly, Jay with the keen interest of one who is evaluating them. Romeo and Mike watched somewhat enviously.

"After we finally got the truck going again," Hicks continued, "Olenski drove off. I was about to get back into the car. I saw some folded papers lying in the snow. They were perhaps tucked into the window of the truck and blew out when the door opened." Hicks held some papers out in front of Tudor. "Exhibit B. An account for Hinder's Hides and Raw Furs Co., Edmonton, for the sale of forty beaver pelts, and signed, 'Gustav Hanson.'"

Everyone was tense at this moment. Gus gave Mike a look of fury. Mike looked sick.

It was Bill who kissed the filthy dog-eared Bible next. Jay stood beside him, ready to interpret.

"He doesn't need an interpreter. He can speak and understand English," Hicks said sarcastically.

Tudor lifted his head, a pair of silver-rimmed glasses set far down on his nose.

"If he feels he can talk more fluently with an interpreter, by all means let him have one."

Bill at once addressed himself to Jay with a swift rush of Cree words. He flung his old knotted hands about, and moved his head and shoulders in strange gestures. The young man listened thoughtfully, then he turned to Tudor, and began in a husky voice.

"He says that the winter has been a hard one. And the children have been hungry too, and Bill had to do what the white man wanted, and bring the beaver pelts."

"This is all out of order!" Hicks said, jumping up impatiently. "Tell him to keep quiet until he's asked to speak."

Tudor leaned back, chewing the end of his pen.

"If he wants to get it off his chest, let him say it."

"I'll talk to them," Ross said quietly. Gradually he drew the story from them.

". . . It was Mike who made the deal with Bill," Jay said. "Bill was to bring in all the beaver he could, and hide them in the back of the truck in the garage. Mike would put them in the empty beer kegs and bring them to Bridgeville to send them out on the freight."

"He can't say things like that about me!" Mike shouted, jumping to his feet with clenched fists.

"Order in the court," Tudor said sternly. "You'll get your turn to speak."

"Sit down!" Hicks said, striding towards him.

"He says," Jay went on, looking only at Tudor, "that Gus was the real boss of the outfit. Gus would come out into the garage and ask him how many pelts there were."

When they had finished cross-examining Bill, he limped back to his place with his head in his hands, muttering in Cree. Romeo was called upon next. Tudor found he had a hard time keeping his mind on his writing. Romeo's long fangs, his slanting yellow eyes and snout-like nose, rather than his words, held Tudor spellbound. He thought it strange how a familiar face can become suddenly unfamiliar and different as though you were looking at it for the first time.

"I seen Gus myself, Thursday morning, putting beaver pelts into beer kegs in the garage," he was saying. "I was over there to borrow a wrench, and I see Gus and Mike—"

"You dirty dog!" Mike cried. "Why you go squealing?"

"Why you go taking my trucking trade?" Romeo snarled, narrowing his eyes to slits. "You don't work for yourself. You only work for Gus. Why do you take my trade?"

"Order! Order!" Hicks rumbled, and Mike subsided into a furious silence.

Dizzon passed his hand nervously over his bald head, and shrank further into his chair. Gus and Jay continued gazing ahead, aloof and expressionless. Bill bowed himself with weary sighs. Sym smiled, stretching his long legs and leaning his arm on the back of his chair. Tudor and Ross exchanged looks of subtle humorous understanding.

Cross-examined, Sym said cagily that he did not know what went on in the garage, since it was rented to Gus. He admitted only that he had once seen Obadiah with some beaver, but he did not inquire where the Indian got rid of them. Mike's face grew white with terror when Obadiah's name was mentioned.

Called to the desk, Gus looked disgustedly at the Bible, lifting it half way to his lips as he swore an oath.

"Do you plead guilty, or not guilty?" Ross asked him.

"Guilty. I admit everything." Yet he looked at them with a superior indifference, a tailored cigarette between his lips, his hand reaching into an inner pocket. "How much will the fine be?"

Mike was getting to his feet in triumphant relief.

"Wait!" Hicks turned to him in exasperation.

"Just a minute, Mike," Ross said pleasantly. "We've a lot to do yet."

After the big Swede had signed a complete confession, Olenski readily told his story, of how he had worked for Gus in the illicit beaver trade.

"Course, I only got a commission," he explained. "Gus done all the big shot work."

Hicks was staring at Dizzon's bald head.

"That guy got his commission too, eh?"

"He didn't have nothing to do with it!" Mike cried. "He's only my pal, come along with me. You got no goods on him."

"Oh—not needed to lie for you now."

Dizzon looked furtively at the floor.

"Sit down, everyone," Tudor said, shuffling through his pages of evidence. "Bill, your fine is twenty-five dollars or thirty days. Can you pay?"

Jay hastily took some bills from his wallet and gave them to the old man who pottered up to the desk with them. The two natives began preparing to leave.

"Mr. Hanson, you will be fined according to Statute No. —. Just a minute now—." Tudor began thumbing through a black book, peering over his glasses. "Yes, here it is. I find you guilty of trafficking in beaver out of season without being licensed so to do, pursuant to Section 97E of the Game Act; and fine you one hundred dollars and costs, or three months—. That will be one hundred and twenty dollars."

The room became very silent. Gus opened his wallet and counted out twelve ten dollar bills, his face expressionless. Tudor put the money into the desk and turned again to his book.

"Mike," he said, "for you it's twenty-five dollars or thirty days."

"But I'm not guilty."

"You were implicated in the crime."

Mike looked distraught among the moving figures of the men who were heaving themselves into their coats.

"I haven't got any money!" he cried out, looking from one to another. Gus was following the two natives out of the door. The bitter night's cold swept into the room, cleansing it of stale odours. Romeo grinned, and Dizzon looked helpless. "Sym—"

Ashley shook his head.

"It's the coop for me!" Mike said bitterly as Gustav's truck roared away. "He gets away, and I go to the coop."

"I'm sorry, Mike." Tudor rose from the desk.

When Romeo's truck had moved off, Ross smiled, jingling his keys.

"Breakfast at eight, and then the train out," he said mildly, following Mike to the prison cell. "It'll pass, Mike, like no time."

2

At Bear Claw, Jay and Tudor got down off the back of the truck, stiff with cold. Bill tumbled out of the cab in high spirits, doing a kind of war dance in the snow in front of the hotel in the glare of the headlights of the truck. Sym and Dizzon paid their share of the gas, and bade the others good-night, disappearing down the alley.

"Where are you going now?" Tudor asked his companion, as Romeo's sour face appeared at the open door of the truck, and the two men felt for their wallets.

"Bill wants to go to Obadiah's and show them he's free. We're staying the night there." Jay handed the driver fifty cents and turned to go.

"Just a minute, Jay," said Tudor. "Wait till I give this fellow his pound of flesh."

"Mighty light for a pound," said Romeo, tossing the coin up in the air, and catching it in his cold bare hand.

Tudor followed Jay to the back of the truck.

"Come and have supper with me."

The motor of the truck roared, the back wheels throwing snow into their faces. Bill joined them to get out of the way of the vehicle, which moved off, leaving them in the grey starlight. Tudor stamped his feet, huddling himself deeper into his parka.

"I'll be seeing you at Obadiah's," Jay told Bill, and they parted.

The town was in darkness, completely silent. Every step the men took made crunching noises in the hard-packed snow. Folkes led the way down a side street, through some bush to his home, a snug log house of three rooms. The entrance led into a kitchen full of peaceful warmth as the two men came in from the bitter cold. Tudor lit the coal-oil lamp, whose light revealed the large stove and the steaming kettle, the kitchen table with a gay oil-cloth, the cabinet with piles of ill-matched and various-sized plates. Jay stood quietly in a corner, while his host began replenishing the fire.

"Almost on the boil," he remarked, lifting the lid of the kettle. "I'll just put some coffee on, and we'll have supper in no time."

He took off his parka, and washed at the wash-stand near the stove. Clean towels hung on towel racks above it, and a good-sized mirror in a fancy silver frame gleamed on the wall between the racks. Everything looked freshly scrubbed.

"Take off your things and make yourself at home," Tudor invited. He reached for the frying-pan hanging on a nail behind the stove. "I hope you like sausages, for sausages it is tonight."

Jay smiled a little, slowly undoing his white coat, looking intently at everything. Tudor set the table in the next room, covering the heavy wine table-cloth with a clean white one, and bringing out some large blue cups from a cupboard in the corner. In the centre of the table the soft light of an oil lamp with a daintily flowered china shade showed the walls lined with book-shelves full of books, and several model ships hanging from the ceiling. There were two or three well-worn and comfortable easy chairs, as well as four stiff-backed dining room chairs of ancient but substantial make. Jay made up the fire in the heater, looking over the place with a kind of wonderment.

After a good meal of bread and sausages, and cups of strong coffee, the men retired to the arm-chairs for a peaceful smoke.

"Tell me—" Tudor leaned back with his hands crossed under his head, his feet dangling over an elegant footstool with carved legs, "Jay, did you ever think of using your ability to interpret? I mean in getting some kind of job. It seems to me that a fellow who can speak fluently in Cree, Chyp, English, French—and you're really quite eloquent—" He paused, looking through the pipe smoke at his companion.

Jay took his limp brown cigarette from his lips, holding it lightly in his well-shaped hands. His every attitude was one of grace. He studied the ash-tray with half-closed black eyes. There was something bitter about the expression of his mouth, something still and closed about his dark face.

"I did think of it." He flicked some ashes off the end of his cigarette into the ash-tray. "But I've been to the Outside, and now I know what I am. When I am a boy in the bush, I don't know it. Only sometimes, I feel it, just a little. But I don't understand. When I go Outside, then I really know. I am a breed. A dog."

"You're very bitter," Tudor said sadly. "So you hate us white men?"

"No. No. It's just—I see both sides. We are sometimes, I know, like children. But it must be wrong that we are dying, and full of disease."

"Yet you yourself are exceptionally sound."

"That is only because of my grandmother," Jay said with swift pride. "She knows the old Indian ways. She gets the poplar butter and the syrup. We are weaned to meat. Now, a breed, he doesn't want to be an Indian. He wants to be a white man, and he doesn't know how. And he is, anyway, a hunter."

Tudor looked at the young man with wise kind eyes.

"What would you say is the answer, Jay? What should be done about the half-breeds?"

"I don't know. Only I think in myself many times, everything they try to do for us, it is the wrong thing. If a breed did not have to be—a dog."

Jay's face twisted as though with great pain.

"Oh, it is too bad!" Tudor said to him. "You could be a valuable man."

"Yesterday I brought in six wolf pelts, two females, four males. And they give me money, and bounty. The wolves, they don't know I'm a breed."

Tudor sat up suddenly. "Where did you get that name, Baptiste?"

"I don't know. Isaiah says it was my grandfather's name. He never tells me who my father is. Perhaps he doesn't know. He says I'm just one of the orphans grandmother took in to raise. She's raised about five like that, all older than me. Martha too, before Isaiah married her."

Folkes knocked out his pipe into the ash-tray. "Why don't you stay the night here? It'll be cold going to Obadiah's, and crowded when you get there. I could put you up."

"You mean you'd have a trashy breed in your house?"

"Jay, there are white men I know that I wouldn't have in my house."

The young man smiled, and the smile lit up his dark face like a lamp turned on inside.

"I cannot stay. Only because of the old man. I think I better be with him. He gets in trouble so easy."

When he had put on his beautiful white coat, and pulled the embroidered parka over his dark head, he held out his hand to Tudor.

"You are a real white man," he said. "Wherever we are, I am your friend."

3

Bill Manydogs lay on his bed, snoring, deep in slumber, while Martha and her two little boys slept on a bed in another corner, breathing heavily. The cabin was lit only by the light from the low burning logs on the fireplace, in front of which Mrs. Waters sat smoking her pipe, and looking into the fire. Jay lay on the floor beside her, his hands under his head. He talked quietly in Cree.

"I got money for my wolf pelts," he said. "Some for the police, and some for you." He stretched out one hand, and put some bills into her lap. "That is for you, Grandmother. For something you need. Not for Martha and the boys, but for you."

The old woman took the money into her misshapen hands. The light from the fire was reflected in her eyes, making them seem full of bright flames. Jay rolled over, leaning his chin in his hands, and his elbows on the floor. In this attitude, and in the firelight, he looked strangely young and boyish. The old woman gently touched his dark hair.

"Grandmother, will you tell me something?"

She took the pipe from her mouth.

"What shall I tell you?"

He looked up at her. "Tell me how I was born."

Mrs. Waters took a stick and stirred the fire. She said at last,

"You were born here, in this house. In winter. A night like this."

The flames leaped, licking the dry logs, but blackness clung in the corners of the cabin. The sleepers did not stir.

"The wolves were howling, and Isaiah's dogs kept barking."

"But who was my mother?"

"Simone."

"And her father's name was Baptiste?"

"He was a Frenchman, and he played the fiddle. Simone's mother was Cree."

Jay leaned on his elbow, looking up at his grandmother. The lines in her face were almost like folds. She was old. Perhaps she had forgotten. He waited, watching the firelight play on her twisted hands.

"Was Isaiah here?" he asked softly.

"Yes. He was cutting wood. The axe went into his foot through his moccasin. It was very bad. All winter he was with me. Bill went on the trap-line."

"And Simone came here?"

"We saw her at Treaty when Isaiah was fiddling for the dance. When he saw her, he was going to cut the logs to build a house. But he did not tell her that. He played the fiddle for five nights and watched her dancing, and he did not speak to her. And then she was gone."

Outside, the dogs began to howl dismally. The logs of the cabin creaked with the cold.

"It was a winter night when she came here," the old woman said. "Isaiah's two dogs barked. And then she came in. You were born that night."

"And Simone died?" Jay asked, looking into the glowing embers.

"She was so young, so young. And weak. My son named you when he heard the jay in the trees."

"Grandmother, who was my father?" He sat up, imploring her to tell him.

"I do not know," she said, drawing her blanket about her shoulders. "I do not know."

"Some white man?" said Jay bitterly. "Does Isaiah know?"

"I do not know; but Simone came here, to us, when you were born."

Jay lay down before the fire again, his hands under his head. Mrs. Waters took the money into her hands, counting it by the fitful light.

"You are good to an old woman."

He was silent. The long-drawn howling of the dogs outside was a heart-breaking sound. Bill began tossing about, moaning in his sleep. Then quietness settled upon the house again.

"Your father would have had a good son." Mrs. Waters filled her pipe, lighting it with a chip which she kindled from the glowing logs.

The young man smiled.

"I have a good grandmother."

The pleasant aroma of the tobacco and of the burning logs filled the warm air. Presently only the old woman was awake, smoking peacefully, gazing into the dying fire.

Chapter XXIV

Didn't figure you'd come back," Dizzon muttered. "Not after such a long time. Sure was a surprise when Sym told me what your letter said."

"You took my letter to Sym?" Mike asked, almost menacingly.

"I can't read. Remember?"

"I'd forgot. But Sym!"

The two men were reclining on the grass, one on each side of a campfire. Supported on a green willow stick, a smoke-blackened tin filled with water, hung over the bright flames. Among the bushes, a rude shelter of spruce boughs and poles was barely visible. All round, the wooded country seemed to press upon them with its remote loneliness. In the sky, large puffy clouds tinted with the vivid colours of the sunset, were beginning to take on the blues and greys of evening.

"Where you been all this time?" Dizzon asked, looking across at his companion.

Mike sat up to rearrange the burning logs. He looked unkempt and dirty, and his mouth had a nervous twitching.

"Oh, I worked out round Edmonton after I got out of the coop. Got me some money, and took up this here homestead."

"Lonesome for the bush?" Dizzon asked, moving to escape the smoke which had changed direction with a puff of wind.

"It's no good Outside. It's better here." Mike made a gesture with his hand, indicating the acres about them. There was a fierce pride in his ugly face. "Not far from here where my old man used to be. I was always wanting to be back on the farm, Dizz."

Dizzon put a dirty finger on one side of his large hooked nose, and said, "Know all what's went on since you was gone?"

"Course not. What did you think I wanted to see you for? Come on now, tell me everything." Mike leaned on his elbow, watching the other man.

"They found the still, couple weeks after you went."

"Dizz! Why didn't you take it away? I counted on you!" Mike cried angrily. "What a pal you turned out to be!"

"Couldn't help it," Dizzon muttered, keeping his head down. "Hicks, he watched me. Every place I was, Hicks he was there too. If I empty a coke-box at Wo Ling's, I see Hicks looking at me from a booth. If I load a truck at Wong's, Hicks looks up at me from under a fender. I couldn't get to the still nohow."

"How'd they find it?" Mike asked, biting his thumb nail.

Dizzon began to laugh nervously, pounding the ground in front of him with his fist.

"Funniest thing I ever know! Brother Conrad found it, that's who. Brother Conrad."

Mike laughed shortly. "Come on! What happened?"

Dizzon sat up, choking back his laughter.

"Well, Brother Conrad, he's going to get all the sin out of Bear Claw, see? He tells us so, shaking his fist. Well, snow's melting this day, and Brother Conrad, he sees Sym Ashley on horseback taking a short-cut from Bridgeville over to Bear Claw. So Brother Conrad starts through the bush, following, and he gets lost. He trips, so he tells the

263

police. And he says, 'I've been a sinner once, a great sinner,' he says, 'and I knows that smell. Moonshine!' he says, 'and this here's got to stop.'"

"What'd they do, Hicks and them?" Mike asked anxiously.

His friend passed a hand over his forehead, and his laughter was gone.

"They find out it's poisoned and no good moonshine. And Hicks, he busts over to the pool hall and collars Sym Ashley. And he says this here still must be Sym's, on account of nobody else uses that short-cut. Sym says he don't know nothing about no still."

"I hid it good," Mike grunted. "What happened then?"

"Well, Hicks, he don't believe Sym, and they get mad. Sym, he says if Hicks don't believe him, let him find out who's been using all the sugar round here. Hicks, he says that's a good idea."

"Squealer!" Mike snarled, starting up. "Sym Ashley's good as squealed on me. He seen me get two hundred pounds down at McIvor's that day we was in Bridgeville, blast him! And the police found out?"

"Might be they never would of found out, only the sugar wasn't paid for. Hicks, he goes to McIvor's at Bridgeville, and soon's the old lady seen him, she comes running out from the counter, and she says, 'When's that Mike Olenski coming back? Went off owing me a mighty big bill,' she says. 'Two hundred pounds of sugar he never paid for, and a heap of other things too.'"

"The dirty rat! I always paid her some time, when I got it. Lots of them don't."

"Searched the shack, too, Hicks did," Dizzon went on. "Found that bottle Obadiah drank out of. She was right smack in the middle of the table where you left her."

"Dizz! Couldn't you of done *nothing* for a fellow?"

"I didn't know you left the bottle," Dizzon whined. "Don't prove nothing anyways."

"Dizz," Mike whispered, "they'll hook me sure."

Dizzon looked up at him.

"It ain't so long they know about the sugar. Hicks, he goes all up and down the line before he thinks of McIvor's. Lots of people makes moonshine. And anyways, he ain't got the goods on you. How'll he know you gave Obadiah the moonshine? Dead men, they don't talk."

"Sym knows," Mike said, very low.

A sudden breeze fanned the flames, so that they swept upon a fresh dry log with a dry crackling. There was a rushing sound of leaves in the high branches above, while a damp evening coolness stole into their little glade. Dizzon moved closer to the fire, but Mike continued to sit quietly, staring out into the shadowy trees.

"Sym's all right," Dizzon said at last cautiously.

Mike sprang to his feet with an oath, and stood looking down over the flames at the other man. His hair was scattered about in untidy locks, and thick reddish stubble stood out on his jutting chin.

"Don't be sore, Mike. What are you sore about?"

"You rat!" Mike stormed. "Took my letter to Sym. Now he knows where I am!"

"He won't say nothing, Mike. And Hicks would of thought of the sugar himself."

"Yeah, I know." Mike clenched and unclenched his hands. "But I been thinking and thinking. All the time I was in the coop, I was thinking."

"It's bad for a man to be thinking like that."

"I never got a break in my life," Mike said bitterly. "All because of Ashleys. Since they came into this country, nothing's been right for us. Sym, and that woman, Lina." Mike spat into the fire. "Took the hayland, she did, right as soon as she came into the country. Set Isaiah Waters after my old man with a shot-gun. Only nobody gets the goods on Lina. Too smart, she is. Then when Sym comes back, she up and takes the farm too, off my old man. Got in there quick when the lease was due. So then we got to go to town. You think I get a break with Gus? Worked me worse'n a dog for only a few bucks pay. Hardly can get even work clothes with the money."

"He's the devil to work for. I couldn't stick him." Dizzon raked at the fire with a stick.

"Then I got to get money some way," Mike said, "when I know I'm going to get stuck about the beaver. And then Sym butts in. He sees Obadiah getting drunk on my bottle. Then he plays a tricky game and wins all the money off me so I got to go to the coop."

"He ain't never told." Dizzon sounded hopeful.

Mike sat down by the fire again.

"He won't give me a break, you'll see. He'll be waiting to see me turn up, and squeal on me. I never squealed on nobody. I never squealed on you, Dizz."

"He won't squeal, Mike."

"He's got me!" Mike said. "He's got me! We have another fight, and he'll squeal."

"You can hide out here," Dizzon suggested.

"Yeah, nobody can find me here. I know this country like my right hand. Every tree. I trapped here when I was a kid. Like to see Hicks and them find me here." Mike glanced around, eyeing a half-hidden trail leading into a grove of spruce. "But what's the good, Dizz! I want to have a homestead. Go to town sometimes and have a beer, without Sym Ashley to tell me off. I don't know. That guy—his wife couldn't stand him. My mother stood by my old man, and he was a heller! Get drunk, and he'd up with a horse-whip or anything. But sober, he was all right. A woman could stand him. But Sym. Drunk, he's OK. Sober, no. Snuck up on me and Obadiah like a snake. Pulls a tricky game with a new deck of cards."

"Lucky Strike."

"And that stuck-up Poppy. Acted like I was a lizard when the slides was showing. Thinks she's too good for me."

Dizzon moved to take the tin from the fire, for the water was boiling over with a steamy sizzling on the flames. He took a package of tea from a grub box on the ground.

"And at that there trial," Mike went on, "Sym wouldn't help me. I says, 'Sym,' I says, when they tells me about the coop. I couldn't ask Gus. I slipped up on the job and lost the papers. But Sym, he could of paid. He wins all the money off me and Obadiah. He could pay twenty-five bucks to get me out of the coop. He shakes his head and goes out."

"Where's the mugs? I'll make some tea. Then we can go fishing. Fish are running good right about now."

Mike chewed his nails. "I get all the tough breaks."

"What are you going to do?" Dizzon asked fearfully, putting a handful of tea into the hot water.

"Dunno. But keep me in the know, Dizz, where he's at, and what he's doing. If he can hold the whip over me, I can watch his trail too."

"He's went to Tudor's tonight. Heard him tell Romeo to see to things while he was gone."

The men sat in silence for a while. Then Mike said,

"You never told nobody where I'm at? Just Sym?"

"I can't read," said Dizzon. "Just Sym."

"Maybe I could get away." Mike dipped a tin mug into the pail of tea. "Mackenzie valley or somewhere way down north. But I ain't got the jack. Got any you could lend me?"

"Guess not, Mike."

Mike swallowed a mouthful of scalding tea.

"Well, keep me in the know, anyways."

Chapter XXV

1

Come on, Poppy, finish up them eggs," Lina urged. "Benny, get your sister another cup of coffee off the stove there, will you?"

It was Friday evening, and Poppy sat at the kitchen table having a meal after the long ride home on horseback from Bear Claw. Benny had curled up in the chair beside her, nibbling a cookie. But he scrambled down quickly when his mother spoke, and brought the big grey pot, carefully pouring out a cup of coffee. The girl smiled at him as he pattered back in his bare feet over the linoleum. Under the bright light of the gas lamp, there was such happiness in her look that Lina stopped sewing, eyeing her speculatively. She was thinking how secretive Poppy was, never bursting out with excited talk about her doings as Olga, for instance, did.

"How was that dinner party at Tudor's?" Lina asked, licking her finger to make a knot at the end of her thread. "He told me he was having you and Olga over."

"It was last night," Poppy answered eagerly. "I—I liked it fine." But as she spoke, she felt a sinking sensation within her. Would her mother like it if she knew all about it? And how difficult it was to say how she felt.

"Who all was there? Just you and Olga?"

"No." The girl looked up uneasily. "Mother, Sym was there. And Tommy." She paused, thinking how hard it was to explain, to make it all sound as right as it really was. "It wasn't the pool-hall, Mother."

Lina arranged a patch on the back of a shirt of Benny's in her lap.

"That's all right. Well, won't you tell us about it? What was it like?" There was a sharp edge to her voice.

"Where did everybody sit?" Benny said, curling his bare feet under him as he sat down beside her.

Poppy set down her cup, with a warm smile for her brother.

"Well, Tudor was like at this end of the table, and Sym at that end. I sat here, next to Sym, and Olga beside me, and Tommy over there, looking at us." She nearly added, "And I felt grown-up, sort of." But the thought of how her mother might laugh at that, stopped her.

2

Tommy brought in a dish of steaming stew from the kitchen and set it on the table.

"There's something about lamplight."

"Oh, it's such a pretty lamp, Mr. Folkes." Olga tilted her dark head. She had pink bows in her hair, and the older men smiled at her approvingly. But the boy watched Poppy. He seated himself opposite her, his clear honest eyes on her face. She looked down shyly at her plate.

"What did everybody say, Poppy?" Benny asked.

Lina paused in her basting, while the girl leaned her elbows on the table.

"It was nice. Olga, she talked about books. Mr. Folkes has all kinds of books, just everywhere you look. And Olga kept on looking at this one and that one, and taking out books and putting them back."

"Was Mr. Folkes mad?" Benny asked. "Heck, at school we can't look at books. Miss Featherstone, she gets mad and throws chalk."

"No, Tudor wasn't mad," Poppy said. "He talked about ships. He's got ships hanging from the ceiling, and he took Tommy over and showed him."

"Ships! Gee whizz!" Benny looked up in wonderment.

"What about you?" Lina asked, glancing up from her sewing. "Didn't you say something too?"

"Yes. I—I talked to Sym." Poppy thought, "But Mother will want to know all about it, and how can I tell her, 'I made friends with my father, and I like him, oh, so much!'?" Aloud she went on, "After supper, Sym and I went out to the kitchen, and made the tea ready. We had after-dinner tea, Mother. Tudor said it should be coffee, but they all liked tea better." *Making the tea, that was the safest thing to tell.*

"And what did you and Sym talk about?" her mother asked relentlessly, wondering with some resentment if Poppy were trying to hide something.

"Oh, school, and Benny—."

"Now Sym, you can brew up a good cup of tea; I know you can." Tudor pushed his chair back from the table, throwing his napkin down in an untidy heap. "Go and help him, Poppy. You know, the woman's touch. Like to see my ships, Tommy? That's a mighty fine model right there."

Poppy hesitated at the doorway. Olga held a heavy book on her arm, and was lost in some treatise on the Greek wars.

"You're not shy of me, are you, Poppy?" Sym asked from the kitchen.

"Oh, no." She went to the cupboard and counted out cups and saucers onto the kitchen table.

"How's school and all that?" Sym put a dry stick of kindling in the stove under the kettle.

"I don't like it very much. The sugar bowl's empty."

"Up here in this tin. How's Benny?"

"Oh, Benny's such a good friend to me, Sym, I miss him so much."

"Poppy, couldn't we be friends, too, you and me?"

She looked up into his hard face with its sad lines.

"I'd like that." Somehow, she found herself swallowing back tears.

"The kettle's singing." Sym lifted it from the fire. "Is the tea in the pot?"

"Sym."

He filled the tea-pot and set the tea to steep.

"What is it?"

"Did you have to go away that last time?"

They looked at each other with troubled eyes.

"Yes, I did, Poppy. I had to do it. It was better for you to have Lina bring you up alone, than for us to be fighting over you. I know it was hard on her, Poppy. But my kind of life wouldn't do for her, or for you either. You got a good clean bringing up."

"Mother's good, Sym. She is. Everything's nice at home. We got a sink, and everything. Only—"

"You need me too, Poppy," he pleaded. "I could talk to you here in town so you wouldn't be so lonely."

5

"Did you say I was a good boy?" Benny demanded.

"Oh, yes!" Then catching her mother's glance, she added quickly, "And Tommy wiped the dishes. I washed, and Olga put away."

Lina smiled, breaking off a fresh piece of thread.

"Tommy's a nice, clean-looking boy; Gus done a good job by him."

"Mother!" Benny interrupted suddenly. "I forgot to put my pigeons in. The cat'll get them!"

"Land's sake, son. You do give anybody a turn. Go and put them in, then. And Benny! How come you tear all your clothes across the back?"

"Getting the ball under the fence."

"You tear another shirt, and you can go to school ragged."

His gay laugh rang out as he skipped across the floor.

"Come and help me, Poppy! How can I reach? I can't reach to the roof."

"Go ahead," Lina sighed. "He'll never get to bed if you don't help him."

Poppy ran out after the little boy into the coolness of the night. A few large stars, cold and brilliant, shone in the sky. The light from the window glowed warmly. In the twilight, the wild roses could not be seen, but their sweet perfume filled the air. Benny caught her by the hand and led her down the path to the granary where two white birds were roosting on the dark roof.

"We got to put them inside and shut the door," Benny told her. "That blamed orange cat, she got my other bird."

The creatures stirred and cooed softly when Poppy put her hands out to take them off their perch. She lifted them carefully down to Benny one at a time.

"Don't they feel nice in your hands? Poppy, Jay's home. He's up at Snakeshead Hill."

"Benny!" She hooked up the door with shaking fingers.

"He's going to Treaty. Amos and Sammy's going too, and me."

"Did Mother say you could?"

"Not yet. She don't even know about Jay."

They walked slowly towards the house.

"Shall I tell him something?" he whispered.

She stopped for a moment in the darkness with her hand on his shoulder.

"No, Benny. No. And don't tell anything to anybody. Come on, let's go in now."

"By the way, did you bring the coffee and sugar?" Lina asked when they entered.

Her daughter looked up in blank dismay.

"Poppy! Why do you always forget things?"

"Mother, I'm sorry."

"Bring in a pail of fresh drinking water, will you? I'm that parched for a cool drink. And Benny, off to bed with you!"

Lina took some torn coveralls from the kitchen line while Poppy went out as silently as she had come in. Like an Indian, her mother thought, shaking her head over her mending. Later, she watched the girl doing the dishes, her eyes shrewd and thoughtful.

"Poppy," she began abruptly. "I want you to tell me something. You seen Jay at all this winter? The other day I heard tell he was in town one time at a dance."

"He was in town," the girl answered casually. "I did see him, Mother. Everybody did. He was at the Valentine dance. He danced with Olga. You know about the trial. Old Bill got mixed up in it, Tudor says, and Jay went there. He's got a woman in the north, so they say." Poppy took the kettle from the stove and carefully scalded the heavy white plates. "I forgot to tell you," she went on rapidly, "at the dinner party, Tudor told our fortunes in the tea-cups. I'm supposed to be taking a trip, and Olga's working in mud to her knees."

"Seems like it was quite a party!"

"And Tommy asked me to go to Treaty with him. That is, if it's all right with you."

"It's perfectly all right with me if you go to Treaty with Tommy. I'm glad to see you taking up with a decent man. When I think of that Dizzon and Mike in town! By the way, what's happened to Mike since the trial, anyways?"

"Nobody round town hears about him."

"Poppy, there's something else I want to talk to you about."

The girl took a dish towel from the line and turned to her mother.

"I seen Tommy in town, and I talked to him." Lina slashed at a ragged trouser-leg with the shears. "I figgered I had a right to know why a young man would be so thick with my daughter. Tommy could see that; you don't need to look so mad. Any decent man would see why a mother would want to know. And Tommy told me right out his intentions is to marry you some day, though he never said nothing to you about it yet."

"Mother! You asked him that?"

"I've every right to know, what with you just seventeen, and miles off in that dump of a town. And I must say I like Tommy just fine."

"But Mother, I'm too young yet to be thinking of getting married."

Lina looked thoughtfully at her daughter.

"Oh, I don't know. I was only eighteen. And you keep beefing about going on to school. What d'you figger on doing next year if you don't get married? You don't want to go out working for some crank of a woman, do you?"

Poppy wrung the dish towel in her hands.

"But I'm not sure if I care about him. I mean, I don't know if we'd be happy."

"Most marriages aren't happy," her mother told her. "You may as well take your chance when it comes."

"Don't you think the folks round here are happy?"

"I was speaking of decent white folks! You wouldn't want to end up married to one of the Panachuks would you? And what else is there in this country but breeds? At least with Tommy you'd have a chance for a decent life, with everything paid for and money in the bank. He's a nice clean boy with a chance to get ahead. Well, what do you think of it?"

"I don't know just yet. Mother, couldn't I just stay home next year? I could help you."

"Mm, you'd find it pretty dull here after living in town. Anyways, you'd have to make up your mind one way or another."

Poppy turned back to the dishes in silence.

"Well, you see you treat him nice," Lina warned. "You'll not find a better man than him."

6

Sym Ashley was surprised to hear a knock at the door. He sat alone, playing solitaire under the light of a green-shaded lamp at the back of the pool hall. The clock had just struck the hour of eleven, and in the little town this Sunday night, there was no sound of horse or wagon, or even of footsteps. When the knock came, Sym got up, threw his cigarette butt on the floor, and ground it out under his heel. Taking an imposing bunch of keys from his pocket, he got the door open with much rattle and noise. From out of the darkness, his daughter slipped inside.

"Poppy!"

"Sym, I must talk to you."

He clanged shut the heavy door, and took her gently by the arm.

"Come in, over here by the light where I can see you."

"I shouldn't have come like this. It's so late."

"I like you to come any time."

He sat down opposite her, full of concern.

"Sym, I don't know what to do."

He reached for a fresh cigarette from his pocket, lighting it deliberately, waiting for her to go on.

"Sym, Mother's been talking to Tommy. She jumped him about going out with me, and he—he told her his intention was to marry me."

Her father put a hand on her shoulder. "Well?"

"*How nice he is,*" she thought. "*I should have come to him before, ever so often.*" Aloud, she said, "But Sym, I don't know whether I want to. And I just don't want to go on to school. Sym, I can't stand it." She looked forlornly up at him. "I just don't know what I want."

"Are you sure?"

She looked away from him.

"And Mother doesn't want me at home."

"Nonsense. Lina isn't going to make you marry some man you don't want."

"She thinks I ought to marry Tommy while I have the chance. She doesn't want me at home," Poppy insisted.

"Why not?"

She said slowly, "Mother's afraid that if I stay home, Jay will come back, and I might be seeing him again." She was surprised at the words as she said them. She saw her father's concern for her.

"Poppy, life's much of a gamble, but there's some chances it don't pay to take. I don't aim to jaw you, but Tommy's a swell kid. You don't half know him yet. Tudor done lots in raising him. Couldn't you come back to school just for another year?"

"I hate school."

"I know. But Poppy, maybe in another year things'll look different again. You'll grow up some, and you'll change."

"Will I, Sym? Do you really think so?"

"Of course you will."

"I get so homesick, Sym. Mother says that's just babyish."

"Well, I'm here. You can come and talk to me whenever you get lonesome."

"Sym, you're wonderful to come to. I feel so much better. I wish I'd come before, only I never felt like I knew you."

"But what are you going to do?"

"I'll think about going back to school. Maybe it wouldn't be so bad."

"You could get a better place to stay," her father suggested. "There's that Mrs. Crossfield just moved into town. She's a real nice woman, and Tudor was saying she thinks she'd like to take a couple of school girls for the winter so she can work in the Post Office."

"That would be nice, if Olga and me can both go."

"Well, young lady, it's high time you were getting along. I'll just step down the lane with you. It's mighty dark." He took out his keys.

"D'you mind if I come in again some time this week?" she asked timidly.

He took her arm as they went out into the street. "You must come. Now don't disappoint me. I'll be waiting. Hm, black as the ace of spades tonight."

They heard the whistle of a train in the distance, and the heavy sound of the approaching locomotive.

"There's our new freight train," Sym remarked. "Goes with the new station they're building. We're to get freight now twice a week instead of once. Quite a metropolis, Bear Claw is."

They crossed the shadowed lane to the back door of the shop. Behind the heavily curtained glass portion of the door, a dim light was burning. At the sound of their footsteps, Mrs. Howe drew back the curtain, opened the door, and exclaimed in disapproval: "Of all the hours to be coming home, I do declare!"

"Quite all right, Ma'am. It's only her dad that's bringing her."

"What do you mean, frightening a body?" the woman asked in a kindlier tone as the girl went inside. "What this younger generation is coming to is beyond me!"

"Don't be too hard on my girl," said Sym. "Not but what I don't think you're doing a good job with her. You are, and I thank you for it. Well, good-night."

As Mrs. Howe watched him go off into the dark, she shivered. "Black as the inside of a squaw's pocket," she muttered, closing the door with a bang.

Sym went slowly down the unlighted street, thinking deeply about this unexpected visit from his daughter. He could hear men shouting at the station where they unloaded. Lights bobbed about there, but not a star shone in the sky, and the clouds seemed to hang heavily close. At the door of the pool hall, he got out his keys, but the door swung inwards before he had turned the key in the lock. A gleam of light from the back shone on his face and then flicked out. There was a groping on the floor.

"Who is it?" Sym asked, moving towards the light switch.

The green-shaded light snapped on. There was no one in sight. The till stood open. Sym looked about him, warily. Then, for just a split second, he saw on the floor under the pool table, the shadowed ugly face of Mike Olenski. He had a drawn revolver in his hand. A shot sounded, and Sym crumpled where he stood. At once, Mike scrambled to his feet, and picking up a ball from the pool table, flung it at the lamp, smashing it with a crash and the sound of breaking glass. Dashing to the back door, he escaped into the night. A few minutes later, the whistle blew, the bell clanged, and the freight train moved forward, gathering speed and momentum, moment by moment.

Chapter XXVI

A long the road between Bear Claw and Bridgeville, an unusual amount of traffic moved in each direction. Cars and trucks veered to pass slow-plodding teams; horse-back riders pulled shying horses into the ditch. Clouds of dust rose under the turning wheels, and from the heavy hoofs. The little cemetery between the two towns lay quiet again under the June sky. There would be time for grass to grow over the new dark mound now heaped with dying bouquets of flowers.

Lina turned her team to the road. Her rig rattled lightly over the bumps.

"Well, I done my duty. Sit still, son! Quit wriggling, or you'll go flying head-first onto them rocks in a minute."

Benny sat up straight. "Wasn't there lots of people!"

"People! we'll be eating dust clear to town. Now what's this coming? Get over, Racer! Steady, Sal!"

She pulled sharply on the lines as Racer reared in the traces and Sal laid back her ears. A huge red truck roared past them with honking horn, while a boy sitting beside the driver put his head out of the window yelling "Yippee!"

"Blasted fools!" Lina yelled. In the choking mist of dust she spoke to her horses above the noise of the retreating truck. They stood trembling. Benny laughed aloud. "What are you laughing at?" Grinning, she cuffed him on the side of the head. "You're some help, you are! Racer! Sal! Get going!"

At Bear Claw, Lina found a place to tie the horses at the hitching post.

"Come on, Benny. You can make yourself useful and carry some things for me. Bring them old shoes of mine out of the rig. I got to take them to Tudor to get fixed." She brushed some of the dust from her rusty black skirt.

"Can't we go to Wong's?" he demanded, screwing up his freckled nose.

"With that dirty face?"

"So is yours."

Lina smiled at him, taking a grimy rag from her sweater pocket.

"Sure is a crowd in town," she remarked, wiping her forehead. "A person will never get waited on."

On the board walk, people stared at the woman and the boy, and fell back in silence to let them pass. Lina looked straight ahead, striding with long steps, while Benny skipped beside her, holding a shoe in each hand. Wong's store buzzed with activity.

"Where's that plunger you was ordering for me?" Lina asked, calling above the heads of the people Wong dealt with at the counter.

He glanced up, bewildered. Then he smiled, a trifle uncertainly.

"Oh, Miz Ashley! No come yet. I order. No come yet!"

"What d'you mean, not come yet? That order was going to go out two weeks ago. It don't take that long. Did you order it?" She shouldered her way among the rough customers to the counter, glaring down on the little Chinese storekeeper. "I'd of been a heap quicker if I had of sent from Radski's at Bridgeville, 'stead of waiting on you."

"I sent, I sent!" Wong protested.

"Sometimes it takes weeks." Sven Jensen spoke up from the crowd in an angry tone. "Some of them parts come clear from the East."

Pete Panachuk thumped the counter with his fist.

"Miz Ashley, dem tings takes time!"

"Who's asking you? When d'you figger it'll come?" she asked, watching Wong's nervous fingers tying up a parcel.

"Next train for sure!"

"It better be! Got any wire screening?" She took a slip of paper from her pocket. "I got a few things here I need."

Wong rang up cash with furious vigour.

"Miz Ashley! People—wait!"

"I'll need some brown sugar and some of these here dried apples, too."

The men about her exchanged angry looks. Ek lifted the lid of the unlighted heater and spat disgustedly.

"Now just who does she think she is?"

Benny wandered about, tapping the soles of Lina's shoes together. Time after time, he returned to the candy counter where Rose Wong weighed out scoops of gum-drops and licorice from the coloured mounds behind the glass. The boy watched women good-naturedly paying money for bags of sweets, and handing them out to their children. Even a big tough-looking man, unshaven and dirty, said to Rose, "Here, Lady. Gimme some of them." And he tucked a bag of licorice into his grocery box before carting it outside.

"Benny!" The boy heard the impatient voice of his mother, and ran to her through the crowd to the door.

"Mother! Couldn't we get some—"

"Candy? I should say not! You got the idea my pockets are plumb lined with pennies. There's berries on trees. Eat them. Hurry up now, we got to catch Tudor before he goes off home." She loaded him up with parcels and took the shoes out of his hands.

As they stepped outside, Gustav tramped towards them on the board walk.

"Mr. Hanson!" Lina moved a few steps away from the doorway,

smiling at him. "I been wanting to see you. Benny, dump them things in the wagon, will you?"

Gustav waited, his hands in his pockets, his sleepy eyes on the woman's dust-grimed face.

"What's this all about?"

"'Bout time you and me had a talk, I should say."

His mouth tightened grimly.

"That so?"

"With your boy and my girl fixing to get married—"

Gus shoved back his hat, no expression on his big face. "It's their affair."

"Well, I aim to treat the thing fair and square to help them get started."

Gustav came nearer, thrusting forward his big head.

"You don't need to worry I won't treat my boy right. He's city educated, and I'm giving him the best quarter in the country. With buildings. Needs a little fixing, but it's as good as that filly of yours has ever known."

"Takes more than land and a house."

He moved back against the store window, looking at her strong shoulders, dusty shapeless clothes, and untidy straggling hair.

"Guess it does. You can surely spare a cow out of that herd of yours. I hear you got an extra team of horses, fat and lazy up at Lilly Lake. House fixing's a woman's job too. They got to have quilts and things." He laughed shortly.

"I said I'll be fair and square, and I will!" Coldly, she cut short his laughter. "I'll see the girl gets a cow when she marries, but I'm damned if I'm giving a team of horses for your boy to plow his own land. That's up to you."

Cars were passing on the road close to them, and suddenly Benny darted out from in front of one, barely escaping to the walk in time.

"Benny! For land sakes! You give a person a turn!" Lina shook the child by the shoulder.

He pulled himself free. "I was just beating Neils."

"What's the use of all this silly talk?" Gustav demanded. "They aren't married, and maybe they won't be. There's nothing settled yet. I can't stand here arguing with a woman in the street. I got things to do."

The cars had passed now, and Mrs. Sven crossed the road to them, holding her little boy's hand.

"Why—why, Mrs. Ashley! How do you do, Mr. Hanson."

Under the brim of a neat black hat, kind grey eyes looked anxiously at Lina. The big Swede smiled, putting out his hand.

"The very one I wanted to see, Mrs. Jensen! How are you? And how's the boy?" He patted Neils on the head. "Where's Sven? He was going to meet me in town."

"He's just in here at Wong's, Mr. Hanson. I—"

"That's right. Shall we go in and find him? Wait, I'll get the door open. Tough catch on it, Mrs. Jensen. Come on, little Jens."

They went into the store without a backward look, leaving Lina and Benny standing in the street. The woman wiped her forehead with the back of her wrist. She looked down at the shoes in her hand.

"Little Jens! Little Jens!" sang Benny, hopping around on one foot.

"Let's get going down to Tudor's. There he is now, by his shop. Run ahead and tell him I want him. Hurry up. Get going!"

The boy ran off. Slowly Lina walked after him.

Tudor and Benny waited for her at the door of the shop, talking together. A coolness had come into the refreshing afternoon breeze that moved the spruce and trembled the leaves of the aspen poplar.

"Hello Lina," Tudor greeted her. "Pair of shoes, is it? Well, that's fine. Let's go in, shall we? I wasn't going to open up at all today. Just didn't feel like it. But don't worry, it's different for you people. I know what a long way you have to come."

The little bell over the door tinkled a welcome as they entered, and Tudor took his hat from his grizzled head. Benny breathed deeply, delighting in the smell of leather that pervaded the atmosphere. On one side, about the work table, lay the things that needed repairing; on the other hung new saddles, new riding boots, and harness. With a wistful sigh, the boy put his hand on the pommel of a saddle.

"Big crowd, eh?" the woman remarked.

"Sym had a great many friends."

"Though what they got that Brother Conrad ranting and raving around for, is beyond me."

Tudor settled his spectacles on his nose, and peered over them at Lina.

"Brother Conrad means well, you know."

The woman glanced quickly at her son. He seemed absorbed in the contemplation of the saddle.

"Folkes, they think it's Mike done it, don't they?" she murmured. "Isn't that what Hicks thinks? I hear he was pumping Dizzon."

"It's hard to say. I don't know. Sym always defended Mike. I don't see what reason Mike would have."

"Except he always was a dirty rat, even when he was just a kid."

"Poor Mike. He didn't get much of a chance."

"Poor nothing! I buried both my men folks. I just got this one left, and look at the size of him."

"Yes." Tudor seated himself at his table with a sigh. "I shall miss my good friend Sym."

Lina suddenly held out her shoes to him.

"I figger they'll need stitching, Tudor. I was going to ask you if you think they'd stand soling again. I could leave them here a week or so."

"Let me have a look at them."

"Can I go tell Poppy it's time to get ready and go?" Benny asked, his hand still gripping the pommel.

"Land sakes, child! Can't you wait a minute?"

"Lina." Tudor looked up at her, the fine shrewd lines appearing about his eyes. "You know, don't you, that Poppy was very fond of Sym? This is going to be hard on her."

"You talk like you thought everything was my fault."

"No, no, Lina. I was thinking of Poppy."

"I know what you mean," she answered, softening. "We couldn't drag her off to the funeral. She's cried herself sick down there at Mrs. Howe's. But the pool room was no place for a young girl," she added. "You can't get away from that."

Tudor turned the shoes over in his gentle hands.

"I think they'll stand soling, Lina."

"Mother, couldn't we—" Benny looked longingly at the saddle.

"Good gosh, how crazy do you think I am? Money don't grow on a spruce bough. Bareback'll be good enough for you for a good many years to come."

Tudor sat filling his pipe, watching them.

"It seems to me this young man is getting to look just like his grand-father. Don't you think so, Lina?"

The boy's face glowed. "Do I, Mother? He was a real cow-puncher, wasn't he, Mr. Folkes?"

"He was, that."

"I reckon he does look like him," the woman murmured faintly, turning away from Tudor. "There's an old saddle of Daddy's at home we could fix up for you, son. His riding-boots are in the trunk. You'll grow into them some time."

"Gee whizz!"

"Now run along and tell Poppy it's time, will you? Good night, Tudor."

Tudor puffed at his pipe, watching her go. He turned over Lina's worn shoes. After a while, he laid down his pipe, and took a large piece of leather from the wall beside him, singing softly to himself:

Cobbler, cobbler, mend my shoe;
Weave the golden thread in so,
Sparkling heel and buckle too.
Milkmaids trip to the King's ball, oh!

With Lord Laney I would dance . . .

Chapter XXVII

1

Groaning along in second over the tortuous trail, the big low grey car lurched precariously on the stumps that stuck up in unexpected places, and scraped over the rocks that jutted among the tufted grass between the ruts. Tommy sat behind the wheel. He travelled through alternate bursts of hot bright sunshine that glinted on the windshield, and cool shadows that gave the grass a blue greenness. The trees rustled in the wind, turning their whitish sides upwards, foreboding rain. Overhead, greyish white clouds were piling up in masses over a brilliantly blue sky. With a quick look at his wrist-watch, Tommy stepped on the gas as he started up a slope. The back wheels sprayed small pebbles, and the car rushed ahead. A large spot of rain fell on the windshield.

At Ashley's, he drew to a purring stop, the car looking sleek and strange beside the rail fence, himself neat and civilized in his good clothes. From his childhood visit, he remembered a little log shack tucked away in the bush, a crude shelter upflung in the wilderness. The house, still of logs, with a good slanting roof of spruce slabs and a brick chimney, now had shape, and was home-like under the old overhanging trees. In the wide barnyard fenced with new-peeled rails, he noticed the new barn, granary, and hog pens. Beyond, lay a field of young wheat coming up like short well-combed green hair, showing the earthy marks of the comb, dark between the straight rows.

Lina answered the door when he knocked.

"Hello, Tommy. We could hear you coming a long ways back. Poppy's getting ready. Won't you sit down?"

He saw the hard lines of her face set in a dogged determination.

"Sorry to be so late. There's a bad piece of road just past the bridge."

"Here, have the rocking chair. Well, it's still a country for horses, I'd say."

In the clean bright kitchen, Lina sat down opposite, giving him the frank shrewd appraisal he had come to expect from her.

"I hope it doesn't rain." Tommy glanced out of the window at the banking clouds.

"Oh, I don't think so. Been looking like this two or three days now. We get a spot sometimes. Weather's been unsettled, like, all spring."

"Mrs. Ashley, if Poppy doesn't care to go out like this so soon after—well, I'd quite understand."

Lina flung out her hand. "Best thing in the world she could do! I been telling her a dozen times. Take her mind off things, she's been that upset."

"Well, she might not feel like having a good time."

Lina looked up at the closed door of the bedroom.

"She'll be just fine. Young Benny's went already. Isaiah took him along this morning with the kids. I reckon they'll be running wild. Well, how's things out your way? Crop looking good?"

"Dandy so far."

"That reminds me." The woman shifted in her chair, and gripped the edge of the table with hard knotted fingers. "I was talking to Gus the other day in town."

Tommy coloured deeply. "You know, there are things that I'd like to say, for myself, now. I don't need any help to get started, Mrs. Ashley.

I've got my own team of horses, and I bought them with money I earned myself; I can make out."

"Takes more than that, let me tell you."

"Look what you did, all alone," he broke in. "And I want the satisfaction of making out by myself."

"And I sure know what it's like, too. You may come to see things differently in time."

Steadily, he met her look.

"I'm afraid not, Mrs. Ashley."

"You been fighting with Gus?"

"No, he had nothing to do with it. I've always had this idea. I don't want his help either."

Lina smiled. "We can see when the time comes. Got any news from your neck of the woods?"

Tommy rocked a bit, his chin in his hand, his elbow on his knee.

"I'm afraid this'll be a shock."

"Go on with you! What d'you think could shock me?"

"It's about Mike. They found him."

"They figger he done it, don't they? Well, I hope he gets what's coming to him!"

"He's got it already, Mrs. Ashley."

Lina stared. "Did they send him Outside?"

"He's dead. They figger he was hooking a freight train and fell down between the box-cars. Got run over by all kinds of trains before they found him. They had to shovel what was left of him into a coffin."

"My God!"

"That's horrible!" It was Poppy who spoke. Looking ill and tired, she stood in the doorway, listening to them.

"Well, it's over," Lina said firmly, getting up. "Now just quit thinking about the whole thing, that's all, Poppy."

Tommy jumped up, going to her with hands outstretched in a gesture of comfort.

"Poppy, I'm sorry it came out like that. I was going to tell you so someone else wouldn't blurt it out. Shall we be going?"

"I'm ready," the girl answered tonelessly.

"Will you be warm enough in that coat tonight?" Her mother handed the boy a generous-sized bundle from the kitchen table. "Here's a lunch for you. Good-bye. Have a good time."

Poppy looked slowly back at her.

"Good-bye, Mother."

"She might have looked a bit happier about it, for Tommy's sake. For her own sake, too," Lina thought, as the young people went off. She sighed. It was such a good match, much better than hers had been.

"I was a young fool," she thought, "and Daddy so trusting of the young men who came round, letting me go my own way. It's going to be different with *my* girl."

But there was no time to sit around day-dreaming, she realized. There were the cows to get in from the pasture, the pigs and chickens to feed. The chores took much longer with only one doing them instead of three. Still, she did not begrudge the girl her outing. If Poppy could only settle down, married to a fine man, Lina thought grimly, then likely gossiping folks would forgive her for being Sym Ashley's daughter.

2

"We won't be getting there very soon," Tommy remarked on their way out. "But maybe we'll see some of the sights."

She said desperately, "Why did he have to kill Sym? Sym didn't mind him. Tudor said that Sym always stuck up for Mike."

The boy slammed the car door and started the motor.

"Nobody can see why he did it. He must have wanted to get even for some reason."

The car rolled smoothly away from the Ashley farm.

"The trains ran over him!" Her voice choked.

"Look, Poppy, would you rather not go to Treaty? We could just have a little picnic somewhere down the creek. Wouldn't you like that better?"

The girl straightened up in the seat beside him, her hair shining in the sunlight.

"No. No, Tommy. Let's go to Treaty if you don't mind."

As he concentrated on the road, he felt the intensity of her look.

"You're being good to me," she added uncomfortably.

3

Grey clouds were piled up in the sky, and the smell of rain was in the air. But at the Indian Reserve no one seemed to notice. It was the last day of the Treaty Celebration. The two officials, white men from Bridgeville, had distributed the pittance to each full-blooded Indian in accordance with the Indian Act, and departed leaving the natives to enjoy their money as they would. Many wagons and one or two cars stood in the fields and along the fence, while hobbled horses limped about, cropping the deep grass. Young bucks in vivid red, blue, and green shirts and cowboy hats, rode on horseback, straight and indifferent, showing off their skill to the Indian girls. The sound of pounding drums, of weird monotonous wordless singing, drifted on a breeze that rustled the leaves and whipped at the loose canvas of white tents pitched among the dark green trees. Groups of Indians and others of mixed blood sat on the ground, huddled in gambling games, their women on the sidelines making quiet bets, and digging into scarlet handkerchiefs to pay up when they lost. Old squaws with brown wrinkled faces and inscrutable dark eyes, smoked cob pipes and played Indian whist with greasy cards. About the booths, made roughly of poles, with roofs of branches on which the leaves were beginning to die, gathered the young people and children, laughing and chattering while they drank pop and ate ice-cream. Mrs. Two Knives boiled coffee over a campfire, serving it in cracked greyish cups. Most of the few white people clung together, watching rather shyly. Frank Pretty-Nice-Man, a young Cree in a blue suit and a new stetson, arranged races for the children. Now and then a pistol barked, and Indian and white boys and girls, in bare or moccasined feet, fairly flew over the dirt track, competing for generous prizes.

Benny leaned against a booth with an orange crush in his hand, watching the race of the seven-year-old boys. Dust matted his fair curly hair and streaked his face about the mouth and eyes. Mud stained his grimy blue jeans at the ankles as though he had just waded a stream without rolling up the pant-legs.

"Aren't you racing?" Martha asked, slamming about the booth beside an Indian woman.

The boy looked indignant.

"Little kids' race." He lifted the bottle to his lips.

Amos bobbed out from among the children and arrived breathless at Benny's side.

"Have some." The white boy held out the bottle invitingly.

Amos shook his head. He hopped up and down excitedly, his black eyes dancing under a dark ragged forelock of hair.

"What's wrong with you?" Benny demanded. Then he tipped back his head, gulping down half the contents of the bottle. "Darn good." He swallowed hard, wrinkling his nose. "Won't you have some?"

The Indian boy grinned, shook his head, hopping a few steps away from him.

"He must be sick," Martha said from the booth where she was working with Mrs. Two Knives. Benny swallowed the rest of his drink in a great hurry and slammed the bottle down on the counter.

292

"C'mon!" Amos cried. "Race. Can't you hear him? He said eight, nine, ten year old. Coming?"

Benny listened. Above the noise of pounding drums and wailing singing, he could hear Frank Pretty-Nice-Man saying in Cree and in English, "Boys eight, nine, and ten year old."

"Why didn't you tell me?" He gave Amos a furious look. "Now I drank my pop and I can't run."

Amos shrieked with laughter and ran off. Benny followed him at a slower pace, feeling himself where he supposed the pop to be by now. At the starting line, he crowded in with the others, digging a good hold with his hard bare heel in the soft dirt. Beside him, Zeke Panachuk inched his foot up in front of the line. Amos crouched low. At one end, little Pete Two Knives kicked out dirt behind him. The line filled with ragged little native children. At the crack of the pistol, they were off, feet flying. Amos skimmed the ground like a deer, cutting in ahead of Zeke and blocking his way. Benny pounded after him. As he passed Pete, his lips whitened. He heard the onward surging of the children behind, and the sound of their running feet. Suddenly, a strange Indian boy shot ahead of them all, passing Amos easily at the finishing line.

Smiling, Frank Pretty-Nice-Man advanced with the prizes, while Freddy Two Knives held the winner by the arm. But Amos leapt upon the other boy, kicking and punching where he could. Benny stood back out of the way with some of the others who could hardly believe they had been beaten in the race. Freddy gave Amos a rough push with the flat of his hand against the child's mouth just as Jay came sauntering forward. Benny beamed at him, admiring his red silk shirt, his new moccasins brightly beaded.

"I was first! I was first!" Amos cried, tears flooding his big eyes. "He cheated."

"Get the kid away from here," Freddy muttered to Jay, his face darkening with anger. The Indian child stood still in his grasp, composed as though the whole thing were happening to someone else. Jay held Amos firmly by the cross-piece at the back of his overalls, talking to him teasingly in Cree. Frank came smiling up to them, handing the winner some money. The boy took it, ducked his head and spat in the direction of Amos, and ran off. Amos squirmed furiously, scarcely grateful for the fifty cents Frank put into his hand.

"And this boy?" Frank asked, pointing to Benny.

Freddy nodded. Benny looked wonderingly at the shining quarter the Indian handed him.

"I'll get that dirty skunk! I'll get him!" Amos said.

"Let's see what they're doing over there," Jay suggested, motioning towards a wagon where a group of men raised their hands aloft, shouting in excitement. He watched and listened a moment. Above the drum-beats and the high, sweet singing, Jay could hear what the men were saying. His eyes filled with laughter.

"It's a louse and ant fight!" He loosed Amos and left the children. Benny ran swiftly after him, and after a moment's hesitation, the other boy forgot his quarrel and followed.

Bill Manydogs was the centre of excitement. He had a piece of white paper in his knotted dark hand.

"Who's got an ant? Who's got a louse? Who's got an ant? Who's got a louse?" He was shouting, almost chanting, in Cree, with the rhythm of the drums that came from a gambling game near them. His snaky locks jumped about on his head, and many tight lines crinkled his brown leathery face. An old Indian with a pocked, wizened face and greasy black hair showing under his cap, his glistening black eyes fathomless, held an ant lightly between the thumb and forefinger of his grey-brown hand.

"Enoch Owns-Six-Horses, he got the ant!" Bill cried. "Where's a louse? Where's a louse? Tchukeg, you got a louse?"

A young Indian plunged a hand down inside his shirt, while the men hooted and jeered. Tchukeg grinned, drawing forth a louse from somewhere on his body.

"Who'll bet on the ant? Who'll bet on the louse?" Bill chanted, flourishing the paper.

"My fiddle on the ant!" Biggeman, the big native from the north shook the violin in the air.

"I'm for the louse!" Bill's eyes were covetous on the instrument. "My bear-trap on the louse!" He jumped into the wagon, throwing out a trap with the sound of clinking chain on metal. "My lucky trap, wins everything!"

Enoch looked from the ant in his fingers to the louse in Tchukeg's.

"My bridle on the ant," he said softly.

Bill looked worried, coming down to gaze at the insects himself. Then he shook his head decidedly. "The louse."

Isaiah squatted on the ground, smoking, with a wagon wheel at his back. He looked into Enoch's old face, and placed his bet on the ant. Most of the other men did too, except for Tchukeg, and a young Indian named Whiskey Bottle. Jack Two Knives wavered uncertainly and finally bet on the ant. Bill's face fell, and the paper drooped in his hands.

"I'm for the louse," Jay declared, coming up to him reassuringly. "You'll get your fiddle, you'll see."

The old man laughed delightedly, setting the paper carefully on the ground. Everyone dropped on hands and knees in the dust while Enoch shook the large ant onto the paper. Tchukeg dropped the louse beside it. With a grass stem, Bill pushed the two combatants together. The men watched tensely, their faces nearly on the ground.

Benny and Amos found themselves shut out by a closely-packed circle of bodies, but they squirmed down, Benny under Enoch's arm, and Amos by Isaiah. Benny watched, fascinated, as the two tiny creatures strove with one another. The ant, handsome, shiny black-and-red, looked a so much superior fighter, with his big mouth opening, and the jaws moving as though they would chew the louse to pieces. The louse, smaller, a tramp of an individual of shabby brown, seemed always to be on the bottom, on his back. Their fine legs tangled. Bill nearly sobbed. Tchukeg muttered in his own dialect, his slit-like eyes nearly closing in his little flat face. Enoch's aged face betrayed nothing. Isaiah enjoyed the scene, with Amos watching from under his arm. But Jay looked on as one who knows some secret. Beyond them, the drumming seemed to be louder, the singing rising to a wild pitch.

"I can do better than that!" Whiskey Bottle suddenly burst out, diving his hand into his own shirt, the sweat standing out on his brown face. "Here's a better one! Tchukeg's lice don't get fed enough!" He put a larger louse on the white paper. The men argued hotly while Bill disentangled the first one from the ant, and brought forward the new opponent with the grass stem.

Benny thought he would stifle in the crowd, but he could not draw back. He must see the end of it all. His eyes followed the first rejected fighter as it crawled off the paper and reappeared on Enoch's hand, disappearing into the sleeve of his buckskin jacket. The little boy looked up curiously into the old Indian's face, but there was no sign that he had noticed. His deep eyes were on the contestants. The big ant, plunging like a bucking horse, fought like a veteran, with the louse underneath. The ant's antennae moved angrily, Benny thought, and there was an almost savage look about the creature. The louse struggled feebly under the weight of the ant's body. Jack Two Knives and Isaiah began to chuckle, and a smile flickered over Enoch's face. Then a curious thing happened. The louse moved down under the ant until its own head was even with the narrow waist. The ant stopped fighting, and writhed as though with terrible silent agony. Seeing this, Benny moved back a little, a kind of horror in his eyes. It was all over in a moment. The louse had bitten the ant in two and the brave fighter's mutilated body moved no more.

"They always do that, every time," Jay said quietly.

Bill whooped for joy, and the men got to their feet, yelling and quarrelling. Benny stayed on his knees in the dust. Suddenly he seized the tough little louse between his fingers, squashing it hard, digging his thumb nail into its body, and wiping it off on the leg of his jeans. He looked back at the ant's body lying in pieces on the white paper. But Amos's dirty bare foot trod upon it, blotting it all out. He gave Benny a shove.

"Let's have some ice-cream," he suggested, tossing his money from one hand to the other.

Benny got to his feet. Most of the men, still arguing, moved off to the gambling game where the drums were. With a preoccupied air, Bill stroked the strings of the fiddle with the bow. Jay inspected the fancy bridle, laughing to himself.

"It'll look nice on Goldy," he said in Cree.

"It sure will," Benny piped up.

Jay looked across at the boy, and then beyond him, and he did not laugh any more. His mouth had a bitter twist as he flung the bridle over his arm and went away. Benny turned round quickly.

"Poppy!" he cried, and ran towards her, while Amos hid behind the wagon.

She seemed so distant, standing there beside Tommy, that Benny stopped a little way from her, staring curiously at the stranger. Poppy walked slowly to her brother, putting a hand on his shoulder, touching a scratch on his smudged cheek.

"What goes on?"

"It was an ant and louse fight. The louse bit the old ant clear in two." Benny's bright eyes kept straying to Tommy while he talked.

"Hello, Bill." The girl looked intently at the old native as though trying to give him some secret message.

He grinned at her, showing his brown teeth.

"Did you win, Bill?"

He held out the fiddle. Poppy touched it lightly with her fingers.

"Why, Bill! That's Gramp's fiddle. I always remember Gramp's fiddle. You lost it a long time ago, didn't you?"

Fine lines creased Bill's face in laughter.

"Biggeman, he say the ant wins. I bet the louse." He plucked gently at the strings. "Benjie's fiddle."

"Is it really your grandfather's fiddle?" Tommy asked with interest. "He was well known all over this country for his fiddling, wasn't he? I've heard Tudor say so." He looked at the battered instrument.

"He got it betting on the louse!" Benny cried. "I killed it dead."

"Benny big hunter!" Amos squeaked from behind the wagon.

Poppy remained silent.

"Let's go and see the stick game," Tommy suggested, taking her arm.

"D'you know what?" Benny cried, trotting beside them. "I came in third in the race and got two bits. See? And I had lots of pop. It makes me feel sick, though. You missed the horse-races."

"I'd like to have seen those," Tommy remarked. Benny half smiled, but the girl looked straight ahead, her fair hair blowing back in a sudden gust of cool wind. The clouds above were gloomier, more threatening.

"Here comes Bill too," Benny chattered on. "He's got his fiddle and his trap. I bet he's going to play the stick game."

Biggeman picked up the drum, and banging it gently with a stick, began to sing the wordless song, low and sweet. Men sitting cross-legged on the ground formed two rows, facing each other, while their women sat on the sidelines, betting, and the crowd pressed about them. Grinning widely, Bill Manydogs squatted beside Enoch Owns-Six-Horses. Jay chose the side of their opponents. With a wild shout, Tchukeg threw the peeled willow sticks into the middle, while Enoch took the two worn bits of wood in his hands. One piece was deeply notched, the other smooth. Eager excited betting went on among the players.

"Here's a place, Poppy." Tommy moved out from between two Indians and stood behind the girl. "What are they talking about?"

"We know what they're saying," Benny answered somewhat contemptuously. He pushed his head between two men, and pummelling with his fists, wormed his way to a place beside Bill.

Jay's scarlet shirt made a vivid spot of colour among the players. Poppy looked only at him. But his half-sleepy eyes were upon Enoch. Beside him, Whiskey Bottle brought out some money from a pocket in his shirt. Tchukeg undid his beautiful beaded belt and sat looking at the fine design done in pale blue and white and silver beads. An Indian with a strong craggy face and long black braids, took off a tarnished silver ring with a bright green stone from his finger. The men put their bets in a pile on one side, the beaded belt, the money, the ring, the fancy bridle Jay had won, Bill's fiddle with the bow tucked carefully under the strings, horse-blankets, knives, beaded gloves.

Then all the men with Enoch took up the song, swaying from side to side, while Biggeman pounded the drum wildly. Enoch tossed the two bits of wood in the air, swiftly juggling them, his old hands moving with quick sureness, throwing the bits of wood from one hand to the other, interchanging them, doing a kind of rhythmic dance with his withered fingers, at once subtle and graceful. His eyes were deep and unfathomable, his face expressionless. The men on Jay's side bent forward, watching, following the notched piece of wood with their eyes, while the maddening singing confused them. At last Enoch's hands came to rest, closed and still. The song and the drumming died. Jay made a sign and spoke, and Enoch opened his fingers, revealing the notched piece of wood in the right hand. Jay smiled, his dark face lighting up. He reached for one of the peeled willow sticks and stuck it upright in the ground before him. Poppy tensed in the crowd, waiting for him to look up at her. But he was as aloof as though he were alone. On the sidelines, the squaws unknotted their handkerchiefs and clinked small change. Immediately, the singing and the pounding of the drum began again.

Tommy turned away to get a breath of fresh air, and then looked back at the game.

"Looks like fun."

"If you win." She spoke without looking at him, wedged between a young Indian woman, Mary Pretty-Nice-Man, and Enoch's wife, a gaunt wizened squaw in black, with white hair braided about her grey-brown face.

"Which side you bet on now?" Tommy asked.

Poppy turned her face towards him with a sigh.

"Oh, I don't know." She saw his disappointment. "Well, Enoch's."

Tommy showed his pleasant lop-sided grin.

"The old boy looks shrewd enough."

Poppy leaned against Mary Pretty-Nice-Man, looking over the heads of the crowd to see the pile of bets. A whirl of dust blew over the fiddle. Again she watched Jay who sat motionless, his eyes on the moving hands. The smell of buckskin and of unwashed bodies nearly overpowered her.

"I've lost track of the sticks," she heard Tommy say behind her. She wrenched herself free from her place between the two Indian women.

"Maybe we should go eat. With the clouds like that, it'll be dark real early, and then they'll start the dancing." Her voice faltered.

"Sure thing," he agreed. "I'll get some cokes."

"Benny." With the toe of her shoe, she touched a small bare foot that showed on the ground between the embroidered mukluks of old Jack Running Rabbit and the dainty moccasins of Mary Pretty-Nice-Man. Benny wriggled out backwards. "Are you hungry? We're going to eat now."

"I'm awful hungry," he cried, getting to his feet. "Can we make a camp-fire, Poppy?"

"Sure. Over in those spruce would be good."

It was peaceful with the wind soughing in the branches, water lapping in the creek beside them, and the sound of the Indian singing in the distance. Tommy fetched a couple of blankets from the car, spreading them before the fire.

"Are you warm enough, Poppy?" he asked. "Let me put my jacket round your shoulders."

"I'm plenty warm," she answered irritably. She leaned back against the trunk of a tree, poking at the flaming log with a stick, moodily watching the sparks fly up.

"I like a fire," Benny declared, stretching himself out.

"Don't get jam on the blanket," Poppy warned him, as he took another large sandwich from the bundle.

"Come on, Poppy," Tommy pleaded. "You're not eating. Have a sandwich, won't you? And drink some of the coke?"

"I'll eat when I'm ready, thanks."

"If you don't want it, just give it to me," Benny sang out. "I've got lots of room."

Drawing closer to the fire, the girl took a thick peanut-butter sandwich and began eating hungrily of the fresh home-made bread. The wind moaned in the strong branches. The drumming and singing went on and on. Through the trees shone the warm blazing of other campfires, with figures moving about them. The darkness was beginning to close in.

Isaiah tightened the bow of his violin, while Whiskey Bottle plucked at the strings of a banjo. The two men seated themselves on sawn logs in a corner of the open-air dance-hall, a floor surrounded by a railing of poles. Pretty-Nice-Man hung a lighted lantern on an upright post behind them, and a crowd began to gather. Off in the darkness, by the fitful light of a dying fire, the stick game went on interminably with the drumming and singing, but only a few old Indians were left playing. Bright lights appeared on the road, and a truck groaned to a stop just outside the Reserve territory. Isaiah struck up a quick foot-teasing tune on the fiddle, while Frank called in Cree and in English, "Get your partners for a two-step!"

Under the threatening sky, and among the rustling trees, the dancing began, while many people stood around watching and talking. Jay came into the light shed by the lantern, carrying a fancy bridle, a bear-trap, and a fiddle. Bill Manydogs followed him up on the dance-floor and into a corner, where Jay sat down on the railing. The old man pleaded with him, throwing his hands about, his voice rising to an angry pitch. Finally Jay handed him the bridle. Bill took it, muttering to himself, and disappeared into the darkness. Jay flung the bear-trap by its chain over the railing, and holding the fiddle on his knee, rolled himself a cigarette.

On the other side, Poppy came up to the railing with Tommy and Benny. The girl watched the couples swinging wildly; Frank Pretty-Nice-Man and his young wife. Biggeman with his laughing squaw, other young native couples, and white people about the edges.

"I'm not dancing tonight." She spoke distantly. "It's too soon after— Anyway, I'm not dancing tonight."

"That's all right, Poppy. I understand. But we can watch them."

"All right," she answered dully. "Anything you say. Do you want to see the Red River jigging? Enoch Owns-Six-Horses does the best jigging in the country."

"Sure. He's quite a character, isn't he?"

Benny slipped away then, worming his way through the watching crowd. Poppy stretched her hand out after him in a helpless gesture.

"I say, you do look cold." Tommy looked anxiously down at the girl.

"I'm all right," she muttered, leaning against the railing.

"We should have had some coffee over at our campfire, something to warm you up. I could get you something from Mrs. Two Knives over there. How about it?"

"Well Tommy, I'd rather watch the dancing."

"That's all right. I'll get it."

From the darkened booth, Mrs. Two Knives gave him two cups, and bent among the shadows, raking the dying embers of her fire, and feeding them with dry kindling. She set the blackened coffee pot among the leaping flames.

"Hi, Tommy!" said a voice behind them, and Romeo appeared, showing his long teeth in a cunning smile.

Tommy glanced up from the fire, frowning.

"Hello."

Romeo slapped him on the shoulder.

"Well, how's the boy? Getting a nice cup of coffee for his girlie?" Romeo guffawed. "You're wasting your time, brother. The bets in the beer parlour is all against you."

"What bets?" Tommy asked, staring.

"We bet in the beer parlour today. Dizz and Ek and me, we bet ten to one on the breed. Panachuk, he's the only one for you."

"The breed?"

"Dizz and Ek and me, we got our money on Jay Baptiste." Romeo's slanting yellow eyes were bright in the firelight, with dark bits of hair falling over them from under his cap.

Angrily, Tommy flourished the cups in his hands.

"You low-down hog, you! Look at the poor kid! Does she look to you like she has any such crazy ideas?"

Romeo peered through the crowd, taking a long look at the girl standing so still at the railing.

"Well, I dunno."

"Get your partners for a waltz!" Frank Pretty-Nice-Man called.

Poppy felt her arm being shaken. Benny stood beside her.

"Jay says," he whispered, "why for did you come to Treaty with that mangy coyote?"

The dancers were clearing off now, and the girl could see Jay sitting smoking with the fiddle on his knee, gazing out into the blackness beyond. She bent down and said in Benny's ear,

"Tell him, why not? He's got a woman in the north to make him nice jackets."

The sweet notes of the fiddle made a tune full of heartache, and the noisy dancers began circling the floor.

"Isn't it ready yet?" Tommy asked, bending over the coffee pot.

"Soon coffee ready," Mrs. Two Knives assured him.

"Got you plenty worried," Romeo jeered.

Tommy waited restlessly, watching the girl.

As she leaned on the railing, listening to the fiddling, Benny appeared at her side again, tousled and breathless.

"He says," the child panted, "he says, well at least he don't bring another girl along when you're going to be here."

She looked down at the little boy's eager face.

"Tell him, how could I help it when I couldn't even come here unless I come with Tommy. I got nobody, nobody," she said bitterly.

"She ain't going to dance," Romeo declared impatiently. "Standing there like a stump."

The wind was rising, rustling myriads of large leaves, sighing through the evergreens. The music sounded as though it came from some far-off hidden place, and the drums and the Indian singing seemed to die away. Poppy shivered, looking at the strange dark faces beside her. Sometimes, between the moving figures of the dancers, she could see Jay's red shirt. With a beating heart, she waited for Benny. He was back very soon, stretching up to whisper.

"He says, it's so terrible to be a breed, he says."

"Oh, Benny!"

"That's what he says, Poppy."

"Tell him—tell him, being a breed don't make no difference. I'm white, and it's terrible anyways."

As the child disappeared again, she turned her face from the lamp-light.

"He ain't going to dance neither!" Romeo said fiercely. "Sitting there like a stump too. I lose ten bucks. So does Dizz and Ek. Panachuk's a lucky guy."

"Teach you to mind your own business," Tommy muttered, as Mrs. Two Knives removed the coffee from the fire.

"Well, I got to go. There's Dizz. Guess what Dizz and me got in the truck?"

"You didn't bring your damn rotten moonshine with you to the Reserve?"

"Look out, little boy," Romeo sneered. "You might get mixed up in something."

Tommy turned his back, setting down the cups on the bench while Mrs. Two Knives poured out the coffee.

Out of the breath of the wind, a few large drops of rain began to fall, spattering amongst the dancers, and dropping with plunking sounds in the dust. Isaiah quickened the tempo of his music, and the dancing couples gave wild yells as their feet pounded the floor. Benny wiped a raindrop from the end of his nose with the back of his hand.

"What did he say?" Poppy asked him, very low.

"Bend down and let me whisper; he said, 'Netimos. Ka sakehit.'"

"Oh, did he, Benny?"

"I know what that means," the child said. "And he said he'd fix it."

The girl smiled, looking among the dancers to find Jay. She saw Bill Manydogs putting his head between the railing, and old Enoch and his wife came into the light near him. As the waltz ended, Jay wandered over to Isaiah and Frank. After they had talked quietly together, Frank called the Red River jigging.

"Netimos!" Benny sang, his eyes sparkling.

"Here's your coffee," Poppy heard Tommy say behind her.

"They're just going to jig." Taking the cup, she gave him a wide slow smile. "Look, it isn't going to rain after all. It's quitting again." She held her face up to the sky.

Frank Pretty-Nice-Man stepped to the middle of the floor just then, and began talking earnestly in Cree. The crowd became silent.

"What's he saying?" Tommy whispered, sipping the coffee.

"He says the police will be looking around and everybody to be good and not get into trouble," Poppy told him.

"Police? Gee, I hope they behave and we can see the jigging."

Isaiah and Whiskey Bottle began some quick music, while everyone pressed back to clear the floor.

"Enoch! Enoch!" Frank called amid eager clapping.

With a pleased smile on his old wrinkled face, Enoch Owns-Six-Horses came up on to the dance floor, hesitating there a moment until his old wife was beside him. Then, on moccasined feet, he danced. His feet moved with incredible swiftness. Gracefully, he held out his hands before him, and his shoulders were still. Close at his side his old wife danced too, watching to follow his steps. Almost noiselessly their feet moved, hardly seeming to touch the floor. The dance went on and on, the steps varying and changing to the same monotonous rhythmic music. Then Bill Manydogs began jigging beside them, and old Enoch was clapped off. As the older woman tired, Mrs. Waters took her place, following in turn Bill's complicated footing.

"They sure can dance," Tommy remarked. "Can you do it too?"

"Done it for ten years."

"I wish I could see you. Gee, you wouldn't think a squaw as big as that one could be so light on her feet," he added as Mrs. Poudre began to jig. "Say, is it really going to rain?"

"I don't think so." She set their empty cups on the ground at their feet.

Wind rocked the lantern, and the music began to sound thin and far away. Sheet lightning flashed, making a ghostly greenish light for a second, and then all was black again. Thunder roared dully in the distance. And now the wind blew in great gusts, bringing the rain with it. Isaiah put up his fiddle, glancing at the sky. Suddenly, Biggeman plunged drunkenly into the middle of the floor and lurched up to Frank.

"Where's your ol' pleece?" he shouted.

"Get away!" Frank struck at him with his fists. "You want us all in trouble?"

"Fight! Fight!" Jack Two Knives came yelling in from behind, his eyes bright, his mouth wet. The crowd surged upon them. Tommy felt the girl dart from his side. She jumped up on to the dance floor to Jay who was calling to her in Cree.

"Hold this, and keep behind me." He thrust the fiddle into her hands. Then he snatched up the bear trap from the railing.

"What are you doing?" Tommy cried, getting up on to the floor.

"I must stop the fight!" Jay shouted. "The police will come!"

He advanced upon the fighting men, swinging the ugly steel low on the floor, striking moccasined feet. The men fell back, leaping over the railings. Rain began lashing down with the wind. The lantern blew about, throwing the light eerily from one place to another. Benny clutched Poppy's arm, watching the fight.

"You got a coat?" she asked him.

"Yeah, at the tent."

"Take the fiddle!" she cried, while the rain streamed down their faces. "It's Gramp's fiddle. It'll get spoilt. Wrap it in your coat. Go on now, run!"

"Poppy!" Tommy seized her shoulder. "We got to get out of here!"

"Let me alone!" She jerked herself free. "I'm not coming with you!"

"Not coming?" He stood in the pouring rain, soaked to the skin, his hair plastered to his head. She faced him, wet and dripping.

"Go away! Go away!"

The clanking sound of steel clattered over the rough boards. Yelling and shouting, the men were disappearing into the dark. Only Biggeman stayed, crouching as though getting ready to spring. Jay swung the trap high, and the drunken native retreated between the rails.

"Poppy, I can't leave you now!" Tommy cried. "Wait!" he pleaded, "think what you are doing."

Isaiah had reached the lantern. Jay spoke to the girl in Cree.

"You dirty breed!" Tommy shouted, putting up his fists. "Put that damn thing down and fight!"

The menacing trap swung high, catching Tommy a cruel blow on the shoulder. He fell back against the rails. The flame of the lantern blew out. In the darkness and the pouring rain, men and women cried to each other. Headlights flashed briefly, and a motor roared as the truck started off. Soon wagons rumbled over the uneven ground, hoofs thudding heavily in the rain. Riders galloped fast down the road. Then all sounds faded in the unleashed wind.

On a forest path springy with fallen needles, her hoof-beats muted in the soft earth, Goldy trotted under her double burden.

Chapter XXVIII

1

Lina woke to hear the rain beating down and overflowing the tubs she had put out under the eaves. Since the children had not yet come home, she thought that they had probably taken shelter in one of the tents, maybe with Jack and Mrs. Two Knives who were camping at the Reserve. It was certainly no place for cars in such weather. She wondered if Tommy would try to get out to the Bridgeville Highway and take Poppy to Bear Claw. At any rate, he had a lot of good sense. Often, though, Lina looked down the wet trail hoping for a sight of a team and wagon, or a rider on horseback.

By late afternoon, the storm had passed. A fresh westerly breeze rolled back the grey curtains of cloud, shook the trees, bringing down showers of raindrops from the leaves, and blew low along the flattened grasses. The wet pine gave off a sharp pungent odour that mingled with the scent of rainwashed wild roses, and of the damp earth of the fields. Vesper sparrows sang high piping notes, and robins crooned liquidly in the coolness of the forest.

Along the mired road winding among the trees, a large truck wheezed and floundered, roaring loudly in the quiet country, leaving a twisted trail in the mud, up to the gate of Panachuk's farm. In rubber boots and overalls, Olga stood almost knee-deep in muck at the water-trough, while the work horses about her drank long and noisily.

"Pop!" she cried out. "Here comes Romeo and Dizz. What do they want here?"

Pitchfork in hand, Panachuk came out of the barn to take a look.

"Look at them, staggering like hooligans!" Olga swung her black braids in disgust. "You can smell their moonshine a mile."

Her father moved towards the gate.

"You get stuck?" he shouted.

Romeo and Dizzon slithered and stumbled, their arms flying about grotesquely.

"We got news!" Dizzon rubbed his forehead, leaving a streak of mud on it from his filthy hand.

Romeo stood grinning like a playful dog, his teeth sharp in his muddy face.

"We came to collect!" he shouted, and licked his lips.

"What you come to collect?" Panachuk asked, staring.

Romeo took an uncertain step and waved his arms.

"You lost the bet! We got our money on Jay Baptiste, and Jay Baptiste, he got the girl! Ten to one on the breed, we bet!"

"Got your money on the wrong horse, Panny!" Dizzon laughed, his mouth hanging foolishly open.

"Go 'way wit you! Lina, she no let Poppy go wit a breed. She got Poppy tight in de fist!"

Dizzon gave a shout of drunken laughter.

"Poppy's gone into the bush with a breed, though. Forty bucks easy money. Come on, Panny!"

Panachuk blinked fast. "Ek, he say sometime he see Poppy and Jay. But Lina, she got everyting tight in de fist, Poppy too."

Waving a dish-towel, Mrs. Panachuk crossed the yard to the men, her bare feet thrust into low rubbers.

"What is it, all dis talk?" she demanded shrilly, watching the two scarecrows of men staggering and bellowing on the road.

"They're just slap-happy drunk, Ma," Olga cried, following the woman slowly in her high boots.

Panachuk turned sharply, quivering with excitement.

"Dey say Lina's Poppy she run off wit Jay Baptiste, like Ek say!"

"Poppy!" Olga gasped, her hand on her throat. "Lina'll give her hell now."

"Big farmer Lina," Mrs. Panachuk grunted, putting her hands on her hips. "Now we see if she so fine woman. My Olga she no run wit de breeds."

"Give us our money!" Romeo shouted, leering. "We bet on the breed ten to one. We put our money on the winner!"

Dizzon struck an attitude.

"Ladies and Gen'lemen, the winner, Jay Baptiste!"

"You bet in de beer parlour, you big fool, you?" the woman cried, glaring into her husband's face.

"Go 'way wit you!" Panachuk shook the pitchfork at the men. "You big liars!"

"Look." Romeo pointed across the fields, his long teeth showing in a grin. "There goes the loser, Tommy Hanson! His daddy's nice car stuck in the mud. Now he'll be going to Sven's to get a team to pull 'er out."

"It's him, Tommy," Olga whispered to her mother. "It's true. It must be." They all looked over at the figure which appeared and disappeared on the well-bushed trail beyond the wheat field.

"Go 'way wit you!" Panachuk ordered the men, advancing with the pitchfork. "I see you in town. Go 'way!"

"That's Tommy," Olga muttered. "She went with Tommy. She ain't with Tommy now. Lina'll kill her." She stood in the mud, watching the boy until he was out of sight.

He walked slowly, his shoes heavily loaded with mud which he sometimes kicked off against a stump before plodding on. Weariness showed in his walk, and in his young face. His mouth twitched as though in pain, and he held his right arm stiffly bent at the elbow.

Mrs. Sven met him at the door.

"Tommy!" She looked at his mud-streaked clothes and white set face. "What in the world? Did you get stuck with the car?"

He nodded mutely.

"Well, come in. No, never mind about the mud, I'm not even trying to keep the place clean today. Here, sit down, and I'll get you a cup of tea. You must stay to supper. I'll have it on in no time." She bustled about, stirring up the fire and settling the kettle to boil. "Were you at Treaty?" she asked him.

"Yes."

Sven appeared in the cellar doorway with a handful of tools.

"Well, Tommy! Treaty must of been pretty rough, judging by the looks of you."

"Pretty rough," the boy answered in a muffled tone.

Sven smiled. "We was just about flooded out downstairs. I been siphoning pretty near all day. It'll be all right now, Ethel," he told his wife. "We could of had a real indoor swimming-pool for the kids." He winked at Tommy. "These women don't want no progressive ideas."

"Could I borrow a team from you, Sven?" the boy asked. "I got the car stuck a piece down the road."

"Why sure. Maybe you better bring the car up here till the roads dry up some. Well, wait till after supper. I got a lot to do yet." He put a cap on his blond head, and went to the porch for his rubber boots. "I'll see you at supper," he called through the screen.

Mrs. Sven peeled potatoes with great energy at the sink, but she looked anxiously at the boy. He put his hand on his shoulder, his face twisting with pain.

"You're hurt!" she exclaimed. "Tommy, what happened? Is it your shoulder?"

"It's all right," he told her. "No blood. Just a bad scrape and a bruise. Do you mind if I wash?"

"Of course. Just a minute. I'll give you some hot water. Did you get Poppy safely home? Olga said you were taking her along."

Tommy did not look at her.

"She isn't with me."

Mrs. Sven came over to him, touching his lamed shoulder lightly with her hand.

"My dear, what is it?"

The boy began washing his hands in silence.

"I guess I may as well tell you," he said at last, looking up miserably at her. "Poppy's run off with Jay Baptiste."

"Poppy!"

"At the dance last night." He wiped his hands, swallowing hard. "She's always known him, Mrs. Sven."

"The poor child. There was nothing you could do?"

"I tried. But, if that's what she wants, well—"

"Oh, Tommy. I'm terribly sorry!"

"Mrs. Sven, I think I better go and tell Lina. D'you think I could borrow the saddle-pony?"

She looked at him.

"You think you should go?"

"Yes, I must. I took Poppy off with me and never brought her back."

Mrs. Sven turned to the sink again.

"This will be a terrible blow for Lina. I don't know how she'll take it."

"I'm not afraid of her, if that's what you mean," Tommy declared.

Mrs. Sven put the potatoes into a saucepan and set them to boil.

"Wait, dear. Wait till we've had supper, and we'll talk things over."

"Oh, please!" the boy implored. "Let's not talk Poppy over."

"I'm so sorry, Tommy." She faced him in the quiet kitchen. "I've

been afraid of this for a long time. My dear, I've watched her grow
up. Lonely. Jay was everything to her, always. What she needed was a
mother!"

Heavy footsteps stamped up the steps onto the porch. Through the
screen, Mrs. Sven saw her neighbour, Mrs. Panachuk, her untidy hair
hastily tied back with a bright handkerchief.

"Miz Sven!" she called into the kitchen. "I make cake for de supper,
and I got no de sugar. You lend me sugar, yes?"

"Come in, Mrs. Panachuk. Of course I can lend you some sugar.
Have you a cup there?"

Banging open the door, the big woman lumbered in, not seeing
Tommy who leaned against the wall behind her.

"What you tink, Miz Sven?" she cried. "Lina's Poppy, she run 'way
wit Jay Baptiste! Romeo and Dizz, dey told. Lina's Poppy run 'way
wit a breed. Dat Lina, she tink she too fine for us. Now she see!"
Mrs. Panachuk flung her hands wide. "A breed!"

"Leave the girl alone." Mrs. Sven spoke severely as she measured
out the sugar.

"But Tommy Hanson—he is here?" She turned about and saw him.
"Why you no keep your Poppy? Why you let a breed take her?" She
laughed.

The boy looked levelly at her without speaking.

"Here's the sugar, Mrs. Panachuk. I hope you get your cake made in
time for supper." Mrs. Sven smiled. "The weather seems to be clearing,
doesn't it? Dear me, I must call the children in; they'll be mud to the
eyebrows. Shall I walk down to the gate with you?"

Almost bewildered, the other woman found herself being led
outside.

"Dere's Ek on de wagon!" she exclaimed, sighting a team coming
down the road. "I get de ride home." She plowed through the mud,
waving and calling.

On the saddle-pony, Tommy slithered his way to Lina Ashley's. The wind had swept the grey clouds from the sky, and died now to a gentle rustling in the leaves. The last rays of the setting sun had disappeared. All along the way, he could see fresh wagon tracks in the mud, and presently, turning the last bend in the road, he saw Isaiah's wagon and team stopped at Lina's gate ahead.

With his jacket bundled up under his arm, Benny jumped down over the wheel, scuttling quickly under the fence and over to the house. Starting with a lurch, the wagon creaked on. Cows stood inside the gate, bawling to be milked. As Tommy dismounted and tied the reins to a fence post, a large ugly dog rushed out, barking and growling. The boy crawled through the railings of the gate just as Lina appeared with milk pails in her hand. He stood waiting.

She buttoned her ragged sweater at the throat.

"Well! So you come horse-back. Bad storm, that one was."

"Yes."

"I guess your car got stuck, eh? Still a country for horses, this is. Well, where's Poppy? Left her up at Sven's, I s'pose? I see you got Sven's saddle-pony there."

Tommy shook his head.

"Mrs. Ashley, Poppy didn't come back with me."

Lina dumped the pails on the ground with a rattle and clang.

"My God, what are you talking about now? Can't a woman trust a great big fellow like you to see a girl home proper?"

"I did the best I could. But—I've come to tell you. Poppy— Mrs. Ashley, it wasn't me she wanted; it was Jay, all the time."

"Jay! That breed! You're crazy! For God's sake, what are you saying?"

"I've come to tell you, she's gone with Jay."

The woman stiffened, her fists clenched as though she would strike him. She was a tall woman, but he matched her in height, and he did not shrink from her look. In the oncoming twilight, they faced each other, while the restless cows moved about them, mooing plaintively.

"I—don't—believe—it!" Lina choked. "She wouldn't—she wouldn't be such a fool!"

"It's true. She's gone with Jay, off to the bush, God knows where," he said in a level tone.

"It's a lie!"

He shook his head. She saw the grim lines of his young face.

"You blasted lumel!"

As though deaf to her words, he got back onto the road, and mounted, wincing against the pain in his shoulder. She watched him ride off, her face suddenly drawn and old. When he had disappeared from sight, she drew away from the gate and strode to the house.

"Look what I got, Mum!" Benny exclaimed when she came in.

She stood still in the kitchen, watching him. Filthy beyond description, he bit hungrily into a large hunk of bread and butter, holding out a violin in his free hand. "Gramp's fiddle. D'you think I can learn to play it?"

"Where did you get it?" Lina asked harshly.

The child looked up, surprised.

"I got it at Treaty. Poppy gave it to me. Jay won it in the stick game. And I got two bits in a race, and—"

"Jay!"

At her tone, the child's face went white. He put the fiddle down on the table.

"Where's your sister?" Lina demanded.

"I don't know."

"What do you know about Poppy and Jay?"

Benny rubbed one bare foot against the other, his eyes on the floor.

"I don't know nothing."

"That's a lie!"

In two steps she reached him, grabbing him by the front of his shirt in a hard strong hand.

"If you don't tell the truth, I'll smash you down till you never get up. By God, it's time I took you in hand!"

"You're hurting!" Benny cried out, struggling in her grasp.

"And I'll be hurting more before I'm done. Did Jay and Poppy tell you things? Answer me!"

Tears came into the child's eyes.

Lina loosed him with an angry shove.

"What did they tell you?"

Benny broke into harsh sobs.

"I don't know. I don't know. I crossed my heart to never never tell." He threw himself down in a huddle on a chair, crying bitterly.

"And I was thinking you was like Daddy, like Benjie." The woman's quivering face went hard. "Why, holy bald-headed! You're nothing more'n another of Sym Ashley's brats, that's what you are. I can't stand the look of you. Get out of my sight!"

White and trembling, the little boy ran sobbing into the next room. For moments, the woman stood transfixed in the darkening kitchen. Then she moved woodenly to the door, and walked with dragging footsteps across the yard to the cattle.

Breathing the fresh cool air was like dipping into cool waters. The land was in twilight now, with grey shadowiness over the acres of young wheat, and the pasture, and the untouched timber beyond. Shadows would be gathering over the hayland too, with its new growth of luscious grass, and over the acres that were once Olenski's where his old shack was tumbling into decay. The whole land lay tranquil, beautiful, utterly still. A single star shone in the clear sky above the tree-tops.

At the water trough clustered the strong forms of the work-horses, and in the little pasture by the yard, the bells of the mares with their colts tinkled among the willows. The bulky, awkward bodies of the cattle lay humped near the gate. The beast nearest Lina turned a horned head with a low, plaintive note. Lifting a pail from the ground, the woman kicked the cow to its feet.

Crouching, she began mechanically to milk.

Afterword

I n Canada as elsewhere, literary modernism is currently
undergoing revaluation from many different perspectives,
providing an opportune moment to bring fresh attention to
Christine van der Mark's prize-winning novel, *In Due Season*
(1947). This book challenged the norms of mid-twentieth-century
Canadian prairie fiction by breaking new ground in its treatment of
gender and in its representation of Indigenous people in the Canadian
Northwest. Today, we can see that van der Mark was well ahead
of her time with her unconventional characterization of pioneer
Lina Ashley and her appreciative portrayal of the multicultural
communities of northern Alberta created by the interactions of
resident Aboriginals and Metis with incoming Europeans. When the
book first appeared, it was very well received and was commended
by Professor Claude T. Bissell as "the tragedy of a courageous but
erring woman" whose story, shaped by "the bitter irony of fate," is
recounted in "precise, unadorned prose" (268–69). Influential *Globe
and Mail* critic William Arthur Deacon, pleased that "[n]o false
romance intrudes" in the book, heralded the "emergence of a young
writer of more than usual competence and deep devotion to her craft"
(32). Juanita O'Connor of the *Halifax Chronicle* praised it as "one of
the most realistic and vivid pictures of conditions in a raw Canadian

northwestern settlement that has yet been written" (10). Likened
to such classics of social realism as John Steinbeck's *The Grapes
of Wrath* ("'In Due Season'" 11) and Gabrielle Roy's *The Tin Flute*
("First-Rate" 10), *In Due Season* tells us about the lives and attitudes of
marginalized individuals and communities as they cope with difficult
socio-economic circumstances that are aggravated by the Great
Depression and the prairie dustbowl of the 1930s. In addition, the story
of van der Mark's life and writings provides a cogent illustration of
women's options during the era before second-wave feminism, as well
as insights into the history of Canadian publishing.

Literary Contexts

The romantic fiction written about the Canadian West at the end of
the nineteenth century and the beginning of the twentieth by such
well-known authors as Gilbert Parker, Ralph Connor, and Arthur
Stringer created a man's world of dashing adventure, idiosyncratic
personalities, and rich agricultural opportunities for European fur
traders, fortune seekers, and settlers. While remaining popular with
general readers, such stories lost academic favour as the mid-twentieth-
century preference for stylistic restraint and social realism granted
canonical status to novels and short stories about the hard lives of
homesteading prairie pioneers. This West was likewise dominated
by men, those who broke the sod (and often fractured their personal
relationships) as they worked obsessively to transform unploughed
terrain into lucrative wheat fields. The commonalities of these fictional
characters shaped the trope of the "prairie patriarch" who was "almost
always portrayed as authoritative and unbending, consumed with
the perpetual acquisition of property and wealth" (Querengesser and
Horton xxiv). Hence the gendered title of Laurence Ricou's 1973 study,
*Vertical Man/Horizontal World: Man and Landscape in Canadian
Prairie Fiction*, is no accident. A common theme within the genre is to

show how the combination of psychological alienation and geographical isolation leads to the collapse of men who are physically strong but emotionally stunted, such as naive Neils Lindstedt of Frederick Philip Grove's *Settlers of the Marsh* (1925), brutal Caleb Gare of Martha Ostenso's *Wild Geese* (1925), overly ambitious Abe Spauling of Grove's *Fruits of the Earth* (1933), and conflicted Donald Strand of Robert J.C. Stead's recently reissued *Dry Water* (2008). In a similar vein, the drought and the Great Depression of the 1930s take their toll in the stories of Sinclair Ross that focus on men's artistic and spiritual failures (*As for Me and My House*, "Cornet at Night") or emotional downfall ("The Painted Door").[1] While the landscape is benign in W.O. Mitchell's *Who Has Seen the Wind* (1947), the perspective of young Brian remains resolutely masculine. Whether the narratives conclude in idealized success or realistic failure, canonical Canadian prairie fiction was dominated by male authors foregrounding male characters, until the advent of Margaret Laurence in the 1960s brought us the varied women who inhabit her fictional town of Manawaka, Manitoba.

Despite the prevalence of male characters and perspectives in canonized literary representations of Western Canada from the first half of the twentieth century, there is no shortage of women's accounts of their prairie experiences. Much of this writing is documentary rather than creative and was penned by educated women from Britain. Some of these texts address the imbalance created by "surplus" women in Britain toward the end of the nineteenth century and the concomitant dearth of women in Western Canada by recommending female emigration to the prairies to provide wives for single male homesteaders. Narratives collected in 1982 by Susan Jackel in *A Flannel Shirt and Liberty*, written by visitors and short-term residents such as Agnes Skrine, present the West as a virtual paradise for female immigrants with money, ambition, and a taste for outdoor recreation. Georgina Binnie-Clark's *Wheat and Woman* (1914) dwells on the more humorous aspects of her three years as a solo woman homesteader in Saskatchewan while mounting a firm critique of the laws that denied women (whether single or married) the right to a homestead grant of 160 acres that was available to any man, regardless of marital status. Despite her initial investment in becoming "a very modern farmeress" (Graham 2), Binnie-Clark did not remain in Canada and spent much of her later life back in London. Some twenty years later, another Englishwoman, Kathleen Redman Strange, published her prize-winning memoir *With the West in Her Eyes: The Story of a Modern Pioneer* (1937), a wry account of eleven years on an Alberta farmstead where she and her husband, a British war veteran, established a successful seed and poultry business before they were devastated by drought and the Great Depression. Pre-Depression writings by Canadian-born women such as Emily Murphy's travel sketches in *Janey Canuck in the West* (1910) share the optimism and the Imperialistic perspective of their British-born counterparts as they celebrate the opening of the Canadian West to European settlement, while seldom acknowledging the catastrophic displacement of the Indigenous population that had lived on the land for thousands of years.

Educated and articulate women like Binnie-Clark and Strange, who came to farming in Western Canada by choice and then moved on to other pursuits when faced with difficulty, are polar opposites of Christine van der Mark's Lina Ashley, a working woman of few words whose thoughts are seldom revealed to us as she manages her limited options. Superficially reminiscent of American author Willa Cather's *My Ántonia* (1918) in its focus on a proficient prairie farm woman, van der Mark's book eschews Cather's portrayal of the open-hearted immigrant to conceptualize Lina as a woman who displays the physical and intellectual strength associated with successful male pioneers, along with the emotional austerity that leads to their undoing. Such an unconventional character challenges our foundational notions of maternal behaviour. In contrast to the stereotype of the self-sacrificing mother as celebrated in Roseanna Lacasse of *The Tin Flute* (1945),

Lina does not succumb to ill fortune. In his review of *In Due Season*, Deacon suggests that readers prefer maternal protagonists who evoke emotion and pity, not women who know "little love" in "dreary" lives in northern Alberta (32). A single mother "forced to work like a man to wrest a living from the land," as van der Mark declares in her author's note at the beginning of the book, Lina "degenerates in spirit" and alienates her children (3).[2] The result is what Colin Hill describes as a "double-edged" feminist message: "on the one hand, Ashley's material success suggests that motivated women can achieve much in the face of powerful opposition; at the same time, the emotional toll that Ashley's pursuits exact on her suggests that such victories are often pyrrhic" (99). The book's title reinforces this moral vision. The phrase "in due season" comes from Galatians 6:9—"In due season, we shall reap"—an image picked up in the book's epigraph from Galatians 6:7: "Be not deceived; God is not mocked; for whatsoever a man soweth, that shall he also reap" (3).

At the same time as she embodies a masculine kind of moral failure, Lina challenges patriarchal norms and economic principles entrenched in legislation that prevailed until recently. Although married women in Alberta could own land after 1922, the attitude persisted that husbands should control finances and property rights. In 1975, the Supreme Court of Canada ruled that, in the case of divorce or separation, an Alberta ranch wife had no right to a share in the sizable property accumulated during the marriage (Bissett-Johnson). Thus, the Ashley homestead would have remained Sym's property even after he had left his family, whereas property that Lina acquired subsequently in her name would likely have been her own. Within the novel, Lina's hard-nosed perspective is balanced by the viewpoint of her small daughter, Mary Belle Ashley, known as Poppy. This name repeats van der Mark's childhood nickname for herself as preserved in archival correspondence with her sister[3] and suggests a personal investment in ensuring that Lina's increasingly narrow focus is balanced by Poppy's maturing self-awareness and eventual independence in choosing her own course of action by eloping with her Metis lover.

One looks in vain for Lina's predecessors in works by Canadian writers. Some parallels appear in the determined immigrant women in the fiction of Laura Goodman Salverson and Nellie L. McClung (notably Helmi Milander of *Painted Fires*), but due to their inability to speak English and their lower social class, these characters are generally restricted to working for employers and none possesses the sheer determination that propels Lina. In her introduction to the 1979 reprint of *In Due Season*, Dorothy Livesay notes some affinity with two female-authored accounts of pioneer hardship in Saskatchewan— Mary Hiemstra's *Gully Farm* (1955), a memoir of the Barr colony, and Vera Lysenko's *Yellow Boots* (1954), a nostalgic story of Ukrainian immigrants—only to conclude that these books' "loving concern for detail" (i) contrasts sharply with van der Mark's terseness.

While Lina may have no evident predecessors, Margaret Laurence would seem to offer a possible line of succession in Hagar Shipley of *The Stone Angel* (1964). Hagar possesses a number of Lina's character traits, such as independence and stubbornness, and experiences similar estrangement from her husband and misunderstanding of her children. At the end of her long life, Hagar is granted restitution when she learns the value of human relationships, but such reconciliation remains unavailable to Lina, who simply continues to milk her cow after she hears that her daughter has gone. Van der Mark's writings also echo in Laurence's last novel, *The Diviners* (1974), which builds connection between Euro-Canadians and the Metis. But here we face a conundrum in that it is difficult to pin down Laurence's acquaintance with *In Due Season* or with van der Mark's other writings. When *In Due Season* appeared in December 1947, Laurence was newly married, living in Winnipeg, and working as a journalist. As an aspiring writer, she must have paid attention to book reviews and would likely have noticed that *In Due Season* was warmly received in newspapers across

Canada, including a glowing review in the *Winnipeg Tribune*. She may also have read van der Mark's stories about the Metis in Western Canada, notably "Catch-Colt" in *Here and Now* and "Brothers" in *MacLean's Magazine*, which both appeared in 1948, or she may have read van der Mark's articles in the *Christian Science Monitor* in the 1950s.

While it seems unlikely that Laurence was unaware of van der Mark, no response is documented in Laurence's published letters or essays or in her fonds at York University. In the late 1970s, when New Star Books prepared a new edition of *In Due Season*, Laurence was the first person invited to write the introduction. She politely declined on the grounds that she was too busy with her own work and evinced no direct acquaintance with a book that she simply described as "clearly of importance."[4] Ironically, Laurence's success as Canada's leading prairie woman novelist of the 1960s contributed to the erasure of her predecessor, as demonstrated in Edward McCourt's influential study *The Canadian West in Fiction*. In the first edition of 1949, McCourt devoted five pages to van der Mark; in the second edition of 1970, this section was replaced with ten pages on Margaret Laurence and van der Mark's name vanished from the volume. This erasure has been surprisingly effective. *In Due Season* receives minimal attention in Ricou's *Vertical Man/Horizontal World* and in Dick Harrison's *Unnamed Country: The Struggle for a Canadian Prairie Fiction* (1977) and earns brief acknowledgement as an "almost unknown" prairie-realist novel (99) in Hill's *Modern Realism in Canadian Fiction*.

Social and Historical Contexts

Long before Christine van der Mark was born in Calgary in 1917, most of the western prairie region was covered with grasslands populated by massive bison herds that were the primary source of food and material goods for Assiniboine, Cree, and Blackfoot hunting cultures.

In the seventeenth century, the fur trade became the major point of contact between Aboriginals and Europeans. Settlers started to trickle into the region as its agricultural potential grew evident, beginning with the founding of Lord Selkirk's Red River Colony in 1812, in what is now Manitoba. Euro-Canadian encroachment on Aboriginal and Metis lands eventually culminated in the Red River Rebellion of 1869–70 and the Dominion Lands Act of 1872. This homestead program granted lots of 160 acres to male settlers in return for a fee of ten dollars and a commitment to cultivate and live on the land. With the establishment of the North West Mounted Police in 1873, the expansion of railways across Canada, and the virtual extinction of the bison—which led to the starvation of the Aboriginal population and facilitated confinement of the survivors on reservations—the prairies were opened to waves of land-hungry European settlers, the first of whom came largely from Ireland and the British Isles. The prairie population swelled from 400,000 in 1901 to two million in 1921 and 2.4 million in 1931 (Friesen 242) as new groups were welcomed, including people from Iceland and Scandinavia as well as "men in sheepskin coats"[5] from Eastern Europe. *In Due Season* faithfully follows this settlement history. In its opening chapter, the established farmers in the long-settled region that is now devastated by drought bear standard British surnames such as Ashley,[6] Brown, Carter, Graham, and Kent. However, in the northwestern area to which Lina relocates, the settlers include more recent newcomers from Ukraine (farmers Zachariah Olenski and Pete Panachuk) and Sweden (farmer Sven Jensen and hotel owner Gustav Hanson), the English harness maker Tudor Folkes, and the Chinese storekeeper known only as Wong. The schoolroom roll call adds Norwegian, French, Polish, German, and Russian names to create a rich ethnic mix (58–59).

The decade following the First World War was an era of unprecedented agricultural abundance in Western Canada, documented in many personal narratives such as Strange's *With the West in Her*

Eyes. Bumper grain crops and high prices contributed to a sense of complacency that quickly evaporated when the stock market crash of 1929 was followed by years of drought. Many farmers, especially those who had invested in new equipment and extended land holdings, lost everything: "The prairie wheat economy tottered as the $1.60 a bushel price of 1929 skidded to 38 cents in 2½ years" (Broadfoot xii). Barry Broadfoot's *Ten Lost Years, 1929–1939* documents how Canadians in all walks of life suffered substantial loss; worst hit were residents of the Palliser Triangle region of southern Alberta, Saskatchewan, and western Manitoba, where dustbowl conditions led to the departure of 250,000 people between 1931 and 1941. Many left "the short-grass plains of the south" for "the wooded parkbelt farther north" (Friesen 388), the choice enacted by Lina Ashley, who treks some three hundred miles across Alberta to create a new home in the Peace River region. The reality of these conditions, which van der Mark witnessed first-hand, would imbue much of her creative and journalistic writing.

Biography of Christine van der Mark

As a shy, self-conscious adolescent, van der Mark began to write poetry and short stories about the Alberta landscape, Indigenous people, and European settlers when she was just thirteen. She was born in Calgary on 17 September 1917, eight years after her father, Christian van der Mark (1879–1954), emigrated from Holland. A trained accountant, he supplemented the family income by raising chickens. Her mother, Mary Widdop (1886–1964), was born in Worcester, England. She worked as an office clerk prior to immigrating to Canada in her mid-twenties and married soon after her arrival. The van der Mark family valued art, music, and education; like most Canadian families, the household had little disposable income during the 1930s, but the parents surrounded their children with culture through music lessons and "prints of good paintings" (D. Wise 365). Christine was the middle child between her older sister, Katarina (Kay, b. 1914), with whom she was close, and her younger brother, Charles (b. 1919). Both Kay and Christine became teachers; Charles served in the Second World War and then followed his father's path, working as a bookkeeper in Alberta. Christine attributed her enduring conscientiousness and work ethic to the family ethos modelled by her father and described later in her short personal essay "A Discourse on Pride and Restraint."[7] In her teenage years, her diligence helped her obtain summer employment on farms, where she enjoyed the solitude of wandering the grain fields and collecting insects that would later serve as specimens in her science lessons in Alberta's sparse rural schoolhouses.

Imagining her future as a published writer, the adolescent Christine created little poetry booklets complete with illustrated cover pages, dedications to her mother, dates of issue, and sometimes her photograph. Her early verses reflect her sensitivity to the personal and political struggles of others. Later, during her undergraduate years at the University of Alberta, Professor F.M. Salter praised her poetry for having "a most peculiar, haunting flavor . . . that I cannot quite get hold of or analyze."[8] Her first publication, at the age of fourteen, was a poem, "To a Bluebird," in the *Calgary Herald*, followed by "The Prayer of a Tree" three years later. At sixteen, she attended a junior authors' poetry group in Calgary, where her literary inclinations were nurtured by Catherine and Mary Barclay,[9] members of the Calgary branch of the Canadian Authors Association. Like the Barclay sisters, Christine's mother was a devout Christian Scientist who raised her daughters in her faith.

Following the path taken by her older sister, Christine van der Mark received teacher training at the Calgary Normal School. After the usual eight-month course of study, she graduated in 1936 with a first-class teaching certificate, apt demonstration of her ability in an environment where female students were "invariably prepared for second class certificates" (Stamp 3). As she turned nineteen in the autumn of 1936, Christine began her teaching career in an abandoned farmhouse that served as both schoolhouse and teacher's living quarters in Cluny, Alberta, situated in the dry belt of the Palliser Triangle. She felt the effects of drought and the Great Depression alongside her students and their families during the longest heat wave in Canada. For the next six years, she taught in eastern Alberta farming communities Bonnyville and Glendon, the setting for the opening chapter of *In Due Season*. She enjoyed the challenge of instructing the children of European settlers and Metis families in outlying communities where the teacher's responsibilities included chopping wood and hauling coal to warm the school before the children arrived in the morning ("My Day" 23). Her correspondence with her parents reveals that the people in these rural communities did her as much good as her patient pedagogy did for their children. In a 1941 letter to her father, she notes her growing ease at conversation as she goes about on horseback, requests donations for the school picnic, and reports feeling "released from the shackles of self-consciousness and shyness."[10]

In the late 1930s, Christine took creative writing courses by correspondence before she and her sister commenced degree programs in September 1938 at the University of Alberta, where Kay enrolled in home economics and Christine in English literature. The sisters consistently attained high academic standing and each won several awards. They also made time for community service: Kay helped prepare bandages for the war effort ("Wauneita" 1) as Christine organized radio programs for furloughed soldiers on the university station ("WW's" 1). Alongside her academic studies and her summer teaching, Christine consistently sought publication opportunities, a practice she would continue throughout her life. In 1936, *The Chinook*, her Normal School Yearbook, included some of her poems, and her work appeared regularly in the University of Alberta's student magazine, *The Gateway*. Her article "My Day: Teaching against Odds on the Prairie" was published in Britain's *Overseas Daily Mail* in August 1938. Early in her undergraduate studies, she attended Professor F.M. Salter's English 65 course, the "first creative writing course offered by any Canadian university" (Melnyk 35). After completing her B.A. requirements in May 1941, she returned to the university in 1944 to focus on creative writing, and in 1946 she became the first student at the University of Alberta to earn an M.A. with the draft of a novel for a thesis: "A Study of Conditions of the Last Frontier during the Depression and Following, in the Form of a Novel Entitled, In Due Season." Between her undergraduate and graduate studies, she continued to submit work for publication and to compose short stories while teaching in the north. A number of the poems written for Salter's course were subsequently published and reveal van der Mark's determination to address social issues that were rarely discussed in public. For example, "She Answered" gives voice to a woman who takes her own life, unable to bear spousal abuse, poverty, and rural isolation; in contrast, "On Leave" tells about "a part of our country that is little known" and acknowledges the "rich story" of the Alberta Metis who served in the Second World War (5).

Van der Mark's summer teaching stints included a placement at Keg River in northern Alberta's Great Bear region of the Peace River District, the destination of many prairie farmers who migrated to escape the drought. Here she grew to know the place and population that inspired her fictional community of Bear Claw. Her consciousness was raised further during the 1940s, through her friendship with the local medical doctor, Mary Percy Jackson, who acquainted her with the work of James Brady, founder of the Metis Association of Alberta. In the summer of 1946, van der Mark took a different job, as a stewardess on the Mackenzie River paddle steamer of the Hudson's Bay Company. By day, she carried linens to passengers, while in her spare time she recorded the customs and concerns of the Indigenous people she encountered. In the summer of 1947, while fine-tuning the manuscript of her book, she returned to the rural school in Keg River and wrote to her family about the social issues facing the community, including the apprehensions of returning veterans who felt misled by false government promises over the Veterans' Land Act and the treatment of tubercular Metis children. Rural Albertans and Indigenous people would inhabit much of van der Mark's subsequent writing. Her short stories of 1948, "Catch-Colt" (a euphemism for a child born out of wedlock) in *Here and Now* and "Brothers" in *MacLean's Magazine*, both critique discrimination against children of Metis descent.[11]

Until her death in 1970, van der Mark actively pursued publication of several dozen short stories, numerous essays and poems, and three other novels; many of these remain in manuscript or typescript among her papers at the University of Calgary.[12] She further extended her range with her play "Nick's Daughter," dramatized on CBC radio on 2 September 1949.[13] Her article "Teaching in the North" began as a speech to the Alberta Educational Council and appeared in both the *Calgary Herald* and *The Alberta School Trustee* in 1948. After the acceptance of *In Due Season*, she continued to support the University of Alberta's alumni publication *The New Trail* with such contributions as "Church Service at Tuktoyaktuk" in 1947.

While van der Mark was refining *In Due Season* for Oxford University Press, editor R.W.W. Robertson, who would describe this novel as "rather a prestige item"[14] and van der Mark as "a new young author" who "has quite a future,"[15] expressed interest in her work-in-progress.[16] She suggested that a collection of her stories, entitled *Hidden Trails*, would be timely, given the climate of increasing public sympathy toward the problems of Indigenous people and the 1947 parliamentary presentation on living conditions in the north from an Alberta delegation of First Peoples who travelled to Ottawa.[17] Nonetheless, the manager at Oxford, W.H. Clarke, decided that it would be "little less than tragic" for her "reputation as a writer if the [second] book were published at this moment."[18] However, publication of two stories from the collection, "Brothers" and "Catch-Colt," brought only praise. The latter appeared on the 1948 "Roll of Honor" in Martha Foley's annual *Yearbook of the American Short Story*, where van der Mark enjoyed the illustrious company of Elizabeth Bishop, F. Scott Fitzgerald, Mary McCarthy, Flannery O'Connor, J.D. Salinger, and Tennessee Williams (323–24).

While neither Clarke nor Robertson appears to have provided van der Mark with a critique of *Hidden Trails*, a previous difference of opinion over revisions to *In Due Season* had strained the author–editor relationship. Although she deferred to her editors' choice of illustration for her book's dust jacket and accepted their refusal to issue a condensed advance magazine version, van der Mark firmly resisted their objections to the positive representation of Metis characters, especially Jay, whom Robertson described as "altogether too attractive." He argued that "if the measure of Lina's spiritual degradation is the fact that her daughter runs away with a half breed, then . . . the half breed should be painted at his worst."[19] Standing her ground, van der Mark stated, "I would rather the book not be published at all than feel that I had been unjust to such people as Jay." She added that "if such discussions were to be omitted, the impression the reader will have of the native and his place will be Lina's own. And her prejudices are of the worst."[20] As well, Robertson requested that van der Mark modulate the focus on the love affair between Jay and Poppy and reduce her attention to the complex community of Metis people and settlers. She firmly replied, "It is true that *In Due Season* is the story of Lina Ashley, a woman whose character hardened as material prosperity came to her. But the book is also the story of a community. There is a kind of balance between the opening up and growth of the community, and the degeneration of the woman's kindlier nature."[21] While Robertson yielded to her concern for "doing justice to the whole problem of the half breed and the Indian,"[22] Oxford appeared to be uncomfortable with her interest in Indigenous people. Yet it is the novel's positive representation of Metis culture and its insightful portrait of rural northern communities that so strongly recommend its reprinting today.

In their contractual publishing relationships, van der Mark's most successful Canadian contemporaries, Gabrielle Roy (whose *The Tin Flute* was an international bestseller in 1945) and W.O. Mitchell (whose *Who Has Seen the Wind* had appeared earlier in 1947), were guided by experienced mentors and agents. In a 1943 letter, her professor of creative writing, F.M. Salter, cautioned van der Mark against giving reviewers an excuse to take her novel as autobiographical, but offered no further advice about publishing.[23] At the same time, Salter mentored Mitchell long after his 1942 graduation from the University of Alberta, where van der Mark and Mitchell had been fellow students in Salter's Shakespeare course in 1940–41.[24] They may also have known each other as aspiring writers, as Salter welcomed Mitchell as an occasional visitor to his creative writing classes (Mitchell and Mitchell 248). Salter thought of Mitchell as a "boy" in need of "fatherly advice" (Mitchell and Mitchell 250) and did much more to foster his literary career than he did for van der Mark, his current graduate student. Very involved in *Who Has Seen the Wind*, Salter "looked over [Mitchell's] shoulder from the beginning to draft stages to publication" and "edited every page of his manuscript before it was submitted." Indeed, Mitchell thought of Salter as his "agent sans ten percent" because he used his publishing contacts to promote Mitchell's book (Mitchell 9). Such personal support and business advice can have a significant effect on canonicity. Although van der Mark inquired about her rights, she lacked outside guidance when she agreed to Oxford's contract, which included British and American rights, even though there was no apparent plan for publication or distribution of *In Due Season* in either country.

Following the release of *In Due Season*, van der Mark held a teaching position with the English department of her alma mater, where she met her future husband, Thomas Wise, a staff lecturer in

economics who was seven years her junior. Their daughter, Dorothy
Wise, describes her father as idealistic, attractive, and extroverted
(368). A Cambridge graduate, he was the son of Edward F. Wise, British MP and chairman of the Socialist League, who had died when Tom
was nine years old. After their quiet wedding on 15 August 1949 at
St. Stephen's Anglican Church in Calgary, Tom and Christine resided
in Edmonton, where their first daughter, Dorothy Maud Shoshanna
Wise, was born 3 November 1950. The following year, they travelled
to England to introduce Christine and their child to Tom's mother
and sisters (C. van der Mark, "Bon Voyage" 21). While abroad in 1951,
the couple attended a summer school in the Netherlands on global
economic development. Dorothy Wise described this as a turning point
in her father's life, inspiring him to work in non-industrial countries;
for the next decade, Tom's preferences mapped the course of what his
daughter called their "nomadic" existence (368). In 1953, the family
left Edmonton as Tom began a Ph.D. at McGill University in Montreal, where their second daughter, Thelma (Tammy), was born 17 June
1954.

In 1952–53, van der Mark began writing for the *Christian Science
Monitor* (*CSM*), where she would publish twenty-one articles over the
next decade, the majority being travel narratives. Two longer articles
appeared in instalments: "We Worked toward the Arctic" introduces
the Inuit customs and communities she observed while working on
the paddlewheeler, and "Tales of a Prairie School Teacher" chronicles
her experiences during the worst drought years. Although some of her
later *CSM* articles express implicit social commentary, she adjusted the
tone of her work to the periodical's editorial requirements by reducing
her outspokenness. Three months after Tammy was born, Tom Wise
took a teaching position at the University of Peshawar, moving his wife
and small daughters to Pakistan near the Khyber Pass, where he could
research rural labour practices and economic development. Far from
North American publishers and the rural people who inspired her, van

der Mark continued to write and publish as best she could. She taught English at the University of Peshawar, which published her short novel *Hassan*, intended as a textbook for the young men in her classes, and contributed a series of articles about Pakistan to *CSM* under the name Christine van der Mark Wise.[25] Publishing from this distance required persistence and adaptability, given the complications of mailing packages from the Khyber Pass, which could take up to six months to reach North America (M. van der Mark 12). By June 1957, when the family left Pakistan, Thomas Wise had been appointed director of the Board of Economic Enquiry and Chairman of the Department of Economics at the University of Peshawar.[26]

The Wise family then moved to New Haven, Connecticut, where Tom planned to write his thesis. He gratefully acknowledged Christine's hand in preparing a readable dissertation that pointed out the diminishing economic circumstances of Pakistan's rural peasant farmers and the economic impact of cultural constraints on women and children.[27] While in Connecticut, Christine took up the burden of care for her ailing mother. The family then moved to Montreal, where Christine taught an English course at Sir George Williams College (now Concordia University) in 1958–59. Plans to return to Pakistan in June 1959 fell through by the time they reached England (D. Wise 368). The following year, the family travelled to Khartoum, in the Republic of Sudan, where Tom and Christine taught at the university and Tom continued his research. Here Christine began her second significant novel, *Honey in the Rock*, and wrote four articles about Sudan for *CSM*.[28] While in Khartoum, Christine discovered she had a tumour that later became malignant (D. Wise 369). Due to her Christian Science beliefs, she did not pursue medical treatment but relied on prayer. In her correspondence regarding the New Star Books reprint of *In Due Season,* Dorothy Livesay lamented Christine's untimely death on 13 January 1970, finding it "strange and upsetting" that "Christian Science adherents refuse to recognize other health resources."[29]

In 1962, the Wise family returned to Canada. For two years, Christine taught in the English department at Memorial University in Newfoundland and Tom taught economics. They finally settled in Ottawa, where Tom worked for the Federal Fisheries Department and Christine taught in a suburban elementary school. She continued to write: "Khyber Bride" appeared in *Chatelaine* in June 1963 and "Memories of a Country School Teacher" was included in *The Hussar Heritage* in 1965,[30] the year before McClelland and Stewart issued *Honey in the Rock*, a condensed version of which appeared in the *Star Weekly* in December 1966. These later writings are set where Christine began her teaching career, in the one-room prairie schoolhouse. *Honey in the Rock* recounts the experience of a young male teacher who spends 1936–37 in a prairie hamlet where courtship and social activities are the prevailing interests among recent immigrants from Eastern Europe. Van der Mark's creation of a narrow-minded religious community successfully portrays the limited horizons of young women for whom marriage is the only option, but without the stylistic tension and distilled characterization that distinguish her first novel and without any references to Native or Metis people.

Van der Mark's unpublished stories, journals, and family correspondence in her fonds at the University of Calgary reveal that over her short lifetime of fifty-three years, she was sensitive to many forms of abuse of power. Although Dorothy Wise describes her mother as "not political" (370) and James Doyle maintains that van der Mark was uninterested in "a Marxist or other socialist perspective" (184), her writings brim with concern for marginalized people.

Settlers, Metis, and the Creation of Community

The social fabric of settlement communities—the complex relationships among rural ranchers, townspeople, Metis, and Aboriginals that van der Mark insisted must remain in the text of *In*

Due Season—is also a recurring topic in her unpublished manuscripts and personal correspondence. In letters to her parents from Beaver Crossing and Keg River, Christine wrote about hungry Metis children on relief who "stay home from school as it is less weakening than walking miles to school," the exploitation of Metis labour by white settlers who paid them a dollar a day to work all day "like live machines" to clear the land,[31] and storekeepers who "reaped all the profit" buying berries and beadwork from Metis women.[32] These letters include examples of consistent neglect by the educational system: the racist, "stern and severe" teacher who hated teaching in the region and in turn was hated by the Metis community;[33] dilapidated desks that students had to repair regularly and crooked floorboards in the poorly constructed rural schools; the scandalous story of her predecessor, a thirty-four-year-old teacher impregnated by an eighteen-year-old Metis student;[34] the fate of a bright, uneducated, forty-year-old deaf-mute woman who kept house for her bachelor brothers and wanted only to "learn" from the local teacher.[35] Other letters and notebook entries address gender politics in her stories of rural women's struggles: a woman whose common-law spouse died, leaving her without property rights or a home for their children,[36] and the plight of daughters subjected to strict paternal rule.[37]

In her introduction to the 1979 New Star edition of *In Due Season*, Dorothy Livesay underscores the "sociological as well as literary significance" (ii) of a book that she describes as "one of the first, if not the first Canadian novel wherein the plight of the Native Indian and the Metis is honestly and painfully recorded" (iv). Likewise, Pamela Karlenzwig's historical analysis of the documentary importance of Canadian women's prairie fiction finds *In Due Season* "extraordinary for its sympathetic portrayal of the Metis from their point of view" (48). While this novel directs attention to the poverty and marginalization of Metis people and the consequences of settler and state encroachment on their traditional trapping grounds and way of life, it is equally remarkable for its subtle representation of a dynamic Metis community that moves fluidly among European settlers and status Indians, creating an unmistakable presence in the prairie culture of Bear Claw.

Karlenzwig's research demonstrates that much of the prairie fiction of the period promoted a "social and literary conservatism" (30) that fostered gender and racial stereotypes. Unlike her contemporaries, van der Mark makes visible the tuberculosis epidemic of the first half of the century and the dehumanizing effect of racist epithets in schoolyard violence and common parlance. Lina Ashley rages against the Metis who have worked diligently to help her clear her land and care for her children when she catches Poppy, now sixteen, with Jay Baptiste, "in the arms of a dirty half-breed" (200). Ignoring his years of dedication to milking her cows and protecting Poppy, Lina adds a final insult: "The number of times I fed you at my door. I might better of fed a stray dog" (200). The impact of this traumatic scene surfaces nearly sixty pages later, when Jay, now a capable trapper, rejects Tudor Folkes's suggestion that his fluency in "Cree, Chyp, English, French" (258) should qualify him for an interpreter's position, saying, "I've been to the Outside, and now I know what I am. . . . I am a breed. A dog" (258). Jay's internalization of Lina's epithet is reinforced by the discrimination he meets Outside, working in predominantly white prairie towns and cities. But as the conversation ends, Jay becomes his community's spokesman: "It's just—I see both sides. We are sometimes, I know, like children. But it must be wrong that we are dying, and full of disease" (258).

Van der Mark vigorously voiced her desire to combat racism in two essays, "Save Our Metis People by New Brand of Aid" (published in *Saturday Night* in 1948) and "That They May Learn Tolerance" (published in the journal of the Alberta Teachers' Association in 1947). In the latter, she condemns a text used in Alberta schools that derogates Natives and demands that Robert Watson's storybook *When Christmas Came to Fort Garry* be "stricken from the books" because it "leaves ideas of racial intolerance in the minds of young students" and "subtly preaches the 'superior race' theory so conspicuous in German propaganda" (23). Contending that Watson's unchallenged racial insults are detrimental to all young minds, she argues that "not only are the students of white blood finding terms in which to express contempt for natives, but many young native pupils have a sense of their own inferiority borne in upon them" (24). She understands that when racist derogation is sanctioned as required reading by school authorities, these ideas will "lie under the surface . . . unconsciously forming prejudices in the mind" (24).

In this story, the McAllister daughter is forbidden to marry the boy she loves because he is thought to be Metis, an outcome that van der Mark counters at the close of *In Due Season*. During the local celebration known as Treaty Days, Poppy flees her mother's control when she rides away with Jay to join the Metis community that welcomes her. This scene reframes and destabilizes the prohibition against mixed marriage in Watson's story, thereby subverting the cultural discrimination that was seldom challenged in Canada during the 1940s. Both *In Due Season* and "That They May Learn Tolerance" strategically apply van der Mark's insight that people do not fully realize what happens as they read. In place of Watson's story, van der Mark recommends Pauline Johnson's "The Shagganappi" (1913) because Johnson's story "puts into the mouth of the Governor-General of Canada, Lord Mortimer, these words, 'I do not like the word *breed* applied to human beings. It is a term for cattle, not men'" (25). Here, van der Mark layers Johnson's authority as a part-Native woman over the authority Johnson bestows on Lord Mortimer, in order to instruct her audience about the dehumanizing power of the term "breed."

In a further example of her writing on key issues affecting Indigenous communities, the essay "Save Our Metis People by New Brand of Aid" raises the alarm about the tuberculosis epidemic among the Metis, to which *In Due Season* alludes when Jay says, "[I]t must be wrong that we are dying, and full of disease" (258). Van der Mark attributes this epidemic to lack of state medical protection as well as to changes in lifestyle and diet stemming from Indigenous people being pushed to the "fringes of settlement, on the outskirts of white communities near Reserves, or as in some regions of Alberta, in the recently organized Metis colonies" (11). She notes that although free hospitalization was available for TB patients in Alberta, the practices and atmosphere in the converted military barracks that served as TB hospitals had the inadvertent effect of spreading this highly contagious disease. As an example, she describes how the Keg River general practitioner, Dr. Mary Percy Jackson,[38] diagnosed a little Metis boy who was sent to one such hospital. He was cured of tuberculosis and of the measles he contracted while hospitalized, but he suffered from loneliness and was terrified of the darkened isolated room prescribed for his measles. Back home, he contracted TB a second time and died because the family would not consult the doctor, as they could not put him through the trauma of hospitalization again. As word of the child's horrific experience spread through the community, well-intended parents and sick children did their best to hide their symptoms, resulting in the exposure of more families. Van der Mark details Dr. Jackson's vision for bringing the disease under control with a hospital "built on a river. . . . Relatives and friends of the patient could then come by canoe . . . and have a place to camp when they arrived. If the patient could . . . see the tents of his friends . . . he would be able to endure more easily the confinement necessary for his recovery" (11).

This vision was revolutionary in its holistic approach to the culture of the patients. A further example of her commitment appears in Dr. Jackson's letter thanking van der Mark for sharing her twenty-five-dollar payment for the *Saturday Night* article. Surprised and grateful, Jackson planned to use the twelve dollars and fifty cents to buy vaccine. She had recently proposed to inoculate all Metis babies in Keg River if the Alberta government would provide the vaccine; when their refusal included the address from which she could buy supplies herself, Jackson was determined to do so, to "see TB rates drop significantly as my immunized babies grow up."[39]

It was through her friendship and common cause with Dr. Jackson that van der Mark learned about James Patrick Brady, one of five social activists who were able to secure land rights for Metis communities in the 1930s through the Population Betterment Act of 1938.[40] The main result was negotiated land and resource rights that still have no parallel in other provinces as well as the founding of ten Metis settlements on leased land, eight of which survive today (Brown 403). Van der Mark's 1941 teaching post in Bonnyville was near two of these settlements, Fishing Lake and Elizabeth. Her Keg River post was approximately fifteen kilometres from the northernmost Metis settlement at Paddle Prairie. In another example of her commitment to social betterment, van der Mark's 1948 speech to Alberta librarians, found among her papers, cites James P. Brady and Johnny Callihoo as examples of educated Metis men who worked to counter racist treatment of their people.[41]

Van der Mark's anti-racist advocacy is paralleled by her demonstration of the resilience and motility of the Metis community. As Jay and Poppy slip back and forth between the town and the bush and in and out of each other's homes, they sustain one another, their movements in tandem along the bush trails becoming a synecdoche for the mutual interdependence that makes up the social fabric of the region. Moreover, van der Mark illustrates the significance of Metis women in the personal lives of new settlers such as Lina Ashley: Mrs. Two Knives is the first person to welcome the Ashleys; Jay's grandmother, Mrs. Waters, the local medicine woman and midwife, tends to Olenski's fever and to Lina's dying father; the young mother, Martha, shows up on a moment's notice to help Lina and care for her children. Such representations impress upon readers the continuity of social interactions within the community.

The role of Metis women in van der Mark's novel accords with documentary evidence regarding the significance of the Metis in Canada's socio-economic history. Sylvia van Kirk's research into the participation of Indigenous women in the fur trade during the late eighteenth and early nineteenth centuries reveals that the foremothers of the novel's Metis characters facilitated interaction between Indigenous trappers and Euro-Canadian traders (83–84). Metis women, whose Aboriginal mothers and grandmothers passed on traditional skills, languages, and customs, were essential to the fur trade and to survival at the trading outposts (110). In addition to making clothing and pemmican, they served as intercessors, translators, and negotiators in European and Native relations (111), much as do Jay and Mrs. Two Knives in van der Mark's novel. When Lina arrives, Mrs. Two Knives offers a "beautiful pair of beaded moccasins of Poppy's size" to "[m]ake you welcome" (30). This moment and others involving moccasins or references to footwear offer a motif of inclusion, literally putting Poppy into the shoes of the Metis. Further assimilation of Poppy and her little brother, Benny, into the local culture appears in their understanding of the Cree language shared by the Aboriginals and the Metis.

The social fabric of Bear Claw interweaves everyone who lives there. In the latter half of the novel, both Sym and Lina guess that when Poppy does not return home to her chores she has gone with their Metis neighbours. When Sym finds her sleeping by the fire under a blanket with Martha's child at the all-night Tea Dance celebration of a new baby, Isaiah simply says, "Poppy come with us. Have fun" (132), words that suggest that Poppy lives in a cohesive community that functions as an extended family. Tea Dances and Treaty Day festivities show an interconnected society where the languages, the music, and the dancing of the European immigrants mix with Native games of skill and chance. In a particularly telling representation of seamless social relations, Benjie's fiddle moves from Lina's home into

Native and Metis hands, passed back and forth in gambling games, connecting cultures through Treaty Day games, dancing, and singing. When Jay gambles at the Metis game of sticks, he ends up with Benjie's fiddle, and then returns it to Poppy and young Benny. Such details of a dynamic intercultural community will, as van der Mark says, "lie under the surface" ("That They May Learn" 24) of readers' involvement with the novel, countering prejudices and leaving an impression that promotes tolerance, just as Metis women, men, and children left a lasting impression on Christine van der Mark.

The Publishing History of *In Due Season*

While still in manuscript, *In Due Season* won two awards. The first was a $200 prize from the Alberta chapter of the I.O.D.E. in its annual fiction contest of 1946; the second led to publication with considerable fanfare in 1947, as co-winner of the Oxford–Crowell Competition for Canadian writers. There is little surviving documentation about this contest, which ran just once, as a collaborative effort between the Toronto-based Canadian branch of Oxford University Press and the New York publishing house of Thomas Y. Crowell.[42] The timing of the award suggests that the competition was designed to invigorate the presses' publication lists as they recuperated from the economic casualties of the Second World War, which had severely constrained the production of recreational reading on both sides of the Atlantic.

While this particular competition was not repeated, such contests had become common in North America during the first half of the twentieth century as a way for publishers of popular fiction to attract new manuscripts that might yield potential bestsellers. In the 1920s, several Canadian authors became instant celebrities when they received large awards from American publishers: in 1925, Martha Ostenso's *Wild Geese* won the Dodd Mead Best Novel of the Year

Award, and in 1927, Mazo de la Roche's *Jalna* won the $10,000 *Atlantic Monthly* Novel Award. The lifelong career of Constance Beresford-Howe was kick-started in 1946 with an Intercollegiate Literary Fellowship from Dodd Mead. From 1942 to 1960, Canada's Ryerson Press followed a similar strategy when it intermittently bestowed the Ryerson Fiction Award, which offered authors $1,000 and publication with a respectable Canadian firm. The latter was likely the inspiration for the Oxford–Crowell Prize, given the friendly rivalry between the two Toronto-based publishers and the similarity of the terms of the two competitions.

With a submission date of 1 July 1946, the Oxford–Crowell competition was open to any prose manuscript (fiction or non-fiction) in English or French whose author was a Canadian citizen or had lived in Canada for at least ten years ("Concours"). Its judges were B.K. Sandwell, editor of the longstanding Toronto magazine *Saturday Night*; A.W. Trueman, a former English professor who was currently president of the University of Manitoba; and Professor Guy Frégault, an author and a historian at the Université de Montréal. The response was strong: 196 manuscripts were submitted, of which sixteen were in French. The prize was shared by Christine van der Mark for *In Due Season* and Angeline Hango (1909–1995) for her family memoir, *Truthfully Yours*; each received a "fellowship" of $500 and publication with OUP Canada.[43]

Between the receipt of her award and the publication of her book, van der Mark suggested that a shortened magazine version be issued in advance. OUP rejected the proposal as likely to diminish the small Canadian market, even though examples abounded, such as the advance appearance of Constance Beresford-Howe's prize-winning first novel, *The Unreasoning Heart*, in a condensed version in *Redbook* in 1946. Despite strongly positive reviews, *In Due Season* fared badly. While OUP did show it to potential American benefactors and film producers,[44] they sold only about 3,600 copies and claimed that they "lost very heavily on the book."[45] It was declared out of print in 1952, with 1,300 unsold copies in their warehouse. A proposal for well-known Alberta playwright Elsie Park Gowan to dramatize the story for radio unfortunately foundered.[46]

In 1978, van der Mark's daughter, Dorothy Wise, aware of the decade's fresh interest in Canadian literature, sought to republish *In Due Season* as "an enduring book, ahead of its time in its sympathetic portrayal of the Indian and Metis characters."[47] After hearing that OUP no longer published adult fiction and that the copyright now belonged to her mother's estate,[48] Wise obtained a commitment from New Star Books in Vancouver, a small, left-wing publisher with a diversified list of literary and non-fiction titles. Knowing that the book would fare better with an illustrious endorsement, its editor, Rolph Maurer, first invited Margaret Laurence to write the introduction and then approached Margaret Atwood, also without success. Next on the list was Dorothy Livesay, who was happy to support a writer she described as "another woman casualty of that era: 1930–1960" who "never put her own creative needs first."[49] The biographical notes that Wise prepared for Livesay became the book's afterword, complementing the introduction in which Livesay heralds *In Due Season* as "a Canadian prairie epic, a parallel to *My Antonia* in American literature" (i). Despite Livesay's amazement that "a work of such significance received praise and awards when it was first published in November, 1947, but has never gained much attention since" (i), the spare-looking volume produced by New Star sparked little response. Of the planned print run of three thousand copies, only about eleven hundred had sold by 1988.

Christine van der Mark received recognition in 1997 as one of the Alberta women writers commemorated in prizes awarded at the end of a summer writing workshop given by the division of extension studies at the University of Alberta ("Women's"). Now, in 2016, this series of reprints of early Canadian literature creates a fresh reception context for *In Due Season* as we reconsider the Canadian women writers who preceded the second-wave feminists of the 1970s and as we look again at the history of Indigenous and Metis interactions with settler cultures in the West.

CAROLE GERSON AND JANICE DOWSON, *Simon Fraser University*

Acknowledgements

We would like to thank the late Dorothy Wise for permission to republish her mother's book. As well, we are very grateful to a number of people who enabled the preparation of this afterword. Our list includes Phyllis Wilson and her staff at Oxford University Press for providing access to archival material concerning the production of *In Due Season*; Annie Murray, Curator of Rare Books and Manuscripts, and Allison Wagner, Senior Rare Books and Manuscript Advisor of Libraries and Cultural Resources, University of Calgary Archives and Special Collections, for their generous assistance in accessing the Christine van der Mark fonds and responding to our subsequent queries; Nancy Blake and the Inter-Library Loans staff at Simon Fraser University for their helpful persistence in tracking down a long list of obscure requests; Linnea McNally for genealogical research; Nicholas Beauchesne for research at the University of Alberta library; Karyn and Geoff Huenemann for helping with the cover photo of Christine van der Mark; and Benjamin Lefebvre for his editorial expertise.

Notes

1　These two stories by Ross appear in his collection *The Lamp at Noon and Other Stories* (1968).

2　Page references to all quotations from *In Due Season* correspond to this Early Canadian Literature edition.

3　See Christine van der Mark to Kay van der Mark, 10 Mar. 1935 and 29 Apr. 1935. File 1.3, Christine van der Mark fonds.

4　Margaret Laurence to Lanny Beckman, 22 Dec. 1978. New Star Books fonds.

5　This description of immigrants from Eastern Europe is attributed to Clifford Sifton, Minister of the Interior from 1896 to 1905.

6　It is tempting to speculate further on the symbolism of van der Mark's choice of names for her characters. Lina's father is Benjie Farrel (6), his Irish/Celtic surname connoting bravery. Ashley, her husband's surname, suggests the mystical ash tree of Celtic mythology, while his first name, always abbreviated to "Sym," remains obscure. Lina is a common Nordic name, but given that her family is English, it too seems to be a nickname of uncertain origin, and may even connote Mary Magdalene.

7　van der Mark, "A Discourse on Pride and Restraint," 1946. File 1.5, Christine van der Mark fonds.

8　F.M. Salter to van der Mark, 22 Feb. 1943. File 2.1.1, Christine van der Mark fonds.

9　The Barclay sisters were founding members of the Banff School of Fine Arts and the Canadian Youth Hostelling Association.

10　van der Mark to Christian van der Mark, 3 June 1941. File 2.1.1, Christine van der Mark fonds.

11　These two stories appear to have been intended for a short story collection entitled *Hidden Trails*, which describes the effects of encroaching civilization on the nomadic lives of Indigenous people in northern Alberta. Her notes suggest she also considered *No Man's Land* and *As a Blown Leaf* as titles for this collection, which was never published. See various items of correspondence in file 6.1.1, Christine van der Mark fonds.

12　*Where the Long River Flows* (a novel set on the Mackenzie River), *Paul Goss* (a dark critique of the education system's treatment of the Metis), and *No Longer Bound* (an autobiographical novel about the challenges of parenting adolescents in the

1960s) remain unpublished. Typescripts of these three novels are found in files 5.3, 7.1, and 8.3, Christine van der Mark fonds.

13 Helen James to Mrs. T.F. Wise, 15 Sept. 1949. File 3.8, Christine van der Mark fonds.

14 R.W.W. Robertson to Mr. Bice (designer of the book's jacket), 2 Oct. 1947. Oxford University Press archives.

15 Robertson to Bice, 22 Oct. 1947. Oxford University Press archives.

16 van der Mark to Robertson, 4 Feb. 1947. Oxford University Press archives.

17 van der Mark to W.H. Clarke, 7 Dec. 1947. Oxford University Press archives.

18 Clarke to van der Mark, 9 Dec. 1947. Oxford University Press archives.

19 Robertson to van der Mark, 1 Apr. 1947. Oxford University Press archives.

20 van der Mark to Robertson, 24 Mar. 1947. Oxford University Press archives.

21 van der Mark to Robertson, 24 Mar. 1947. Oxford University Press archives.

22 Robertson to van der Mark, 1 Apr. 1947. Oxford University Press archives.

23 Salter to van der Mark, 8 Aug. 1943. File 2.1.1, Christine van der Mark fonds.

24 "Registration Forms and Calendar 1940–41"; "van der Mark Registration Form #942," 25 Sept. 1940; "Mitchell Registration Form #1720," 26 Sept. 1940. Book and Record Depository, University of Alberta.

25 These include "'MacBeth' at the Khyber," "N'Horse," and "First Khyber Christmas" in 1955, "Pakistan Home Charms Westerners," "Marketing by Tonga," and "At the Gate of the Khyber Pass" in 1956, and "Convocation at the University of Peshawar" in 1957.

26 Ahmed Hassan (University of Peshawar registrar) to Thomas Wise, 9 May 1957. File 4.4, Christine van der Mark fonds.

27 T.F. Wise's dissertation, "Methods of Mobilizing Surplus Rural Labor with Particular Reference to Pakistan," was completed in 1965 at McGill University.

28 "Letter from Khartoum" appeared in 1961, whereas "Seeing the Pyramids by Camel," "Marco Polo Stowaway," and "Sudan Educates Its Women" appeared in 1962.

29 Dorothy Livesay to Dorothy Wise, 15 July 1979. New Star Books fonds.

30 Hussar is close to Cluny, the location of Christine's first teaching position.

31 van der Mark to Mary van der Mark, 7 May 1941; van der Mark to Christian van der Mark, 3 June 1941. File 2.1.1, Christine van der Mark fonds.

32 van der Mark to Mary van der Mark, 5 May 1941. File 2.1.1, Christine van der Mark fonds.

33 van der Mark to Mary van der Mark, 18 May 1941. File 2.1.1, Christine van der Mark fonds.

34 van der Mark to Mary van der Mark, 1 May 1941. File 2.1.1, Christine van der Mark fonds.

35 van der Mark to Mary van der Mark, 26 June 1945 and 3 July 1945. File 1.7, Christine van der Mark fonds.

36 van der Mark to Mary van der Mark, 26 June 1945. File 1.7, Christine van der Mark fonds.

37 van der Mark, draft fragments written for English 65 and correspondence course 1938–39, n.d. File 2.1.21, Christine van der Mark fonds.

38 For a verification of statements attributed to her in "Save Our Metis People," see Mary Percy Jackson to van der Mark, 18 Oct. 1947. File 3.2, Christine van der Mark fonds.

39 Jackson to van der Mark, 12 June 1948. File 2.1.1, Christine van der Mark fonds.

40 The five men were Malcolm Norris, Joseph Dion, Peter Tomkins, and Felix Callihoo (see Wall).

41 van der Mark, "Speech to Librarians" [1948]. File 3.6, Christine van der Mark fonds.

42 For more information on Crowell, see DeLowry-Fryman; for more information on Oxford University Press Canada, see Tritter. The two firms likely found a link through their shared specialization in educational and reference books; both presses made occasional forays into trade and literary publishing.

43 Hango's book was delayed until 1948 due to the time required to prepare the illustrations. It won the Stephen Leacock Memorial Medal for 1949, the first time this prize went to a woman, but Hango did not pursue her writing after this one effort.

44 Unidentified editor at Oxford University Press to van der Mark, 15 Sept. 1948. Oxford University Press archives.

45 C.C. Johnson to Christine Wise, 24 Oct. 1951. Oxford University Press archives.

46 Wise to unidentified editor at Oxford University Press, 24 Feb. 1952. Oxford University Press archives.

47 Dorothy Wise to unidentified fiction editor at Oxford University Press, 15 Sept. 1978. Oxford University Press archives.

48 William Toye to Dorothy Wise, 19 Sept. 1978. Oxford University Press archives.

49 Livesay to Wise, 15 July 1979. New Star Books fonds.

Works Cited

I. Archival Sources

Book and Record Depository. University of Alberta.

Christine van der Mark fonds. Archives and Special Collections, University of Calgary.

New Star Books fonds. Special Collections and Rare Books, Simon Fraser University
    Library.

Oxford University Press archives. Oxford University Press (Toronto).

II. Books, Periodicals, and Electronic Sources

Binnie-Clark, Georgina. *Wheat and Woman*. Toronto: Bell and Cockburn, 1914. Print.

Bissell, Claude T. "Letters in Canada: 1947. Fiction." *University of Toronto Quarterly* 17.3
    (1948): 265–78. Print.

Bissett-Johnson, Alistair. "Murdoch Case." *The Canadian Encyclopedia*. Historica Canada,
    23 Jan. 2014. Web. 18 Feb. 2016.

Broadfoot, Barry. *Ten Lost Years, 1929–1939*. 1973. Toronto: McClelland and Stewart, 1997.
    Print.

Brown, Jennifer S.H. "Metis." *The Oxford Companion to Canadian History*. Ed. Gerald
    Hallowell. Don Mills: Oxford UP, 2004. 401–03. Print.

"Concours Oxford-Crowell." *Le Canada français* 33.7 (1946): 528–29. Print.

Deacon, William Arthur. "Lone Pioneer Woman's Struggle on Northern Alberta Bush
    Farm." Rev. of *In Due Season*, by Christine van der Mark. *Globe and Mail* 13 Dec. 1947:
    32. Print.

DeLowry-Fryman, Linda. "Thomas Y. Crowell Company." *Dictionary of Literary Biography*,
    Vol. 49: *American Literary Publishing Houses 1638–1899*. Ed. Peter Dzwonkosi. Detroit:
    Gale, 1986. 107–09. Print.

Doyle, James. *Progressive Heritage: The Evolution of a Politically Radical Literary Tradition in
    Canada*. Waterloo: Wilfrid Laurier UP, 2002. Print.

"First-Rate Alberta Story by New Canadian Author." Rev. of *In Due Season*, by Christine
    van der Mark. *Winnipeg Tribune* 10 Jan. 1948: 10. Print.

Foley, Martha. "Roll of Honor 1948." *The Best American Short Stories 1949 and the
    Yearbook of the American Short Story January 1 to December 31, 1948*. Ed. Martha
    Foley. Boston: Houghton Mifflin, 1949. 323–24. Print.

Friesen, Gerald. *The Canadian Prairies: A History*. Toronto: U of Toronto P, 1987. Print.

Graham, Isabelle Beaton. "Homesteads for Women: A Western Woman's View of Man's Duty to Women." 1909. Rpt. in *A Great Movement Underway: Women and the Grain Growers' Guide, 1908–1928*. Ed. Barbara E. Kelcey and Angela E. Davis. Winnipeg: Manitoba Records Society, 1997. 2. Print.

Harrison, Dick. *Unnamed Country: The Struggle for a Canadian Prairie Fiction*. Edmonton: U of Alberta P, 1977. Print.

Hiemstra, Mary. *Gully Farm*. Toronto: McClelland and Stewart, 1955. Print.

Hill, Colin. *Modern Realism in English-Canadian Fiction*. Toronto: U of Toronto P, 2012. Print.

"'In Due Season' Rich Novel of Alberta's Bush Country." Rev. of *In Due Season*, by Christine van der Mark. *Toronto Star* 13 Dec. 1947: 11. Print.

Jackel, Susan, ed. *A Flannel Shirt and Liberty: British Emigrant Gentlewomen in the Canadian West, 1880–1914*. Vancouver: U of British Columbia P, 1981. Print.

Karlenzwig, Pamela. "Women in the Mirror: Women Writers and Women's History in the Prairies 1945–1970." M.A. thesis. Simon Fraser U, 1992. Print.

Livesay, Dorothy. Introduction. *In Due Season*. By Christine van der Mark. Vancouver: New Star, 1979. i–iv. Print.

Lysenko, Vera. *Yellow Boots*. Toronto: Ryerson P, 1954. Print.

McCourt, Edward. *The Canadian West in Fiction*. Toronto: Ryerson P, 1949. Print.

——. *The Canadian West in Fiction*. Rev. ed. Toronto: Ryerson P, 1970. Print.

Melnyk, George. "Literary Genealogy: Exploring the Legacy of F.M. Salter." *Alberta Views* 1.2 (1998): 34–41. Print.

Mitchell, Barbara. "The Long and the Short of It: Two Versions of *Who Has Seen the Wind*." *Canadian Literature* 119 (1988): 8–22. Print.

Mitchell, Barbara, and Ormond Mitchell. *W.O.: The Life of W.O. Mitchell; Beginnings to Who Has Seen the Wind, 1914–1947*. Toronto: McClelland and Stewart, 1999. Print.

Murphy, Emily. *Janey Canuck in the West*. London: Cassell and Company, 1910. Print.

O'Connor, Juanita. Rev. of *In Due Season*, by Christine van der Mark. *Halifax Chronicle* 20 Dec. 1947: 10. Print.

Querengesser, Neil, and Jean Horton. Introduction. *Dry Water*. By Robert J.C. Stead. Ed. Neil Querengesser and Jean Horton. Ottawa: U of Ottawa P, 2008. xi–xli. Print. Canadian Literature Collection.

Ricou, Laurence. *Vertical Man/Horizontal World: Man and Landscape in Canadian Prairie Fiction*. Vancouver: U of British Columbia P, 1973. Print.

Stamp, Robert. "Through the Eyes of Students: A Learner-Centred Approach to Educational History." *History of Intellectual Culture* 2.1 (2002): 1–11. Web. 13 Sept. 2014.

Strange, Kathleen Redman. *With the West in Her Eyes: The Story of a Modern Pioneer.* Toronto: George J. McLeod, 1937. Print.

Tritter, Thorin. "Canada, Australia, and New Zealand." *The History of Oxford University Press*, Vol. 3: *1896 to 1970*. Ed. Wm. Roger Louis. Oxford: Oxford UP, 2013. 619–47. Print.

van der Mark, Christine [Christine van der Mark Wise]. "At the Gate of the Khyber Pass: University of Peshawar Pioneering in Pakistan's Ancient Seat of Learning." *Christian Science Monitor* 26 May 1956: 13. Print.

———— [Christine van der Mark Wise]. "Bon Voyage for Baby." *Christian Science Monitor* 2 Apr. 1952: 21. Print.

————. "Brothers." *MacLean's Magazine* 1 June 1948: 14+. Print.

————. "Catch-Colt." *Here and Now* May 1948: 26–36. Print.

————. "Church Service at Tuktoyaktuk." *New Trail* Jan. 1947: 244–45. Print.

———— [Christine van der Mark Wise]. "Convocation at the University of Peshawar." *Christian Science Monitor* 27 Apr. 1957: 18. Print.

———— [Christine van der Mark Wise]. "First Khyber Christmas." *Christian Science Monitor* 14 Dec. 1955: 21.

————. *Hassan.* Lahore: U of Peshawar, 1957. Print.

————. *Honey in the Rock.* Toronto: McClelland and Stewart, 1966.

————. "Honey in the Rock." *Star Weekly* 31 Dec. 1966: 1–12. Print.

————. *In Due Season.* Toronto: Oxford UP, 1947. Print.

————. *In Due Season.* 1947. Vancouver: New Star, 1979. Print.

————. "Khyber Bride." *Chatelaine* June 1963: 24+. Print.

———— [Christine van der Mark Wise]. "Letter from Khartoum: Our Beautiful Nights in Khartoum." *Christian Science Monitor* 22 Nov. 1961: 21. Print.

————. "Loneliness." *Gateway* 18 Nov. 1938: 3. Print.

———— [Christine van der Mark Wise]. "'MacBeth' at the Khyber." *Christian Science Monitor* 30 July 1955: 7. Print.

———— [Christine van der Mark Wise]. "Marco Polo Stowaway." *Christian Science Monitor* 2 Mar. 1962: 16. Print.

———— [Christine van der Mark Wise]. "Marketing by Tonga." *Christian Science Monitor* 6 Apr. 1956: 21. Print.

———. "Memories of a Country School Teacher." *The Hussar Heritage*. Ed. M. Bell. Hussar: Hussar Ladies Aid, 1965. 142–45. Print.

———. "My Day: Teaching against Odds on the Prairie." *Overseas Daily Mail* 13 Aug. 1938: 23. Print.

——— [Christine van der Mark Wise]. "N'Horse." *Christian Science Monitor* 8 Aug. 1955: 16. Print.

———. "Nick's Daughter." *Canadian Short Stories*. Canadian Broadcasting Corporation, 2 Sept. 1949. Radio.

———. "On Leave." *Gateway* 19 Oct. 1945: 5. Print.

——— [Christine van der Mark Wise]. "Pakistan Home Charms Westerners." *Christian Science Monitor* 30 Jan. 1956: 6.

———. "The Prayer of a Tree." *Calgary Herald Magazine* 10 Mar. 1935: 26. Print.

———. "Save Our Metis People by New Brand of Aid." *Saturday Night* 24 Apr. 1948: 11. Print.

——— [Christine van der Mark Wise]. "Seeing the Pyramids by Camel." *Christian Science Monitor* 3 Jan. 1962: 17. Print.

———. "She Answered." *Alberta Poetry Yearbook*. Edmonton: Canadian Authors' Association, 1944. 30. Print.

——— [Christine Wise]. "Some Impressions of England." *New Trail* 10.1 (1952): 22–25. Print.

———. "A Study of Conditions of the Last Frontier during the Depression and Following, in the Form of a Novel Entitled, In Due Season." M.A. thesis. U of Alberta, 1946. Print.

——— [Christine van der Mark Wise]. "Sudan Educates Its Women: Who Find Joy in Learning." *Christian Science Monitor* 24 Nov. 1962: 21. Print.

——— [Christine van der Mark Wise]. "Tales of a Prairie School Teacher." *Christian Science Monitor* 12 Jan. 1953: 17; 14 Jan. 1953: 17; 16 Jan. 1953: 17. Print.

———. "Teaching in the North." *Calgary Herald* 12 Feb. 1948: 4. Print.

———. "Teaching in the North." *Alberta School Trustee* 28.3 (1948): 11–12. Print.

———. "That They May Learn Tolerance." *ATA Magazine* Jan. 1947: 23–25. Print.

———. "To a Bluebird." *Calgary Herald* 18 June 1932: 19. Print.

———. "Today Is Spring." *Gateway* 25 Mar. 1941: 3. Print.

———. "Tonight." *Gateway* 9 Dec. 1938: 3. Print.

——— [Christine van der Mark Wise]. "We Worked toward the Arctic." *Christian Science Monitor* 10 June 1952: 17; 11 June 1952: 23; 12 June 1952: 23. Print.

van der Mark, Mary. "Calgary to Khyber: Cake Makes Journey." *Christian Science Monitor* 5 Dec. 1950: 12. Print.

van Kirk, Sylvia. *Many Tender Ties: Women in Fur Trade Society, 1670–1870*. Winnipeg: Watson and Dyer, 1980. Print.

Wall, Denis. "James Patrick Brady." *The Canadian Aboriginal Issues Database*. University of Alberta, n.d. Web. 20 Feb. 2016.

Watson, Robert. *When Christmas Came to Fort Garry: A Romance of the Early Red River Days*. Toronto: Ryerson P, 1935. Print.

"Wauneita War Workers All Set Groups Named." *Gateway* 18 Oct. 1940: 1. Print.

Wise, Dorothy. Afterword. *In Due Season*. By Christine van der Mark. Vancouver: New Star, 1979. 365–72. Print.

Wise, T.F. "Methods of Mobilizing Surplus Rural Labor with Particular Reference to Pakistan." Diss. McGill U, 1965. Print.

"Women's Writing Awards Presented." *Folio* 13 June 1997: 7. Print.

"WW's Need Help; On Radio Soon." *Gateway* 25 Oct. 1940: 1. Print.

Books in the Early Canadian Literature Series
Published by Wilfrid Laurier University Press

The Foreigner: A Tale of Saskatchewan / Ralph Connor / Afterword by Daniel Coleman /
2014 / x + 302 pp. / ISBN 978-1-55458-944-9

Painted Fires / Nellie L. McClung / Afterword by Cecily Devereux / 2014 / x + 324 pp. /
ISBN 978-1-55458-979-1

The Traditional History and Characteristic Sketches of the Ojibway Nation / George
Copway / Afterword by Shelley Hulan / 2014 / x + 208 pp. / ISBN 978-1-55458-976-0

The Seats of the Mighty / Gilbert Parker / Afterword by Andrea Cabajsky / 2015 / viii +
400 pp. / ISBN 978-1-77112-044-9

The Forest of Bourg-Marie / S. Frances Harrison / Afterword by Cynthia Sugars / 2015 /
x + 258 pp. / ISBN 978-1-77112-029-6

The Flying Years / Frederick Niven / Afterword by Alison Calder / 2015 / x + 336 pp. /
ISBN 978-1-77112-074-6

In Due Season / Christine van der Mark / Afterword by Carole Gerson and Janice
Dowson / 2016 / x + 356 pp. / ISBN 978-1-77112-071-5